I0588125

Necromancer's Bullet
A NecroTek Novel

JOSHUA E. B. SMITH

Death isn't the end.

But it's not a great start.

TABLE OF CONTENTS

Acknowledgments...   ii

Prologue...   1

1. Ex-Obligations...   8

2. Slash 'n Burn...   37

3. A Quicker Fixxer...   70

4. Warranted Bondage...   111

5. Gangland State of Mind...   142

6. Mortality Moratorium...   179

7. A Criminal Informant...   218

8. Corpse Capitalism...   256

9. Fire Fight-er...   282

10. Little Battery-Powered Army Men...   297

11. Necromancer's Bullet...   314

12. Reboot...   334

Epilogue...   346

The Saga & Other Books...   351

Copyright and Corp-Crap...   353

ACKNOWLEDGMENTS

I like guns, but I am not a gun guy.
I like the military, but I am not a military guy.
I like writing, but apparently I'm bad at spelling.
I like eating dinner, but apparently I'm bad at affording it.

The last two years of my life have been a nightmare of details and determination and bad choices and good ones. This book would not be here in the state that it's in without an extensive Q&A session from Alysa Crews-List (who provided me extensive pew-pew info when I first started writing it) and Brandon Taylor of the WV National Guard (who answered enough military-branch questions that I am sure got me on another watchlist).

This book also wouldn't be here except for the brutal yet necessary feedback from Amanda Hooser, who is an excellent author in her own right.

And it absolutely wouldn't be here if not for the efforts of Alecia Gulley — best friend, partner, and investor who got me through some tough times when eating books was more affordable than writing them. She read the first chapter when this book was still an infant and not even through Chapter 3...

...and embarked on a crusade that included weekly threats of violence to continue pushing through on it every week since.

I couldn't do it without all of their powers combined, and for that, my gratitude is undying.

Thank you.

And now, I hope you enjoy.

~Josh

PROLOGUE
FRIDAY, MAY 25TH, 2057. 9:19 PM

UNKNOWN: *"Bless me, Father, for I am sin."*
PASTOR JORDAN FISHER: *"It is to say, for you have sinned."*
UNKNOWN: *"No."*

The sound wave overlaid across a green backdrop disappeared as the replay ended in steady static. *"That exchange provides the last known statement of Pastor Jordan Fisher of the Church of Angelic America, a man described by all those that knew him as a true beacon of light in an otherwise dark world."*

"What kind of 'zul'd out bullshit...," Anthony exclaimed as he squeezed the steering wheel until his knuckles went white. "Some shithead ganked Jordan? Damn. That's just... damn."

"Now, now, my good man. Take a moment. I know. News reports bein' personal do kinda suck," the man in the passenger seat opined with his voice weirdly echoing from behind the car and out the window. *"But you're drownin' out the reporter. She's an absolute doll."*

"You can't see her."

"Yeah, but I can hear her," the disembodied voice retorted. *"Just listen."*

The car's panel display switched from an empty blackness to an overhead view of Los Santuario. The garish, neon-white K-GWN logo popped into existence over the bottom right corner of the screen as a news ticker scrolled across the bottom. **"BREAKING: BELOVED PRIEST MURDERED - - - LSPD AB/PSY DIV HEADING INVESTIGATION"**

The driver grunted and tapped a metal finger on the screen. "Is that what they're... oh, fuck no. Beloved my ass."

The drone recording the crime scene tracked through the sprawling urban canyons of ste-crete and glas-plas with ease before it came to a stop a hundred feet over Allenway Drive. The veritable army of squad cars and 'Technology/Engineering Consolidated' vans (aka the TEC-Dets, if you felt like being polite) scattered along the sides. The entire street had been cordoned off, and LSPD had gone to great lengths to make sure that in a sea of blinding LEDs and neon advertisements that covered damn near every flat wall on the street, *their* flashing bits would reign supreme, even if it blinded everyone else.

"*Sources tell us that LSPD is interested in a black van…*"

"Well, that narrows it down tremendously," the driver quipped.

His passenger, for once, ignored him.

"*Not much is yet known about Pastor Fisher's death, but Los San PD has provided the voice sample you just heard with instructions to all major media outlets to play it as often as able. You can cloud-store the audio by clicking on the chyron at the bottom of your screen, or if you happen to recognize the other voice, please contact your local precinct or the LSPD tip line at…*"

The figure in the Venus's passenger side leaned back and soundlessly cracked his neck. It had the effect of showing off a faint red gash that glowed in the car's otherwise dark interior, not that he cared. "*Oh no. Someone missed a sec-mic. And that voice? That's gonna make it harder to hide in the local turfs.*"

"Local hell," the driver remarked after he took a long drag on a thick white stick of pure cotton-wrapped menthol. "That's gonna go national. You fucking ice a priest? In *this* town?"

"*It does pose a few questions, no doubt. May even pose a few for you.*"

The driver grimaced and flung open his door with a kick and stretched out his leg before he stood up. "Haven't seen the fucker since the divorce, thank God. Think Kath'll bitch at me to go to the funeral?"

"*Think you'd be a shit husband if you didn't.*"

"*Ex*-husband," he countered. "Besides, the Church will try to set me on fire if I get anywhere close to it," he added as the broadcast switched to an interview – though that was probably too kind of a word for it. Some cam-head had managed to force his way past the police line and gotten up close and personal with an LSPD detective known and loathed by half the city. It wasn't that she was terrible at her job – it was that she existed. Society loved mages, except when they turned out to work for the cops.

The fact that she was the best mage on staff for the LSPD just pissed them off even more. "Lieutenant! Lieutenant Dimir! What can you tell us about the murder?"

"It's against policy to discuss an active —"

"But if you're here, then that must mean that Ab/Psy is working the case? What could the Abby Squad have to do with this? Is it because he's a priest? Doesn't the Abby Squad have a long-standing hostile relationship with the Church of Angelic America?"

The Lieutenant halted her retreat from the reporter and pointed her finger at him menacingly. All it took was one squeeze of her shoulder by a uniformed officer behind her to get her composure before she lived up to her nickname of 'the Delight,' or more specifically, 'The Turkish Delight.' She was the one woman on the police force that could turn your guts to jelly with a look and a wave if she wanted.

More often than not, she wanted.

"The Abnormal/Para-Psychology Squad is assisting the hardworking men and women of LSPD's homicide division as a courtesy. All branches of law enforcement are happy to work together to resolve any concerns that may erupt in the city."

The telecaster's disembodied voice chimed in once more with an overly eager, "*You just heard from Lieutenant Alara Dimir. Regular watchers of K-GWN — your #1 source for news in the West Gulf — may remember Lieutenant Dimir from the Strawberry Grove incident, where the Ab/Psy squad was implicated in the deaths of two bystanders during a routine warrant recovery operation. It is unclear to our sources exactly why someone with her reputation has been assigned to such a potentially volatile scene, but rest assured — we will make sure that When We Know, You Know.*"

"*Oh boy. They put Madam Unpleasant herself on the case. Ya know,*" the driver's companion mused without getting out of his seat, "*back in my day, none of my colleagues looked half that cute. What in the hell is a Turk doing in fuckin' Texas anyway?*"

"Blackburn, you know damn well who she is and your 'day' was back in the '90s, and I'm going to tell her you said she's cute," Anthony retorted. "I'm sure she'll be enthused."

"*Lot of things ain't my fault. Doesn't stop me from —*"

"It should. You were old enough to be her grandpa *then,* let alone *now.* The fact that you haven't been able to get laid in sixty years isn't my fault. Next time, *run* from a fucker with a knife."

The cold 'harrumph' from his passenger neatly ended that part of the conversation. Just as well. Some rent-a-cop border patrol agent had sauntered up to the old Venus, a bright and shiny headlamp shining from an ocular implant on the side of his temple. "Pierson? Anthony Pierson?"

"Unfortunately," Anthony answered as he adjusted his duster and flipped off the engine. The broadcast continued to play in the background, though everyone ignored it. "Sheriff or Fed?"

"Neither," the pudgy cop snapped in reply. "Lieutenant Dave Wesley. Corbitt Security. We're doing work for Cloud-9 Comms."

If the name-drops were supposed to provide anything useful, they failed. "I don't contract for Corbitt. What the hell am I doing here?"

The sec-officer shrugged his shoulders and dialed down the brightness of the light. "You contract for the state?"

"Not by choice."

"Take it up with them. We put in the call; I ain't their fuckin' dispatch."

The broadcast from the car continued as both men began the less-than-delightful process of pulling out their IDs to verify that yes, honestly, neither of them wanted to be there, and neither of them were getting paid enough to care what the other thought.

"However, the Church has an entirely different opinion. Our on-the-scene reporter caught up with the venerable Sine-Pastor Charlie El-Rhodes, who drove up on the scene mere moments after LSPD tried to force our coverage to end."

A man in a suit tailored to hide an army's worth of augments tried to push the cam-head back before he could get a word out. *"Move, by the Grace of –"*

The reporter didn't budge. Anthony could only imagine the smug look on his face as he shoved his way past the bodyguard with deft ease. *"Sine-Pastor, what can you tell us about –"*

"What can be said?" The mountain of a man intoned the question, sounding bored. He wasn't fat – not by a long shot – but Charlie El-Rhodes was one of the biggest men either of the Venus's passengers had seen before. Even hidden inside his flat-black limo, he looked tall enough to be intimidating as hell: more of a linebacker than someone in the rankings of the region's top three poli-soc elite. *"Los Santuario has long been a hotbed of violence. Bigotry. Hatred."*

As soon as they finished showing off, the rent-a-cop motioned for Anthony to follow him. He did, though he tapped a button hidden just behind his ear to keep the news going in a private screen just off to the edge of his vision. Having head-tech had perks; you never had to miss a minute. *Fuck* the advertisers that had figured out how to get around ad-block apps, though.

A second chime came through over the broadcast to acknowledge that the wandering cop really was a security consultant and he wasn't trying to lead Anthony off to his death somewhere. "Okay, so I'm me; you're you. Why are we *here*?"

"Found a problem. Up ahead. Shipping container. We're way off the highway and the closest mono-lines are ten miles that-a-way, so unless someone dragged it out here…"

Anthony took a long look around the immediate area. All that surrounded him was an expanse of dry dust, drier sand, and a small gravel access road. Some half mile beyond lay a fenced-off remote relay station the size of a double-wide trailer. It fit the unofficial state motto: *Texas: The Dirt's Part of the Charm*! The only other notable feature was a pile of debris dead ahead and smaller trails of construction garbage lining the path. "Who's gonna drag a pile of shit that big out here? We're hours from civilization."

"I assure you, the loss of Pastor Fisher opened a gaping hole in the hearts and souls of not just his congregation but the community at large and this neighborhood as a whole. It is my promise to you that the full might of the Church of Angelic America will be brought down to ensure that the Sanctuary on Allenway will continue to serve as a beacon of hope for the souls lost in the darkness."

"Sine- Pastor, do you know who the suspect is?"

"Violence is violence. It matters not who and what the cause is, only that it exists. Still, the one responsible for such an act must be brought to justice and face the full extent of the Law — God's and Man's. Gang-on-gang violence, in particular, has been on the rise, and it is no coincidence that such animalistic behavior has made its way to a haven for those who would hide from it. Perhaps the Grimshanks are to blame? It's been well documented that their hedonistic behavior is in all quarters of Los San."

The screen instantly cut away from El-Rhode's bald head and shining eyes, returning to a studio setting where a young blonde woman with chrome-dyed dreadlocks smiled for the camera. *"When contacted for a response, Lieutenant Dimir categorically denied that gang involvement was suspected at this time. Still, our Live-Air Man on the Scene caught a caravan of AGU transports as they arrived moments later. Watch the extended —"*

The sec-officer shrugged as he wandered to the biggest pile and pulled off a tarp. "Happens a lot, really. Not here, you know. Corbitt keeps shit secure. But up and down the 'skirts? Fuckin' rail companies and the other com-lines. They'd buy up half a mile of scrub, dump their crap in it, build a segment, and do it again. Then, they'd claim 'environmental impact damages' and make the state take it off their hands when they were done."

"Corp-shell-games and dumpster fires: Welcome to America."

"Yeah, well, they dump their garbage, then the traffs come in. They do this," Dave explained as he pulled the tarp down to expose an old steel-style shipping container. With a kick and a grunt, the door popped open and a *smell* rolled out.

As Anthony stepped back with a gag, Lieutenant Wesley pulled out his G-Locke 9 and gestured at the corpses inside. There were three of them that he could see right off, but there was something else in there that *moved* as Dave's headlamp panned across the piles of desiccated flesh.

"Ab/Psy said they'd send someone to do something about this. Kinda was expectin' Reclamation. You ain't one, are you?"

"Not... not quite," he replied as he gagged anew and reached into his duster for his own gun. "This happen a lot out here or...?"

The lump started to stand up as Dave moved back and answered his question. "Gift boxes? Too often. Not to us, but... too often. The moving? Been hearing rumors. Didn't think they warranted a... what? You some kind of nth-freelancer? Mage-cop? What?"

"*You'll have to tell us all about 'em,*" Anthony's passenger replied as he simply appeared behind the cop. "*None of us want to get called back out here if we can avoid it.*"

Dave turned around and nearly pulled his trigger when he realized he couldn't just *hear* the man, he could see clear *through* him. "What the *fuck* are you?"

"Marshal!" Anthony barked as he pulled a shotgun from its mag-holster on his leg. "You know better."

The specter smiled and waved his arms like a delighted child. "*And miss this part? You gotta be kidding me.*"

Anthony quietly loaded a silver-filled slug into the scattergun and pumped it once. "I'm a li-nec, Mr. Wesley, and the spook's right; you'll have to tell us *all* about it." The vaguely humanoid figure in the back of the box tried to rise to its feet and hissed as Dave's headlamp illuminated it for the sad wretch that it was.

It was human, or at least, human-related. The horn sticking out of the side of its half-fleshed skull suggested more 'related' than 'human', but that was a detail for later. Either way, it was awake, slavering, and had more obviously broken bones than not. *"Anthony! You got us called out here for a dead Daem of all things?"*

"Not dead enough," he muttered.

"Now now, don't wanna be accused of rac-"

"I'm ex-Army, Blackburn. Of course I'm anti-Daem. Besides. I'm late on the rent again and you know damn well the state'll pay enough to take care of this."

His familiar didn't have a response to that. Instead, the news continued to drone on in the background as the demi-human's restless corpse tried to pull itself free of a broken steel beam that had it pinned to the ground. God only knew how long it'd been trapped here, let alone where it'd come from.

That was a question for another day at another time.

"And in other news, representatives from the Heart and Spade Foundation have scheduled a press conference tomorrow to address public concern over growing rumors of unexplained disappearances in the Daem-Sapien community. Otherwise known as 'crackbreeds,' the Foundation has been vocal about –"

The news-drone was drowned out by the shotgun's thunderous report.

1. EX-OBLIGATIONS
Sunday, May 27th, 8:22 PM

For a change, it was a pretty damn good Sunday night in the city. Not the 'fun' part of the city, populated by entertainment venues and bars. Not down at Sunset Point, or up at Wacky Wally's Wondrous Wonderland, or over at the Hawks versus Horns game at Meltdown Park. Hell, it wasn't even a night over at the Synth-Beach getting your brain blasted out your ears by whatever hip-hop-techno-cyber-soul jolt DJ Damned Dave was cranking out.

No, it was a pretty damn good Sunday night in the city because Callie Neale — her real name, not even her stage name — was down on her knees, happily earning the hundo-credit and a half she'd requested for tonight's date. Honestly? She was worth every penny.

Even more for remembering to wear the staining lipstick.

From where she knelt, Anthony wasn't a bad guy. He wasn't a good guy, but he wasn't bad. As she bobbed her head up and down, she gave him a quick glance and smiled. He hadn't shaved in a week, and too-early gray hairs decorated the short and patchy beard along his jaw and neck. Still, he had a way of looking at her that warmed her heart.

It was nice to be appreciated, even at work.

As she blew him, he adjusted his button-down shirt and lifted it up a little for her. He looked like some middle-aged off-duty wage slave with it on; just an average John who had seen better days. No tie, though sometimes he had one to tie up her wrists if she felt spunky.

He never stripped. That was his number-one rule. She'd asked why, at first, and he said something about a scar or two.

"Last tour... yeah... made a mess of things." He'd flexed the fingers of his left hand when he said it; his chrome-plated fingers took care of the rest.

Which was, she had since come to realize, an understatement.

When he curled his fingers up in her slicked-back red hair, Callie responded with a happy little sigh. He was a John, sure — she couldn't remember the last time she'd been with someone who wasn't. Still, he'd never been an asshole, never slapped her around, and always took care of her. He just wanted the company a couple times a month.

And his dick sucked.

Not that there was anything wrong with that.

She was an escort, thank you kindly, and not one of those bubbly neko cuddle-sluts across town in New-Tai. If you were known for doing a job, you took the title and did it right. She felt him tense up and decided that, yes, she was doing her job right.

Her satisfaction lasted for a few fleeting seconds before some bint with absolutely atrocious timing started to pound on Anthony's apartment door. He ignored it. She ignored it. He wasn't the greatest at maintaining focus, but she wasn't paid by the hour. Besides, his company wasn't terrible... and his fridge was always stocked with rum, so it wasn't *that* bad.

So, they continued to ignore the pounding until the bitch on the other side opened her mouth and everything went straight to Hell. Literally. "ANTHONY! OPEN UP, PLEASE!"

You know how sometimes you feel all the air leave the room in a heartbeat? Like everything that ever had the capability of experiencing joy suddenly upped and died and left the room full of the stench of broken hopes and dreams? He went as limp as an overcooked wad of ramen, and Callie suddenly felt like she had more in common with the Amazon Dustbowl than she did with the Islands of Old DC when she saw comprehension dawn in his eyes.

"Anthony, you asshole, open up! Please! It's important!"

He was out of his seat before his date had a chance to put her top back into place. There was precisely one type of woman on the planet who could hit that octave and carry that much joy-sucking strength in her words. One and only one — and it'd taken a court order to get her that title.

When Anthony pulled his apartment door open, his ex-wife looked right into his eyes... and promptly dove into his arms with a desperate embrace that stunned the call girl and her client alike. When she started to cry, Anthony awkwardly pat her on the back with his good arm. For a brief moment, Callie felt a rush of heat creep into her cheeks and put a little more bile into her words than she meant to.

"You didn't pay me enough to party with that bitch."

Bitch? That was the other understatement of the night. Katherine Fisher; certified registered nurse at the University of Anthenium-Medical Hospital of Los Santuario (or U-Anth-Med for short), his certified ex-wife, certified holder-of-alimony-demands, and owner of a pair of certified-fake tits.

And even if they weren't fake, Callie was going to call them that anyway, just because.

"Please, shut the door, we can't... I can't... nobody can know I'm here," she sniffled.

"Why, because your boyfriend is looking for you?" the escort snidely interjected. She'd heard enough about the woman to enjoy watching her cry. Callie wasn't about to pass up the chance to pile a little more on her shoulders.

Sometimes, her job tipped in the most unexpected ways.

Anthony sighed as he poked his head into the hall and surveyed the scene before shutting the door behind them. "Callie, hit the fridge. I put something in there for you."

"You cooked?"

"He doesn't cook," Katherine sniffled, "and if he does, don't eat it."

He let out another sigh and crossed his arms. The dim light made his chrome shine and masked the dirty look on his face. "I'm not that bad. What do you think I live off of?"

She glanced up and wiped away some smudged eyeliner. "Cheap beer and *maybe* mac 'n cheese?"

"Ouch. You're not wrong, but ouch." Anthony let go of the shorter woman and looked her over as she struggled to compose herself. She didn't *look* hurt, but more than a decade of marriage had taught Anthony that looks could be deceiving.

"Now, talk," said Anthony, finally. "Why are you here?"

Katherine blinked her big blue eyes and gave a nervous glance at the redhead in the kitchen. His apartment wasn't exactly high-class, and the open floor plan didn't provide much privacy. There was a room to shit in, a room to sleep in, and the living room for everything else. "Not while... I can't while she's..."

The escort rolled her eyes and grabbed the not-exactly-fresh dessert from the fridge. "I literally could not care less. And Anthony! You got me cheesecake? You remembered!"

"I listened."

"That's a first," his ex huffed. "Why is she even here?"

Anthony gave her a blank stare and adjusted the fly on his battered jeans. "Why do you think?"

She sneered and stepped back. "A hooker? You're a pig."

"No, I'm a pig!" Callie countered with a grin. "I mean, I am when he pays enough."

"Fine. You're both pigs."

Callie's eyes flashed as she countered with a smile that stretched from ear to ear. "Oink. Oink."

"Disgusting."

Anthony lowered his head into his right hand, massaging his temples. "We're not doing this," he growled under his breath. "Kath, if you're going to bitch about where I stick my dick, then you shouldn't have filed for divorce."

"I filed for divorce because of where you stuck your dick," she snapped, before fresh tears welled up in her eyes again. She jumped topics like a gymnast. "Jordan's dead. He… he was…"

The admission scuttled any retort he might've had, and his date carefully set down the clearance-marked cake lid as quietly and respectfully as possible. "I… I heard," mumbled Anthony. "I should've called. For the record, I didn't do it."

Not that he hadn't wanted to. Jordan Fisher had been an administrator and pastor for a quaint little fellowship. As such, he was a devout follower of the Church of Angelic America and an all-too-eager advocate for the pious bullshit they practiced. It wasn't even a case of not getting along with his brother-in-law; rather, an issue with the preacher's readiness to remind everyone what the Old Church used to do to people like him.

"*Beware of those calling for the good old days,*" the saying in his circles went, "*Especially when they come bearing pitchforks and torches.*"

None of this was news to Katherine.

"I know," she replied at last. "The cops think… they think it was done by some gang. Anthony? It was… it was bad. *Really* bad."

"It's not like dead guys are normally pretty," Callie muttered under her breath. When the former couple looked over at her, she shrugged. "What? You're a nurse, he's… well, I don't know what he used to do, but I know where he got that arm from, so I'm guessing he wasn't selling shoes. Me? I have an open arrangement with the *Crem la Flamme* down on 10th. Bunch of weirdos, but ya see shit. Lots of dead shit."

Katherine shuddered in revulsion as Anthony wondered what the hell would make the cremators down there *weird* and decided it was better not to ask. "Damn. I know I didn't think much of the jackass, but I'm sorry. Do they know…?"

Katherine sniffled and wiped away a few more tears. "The cops… they said something about it being locals? The Grims. I mean, it'd have to be locals; Jordan didn't do anything that anyone… I mean, that's what I told the anti-gang unit…"

"The Grimshanks? The AGU shits are accusing the *Grimshanks* of offing a CoAA-er?" Katherine just nodded her head. Callie and Anthony exchanged a *look*, relaying a message words weren't needed to convey. Upset or not, Kath wasn't as much of an idiot as his date opined, and she finally interrupted their silent exchange with a frustrated snap. "What? What'd I say?"

Anthony took a long, deep breath and cleared his throat. "There is absolutely no chance in any of the Ten Known Realms of Hell that the Grims would kill a preacher of the CoAA," he clarified, even as he used the Church's abbreviation in the way they hated. They preferred to be called 'The Angelic' or just 'The Church.' Everyone else called them the 'Co-ahh,' because, dammit, that's how the initials were spelled. It didn't go over well with their rank-and-file. Nobody who called them that cared what they thought.

It was a linguistic win-win.

"What's that supposed to mean… why not?"

"Well," Anthony began after another glance at Callie, "the Grimshanks are supervised directly by the Heart and Spade Foundation. They wouldn't pick a fight with the C-o-Double-AA's even if you paid them."

"I mean the Grimshanks… they're a gang? What makes you think that the HaS…?"

"The Grimshanks aren't *a* gang, Kath, they're *the* gang. Heart and Spade runs the city. Grimshanks run the streets. I know you don't get that view from your apartment downtown, but it's not exactly old news," Anthony grunted.

Callie made a few happy noises as she stuffed the cheesecake into her mouth before she mumbled succinctly: "Like, Lady Helesiki has the Grimshanks on retainer, so… they don't shit without permission from the tower. And this is a big-ass kinda shit."

Katherine winced at how casually the escort dropped the name – and with reason. Even Anthony felt his eye twitch at the mere mention. Callie continued to munch away without a single care in the world. Anthony had suspected Callie had an attachment to Desire, but hadn't realized she was that comfortable invoking Her out loud.

Lady H. The fourth of five… *things* that had crawled out from under the asshole of the universe decades ago. Calling them 'demons' seemed to be an understatement for creatures that appeared to have come straight out of the gaping mouth of Hell. You would've expected them to try to take over the world or usher in the Apocalypse. Weirdly, They did just the opposite – and for both Her credit and the probable sake and safety of humanity proper, Helesiki was objectively 'better' than most of Her siblings.

Not that She wouldn't ruin your life, given reason, but there were levels of 'bad' that She stayed towards the bottom of. She just wanted you to buy things. Spend money. Engage in excess. Get laid, do drugs, drink booze, party, play loud music. Have *fun.*

She even encouraged you to do it safely.

Corpses didn't buy porn, didn't you know.

She launched a mega-corp that established itself in the financial and entertainment markets in a way that rivaled only one other big-eared corporate entertainment-class entity on the global stage. Outside of that, Helesiki was reputed to be pretty reasonable. Not that most people would know.

It was said to meet with Her – or one of Her siblings – was to be an ant at the foot of a mountain. She let Her intermediaries do the talking, the fucking, and the fucking-over. It was a tale as old as the concept of Kingdoms and CEOs: the boss doesn't talk unless the boss notices you.

And you don't want to be noticed by the boss.

Realization dawned across Katherine's face as her heart dropped into her stomach. "Then that would mean…"

"That the Grimshanks are the thugs that protect the Daemoness of Lust's street-level operations," Anthony replied with a shrug. "The H-a-S? They're Her official corporate interests. If you think, even for a minute, that they'd sanction a hit on a CoAA priest… that's *beyond* bad for business. It'd be open war to the extent that the other Four would have to get involved." He paused for a minute and gave her a disbelieving look. "How do you not know this? This isn't a national secret or anything. Spend five minutes in a bodega on Hurst and…"

Katherine blanched. "Look. I have gone way outta my way *not* to know, okay? I work in R&D. I don't work in the bloody ER. I don't see people unless they've got three different kinds of insurance and a corporate ID. What the gangs are doing, the gangs are doing. I don't know and I don't care, and I *didn't* care until my brother got... got..." she faltered as she struggled for a word, "...got flattened. In his fucking Sanctuary."

"That's ballsy," Callie added. "Ganking a priest in his own house? Most of the streeters know that 'thumper types are off-limits. Orders from well on high."

"You mean from the well down below," Anthony corrected.

She shrugged. "Even below, they're on top."

Katherine ignored the banter and slowly shook her head again. "No, not his actual... I mean, they did it... they killed him at the Sanctuary on Allenway."

Callie looked up from her desert and interrupted them with a slow whistle. "Damn. I repeat that they're *hella* ballsy. Ain't a single 'shanker in the city that's got a dick big enough to do that. Not even the B&B."

She shot the younger woman an exasperated and confused look as Anthony mumbled a quiet agreement and a wince at the added suggestion – whoever the B&B were supposed to be. "Then why would the cops say that?"

Callie popped open a beer before she answered. "Probably because the cops here are the cops *here*. They only tell you who's guilty after someone pays them to make up their mind."

"Are you implying... no. No, I don't want to know that. I don't want to ask. So, if not the Grims...? If not them, who would?"

Anthony slowly shrugged as he straightened up the old button-down shirt he had on. "I mean, violence is a *thing* in this day and age. Someone mugging a priest isn't unheard of, I'm sorry, but it's –"

"He wasn't mugged," she interrupted quietly. "Anthony, it..."

"It what?"

"They crushed his head," Katherine answered meekly. "I said it was bad."

Callie coughed and slowly set the cheesecake back down, as the strawberry topping suddenly looked a little less appetizing. "Do you mean they beat him to death, or are you saying...?"

"Like it was in a vise, okay? That's what I'm saying. That they broke in, tore up the place, and then crushed his head like they dropped a truck on it!" Katherine shouted before she shot Anthony a furious look. "Why is she even here? She doesn't even look like she's out of high school!"

The escort straightened her petite frame and made a show of untying her hair from a bun. At the same time, she made her chest flare out against the thin fabric of the old black-and-white t-shirt she wore that advertised some long-defunct gaming company. "I am twenty-three, thank you very much."

"Fine," the nurse growled, "she's not out of college, better?"

"You weren't either," he pointed out.

"Anthony! We were the same age, you... you... gross..."

Anthony cringed away from the venom in her voice and shrugged. "What do you want me to say? She's here because I... you know."

"I got this, *mon amour*," Callie interrupted. "I'm here because he's a nice guy who needs a chance to relax and wants the girlfriend experience without the girlfriend *baggage*. Unlike some people, when I show up, he *relaxes*," she explained as she slowly licked her lips and flicked the end of her tongue. "Besides, I'm cheaper than a weekend hunting the clubs and he doesn't have to scrub the bathroom before I come over."

"That's disgusting," Kath growled as she shot the younger woman a vile glare.

"Oh, please! He's got the kinds of tricks you only learn from practice. Don't blame me for letting him do things to me that he learned to do with you."

Kath's eyes went wide and almost flashed with raw rage. "How *fucking* dare you –"

Anthony stepped between them and crossed his arms. "*Enough*, you two," he growled. "Kath. I'm sorry about Jordan. Sounds like the cops have it, and I genuinely hope they find the right guy. I don't know what you think I can do, but being the man in the middle between you two little hellions isn't it."

"It can be," Callie countered with a smirk. "There's this girl I know that visits the *Techno-Voodoo* on 13th, and she –"

"Anthony, someone took a shot at me," Katherine interrupted, "earlier tonight. I came straight here after."

The statement sucked the air out of the room until at last, Anthony summoned the words to ask the obvious. "They. What?"

Katherine stepped back, resting her shoulders on the door to his dingy, junk-filled apartment. "An hour ago. A couple of guys showed up. Tried to break in. Shot off the lock. I had to climb out the fire escape. I didn't know where else to go."

Shock danced across his face as his jaw dropped open. "I don't know, *the cops*?"

"She just said they're corrupt!"

"But you didn't know that until you got here!"

"I *assumed*," Katherine snapped back. "I'm not an idiot."

"Remains to be seen," Callie muttered under her breath.

"Ladies," Anthony thundered. "You should've led with that! 'Honey someone just tried to kill me, can we talk?' is a great conversation starter."

Katherine sighed and dropped her head. "I... I wasn't sure if you'd be willing to help. That's the truth."

"Would've helped faster than you telling me about Jordan."

"Why, were you thinking of opening a bottle of champagne after I'd left?"

Callie perked up at the suggestion. "If he has some, I'm willing to share. I'm not a complete bitch."

"No, just a complete cu-" Katherine started before her ex cut her off.

"You, get away from the door and go sit on the couch," Anthony barked before he turned his attention to his evening's entertainment. "Callie. That cabinet by your knees. Reach in, then up. It's hooked in but it's not anchored."

Callie frowned and glanced down at the grimy cupboard, wrinkling her nose. "It isn't going to bite, is it?" Katherine gave a matching glare of distrust to the pile of old magazines and an empty pizza box cluttering up the seat, before she began to tidy it up a little.

"Just don't read the name on it out-loud, okay?" he directed as he turned his attention back to his ex. "You. Do you know what they looked like, what they were driving, anything at all?"

Katherine swallowed nervously as she sat down on the old, well-worn leather. "No, I... I mean, I saw a car as I was leaving that I didn't recognize. Some old beat-up '22 De-Milo. I only caught a glimpse of one of them... green vest. Denim, maybe? It was dark."

"Okay." Anthony sighed as Callie made a startled exclamation from the kitchen. "Be straight with me: have you pissed anyone off lately? Anyone at all?"

"Anthony, I'm not like you. Normal people don't usually make people angry enough to try to kill them!"

"Bullshit," Callie called out. "Also, *holy shit*, Anth. You been keeping this relic in here the whole damn time?" she asked as she hefted up a pristine, classic, single-barrel, pump-action shotgun. The stock was solid oak and weathered like it'd been to hell and back, but even banged up? The whole thing absolutely *shined*. "When was this thing put together? In the teens?"

"The '90's," he corrected. "Most of it. Had to replace some parts."

She rolled her eyes as she walked across the cluttered room. "Gee, you've had to tweak a half-century old boom-stick with modern parts. Color me surprised. Color me *pissed*, too. You know how I feel about guns in the bedroom."

"That isn't the bedroom," Anthony countered as Katherine rubbed her eyes through the exchange. "That's the kitchen."

Callie handed him the gun and stood on her tiptoes to whisper in his ear, her eyes locked on his former wife. "We treat every room in this house like the bedroom. Couch included."

Kathrine shot up off the couch with a shudder as Callie stepped back with a giggle. "You two are vile."

"And you interrupted date night," Callie countered. "Anth? I'm gone. Seriously, you didn't pay me enough to deal with this."

There wasn't any real way to disagree with her, so he didn't try. "Redo on Friday?"

"Busy. Party with some suits. How about Monday?"

"Game."

"You don't watch," she argued, "Or play. Don't tell me you're after a cheerleader when I'm not around."

"No, but 13-C watches the 'Horns. Cooks a mean kielbasa."

"Then bring me along."

"Don't want them to think we're dating."

Callie leaned up and kissed him on the cheek. "Like you could do better."

Katherine choked back another gag. "Fuck. You *are* dating him. Admit it."

Callie simply smiled. "Girlfriend. Experience. Blurs the lines a little."

As she slipped out of the room, Anthony's black-haired visitor carefully sat back down on the couch. "She's gross. And why do you have that thing?" his ex demanded as she pointed at the gun with a fresh shudder. "Thought you got rid of it."

"*Him*, not *it*," Anthony chided as he patted the old-school cannon. "He decided he didn't want to leave," he answered. "So, I kept him for safety purposes."

"I don't feel safer with you holding it... him."

Anthony shrugged and checked the small magazine attached to the underside. It was one of a couple of mods – though the idea was that you never wanted to use more ammo than what the stock model was made for, anyway. "Good, because it'll raise my damn rent if I have to use it." As

Katherine sighed, he fastened it back in place and gave the antique a quick look-over. "Alright. Out with it."

"Out with what?"

"Whatever you're not telling me."

"What makes you think I'm —"

Anthony tapped the end of the barrel with his left hand and enjoyed the faint metallic clang that resulted. Steel hand on a steel barrel; one a gift from the army, the other, a… gift from someone else. Or maybe, gift wasn't quite the right word. "Because our first date was when you were nineteen and we only got divorced three years ago. What aren't you telling me?"

Katherine withered a little under the irritation in his voice and the look in his eyes. Once his voice dropped to that particular octave, there was no longer a point in trying to argue with him.

"Jordan sent me… this," she replied slowly, fishing a flat-based spherical bauble from the depths of her pocket.

"He was getting murdered but had time to send you a 10/9? What, the cops say the Grimshanks work for the postal service now?"

"He called me in the middle of some confession. I was busy and… he left a voicemail. The cops had already shown up and gone when I found it, and they said it was the Grims, so I assume they had it, and then…"

"And then someone came to shoot your head off tonight, so you saved it on an US-subsphere just to be safe? Not a bad idea, but the N-Cloud would've been better."

"Didn't think it'd hurt. I didn't… I promise I didn't actually get the message until after they left. I'd been busy with work and had missed his call and… I can't help but think it's my fault. If I had answered the phone then…"

"If someone had heard you on the other end while it was happening, you'd be dead. The fact that they just found you means they didn't know, and they don't like the idea of witnesses. Don't argue fate. We don't know why things happen in the order they happen, just that they do."

Katherine grimaced and looked down at the sub-sphere in her hands. "I don't know if that helps."

"I don't know if it does, either. Here. Hold this. Don't say his name."

Of course, she did the exact opposite as soon as she had the shotgun in her hands. At this point, almost out of spite. "I know what his name is. Marshal B-"

"Kath, for the love of *God*," Anthony interrupted. "What part of *don't* did you miss?"

She huffed and set the gun down across her skirt. "It's just a name."

"And he likes you less than Callie does, so stop," Anthony remarked, with a choked-back noise of raw irritation.

He fished his phone out of his pocket and pressed the 10/9's flat base to it. Within seconds, the ball lit up with a faint pink glow and connected with a magnet and a wireless up-link. A digital handshake later, and a host of files popped up on his phone's screen.

"Besides," Anthony mused, "Names have power. Names like… 'SpecialRed' and 'MeshBlack'?" he read aloud. "I see someone's taken up photography," he remarked as the first photo filled his screen.

A red flush of embarrassment filled Katherine's cheeks. "And you've taken up cheap tricks," she spat. "Don't click those."

"Seen it before… not like that though, damn. Plus, for the record: Callie's not cheap," Anthony retorted with a grunt as he scrolled through the list before he found a file labeled 'Jordan5-27-47-VM'. A moment later and his phone started to play back her brother's last words.

"Bless me, Father, for I am sin."

That wasn't Jordan. That was someone with a nasal voice and the slightest of lisps. Or maybe it was some underlying static on the recording. It wasn't a perfect scan and he couldn't quite tell. He could tell he wanted to punch the guy right away though; and that wasn't the greatest sign of how he expected the night to unfold.

"It is to say, for you have sinned."

That was Jordan. He wasn't a loud man, but wasn't quite soft-spoken, either. He'd never had that fatherly tone you'd expect from a priest; he sounded more like a linebacker for a middle-school football team. You'd expect a 'Yes Coach!' from him more than a 'Praise God and His Son, amen,' but he worked that to his advantage. It made him seem down-to-earth. One of the people. He was good at that.

Plus, as much of an asshole as he was, the jerk could grill up a mean slab of Green-Beef Burgers. Made him really popular on game day. His following was small but loyal. That meant a lot, nowadays.

"I meant what I said," the nasal voice argued. *"Sin is who we are, what we do. I am a sinner, and I came to you."*

There was a pause. A nervous hesitation. Jordan wasn't the fight-or-flight type; he was a peacekeeper. Nor was he an idiot, no matter what Anthony thought of him, and so the next words out of his mouth had to have been picked carefully. *"The Church is here for… all manner of souls. We are here to unburden."*

"As am I. You have a secret, Father. One that does not belong to you."

Anthony cringed. This was going downhill fast. If the priest had been packing, a gun would have justifiably been in hand at the mere utterance of such an accusation. *There are no secrets in God's eyes, friend. Only truths. Said or unsaid, there are only truths in this house.*

"I am not here on behalf of God's eyes, I'm afraid," the voice intoned, *"but I am here to unburden you."* There was another pause, a painful one, but it was matched by a faint noise in the background. Katherine didn't look like she realized what it was, but Anthony sure as fuck did.

It was a simple click. The sound of a mag-lock disengaging. The simple 'tink' of a pistol's grip popping into a metal hand. The intent of a slug-shot's safety going off. *"Friend. This is a house of God. There is no need –"*

"But it's a city of devils, Father. I know you will say you can't violate the sanctity of this and that. I know that you'll require motivation. I know that a gun won't do it. I know because I am paid to know how to negotiate with people."

"Friend, I –," Anthony glanced up from the phone and saw the tears forming in Katherine's eyes and paused the recording. A kinder man might've stopped the playback entirely. He intended to; he really did.

Instead, she caught his hand and pushed his thumb back on 'play.' "Keep going. There's something there. I don't know what, but it's something."

He let it play.

A door opened. A big one. That particular sanctuary had only one of that size, so it had to have been the front. It needed oiled. *"I'll be polite, once. Sojourn Enterprises – Project Wetshell. What were you told?"*

"Project…? I don't know what you mean."

The way Jordan faked his response so easily, so casually, it set off all kinds of warning bells. Anthony nearly dropped the phone as he let out a low whistle. In all the years he'd known the aggrandizing little prick, he never thought that Jordan had it in him to lie with such ease.

The nasal jerkoff wasn't fooled either. He sounded like he walked around everywhere with a wad of cork shoved up one nostril and a tissue in the other. It was the kind of voice that made you want to punch a guy the second you heard it.

"Lying is a sin, Father. Unfortunately, it's not a vice either of us have time for." A single shot went off, sudden, direct; the priest wouldn't have seen it coming unless the gun had been pointed at his head. Something told him the gunman had his hands in his pockets to keep Jordan at ease. Anthony could see the scene playing out in his mind from that point on.

Jordan screamed and fell. Bits of stone clattered from the slug as it punched through skin and bone and hit the floor. Probably his knee, if he had to guess. The report itself came from a small caliber gun. Could've been anything from a .32 to a 9mm.

Tears were flowing freely down Katherine's face by now. Her muffled whimpers were matched only by the cries of pain from the priest. Both sounds worked to nearly cover up the slick 'thud' that followed a moment later.

"I don't know anything! Whatever you want, you won't find –"

Another thud. A heavy footstep. Heavier than anything human, that much Anthony could tell. He strained to hear it, but it wasn't hard to miss.

"A good book I once read said that the wages of sin were death. You'll find that your payment will be an installment plan, though I will add: the truth will set you free."

That kind of threat and those kinds of screams were the prerequisites to torture. You hear them once or twice; you learn to recognize them. Even still, it wasn't what he said that made Anthony's stomach tie itself into knots, or the voice of the man grilling him.

That title went to a louder noise in the background and was underpinned by Jordan's terrified utterance of, *"By God's Grace! What kind of hell spawn –!"*

The priest probably hadn't given any care to what the grinding thrum was from a few seconds earlier, judging by the rest of the call. Katherine didn't seem to notice. Beneath the heated argument and the downright disturbing hiss of whatever 'not human' *thing* Jordan had seen in his last moments, there were words. Words that were hidden in a bio-mechanical thump that pervaded the recording.

Bio-mechanical hums, thumps, and the occasional high-pitched whine were nothing new. You live (or lived) in Los San, and you heard it from someone or somewhere every time you stepped out to get the mail. Bio-mechanical *tech* had been around for nearly a century. Bio-*magical* tech, on the other hand? That was an entirely different story.

Nobody had argued about the existence of magic – or as the 'official' sources had branded it, *'nth,'* – since the first of The Five made His inaugural public appearance in the middle of World War II. It'd existed since the dawn of time, but the arguments stopped when Hell opened for business upon the arrival of the Pentaship into public view. It was regulated, it was uncommon enough in most places, it was treated with equal parts skepticism and distrust, but it *existed*.

Of course, it was always easier to prove something you could wrap your fingers around, like a cold, hard chunk of rock that you could point at and go, 'It's right here!'. Enter anthenium – the keystone that pushed humanity into a brand-new age of science and tech. The truth of the mid-1900s was simple: a world full of skeptics needed proof that the rest of the planet hadn't lost their damn minds. So, science and magic delivered them proof.

Combined, science and magic both discovered and created anthenium.

Followed immediately by everything going to shit.

It was raw, concentrated *nth* in a blue-crystal form that you could hold in the palm of your hand. A semi-natural phenomenon that had largely gone unnoticed for *centuries* of human development until magic – and all the ills of the world made manifest – followed the Pentaship out of Hell itself. When They walked free, anthenium deposits around the world slowly activated as they reacted to the change and the charge of the flow of nth across the planet.

Or plane of existence, or dimension, or whatever you wanted to call it. The *here* and the *now*. The world. The world where living, breathing, dumbass humans lived and did dumbass things.

Dumbass things… such as realizing that they could hold magic in the palm of their hands. Followed closely by even *dumber* dumbass things like how people decided to treat the glowing rocks as though they were nuclear reactors (as a bonus: reactors without all the radioactive love and cancer-causing effects used plutonium came with). You could do a lot with magic, assuming you had the aptitude.

People without that aptitude could do a lot with anthenium.

Basically, humanity found glowing rocks capable of holding an electrical charge and decided to turn them into batteries – and promptly shoved them up everyone's ass. Bio-tech, bio-med, anth-med, anth-tech; different faces of the same die. Anthenium wasn't the *easiest* thing to manage in the world, but it could *power* a lot of things – everything from cybernetic implants to cars to satellites and computers.

And weapon platforms, too, naturally.

Because that's just the way Uncle Sam rolled.

Of course, there were rules – primarily about mixing anth and tech together. Anthony cared little about these rules beyond the fact that they existed – and the way that various agencies made sure you played along. You either followed them or you didn't, and since he liked to keep breathing, Anthony chose to follow them.

The nuances weren't important. Just that there were *rules* and they were *rules* established first by the Five and later, by the Church. The governments and their courts followed suit soon after. There were *exceptions* to the rule — like a replacement heart — but those lines were *very* well-defined.

Cross them for anything outside of the narrow scope decreed by the powers that be? That was a no, one accentuated neatly with a bullet. If you were lucky, the State did it. If you weren't, then the State watched, shrugged their collective bureaucratic shoulders, and fucked off.

"What the hell was your brother involved in?" Anthony asked as the recording ended with heavy static and a meaty crunch that made his blood run cold. That was the unmistakable sound of a phone being crushed into bits. Since he was hiding it to start with, it meant he'd been kicked hard enough to break what the Comm-Corps advertised as unbreakable, or someone had stomped on him after he'd dropped. Either way, ouch.

"I don't know. He'd been upset for days. Told me he'd heard a confession that didn't sit right with him. He ended up getting called out to NNI last weekend."

"New Northern Italy?" Anthony asked in surprise. "The only thing up *there* for your brother is the damn College of Eagles and the CoAA's big-boss. What the hell would the Canuck Pope want with a street-level 'thumper like Jordan?"

"He was more than a 'thumper. He was a good man trying to do good things for the city."

"Yeah, by championing legislation to outlaw people like me," Anthony growled. "If he had his way, I'd be stuck in Anchorage being used as a divining rod for fossils."

She crossed her arms and leaned back. "It'd be an honest living. Not that you'd know what that's like."

"Kath, I won't ask again."

She ran her hands through her hair and pulled out a couple of loose knots with a wince. "Recently? He's been working hand-in-hand with the Sine-Pastor. Outreach program. Trying to help find homes for refugees from the Peninsula."

Anthony couldn't hide his scoff. "Oh, I don't believe that for a minute. C'mon. The only people left down there are commune remnants from the 2nd Civil and the 90's Cult/Ure wars. Oh, and crackbreeds. Everyone else moved their shit out if they could."

"Not everyone could. You know that. And don't call them that. They're Daem —"

"They're genetic offspring between humans and demons. Or mutants from the unlucky shits that happened to be living around the biggest anth deposits in the world when that pseudo-scientific shit hit the fan back in the '60s. Either way, they're descendants of demons I don't fuck with, and humans shouldn't have, either."

"Humans will fuck anything that moves and you're living proof," Katherine snapped. "They're not all bad."

"I know. I'm friends with some," he countered. It was weak, but it was the best he could manage. "Bluntly? The only people that hate them more than the guys I served with when we were putting Uncle Sam's boots to the NPC's asses out in the desert? Yeah, your brother preaches from their so-called Good Book. 'Love thy neighbor,' my ass."

"Oh come on, Anthony. The tried and true 'we hate them because they weren't human bullshit? I know you're pissed about the arm but I thought you were better than that."

Anthony's hand went to his shoulder protectively. "I thought you divorced me because I wasn't," he charged with a glare. "Now you're telling me that Jordan, *Jordan of all people*, is working with the hell-muties, I assume you're going to tell me that the sky is green and water is dry."

Katherine shook her head vehemently as she took her phone back. "New initiative. The Church calls it the 'Helping Up Plan.' Show the world that the Daem-Sapien community has other uses and social functions than just... you know. The Pentaship. You could be a little kinder with how you talk about them. I know you're not a fan, but they are people."

"There is extensive genetic debate on that issue and you know it," he countered. "So, what? The CoAA is... offering affordable housing? Doughnuts and beer? And they've got Jordan working on it?"

"More or less. He's been so proud of it. They have a community up in Tex-Armine. It's an hour outta the city on interstate. They come in through... oh, shit. He was so proud of the partnership. ABE? Honest ABE?"

Anthony pursed his lips and worked that idea over a few times. Honest ABE was a logistics firm — a relatively new mover and shaker in the city. You couldn't walk five feet without seeing an ad for the mag-lev passenger hauls they were pushing all over the southern US. '*When Transport is Presidential, Vote Honest ABE: Honestly, it's America's Bullet Express!*'

And no matter what, don't forget about their Chief Engineer. You couldn't turn on a broadcast screen for more than five minutes without seeing his face – and they had him plastered all over so many bus terminals you'd think he was about to drive you down the streets to the rail station in person. Not that you could *see* his face on the ads – he was always covered in some full-face curved visor – but his name?

'Master Chief Orion – The Honest Face of Honest ABE!'

They had money, they made money, and they had trains that were making money off some new kind of engine tech. That was more or less everything he knew about them, though it made sense – if Jordan was somehow involved in refugee resettlement out of the Flo-Penni, trains and monorails were easier to manage than buses.

Kinda.

Usually.

"I'd say it's unbelievable, but that sorta flies in the face of what the Church is supposed to do," Anthony mused. "I can see it making people uncomfortable, but not to the point of... whatever the hell that was. Are you sure you don't know anything else? Anything else at all?"

Katherine raised her hands defensively and shook her head again. "I'm telling you, I have absolutely no idea. He heard a confession. It upset him. He got called to NNI. He got sent back from NNI. When he returned, he was even more pissed than when he left. Then he got killed. What more do you want me to say?"

That was a loaded question and came with a long list of ideas. Not exactly helpful, but extensive. "Then what do you want me to do about it? What am I *supposed* to do about it?"

"I don't know!" she exclaimed as fresh tears rose. "I work at a damn hospital! People don't show up at my house with guns trying to kill me as part of my day-to-day life!"

"What, you think that I'm used to that?"

Katherine sniffled and drew a ragged breath as she tried to calm herself down. "I think you do more work than you report on your taxes. You and... Marshal here."

She wasn't wrong, but it made him irrationally angry to hear her say it.

Without a word, he popped the data-sphere off his phone and dropped it into his pocket. His phone followed a moment later, and he carefully took the gun off of her lap the moment following.

"Fine. Then you sit your pretty ass there, and I'm going to check the underside of the N-Cloud and..."

…and nothing. Before he could get the next word out of his mouth, the door to his apartment swung open and Callie dove inside with more profanity on her breath than Anthony was aware she knew. "I swear to Desire, if you don't have another way out of this shitbox I'm gonna bite your dick off the next time I see it."

Her date had the door shut before she could make it to the lone window in the apartment to pull the old drapes closed. "What happened to you?"

"The fuck didn't happen to me," she snapped. "Her problem? Yeah, her problem just called *my* fucking phone," she growled as she chucked it at him. "Here. It's for you. Do you have any more guns around here?"

"For me?" he mouthed as he brought it up to his ear. "Yo?"

The voice was instantly recognizable, even if he didn't have a name to put to it. It was the same son of a bitch that Jordan had recorded, and that failed to bode well. *"Guns won't solve your problem, Mr. Pierson. But I can. I have solutions for you."*

Anthony didn't respond, but the look he gave both women was enough to put the fear of God into them. "I don't think I want your help. Maybe we can talk about it over dinner? At your arraignment maybe?"

"Don't be cute, Mr. Pierson. You live the life of a jilted husband, and it costs you seven-fifty-three on a cred-stub a month. You can be debt-free in just one simple step, if you'd like."

Katherine couldn't make out what he said, but Callie could. The hooker shrugged slowly and waited for her date to reply. "Something tells me you don't work for family court."

"No, yet the resolution is simple: do unto her as she did unto you. Demand she leave your home, and your alimony becomes a thing of the past."

"I dunno. I mean, I've got her; I've got the lovely piece of ass you just spoke to. Think I've got some booze. Enough of it and I won't want either of them to leave."

As he spoke, the black-haired woman's eyes lit up with a flash of hate and anger that *only* an ex-husband could earn. *"Either she leaves and you are debt free, or she stays and neither of you worry about her next check."*

Callie matched Katherine's glare with her own. "There is not enough whiskey in the world."

"Hate to agree with her, but same," the nurse added.

"I'm sure I can find someone in this complex with enough cocaine," Anthony countered with his voice just over a whisper as he pointed at the hooker, "and two words for you, Kath: *Cuba's. Vegas.*"

They didn't even look at each other before they both quipped, at the same time and in the exact same tone of voice: "Go fuck yourself."

The pair gave each other a surprised but somewhat knowing look as the voice on the other end of the line lost his patience. "*If you're quite done, Mr. Pierson – which option will it be*?"

Anthony thumbed the call-kill button and silenced the jackass without giving him another thought. "That I'm not going to share my whiskey with any of you," he grumbled as he dropped the piece of tech to the ground and calmly punted it across the floor.

"My phone!" Callie shouted with a whine.

"A guy just threatened to kill my wife over it, and you don't think you were going to need to change your number?"

"Your *ex*-wife, and you should've said ye –" the hooker started to retort before she caught herself and gave him a defeated look. "At least I insured it, I guess."

With a noncommittal grunt in her direction, he looked back over at the unwelcome guest who had once again made his life an unbearable hell. "In my room, under the bed. There's a box. The code is our anniversary date. Get the dagger and bring it here, but you take the gun."

The way he said the words sent a chill down Katherine's spine. "So does this mean you'll help...?"

"It means I want you to get the damn knife," he growled as he slid over to the door and glanced out the peephole. "We're leaving, but not until you go get my shit."

"We?" Callie interrupted. "What's this 'we' business?"

"The sound of you getting paid extra tonight."

"How much extra?"

"How much do you value your life?" Anthony countered as Katherine not-so-gracefully stumbled over one pile of laundry after another as she made her way to his bedroom. "Honestly, hon, if you don't..."

Callie sighed and ran her hands up through her hair. She had a way of doing it that put every single freaking curve of her body on display, and absolutely no matter how pissed off he was, she'd learned it had a way of shutting him up. "If you think this is the first time I've had a date interrupted by a handful of gangbangers with shitty intentions, you're sorely mistaken. Fucker on the phone not the kind to care about unarmed innocents?"

"Think the fucker on the phone was more corp than gang, so probably not. Didn't talk like a streeter. You get the same vibe?"

"Educated, smug, and packed with equal parts money and lead? Wish I hadn't. Fuck," she agreed. "Any idea which corp? Since the Grims aren't dumb enough to piss off the Angelic?"

"Sojourn? While you were gone, Kath played a recording for me. Their name came up," Anthony replied, careful to leave off the circumstances of the call. Just for the sake of her nerves.

"Would that be… Sojourn Enterprises?"

"You know 'em?"

Callie shrugged her shoulders and swiped an unopened bottle of water off of his counter. "Eggheads. Don't know which end of a woman to stick their dick in, which is kinda sad if you think about it. Met some at a lame-ass-stuffy-suit convention. Only thing there drier than my cunt was the conversation."

"Well, that's a start," Anthony grumbled as he carefully checked his shotgun over. "Know anything else?"

While she explained what very, very little she knew about them, Katherine managed to kick a pile of filthy laundry away from the end of his bed. The whole room was a mess; titty posters on the wall, loose cigs on the floor, and a half-empty bottle of some off-brand fake beer on the nightstand.

"Anthony, the hell is going on with you? I've never seen you this fucking bad before in my life…" she muttered under her breath as she knelt down on carpet that hadn't seen a vacuum in ages. The box – when she found it buried behind a couple of empty canni-caff bottles and a used pair of underwear – was nondescript. The lock wasn't; it was almost the only thing she'd seen in his pigsty-turned-apartment with a shine on it other than the shotty.

Not just a shine. A… tingle. A touch of something that wasn't quite right. Not that it wasn't of this world, but it felt like something that wasn't supposed to *be* in this world. Nothing about it felt natural, and as she worked on the antique combination lock, the dirty, dingy gray box slowly cleaned itself off, and the dust that covered it simply ceased to exist. By the time she had 07062041 dialed in on the rolling tumbler, the whole chest had taken on a pleasant silver sheen.

As she pulled it out from under his bed and cracked open the lid, she heard a small argument going on in the living… area. *Room* didn't sound quite right. "Whatever she's gotten you involved in, I don't want to be part of it. She's your ex and your problem," Callie complained loud enough for Katherine to hear her clearly.

And probably intentionally.

"Wasn't my phone they called."

"Did you bother to turn yours on for a change?"

"Well, no –"

"Then who's fault is it they called mine? Hm?"

Katherine looked up from the distressingly mystical box and shouted out into the other room. "For two assholes that aren't dating, you sound like you are."

"Girlfriend. *Experience*," Callie shouted back.

Anthony bent forward and tapped his forehead with the tip of the shotgun's barrel. "I just wanted a blowjob."

"Was that all? I shaved," Callie quipped, crossing his arms as she watched Anthony work on his antique boom-stick. "The fact that we haven't run screaming out of your apartment yet worries me."

Anthony made *all* the effort in the world to ignore the pout on her lips as she passed him a small box of shells that had also been hidden under the counter. "They know she's here, whoever *they* are, and they know enough about who else is here to call *you*. What makes you think they aren't outside waiting for us to run?"

"Hope?"

"Springs eternal," he grunted. "No. They want her; they'll have to come get her. *Then* we leave."

"After you give her to them?"

He didn't have a chance to reply before Katherine stepped out of his room with a gleaming onyx-hilted silver knife in her hand. 'Knife' didn't do the ornate dagger justice, but it was the only word she could think of to call it. "Anthony. The gun is one thing. This..."

Her ex carefully took it from her and slipped it gingerly through the belt at his hip with practiced ease. There wasn't a point in finding a sheath for it – it didn't like them anyway. It barely tolerated being in the box. "You came to me for help. You don't get to dictate how I give it."

Katherine didn't answer. She just stared at him. Callie took a slow step back as she *felt* the sparks erupting in the air between them. They didn't move, they didn't shout, they just *looked* at each other. When the silence finally grew to the point that it was absolutely *suffocating*, she nervously cleared her throat. "I don't know what I'm missing between you two, and I don't care. What's wrong is that we're still here and not..."

"Yeah. You are," Anthony agreed as he and Kath broke their stare off at the same time. "My room. Go in, hunker down. One way in, one way out. No windows."

"I noticed that," the escort whined. "Can't say I like it. No natural light or sun or anything, you know?"

"I know. It's intentional."

"Oh."

Kath put one hand on her hip and one hand on the counter. "Go in your room and do what?"

"Wait," he answered simply as he turned to face the door.

"For what?"

Callie swore under her breath and grabbed the older woman by her elbow. "For him to have an excuse to use that gun, I'm guessing. Anthony? I'm billing her ass for this."

"You aren't doing anything with my ass, thank you much," Katherine snapped as she shook her arm free. "I know how to get to his bedroom."

"Apparently not. He'd have stayed with you longer."

"*You bit-*"

A muffled noise and a hastily shut door outside made Anthony shut them both up with a quick thump on the counter. He rushed back out of the kitchen and planted his back against the wall beside the door that led into his place. Thankfully, the pair took the hint and bolted into his room, as shouting from outside woke every damned and tired soul in the apartment complex.

Whatever got his attention made the same noise again, and this time it was as plain as day. It was amazing how well you could hear when you knew someone wanted to kill you. It boosted your adrenaline. It set your nerves on edge. You might not always hear someone when they first approach, but if you were paying even half of a bit of attention...

Click.

The sound of a safety going off.

Vague whispers of people trying to hide who had never once been trained to do so. People who thought they could talk in hushed voices, unheard by anyone within at least five feet. "*Yo... ink... in... there?*" followed by, "*Oi, yeah. Sla... inks... in...*"

A second *click*. The unmistakable sound of a clip being hammered home. That brief moment of time when you didn't hear anything, so you knew something was coming. If you worked with weapons, you got used to the sounds. You knew what they were. You knew what followed, inevitably, in their wake.

No matter how much training was under your belt, you always jumped – even just a little – when you knew the sound that followed was aimed at *you*. It was true in '40 when Anthony enlisted. It was true in '54 when he'd lost his arm.

When the gunfire erupted, it roared through the room with a hail of bullets that shredded his door. The couch? Ruined. The coffee table? He'd bought the poor thing at a yard sale ten years prior and fought like a bastard to keep it in the divorce. It had seen dozens of overpriced pay-per-views and all the beer spills and chicken wing stains you could imagine, but it couldn't hold up against a burst of 9mm.

For one brief second, all he could think was that the damn door was supposed to have been *reinforced*. As splinters covered the carpet and he shielded his eyes, he made a note to send his landlord an email demanding he choke on his security deposit.

A shotgun blast followed a second later. The impact annihilated both the door handle and the locking mechanism. Soon after, he heard the tell-tale noise he was waiting for. Asshole #1 – Anthony decided to call him Mr. Automatic – dropped the empty magazine from his gun and started to slide a fresh one in with a metallic clack. Asshole #2 pumped his weapon behind the broken door and prepared to continue the attack.

These guys weren't dicking around with their choice of ammo. 9mms would do some damage to the furniture, sure. These were punching through wood and everything else like it wasn't there. Armor-piercing rounds? Maybe? It was worth noting for later. Right now?

Right now, they were reloading.

Neither had the chance to finish.

Left foot one step forward. Down. Weight on it. Pivot one-eighty.

Pump quickly. Sweep the barrel up. Stay fluid. Level it at shoulder height. Don't try to look through the holes to aim. The gunfire came from a single direction. They were directly behind the door, even as it started to swing open. Anthony didn't hear any footsteps to suggest they had moved. That was all the aiming he needed to do.

The stock pressed against his shoulder. Anthony's breath caught in his chest. The last step was so simple, anyone could do it.

If the gunfire a moment ago hadn't set the girls scurrying for cover, the explosive, bone-wracking **BOOM** that thundered through the tiny apartment surely did. A chunk of the door simply ceased to be, though it was replaced with the agonized scream of the man behind it. The hole in the wood let him see Asshole #2 scramble away from his friend – so Anthony did what he hadn't done five heartbeats prior.

He aimed.

The fore-stock slid back with practiced ease as he pumped a second shell from the magazine to the firing chamber. Asshole #2 stumbled backward out of control as his arms pinwheeled at his sides in utter futility. Mr. Automatic spat out a mouthful of blood as he died, unceremoniously in the middle of a run-down apartment hallway, in a shitty neighborhood, in of one of the nation's most violent cities.

He wasn't the first and he wouldn't be the last.

Both in terms of 'violently dead in the city' and 'in this hallway.'

Anthony pulled back on the trigger a second time with the barrel pointed down at a slight angle. Another chunk of the door vanished. Another thundering boom ravaged his eardrums and sent a sharp pain that screeched through his skull. As bad as the pain in his ear was, it was nothing that could compare to what the dumb-ass punk felt when most of his right knee splattered across the wall.

The gunfight was over just like that.

Two goons who had stupidly given warning they were coming. Two goons who had decided to pick a fight with the wrong woman and her ex-husband. Two goons who had no idea who or what he was, and they lacked the foresight even to ask *why* she would've gone to him for help.

One wouldn't know.

The other was about to get a crash course.

The jackass couldn't have been older than nineteen. Dumb kid; dumb way to die. A dumb, *scared* kid who knew he had a lifespan that could be measured in minutes, if he was lucky. The look on Anthony's face implied that luck was not on his side.

He couldn't stop screaming.

Anthony helped him with that.

A cry of pain died on the thug's lips as his intended victim set his gun down and wrapped his flesh-and-bone hand around the bloody chunk of muscle and ruined denim that used to be the gunman's lower thigh. A cold rush and an almost electrical *hum* briefly emanated from his palm as a pale-yellow glow slowly radiated down the underside of Anthony's arm to his hand. The former soldier opened his mouth and a very faint, very distant cry of *something* slipped out from his throat.

The sound, the glow, and the unbearable pain were all gone within a handful of heartbeats. The bleeding didn't stop, but a surge of nth pulsed through the ravaged tissue and overwhelmed his nervous system. Before the kid could say a word, his killer interrupted him.

"You've got three, maybe four minutes before you pass out," Anthony flatly informed him. "You've got two, maybe three after that before you die. Talk fast, and it'll stay painless."

The thug looked down at the mess of his leg and screamed. Anthony slapped him across his jaw with his metal hand to try to force the kid to focus enough to use real words. "But you... you just healed me..."

He just sneered at the idiot and moved his hand away. The shooter's leg was still an utter bloody mess. Glowing, yes. Bloody and worthless? Also, yes. "Does it look healed? I just sent a death-shock to your nerves to get them to shut up. You're dying. Do your soul a favor and go gracefully," he stressed, "with truth on your lips."

"Dying? I'm... fuck you. You just... why should... why should I tell you a damn thing?" the punk gasped as his killer rolled back on his heels.

"Die screaming or die sleeping," Anthony countered. "I don't care. You just tried to fucking kill me, and I want to know why. Agony or peace? Your choice, but choose now."

As he spoke, he lifted his bloody hand up again and waved it at the dumbass kid. The same faint yellow glow flickered back to it with little jolts of otherworldly energy dancing between his fingers. "Dude I... I can't. They'll kill... kill me."

"I beat them to it."

"No... nah man, nah man, you don't know. You don't know what they do."

"I'd like to. Tell me about it," Anthony demanded as he pointed down at the ever-growing pool of blood seeping further into the ruined hallway carpet. "Time's running out. Really; I'm going to know what you know. If I have to make you scream, I will. I don't want to, but I will."

The kid tried to shake his head but only managed a slow flop. "Slash... he's... he's got tech. New... new stuff. You don't..."

Anthony pursed his lips and gazed down into the dying man's fading eyes. "Slash?" When the ganger shook his head in a silent no, Anthony pushed on. "Lots of places have tech."

"Nah, man, not... not like this," the punk rambled. "Please, man. In my head. Put one in my head. They bring me back and... and I'm in Hell. Real Hell, man, I've... I've seen it and..."

The request took the ex-soldier back a little. "I don't see the need to waste the bullet."

"*Please* homie, *please.* Like... like I'm *sorry* man," the kid cried as tears dripped from his closing eyes. "I've *seen.* The *centurios.* Make me one or feed me to one. Please, man, plea... I'm sorry. Just... please."

Anthony sighed slowly and unbuttoned his shirt all the way to his navel. He filed the phrase away but as fast as the shithead was fading, there wasn't a point in asking. Besides, getting the answers later would be easier. Or at least, faster.

The would-be assassin couldn't even focus his eyes as he faded in and out of consciousness. "There's an old band. Some 80's shit. Classic. '*Public Image Ltd.*' You know 'em?"

No response but a tired wheezing was offered.

"They've got this song. Always loved it. Really simple. Two lyrics, if you can believe it, just repeated over and over again," he continued as he opened up his shirt and touched a circular scar on his chest. "Awesome beat to it. Should listen if you can, whenever you can." Anthony paused and let his gaze linger on the dying gangbanger briefly. "Then again, don't think they'll play it where you're going."

"Why... are..."

"Oh, why am I telling you that?" Anthony shrugged slowly, hooked the knife at his belt loose, and pressed it across the old wound. Blood welled up from the insignificant cut and the circle suddenly sparkled with a yellow light that quickly turned into a greasy orange. "It's called the *Order of Death*. It's fitting. Trust me."

The scar twinkled as more scratches and old branding marks took on a matching shine across his chest. Streaks of light flowed down between each of his ribs and coalesced just above the center of his sternum. A dark green blob of energy welled up under the flesh of his throat as his eyes lost their color and turned an inky black. The punk screamed. Or tried to.

Maybe he'd seen the spell before. Maybe he'd watched one of Anthony's kind work at some point or other. It wasn't outside the realm of possibility. Or maybe he was just terrified that the man he was supposed to kill wasn't just some ex-mil asshole.

"Homie, no, please, man, just kill –!"

Anthony covered the kid's mouth with his glowing, bloody hand and cut off his weak cries of terror. "They can't bring you back if they can't find you," he replied, as the glow in his chest settled down to a single orange throb that reflected from the kid's eyes.

He tried to scream again. It didn't work. The ex-husband, ex-soldier, current *monster* (by damn near every definition of the word) placed the tip of the silver-bladed, onyx-hilted dagger right over the punk's heart and *pushed*. The blade slid inside the teenager's chest but didn't draw a single drop of blood as it sunk in to the base of the cross-guard.

With a shuddering groan of pain, the would-be assassin died. When Anthony pulled the blade out, it was clean and didn't even leave so much as a cut in the punk's shirt behind. What it *did* bring was a pale white fog that began to stream freely from the idiot's corpse before it wrapped a tendril around the point of the knife and began a slow path back up his arm and to the scars on his chest.

The etheric cloud poked and prodded at his skin before it suddenly *seized* up like someone had grabbed it with a claw. The glowing runes on his chest flared with shining yellow light as the poor idiot's essence was forcibly pulled from where it was, away from where it should've been headed, and right into the heart of the man that had killed him.

Anthony's eyes flashed a sickly green and the glow in his chest briefly flashed bright enough to illuminate the hall. One by one, the glowing marks on his chest faded to nothingness as he focused his breathing and regained control of his heart rate. He slowly swallowed air and spit a wad of vile *gunk* up out of his throat with a disgusting, hacking cough.

"Carlos Reyes. I'd say it's a pleasure to meet you but…"

"Fucking *hell,*" Katherine cursed in a whisper from the other side of the ruined door. "*Dammit.* You promised me. You *promised me* you'd never —"

"Promise was voided after you divorced my ass," Anthony grumbled back, as he slowly stood up and pumped his shotgun again. "You came to me with a problem. The fuck did you think I was going to do about it? Plant sunflowers and ask these pukes to go away?"

Behind her, Callie stood in utter shock. Her hands were clamped down tight on her ears and horror was etched across her face. The sound of the gunfire in the cramped run-down apartment had left her half-deaf, so when she spoke, she almost shouted.

"What in the fucking shit *are* you?"

Anthony didn't answer as he nudged the other body with the tip of his gun before he bent down and started rooting through its pockets. Katherine did, and her voice dripped with more venom than the black magic her ex had just used. "Guess the *boyfriend experience* doesn't tell you everything does he? Well, you irritating bitch, meet the man of my nightmares: Anthony Pierson. Retired Army, Spec-Int."

"That doesn't tell me shi —"

"You've been sucking off a li-nec. A fully Federally-licensed necromancer. Trained by the *finest* grave-robbers and unethical mages that the Army can afford, coupled with the crap they call intelligence work for good measure," she added.

"ParaPsy Intel," Anthony added. "If you're going to piss on my old job, at least get the designation right."

"Oh, of course. *Captain* Anthony Pierson wouldn't want his good name drug through the mud. Don't worry; fucking him doesn't make you a necrophiliac. I checked. Does make you an 'enabler of heretical acts' by Church standards though, if you care."

Callie's jaw dropped to the floor.

"Need recommendations for mouthwash?"

2. SLASH 'N BURN
Sunday, May 26th, 9:01 PM

"C'mon, you two, don't just stand there; get this asshole," Anthony ordered as he pointed to Mr. Automatic, "into the apartment. Loot his *jal* and we'll get the fuck outta here."

"Drag him..." Katherine began before she walked through the ruins of his flimsy door and grabbed the corpse by his leg. "Are you going to do both of them?"

"Different things to both of them," Anthony muttered as he rustled through Carlos' pockets. "Are you going to be a bitch about this or...?"

"You already stole it, didn't you?" she shot back, and then before he could reply, went on with a curt growl, "Then it won't matter what shit we do to the corpse."

He looked up from the body he was working on and rolled his eyes. "He was trying to kill us."

Meanwhile, half-deaf and utterly lost, Callie finally had the breakdown she felt she'd earned, "WHAT THE HELL IS GOING ON? WHAT ARE YOU TWO DOING?"

Anthony started to reply to her before he paused with his hand buried in Carlos's pants, "Wait. You can hear after all that, and she can't."

His ex-wife stopped pulling on Mr. Automatic's leg and gave him a happy smile that went from ear to ear. An ear that she casually turned to him and then tugged on her earlobe. The piece of metal inside didn't glint, but a tiny little red LED flashed twice as he stared. "Found some spare mufflers. Yes, I gave her one. Yours are built-in, aren't they?"

His eyes slowly narrowed as he looked from one woman to the other. "Did you turn it on?"

"Wouldn't I?"

"Dammit, Kath..." he growled under his breath as he let Carlos go and quickly moved over to his date. While she protested with more than a little profanity and shouted way too loudly for him to be comfortable with, he pressed his fingers into her ear and fiddled with a plug that perfectly matched the one in Katherine's head. "We don't have time for you two to waste in a pissing match."

Katherine shrugged her shoulders and adjusted her blue vinyl jacket. It was unusually fashionable for her, and might actually hide a few blood splatters. "Like you're not used to giving a woman a headache."

"Which is why I started seeing other women. Spread the pain around," he muttered as he flipped a tiny switch and stepped back. "Callie. Better?"

"Kinda late now you asshole... no. Not an asshole," Callie grunted as she rubbed at the intrusive noise-filter and gave him a look that mixed a cute pout with open hatred and revulsion for Katherine. "What the hell are you? Don't touch me until you tell me."

"I'm a guy trying to keep you two from getting dead. Do you really want to know more?"

"The short answer? No."

Almost hopeful for a chance to save their not-a-relationship, he gave her a faint little smile. "The long answer?"

"Yes. Yes, I want to know more. And throw in a 'fuck you' for good measure. What the hell did you just do?" That was a question he wasn't entirely ready to answer; in part because he could overhear damn near every person in the apartment complex calling the cops. The *El Puro* projects or not, LSPD didn't appreciate gunfire disturbing the residents. It set a bad example for the other slums.

It also made them get off their asses and actually work. They weren't going to be *fast*, but they'd still *work*. Anthony reached over and tapped at the bit of tech he'd slid into her ear. "That's a Synac-Industries Shot-Breaker III. Made for and by the kind folks at the Department of Defense. Specifically tuned to deaden the aura impact of gunfire. It enhances your auditory nerves somehow. Makes you hear better in general."

She reached up and rubbed at her ear while Katherine growled about dragging the corpse into his apartment. Before she could say anything else, Anthony grabbed Mr. Automatic's leg and helped her drag him inside. "Not that, you ass. The... the... glowing lights and... what did you do?"

"Got some answers, hopefully."

"Are you... human? You're not one of...?"

Katherine rolled her eyes and unceremoniously dropped the corpse onto the carpet. "No, he's nothing special. G'on. Tell her what you used to do. See if she still sucks your dick."

The growl that emanated from the depths of Anthony's throat was impressive as he stared her down and tore into her with gusto. "I need answers, and we need a distraction. What did you think I was going to do?"

"I don't know, and I know I should've known better."

"Yeah, you should've," Anthony snapped. "Callie. Yes, I'm human. Worked for the Secretary of State though, so take that for what you will." When she didn't budge, he shrugged his shoulders. "The army has mages on staff. I used to be one. I know a few tricks."

"That wasn't a trick. I've seen tricks. I *perform* tricks. What the hell was that? She said you were… a necromancer? Are you… really…?"

Anthony chambered a fresh shell and stepped back into the hallway. "We get a bad reputation, but yeah," he answered as he aimed the gun at Carlos's head. "Clear out that asshole's pockets and don't get any of this guy on you."

She looked back and forth between the two bodies and then jumped away as he aimed the shotty at Carlos and pulled the trigger. The gun's thunderous clap and the buckshot it'd been loaded with turned the gangbanger's head into a pile of instant mush. The kid was a dumbass, but a last request was a last request.

All things considered, it further terrified the escort and earned another disapproving glare from his ex-wife. "You already fucked with the guy. Was that necessary?"

"Yes," Anthony curtly replied. "Find anything?"

Katherine held up a wallet and a pair of keys in one hand and a super-fancy phone in the other. "This help?"

"His *jal*, sure does."

"Jal…?" Callie asked as she looked down at the bloody corpse with a mix of disgust and horror.

"Joy and life," he clarified. "Wallet. Keys. Phone. Lighter. Rings. Money. The things your life revolves around that you don't need once you take a bullet to the head. Point blank: we need answers and we need a distraction. I'm not going to be able to do either unless you both get really cool with a bunch of shit really fast. Save the questions for when we get to the car. Can you two do that or no?"

Callie took a deep breath and steadied her shaking hands while Katherine shot back at him with more than a few choice words, "I have dealt with some fucked up shit before," Callie muttered falteringly. "Necromancy? Heard about it just didn't... mage shit, it... that's one thing. I know a couple of mages. Sure. But that... I thought I knew what your type... they say it's just head stuff, internal... but that..." she rambled. "What was that? Was it a soul? An actual...?"

"It's real, honey," his ex replied, "It's real, it's disgusting, and if you aren't careful, it'll go a long way to ruining your life."

"I'm the same guy you knew twenty minutes ago."

"Oh, that's a fucking lie," Callie snarled before she turned her ire to Katherine. "Bitch, if I get killed because of you..." she trailed off as a fresh thought came to mind. "Uh. If I get killed because of her, will you... can you... I don't know? Bring me back? Is this like a 'get out of the Reaper's asshole free' card?"

Anthony blanched and knelt down beside Mr. Automatic. "Can I? Yes. Would you want me to? No. Now, step back again."

"Oh, you aren't... are you?" Katherine began, as comprehension dawned in her eyes.

"We need a distraction."

"You need a priest."

"Why? A dead one got us into this mess," Anthony grunted as he pulled the clothes away from Mr. Automatic's ruined chest. "We've got maybe ten minutes. Doing him is going to take five. When I run, you run with. Any more complaints or bullshit? Just save it until we're safe. Understood?"

Katherine sighed and placed a hand on Callie's shoulder. The escort didn't even flinch. "I know this mood. Do what he says, it'll be over fast enough."

Callie looked down at the body and then back at her date as she nervously wiped her hands on her jeans. "I like that better when he says it."

"Anth? You have everything you need?" Katherine asked as she slid further away.

Her asking that was an old habit and his hands immediately slipped to his pockets before he realized he was doing it. "Kit, gun, jacket and pants," he replied as he patted himself down. "Assorted data chips too. If I need anything else, we're screwed."

The escort took a nervous gulp of air as the pair shared a 'moment' of their old life. "Aren't we... aren't we screwed already?"

Anthony paused and pursed his lips. "Not the way I wanted to be." Katherine shuddered and pulled her hand away from Callie's shoulder.

Confident that the two were done bickering, the necromancer pressed his fingers into the dead man's chest and went to work. It wasn't pleasant, it wasn't pretty, and Callie threw up in the sink before he was done.

But once he was...

***

The Federal Licensed Necromancy Program
Because Dead Men Do Tell Tales
***

A heavy, wet footstep from a limp foot wrapped in an old sneaker.

It was a simple sound. So simple it was expected. So normal that the thugs watching the entrance to Aldour Estates didn't even flinch. Another step. A slight limp, maybe even a shuffle; as if every step was a fight. It was the sound of someone limping across old concrete, completely zoned out on the world.

His friends assumed it was shell shock. They'd heard the gunfire. There was more blood than they'd expected. They'd seen a few people run screaming from the complex already. Their friend looking a little beat up and bloodied from across the lot?

Nothing was off about that at all. The sirens weren't unexpected, either. Their shrill cries warning of disaster and disquiet were nothing new in Los San. To the thugs, they were just a warning that they needed to move fast. Faster than their friend was limping across the lot, that much was for sure.

For Anthony? The sirens always seemed to sound different when they were because of *you.* If nothing else, it was going to wreck any chance he had of getting his deposit back.

Aldour Estates. A two-story apartment complex in the El Puro Projects that was known for a number of features, almost all of which were bad. One of the few good was the spacious parking lot built into the center of the complex. Supposedly, it had been a pair of basketball courts for the kids at one point. Now?

Now you came out and got stoned in your car so the scent didn't get picked up by the buildings HVAC and matching 'Oh No – We Don't Do That Here' environmental control. Only time you came out to play ball was if you brought a wad of greenbacks and left with a bag of azul-spheres to go straight up your nose. For some strange reason, it meant that the property management company couldn't keep the pale blue security lights intact.

The lot was great. Paved, crack free, and sometimes the asphalt would glow if it rained. The light-bulbs-turned-target-practice? For once in the entire time Anthony had lived there, the lack of light played in his favor. Mr. Automatic (revealed to be a punk named Thomas Amyers from freaking Burbank, California) was welcomed by two distinct new assholes from the other side of the concrete pad.

The goons didn't realize what had happened to their friend. They wouldn't for a few moments longer. All they knew was that he looked like shit and that he walked like shit and he hadn't talked for shit. *They* talked enough for everyone else with shouts of, "Yo, Tommy!" and, "Dumbass, hurry the fuck up!" that went unanswered.

Unanswered, but served to point out where they were standing.

That nugget of knowledge was a bit important to the survivors, though not as important as what Tommy (dead and brainless) was doing to help them out. The fact that he was doing it against his will only bothered the ladies. The sheen of sweat across his face and the yellow tint behind his eyes made his face look almost as haunted as the dead man's (and that was saying something).

Most importantly though? All eyes were on the former Mr. Automatic, and *not* on the trio of still-breathing souls that desperately wanted to *keep* breathing...

...even if one of them couldn't believe she was watching an actual, not-exactly-living-or-breathing *zombie* cover their escape. Or, as the other one couldn't believe she was seeing one again. And the third member of their party? He wanted one of them to leave and the other to go back to doing the job he'd paid her to do.

But if wishes were wives, he'd still be married.

"Yo, Tommy? Where's Carlos? You get the slitch or not?"

New assholes, new names. Wheelman #1, stood across the parking lot, next to a white SUV and a line of shrubs directly under a dead streetlamp. It was too dark to make any details out, but given the hardware the other two goons had used, he was probably loaded. "You guys took long enough! Carlos still busy with her?"

That was Wheelman #2. Same spot. It didn't lessen the chances of another asshole or two popping up nearby, but with one small SUV, that meant four seats at best. If there wasn't a second car, it made the odds better.

Necromancy was about telling the Great Beyond to wait in line.

Honestly? The Great Beyond didn't appreciate the attitude.

Anthony's eyes went white and cloudy as he focused on the walking corpse. The play wasn't ideal, it wasn't easy, and he hadn't been prepared for any of it. Making sure that he let loose *enough* but not *all* of his grip was critical. He needed the ghast locked onto a target, not wandering around until its new batteries ran out.

A ghast resurrection was some of the most brutal, brute force work a necromancer could pull off. You didn't try to put the body back together. It wasn't designed to be passable. The Army didn't even like to let their corpse-casters do it unless there was absolutely no other choice in the matter. The Army liked to keep firm control of their toys and a ghast was more like a fire-and-forget rocket that used a giant question-mark for its guidance system.

Taking control of a body required a necromancer to do two things at the bare minimum. The first was to infuse the body with enough life essence to replace what had been lost when its soul detached. The second was to impose enough force of will that it would act as the mage directed.

As Anthony relaxed his control, the corpse reacted as all corpses did.

It tried to fill the void left behind. It couldn't, but it tried.

Without Anthony providing an essence to fill the void, the void looked for other options. Tommy's corpse shook off the last vestiges of Anthony's command like water off a duck's back and lunged for the wheelman in front of him. The walking corpse landed on his terrified friend before the punk could do anything more than scream and cover his face with his forearms.

The necromancer was off on a run before they even hit the ground. The women had a lead on him, but not by much. By the time he cleared the main hallway and was nearly down the second, they were already within earshot. Katherine, bless her, turned to face him as he rounded the corner and had the shotgun pointed at his head before she realized who it was.

Honestly, he was just impressed she'd taken the time to aim.

Without answering either of their complaints or concerns, Anthony lifted up on a round door handle and then slammed his shoulder into the corner of a beaten-up metal door emblazoned with *Employees Only* scrawled across the front in magic marker. "I've been trying to get that open for the last..." Katherine muttered before her ex interrupted her.

"Jack keeps losing the key," Anthony explained as he whisked them both inside, "and for being the building super, he's too damn lazy to go get spares made. Watched him pop the latch a dozen times before he showed me how to do it."

Any other questions she might've had about who Jack was or why he'd helped her ex-husband get into some kind of maintenance shed were glossed over as she peered down a poorly lit half-hallway that dropped down a flight of steps into places and realms unknown. "Oh. This looks safe," she whined.

He rolled his eyes as he pushed past them both and muscled his way through the access corridor. They followed – with objection – but they followed. The tunnel only took a few minutes to navigate, but a few minutes of the flickering halogen lights was long enough to give both women a headache. The hallway dumped them out into some kind of underground workshop, with a dumpster that smelled worse than the corpse Anthony had played with, and a utility truck that didn't look even remotely road-worthy.

Before they could ask, he walked over to a switch panel buried behind a pile of boxes and flipped something on. A moment later, one of the walls rumbled, whined, and eventually began to roll up into the ceiling. "Ditch the Uzi," he ordered, "and hand me Marshal."

"You're awfully attached to that antique," Callie complained as she stuffed the sub-machine gun into an old open cardboard box. "Tell me you've got the keys to the truck."

"You would be, too. He's saved my life more than once," he replied as he took the shotty from his ex and strapped it inside a loose holster of sorts in the lining of his duster.

"It, Anthony. It's a gun, not a person."

"He, Callie," the necromancer countered. "Very much a he."

While she rolled her eyes and said something unrepeatable in polite company, Katherine reached over to help keep him steady. "Anthony, what's wrong with you? You don't look... well."

"He made a dead guy get up and walk; I'm sure that's helping him feel just fucking *fine*," the escort grumbled under her breath.

Before Katherine could chastise her, he agreed. "She's not wrong," Anthony muttered. "Something's *wrong* about these assholes. I can... I can feel it."

"Wrong? Wrong how?"

Anthony rubbed at the tattoos and scarification under his shirt and answered with a quiet but unpleasant belch. "That other dumbass. He's not settling well."

"Settling? What did you do, eat him?" Callie asked. When he belched a second time, her face went stark white. "You didn't."

His ex shook her head and leaned against the truck by her shoulder. "You don't want to ask that question. Anthony – how much time do we have?"

"Not enough, so keep moving," he replied with a grimace. "I know where I can take you two, but… yeah. Hurry."

Before they could ask *where*, he was out of the garage and into a small alley well behind and below the complex. A few minutes later and the alleyway morphed into a small street, and a few moments after that? The trio were well on their way into the city proper on foot – and thankfully, the closest subway stop was a few short blocks away.

Not short enough for Anthony, but, it was better than the alternative.

And the alternative was pissed.

***

As they left, a corporate-clad man in a trilby hat looked down at two dead gangbangers. One fresh, the other… fresh in all the wrong ways. Wheelman #1 wiped nervous sweat off his forehead as he paced around the corpses.

"Slash, what… what do we do now?"

Slash – Mr. Slash, to those who knew better – took a slow drag on a half-used cigarette hanging from his mouth and calmly ejected a spent shell from his rifle before he reached into his jacket pocket with an irritated sigh. "Load these two into her car," he answered. "They won't get up again."

"Not going after them?" the ganger asked, eyes alight with bewilderment.

"He could be anywhere," Slash responded with a shrug. "But he won't be in there, so it's pointless. I'm not worried – the city is big, but the holes he could hide in aren't plentiful. Or they won't be, by the time we're done."

"Slash, I…"

His boss took another slow draw on the glowing cig and didn't repeat himself. Either the punk was going to listen, or he wasn't. The idiot let the words die on his lips and went to work dragging the two bodies towards

Katherine's car – a small, 'responsibly priced' sedan perfect for inner-city life.

Anthony's ghast wasn't moving anymore – the round that Slash had put into the back of its head had obliterated what was left of its central nervous system in a single shot. Anthony's magic could only do so much for so long, and while a corpse didn't have to have a head to force it to get up and walk around, if someone wasn't pulling the strings personally?

It was the little things that mattered. Like a functional motor cortex.

Magic could do a lot, but without a necromancer forcing individual chunks of dead flesh to move or the body's braincase functioning semi-independently, a dead guy was just a dead guy. Slash gave Anthony credit for the amusing little trick; it'd done more than just give the trio time to get away. That he'd killed four of his more useful men was just an outright inconvenience.

Well, three.

Slash thumbed a small detonator in his pocket and Katherine's car exploded in a flash of white-hot fire and hydrogen-cell-powered flames. All of the gangers were turned into little more than greasy vapor and a faint hint of bloody mist that settled across the parking lot a few heartbeats later. The hitter adjusted his hat and calmly walked towards his own car parked down the block and out of sight, as the screams of police sirens filled the air.

Now it was four.

It wouldn't do any good to have stories being whispered between his men about what their mark might do whenever they crossed paths next. Because they would. Oh, they most certainly would.

While the car burned, the hitter very calmly tapped the side of his head and made a hands-free call. A moment later, and the conversation was equal parts short and unpleasant. "Miss Adams, my apologies. Our loose thread just became frayed. Additional resources will be required to resolve this concern."

The voice on the other end of the call said something he didn't appear to like, and ended the chat almost as soon as it had begun. He took another puff off of his cig and very carefully made an effort to slip the butt into a small bag in his pocket. By the time the police arrived, he was long gone.

***

The A-32 subway line was first in the alphabet but last everywhere else. And this time of night? The 32 wasn't a bad way to get stabbed, either. Some meth-head looked a little too long at the trio as they boarded the shuttle and didn't look away until Anthony gave him a glimpse of Marshal's barrel stuffed under his coat.

All Callie had to say about them was just, "Go home, worthless *traff*," and then to Katherine, she shrugged her shoulders. "Sub-border traffickers. Traffs. They make the nights... well, hell, I guess... on the lower lines," she said as she glanced up at a gigantic sign plastered inside the car. "You really don't leave the bright lights of the Uni campus area, do you?"

Hell was right. As soon as the traff got up and walked off, you could see the silhouettes of three over-stylized male figures, a woman, and a gender-less fifth splashed across a gold-and-blue background. *The Pentaship: Do Not Settle for Lesser.* Lesser *what* was the question. Lesser status? Lesser riches? A lesser evil?

Lesser Gods?

With the Pentaship – and Their egos – it was hard to say. The point was as obvious as it was unforgiving: power had many meanings in Los San and, in a way, just as many names. Babal, Yelthid, Arsherack? The self-proclaimed Lords of Peace, Cultivation, and Wealth? While anyone with half a brain knew that the titles were bullshit, the Lords of Conflict, Decay, and Greed – if you called Them what they were – had Their way about things.

If your tastes ran more alongside physical excess, Lady Helesiki could find a position for you. And maybe even a job. It *was* Her damn city, after all.

All told, the Five operated somewhere beyond the realm of simple 'love and hate' with each other and the rest of the known world. They owned property. Investments. Corporations. They had Their own little fiefdoms across the world where They pretended to play by the laws of man as much as They felt it necessary, though there weren't a lot of places They made the effort to even bother.

Sometimes They competed. Sometimes They worked together.

A wise man would say that the Pentaship – when it was a united front – was the most dangerous group on earth. A wiser man would say that the individual members were in competition with each other in a way and for reasons that were beyond mankind's comprehension. Either way, They didn't run the planet so much as they *invested* in the mere humans that thought they did.

Except for one – Their older brother, or whatever the closest approximation you could call Him. The other four were overshadowed by one last figure, an entity and a name of greater strength than all its siblings combined. The Four Points of Post-Humanity answered to one of the eldest sentient minds in creation – Guuuthenber, the embodiment of raw, complete Power. Electrical, physical, magical, it didn't matter.

Gu was power.

And Gu didn't care what you thought of It.

Anthony liked to imagine that in a *sane* world, more of humanity would've taken the literal manifestations of metaphorical demonic concepts as a sign from On High that maybe people needed to get their act together. That would be the sane thing to do, but sanity always had opposition. Instead? Humanity took the hard road.

The world decided instead to suffer through an endless slew of wars and civil disturbances, before the global Powers That Be collectively shrugged their governmental shoulders and passed laws that allowed the five – one after the other, since they took their sweet time to manifest – to become federally-protected members of society. They could legally own property, pay taxes, the whole nine yards. There was probably an argument to be made about 'tolerating the intolerable' or something you could make in there.

Then again, when the Five started to sink their claws into the world, the world sort of already knew They were there, even if they lacked names to put to faces. Or a lack of a face, where Gu was concerned. The history books had foretold of them; old-time cultists, crackpots, and mythological figures had embodied them for centuries. Quiet manipulation, hushed words spoken in shadow, had made it clear for all time that something was lurking just below the surface.

When They crested the waves of reality and pushed through the dimensional walls into humanity's home, it didn't come as much of a shock, the hard road be damned. It turned out that soft branding really did work. Anthony assumed that if you existed because you tempted souls to eternal torment, you absolutely *had* to be good at PR.

"Speaking of Hell, he gonna be okay?" the escort asked with a nod in Anthony's direction. Her voice snapped him out of his reverie and made him focus his attention on the supremely pissed-off soul writhing away in his chest.

"I... I don't know," the dark-haired woman replied as she gave her ex a sideways glance.

Anthony didn't look… well. His eyes had taken on a sunken, jaundiced appearance. His left hand twitched erratically, and he hung his head down like he was suffering from a migraine. That wasn't far from the truth, and when Kath tapped him on his shoulder, he looked up at her with a speckle of drool that trailed from his lips.

"Oh, fuck. You ate him raw, didn't you?" she exclaimed as she pulled her hand back.

"Wasn't like I had time to cook him. You were there, remember?"

The profane response she muttered even took Callie back, who, frankly, was surprised Kath knew those words (let alone the right order to use them in). "Are you going to be okay?"

Anthony grunted and ran his shaking hand through his hair to wipe away a cold sweat across his forehead. "It's not going to kill me if that's what you're asking."

"How about, 'Are you going to throw up on my shoes before or after you bleed out on my shirt?' Is that better?" Katherine demanded as she held his head up and carefully peered into his eyes, one after the other.

"Either or," he tiredly admitted.

"You're going into n-tox. Quickly, and I'm guessing painfully," Kath finally sighed after she pulled his eyelids up and looked under them like she was trying to find something hidden under a rug. "Looking at you? You've got an hour before your heart starts popping off. *Tops.*"

"N-tox? Bleeding?" Callie interrupted. "Excuse me, but…"

"That's not long enough," Anthony grunted. "Joy."

Katherine wiped another bead of sweat away from his eyes with the back of her hand and replied with the kind of sigh that you gave someone when you didn't like how much you knew about their hobbies. "How long do you need?"

The delay in his answer did nothing at all to calm the sour feeling in her stomach. "I need to get you two to Erica."

"Anthony, I'm not going anywhere until you…" Callie interjected before Katherine turned to face her and shut her up with a single *glare* that spoke volumes about the current situation. "The man made a corpse walk. I have concerns," Callie whispered under her breath. "I feel like they're *valid.*"

"She's not wrong," the necromancer mumbled. "Tell her. I gotta make a call."

"How come you get a phone and you broke mine? That's not fair."

"Because your phone wasn't given to you by A-Int. The only people able to listen in on mine are them," he countered as he fished it out of his pocket, "and the Dragon-Czar. But frankly, the Ru-Chi Bloc doesn't care about a corp/gang fuckup in Santuario."

Callie's face slowly went white as she sank down into her seat and asked, "Did he just suggest that he's being watched by –"

"He really didn't tell you shit, did he?" Kath snorted. "You just saw him raise a zombie, he's ex-Army, and his arm is a retirement gift from the Department of Defense. You think he *isn't* being watched?"

"But… our holo-sessions…" Callie pressed meekly. Katherine just rolled her eyes as the escort wracked her brain. Finally, after a prolonged beat of silence as Anthony struggled with the lock on his phone, the escort settled back and crossed her arms with a defeated sigh. "From now on, I'm charging you group rates."

Katherine rolled her eyes with a disgusted 'tsk' as her ex finally dialed in whatever number he was trying for. The voice on the other end of the line answered with far too much perkiness for the time of night, and it was loud enough all three of them could hear it. *"Frank's Hardware Customer Support! We provide all the support you need – but I'm afraid this call is after hours! Please call back during our –"*

Anthony cut her off before she could finish the sentence. "I'm an account holder. ALNEC-APIEO9. Need an emergency assist."

The line went silent for a few short heartbeats before the chipper agent on the other side spoke up again. *"Mr. Pierson! So good to hear back from you. You've changed numbers! How can Frank's Hardware help you tonight?"*

Yeah. He'd changed numbers – and specifically because he didn't want Frank knowing where he was. All of which made the rest of the call a little less comfortable. He looked down the car at the traffs at the other end and slowly dialed down the speaker. "I'm having a cookout. Out of buns for my dogs."

"Oh, I see. Would this be the cookout at 957 East Arbunkle?"

"We've had to move it. Crowd got noisy."

"I understand, Mr. Pierson. As a reminder, we at Frank's always appreciate our clients avoiding situations with our equipment that would cause additional civil complaints to be filed."

Anthony grimaced at his handheld and tapped out a small command onto the screen. "Additional?" A map filled the display and angry little dots appeared across it as he looked it over.

The voice on the other end of the line wavered before it replied with a succinct, *"We're currently out of buns. Is there anything else you'd like to place an order for?"*

"To be honest I might need a new grill tonight. I'll return it tomorrow."

"Unfortunately, Mr. Pierson, your account shows a past-due balance. A grill rental won't be possible at this time."

The grimace turned into an outright look of disgust as he continued to scroll his fingers up and down his phone. "What if I give Frank an invitation? Introduce him to the other guests?"

"Please hold."

Callie reached over and grabbed his wrist as absolutely God-awful elevator music kicked on. "What in the ever-loving *shit* are you doing, Anthony?"

The necromancer carefully pulled free and turned the phone around so she could see it. "I'm trying to rent a grill. Look – it's the ActiveNow report. Whole fucking city is lit up tonight."

That wasn't an overstatement. The app showed a dozen different calls for emergency services across the southern side of the city, but there was a concentration of icons marked 'F-Inv' and 'CCS' that flickered across the map. Most of them were congregated around two addresses she recognized as police stations, but a tight ball of them were gathered at Anth-Med.

"What's that...?"

"It's an illegal knockoff of a scanner app," Kath interrupted. "Up to old tricks?"

"I like not getting pulled over."

"I bet," Katherine grumbled. "CCS – that's Conglom-Corporate Sec right?"

"Rent-a-cops, yeah. They rep about thirteen of the big-name services in town. Lemme guess – they contract for Anth-Med?" he replied as a fresh round of tremors caused him to nearly drop his phone. When she nodded, he went on to ask the next semi-obvious question of, "Any idea why they're gathered 'round the hospital block? Or why they're tagged with markers of 'Federal Involvement' tonight?"

Katherine shook her head slowly and nervously slid her hands into her pockets. "No, I mean... there was an enforcement staging alert about ten minutes before I pulled up at your place, but we get staging alerts all the time..."

Anthony pursed his lips and turned the phone back around as the awful music finally changed tune to something less country and more pop-club. "An ESA, those gangbangers, and now Frank's giving me shit? I do not think I like tonight."

"Who's Frank?" Callie asked.

"A hardware specialist," he answered without actually answering the question. "One I owe money to."

"Who don't you…" Kath started before the customer service agent spoke up again.

"*Mr. Pierson?*" she began, "*I spoke to Frank's assistant. Where would you like to have your grill delivered?*"

Anthony looked up at the painfully glowing map bolted to the inside of the car. "9th and Hackshaw? And if he could rush it…"

"*Rush orders require additional down payment,*" she chided, "*but you'll be happy to know that its already on its way there. The A-32 will arrive in the next ten minutes and your grill will be there within twenty.*"

A little flicker of… something… flashed across his eyes as he replied with an uncomfortable, "I… yeah. Your location-tracking data is impeccable as always."

"*We have to know where our customers are to best suit their needs. Is there anything else I can help you with tonight?*"

"No… no, I think we'll be okay."

"*That's a relief to hear. His assistant had concerns about your cookout. We'd also like to remind you that at Frank's, we appreciate it if our rentals are returned in one piece.*"

"For your clients or for your merchandise?"

You could hear the smile in the agent's voice just before she ended the call. "*Mr. Pierson, shame. You've had an account with us long enough to know there's no difference between the two.*"

A malicious *bloop* sound disconnected the line before he could respond, though he didn't look any happier after the call was done. "I swear to God all I wanted to do tonight was to get my –"

"Anthony, I don't care," his ex interrupted. "What happens now? Where do we go? What do we do?"

He took a deep breath and looked down at his shaking hand. "I've got a friend that can help you two out. Then I guess I'm going to go find out who wants you dead."

Katherine looked down at his hand and watched as an inch of his skin split open, flashed an ominous yellow, and sealed itself closed again. "After you detox."

"Depends on if I get shot at again."

"Anthony, no. I said you had an hour, *tops*."

The necromancer looked up at her with what was nearly literal fire in his eyes. "I didn't ask for this. I don't want it. This is the poster child for 'not my problem.' I'm doing it because you asked for help."

Callie slowly cleared her throat to add, "And because your favorite date got shot at."

"My only date."

"Only? You're not seeing anyone else?" she asked as a brief, bright smile popped up on her lips. It faded quickly with a glance from Katherine. "Why, uh. I mean, thank you for your... patronage."

His ex-wife gave her a murderous look and rolled her eyes as Anthony winced. "And because I was shot at, not that anyone would care about that *trivial little complaint.*"

Both women took the hint and backed off just a little bit.

A few silent minutes later, Katherine finally found it in herself to speak up again. "Anthony, I'm scared. I'm not like you. I don't *get* shot at."

"You said that already."

"Yeah, but I *mean* it," she stressed. "Gang this, gang that, corp this, corp that. I'm a fucking *nurse.*"

Anthony took a deep breath and shook his head slowly. The burning in his chest wasn't getting any better, and leave it to her to exasperate it. "Look, you know how the city works. The corps say bark, the gangs bite. It's hand in hand."

"No, Anthony, I don't. I go to work at my *legal* job that pays *taxable* income. I get insurance. I get dental. I get up, I clock in, I work, I go home. Sometimes, I order Food-On-A-Wing. That's how the city works for the rest of us."

Callie blinked and looked back and forth between the pair. "She gets dental?"

"I get dental."

"Ya'll hiring?"

Katherine ignored her entirely. Her ex spoke up instead. "That's how it works in your tidy little clean hallways, sure. But for the rest of us? C'mon Kath, you're not that blind. The Daemons run the show from the top of their gilded towers. Everybody from DC on down answers to their scaly asses."

"Do they have scales?" Callie interrupted. "I've always wondered."

"Fuck if I know," the necro replied with a grimace. "I've met a couple less-adjusted horn-heads and crackbreeds that did, but I've never laid eyes on anyone even close to the Penta's level."

While he blew his date off with his answer, Katherine looked away from the other end of the subway car and tried to study his sweating, miserable face. "It's not like that. We live in a democr-"

"Kath, seriously. Of the top ten largest Mega-Corps on the freaking *planet*, the Pentaship has direct control over three of them and one of those three is based here in Los San. Heart and Spade is one of the biggest donors to Anth-Med *and I don't even have to work there* to know that. They have controlling shares by proxy in at least four more across the damn globe. You don't get that kinda power just by playing grab-ass in a boardroom."

"If only," Callie happily quipped.

It was Anthony's turn to pretend the younger woman didn't exist, and he sighed as he tried to curl in on himself just to get some relief. "Of the six major international gangs — cartels, families, whatever — active in North America, four of them have pledged open allegiances to the Pentaship. That includes both the Gardeners and the Grimshanks: two of the most active criminal groups in Los San, at that."

"Don't forget the Sub-Soua Carties," the escort added. "I mean, I know they're more into the whole 'Lower Circle Cult,' shit but they'd be pissed if they thought you were ignoring them."

"I'm not, but they don't take their marching orders from the sky-risers downtown," he countered.

It was Kath's turn to say something stupid. "You say that like you think the gangs *work* for the corps."

"You say that like you think they *don't*," Anthony countered.

It was so stupid that even Callie was left feeling a bit speechless. "Fuck, Anth. She really this dumb?"

Anthony glanced up and looked his ex in her eyes and saw something familiar glinting back: a telltale sign there was something she knew and was not keen on sharing. "No, she's just good at playing at it. Kath, I don't want to burst your worldview here, but yeah, *They do*. The megas in this Gulf use gangbangers like the mall uses rent-a-cops. Cheap, disposable, and easy to say they did more than they were asked. The corps keep the rules in place between boardrooms and Wall Street, and the gangs keep it in the alleys."

"Plus, the dumb-asses street-side get to do all the shootin' when the suits wanna go to war," Callie added. "Nobody prim and proper ever faces a courtroom, and the punks with guns get to blow shit up when they all get angry at each other."

"She's got a point. C'mon Kath, you had to know this."

The nurse took a trembling breath and tried to steady her hands. "What I know is that Anth-Med treats everyone equally. I don't worry about boardroom bullshit or gangland antics until someone shows up with a bullet wound or their face blasted off by some pyro. I mean, I know that the gangs do work for the Penta… fuck, my *boss* has an idol of Gu in his office," she admitted. "Still, I… I can't imagine any of them are working for them in some 'vast conspiracy' nonsense."

"Oh, there's no conspiracy. It's all out in the open. Everyone works for the Penta."

"And how the fuck exactly do *you* know about this? The Army?"

"Because your alimony eats up half of my disability check, and bluntly, the rest of it doesn't cover rent," he snapped back. "I did say *everyone*. I'm not cashing checks direct from the Spades or anything, but I've done… work… here and there for… people."

"And I'm not cheap," Callie added with a smirk. "Please, you didn't know? Either you're dumb as a brick, or you're willingly being a moron. What's your angle?"

"I just… with Jordan I…"

"Oh. I get it," the escort realized with a start. "You were hoping that a few punks taking shots at you wasn't as bad as you thought it might be? You *are* playing dumb, aren't you? Or, no. You're *intentionally being* ignorant. I guess life really *is* different downtown in the Corp Towers."

"Let me make it worse for you Kath," Anthony clarified before his ex had a chance to respond, "*nobody* would take a shot at a priest in his sanctuary without express and full permission from either Heaven or Hell to do it. Since I can't fathom the Church putting out a hit on one of their own… it's the gangs. Since those two shits at my apartment were Gardeners, that means we have to wait."

"For what?"

"For the Farmer's Daughter to put out an apology on behalf of Eden Farms," he replied. The first name didn't mean much to Katherine, though Callie's eyes went wide. The second name? Just the nation's number-one agri-corp. "If they don't give a message about an overzealous staffer soon… well, then, that's all the proof we'll need that they authorized it."

Callie nodded along with him for a minute – then opened her mouth. Normally, he was a fan of that. This time, not so much. "You so sure? Didn't the news say the cops are after the Grims?"

"Oh. Yeah. You have a point."

A point that Katherine didn't catch or care about if she did. "Why… I can't stress this enough, Anthony, why the *fuck* would *Eden fucking Farms* put a hit on my brother? Why the fuck would *anyone*?"

"That's a really freaking good question. One I don't think I want the answer to."

"Can… can I admit again that honestly, I'm *scared*?"

Anthony nodded his head slowly and swallowed another lump in his throat. "If it helps, I know someone more terrified than you are."

"I'm not that…" Callie began before he cut her off and pointed to a faint glow emanating from his throat.

Anthony rubbed at the shifting pale white spot and coughed up a flake of blood. "Not you. Him. Your night ain't half as bad as this fucker's."

***

Guth Investment Capital Assets
Power is the Ultimate Investment.
***

Nobody had anything else of note to say until the A-32 ground to a creaky stop at a grime-strewn station on the edge of Midtown. Wasn't the worst place to be, wasn't the best. A couple of homeless kids huddled in a corner of one of the maze-like hallways leading out of the station, and Katherine lingered a few steps behind as she debated whether or not to help them. Callie grabbed her with practiced ease and pulled her along without a second thought.

The necromancer in their party seemed oblivious to everything. The only thing he was focused on was keeping a hand over his chest and his stomach in place as they made their way back to the bright neon-bathed streets above. Once they climbed the stairway and stepped into the cool night air, it was almost impossible not to be taken aback by the sights and sounds around them.

A few minutes in the lower metro lines transported you from a poor, dilapidated, and borderline demilitarized zone straight into the excesses of Los Santuario. At the end of the day, that's all Santuario was: a city of bright neon LED lights that didn't shine anywhere light was actually needed.

Someone had once called it the City of Ads. A city of digital displays that hawked everything from pretty little panties that *promised* to make your partner as hard or as wet as you could want, to the finest in home-defense weapons that could down a full-sized buffo-mutie from the Vegas Glowlands in seconds. Every last one of them a promise. Every last one a whisper in your ear and a blinding light in your eye to convince you to BUY HERE and SELL THERE and GET LAID and GET AHEAD.

Every. Single. Minute.

Every single minute of every single damned day.

It was everything the Neo-American Dream claimed to be. Violent sex. Passionate guns. Fast cars. Faster food. If you wanted it badly enough, you could get it in Los Santuario. All you had to do was sell your soul. Maybe figuratively. Maybe literally. It depended on whether the ghost you walked around with was worth anything to anyone.

"Good luck getting to sleep," Anthony grumbled just under his breath.

What didn't take obscene quantities of luck was the not-so-sudden arrival of his new 'grill,' or as Callie called it, "Hey, holy shit, that's a nice fucking car."

Katherine secretly agreed as she sized up the shiny chunk of carbon fiber and flex-it-glass that rolled right to them not even a minute after they made it onto the streets. A gunmetal gray hood, *pristine* red sides, and a convertible top that was already down to expose the real-leather seats front and back.

They didn't stop drooling until Anthony nodded at the driver and walked to the *next* car that pulled up – a 2020 Kiaiac SUV that had fewer matching tires than it did functioning brake pads. Any temporary joy the pair with him might have had went away as their hearts broke and butt-cheeks clenched over the idea of being caught dead in that thing.

Literally or figuratively.

"You APIE?" the driver of the junker called out.

"Naw, he's A-PIE-of-shit," the driver of the drool-worthy chunk of pristine steel called out. "Yo. Tony."

"Zeek," Anthony replied with a curt nod. "Thanks for the grill."

"Don't thank me, thank Frank," Zeek replied with a nod and a wolfish grin that it up his brown cheeks from ear to ear. "I told him you'd used up all your days at the park. He overruled me."

The ex-int officer grimaced and gave the lead driver an ugly glare. "That's the kind of thing that gets people shot. I thought we liked each other."

Frank's courier shrugged his shoulders and drummed his fingers on his steering wheel. Gold rings 'thunked' against the cool leather as the bigger man in an *incredibly* classy suit shot him an even bigger smile. "I like your money and you haven't been good for a lot of it lately."

"Then why did Frank deliver the goods?"

"Because the boss is a generous man," Zeek replied. "Take a look in the back seat. Thought you might need some refreshments for your picnic."

Anthony caught the keys as the second driver tossed them over and caught a good look at Zeek's escort. He wasn't someone he recognized right off, but the simple crossed hammer and screwdriver tattooed on the side of his temple made it clear who he worked for. "Usually, a grill comes with a threat to bring it back in one piece. We skipping that tonight?"

"It ain't in one damn piece to begin with. Can't ask you to do much worse," Zeek retorted. "Can give you a warnin' about a bad *extended warranty*, though. You know, the kind that'll bring it back from the junkyard? Some new oil in town. Fucks with the engine in ways you ain't seen outside of an M-M-M-F holo-spank."

Callie winced in sympathy while the necromancer paused with one hand on the beat-up, once-white passenger side door. "Frank is offering service plans now?"

Both drivers cut loose with dry laughs that made Katherine's skin crawl. "Boss had a feeling you might've let one of your guests overstay their welcome," Zeek replied slowly as he dropped any hint of his jovial attitude. "He knows you're one to watch your diet but thought he should give you a heads up that there's been someone going around spikin' the punch. You take a sip?"

Anthony slowly opened the car door and ushered Katherine inside as a few club-dressed pedestrians walked by without paying them any attention. "Chugged a whole bottle." He punctuated the remark by pulling open his shirt enough to show off a glow from the scars around his heart.

Frank's wheelman grimaced and revved his engine. "Then Tony? If I were you? I'd pump yo stomach. Like, now."

"Exactly how soon is now?"

"As soon as you can do it away from the grill," Zeek replied. "Give Frank a call when you get a chance. You know the number. Get a good *fix*. That's his suggestion, ain't mine."

Callie slid into the back seat as her john chewed the warning over and felt fresh bile roil in the back of his throat. "Let him know I will as soon as I get everyone dropped off."

Zeek answered with a nod and a mocking salute as he pulled out onto the avenue without another word – or a glance at the oncoming traffic. Anthony walked around the car and dropped into his seat as quietly as he could, but once he was in and down? A short, succinct, and heart-felt *"Fuck,"* left his lips without hesitation.

Neither of his companions did anything but gratefully crack open the water bottles and protein bars that Zeek and his crew had left behind for them. Anthony didn't even bother to do that much; he just cranked the key, listened to the engine have what could only be described as an epileptic fit, and felt the junker unleash a backfire that would've filled the

Field Artillery School with envy. A moment later, and the trio were on the road and in the direction of I-37S to Corpus.

His lack of attention to the foodstuffs didn't get past Katherine's eye, even as Callie wolfed down as many snacks as she could get her petite hands on. "Too full to eat?"

"Meh."

"You know I'm not going to let you skip."

"I said 'meh,'" her ex repeated, with an annoyed side-eye glance.

"And I said I wasn't going to let you," she countered. "If you don't put some water in your mouth, I'm going to dump a bottle in your lap. Your choice."

There was a time and place for an argument, and right now – this was neither. Reluctantly, Anthony took an opened bottle from her and tried to take a drink, although he only managed a bare sip before everything past his lips tasted rancid and foul. His hacking cough and gagging fit sent water spraying everywhere and caused him to swerve into the next lane before Katherine could grab the wheel and force him back into the right spot.

"Fucking dammit so fuc-"

Katherine buried her hand in his hair before he could finish the sentiment. She gave him one long, steadying squeeze and felt his whole body relax at the touch as she quietly asked him, "You fucked up with that guy, didn't you?"

Anthony groaned and tried to get his blurry eyes to focus back on the street. Traffic wasn't terrible, but it wasn't great. Each stop light and street lamp cast a halo around it, making the drive feel like traversing through a kaleidoscope from Hell. "Yeah."

"Damn," she muttered as she began to run her fingernails across the back of his head and down his neck. Each time she touched him, he flinched, but then after, his shoulders sagged a little bit more and more. "You're an asshole, you know that? What can I do to help?"

"Maybe stop touching him like you still love him?" Callie grumbled from the back seat. "It's gross. And it's my job. *Girlfriend expe-*"

"Callie, not –"

"No," she snapped, flatly interrupting him, "I'm not going to do shit until you tell me where we're going and what the hell you are, and what's going on. Fucking forget it."

'Fucking forget it' was easier said than done. "We're going to see a lady I know. She's got a –"

"Anthony, are you taking us somewhere where we might get shot at?" Katherine interjected.

He shook his head and slowly let off the gas as they approached an on-ramp leading to Exit 89. "No. E-Ve has strict rules on –"

"Good. Then I don't care," Katherine retorted, flicking a lock of hair back over her shoulder. "Callie, you shouldn't either. He likes us both well enough not to endanger us more than he already has. I think."

"My apartment is a crime scene, and I heard someone blow up a car in the parking lot. I just lost my deposit and damn near all my worldly possessions to the coffers of LSPD so *yes*, assume I like you *barely enough* not to endanger you further," Anthony snapped, "but don't tempt me to switch lanes and introduce our teeth to the next CarGo-Go! van I see going northbound."

"Someone woke up grouchy," his date whined before she turned serious a second time. "Will someone please tell me what's going on?"

Katherine sighed and let go of her ex-husband's head and put her hand on his shoulder. "You. Drive. I'll deal with this."

"Be gentle."

"That'd be a first and you know it," she quipped. "Callie, shut up and listen, or I'll help him wreck the car and get it over with for all of us. The only thing that's keeping me from having a nervous breakdown is the knowledge that he's cruising to a full-body shutdown and I don't get alimony if he's dead. You don't have that excuse. You got it?"

The escort's eyes went wide at the sudden steel in the other woman's voice. Kath'd reverted to her, *'I'm a nurse and I know what I'm doing so sit back and shut up'* tone, and it worked. "Is he human?" Callie asked.

"Yes. He's just got some powers that most people don't."

"To play with the dead, you mean."

Katherine nodded slowly and let her eyes flick back to their driver. "I mean that there are people in this world that can draw power from the same place that the Five do. Anthony's one of them."

The escort felt her face lose a bit of coloration. "So, he's a crackbreed?"

The car swerved a little as Anthony flinched. It was one thing to *say* it, it was another to be *called* it. Was it speciesist? Oh yeah. Did he care? Not really.

As he tried to get the junker back under control, Katherine shut the question down. "Magic's been around longer than the Five have been here," she admitted reluctantly. "He's not… one of those. Just… trained to use it."

"Trained. To raise the dead."

"He can pull strings on puppets," Katherine replied. "Doesn't make him worse than anyone else."

"That's not what the CoAA says," Callie countered. "They've always said that necromancers are abominations and devil-suckers and…"

Anthony looked away from the highway and over his shoulder with a dirty glare. "The Canuck Pope doesn't have a great view of hookers, either. Don't see me calling you names."

"You do when I'm sucking *your* soul out of your body!" she shouted. "At least I put it *back*. Kinda. If… if you pay extra I mean I guess I…"

The exchange put a very brief smile on Kath's face, but it didn't last long. "It's just nth manipulation. Just his is with bodies and souls instead of lightning bolts and levitation. It's not a *clean* profession, but it doesn't make him any less human. Makes him a sinner and an asshole, but… you can say the same about all of us to some degree. That's what Jordan used to say. He sins more than we do, but still."

"Thought you were on my side," Anthony groused as a shaking fit wracked his body.

"Yeah, well, your side smells like a week-old autopsy," she countered before she turned to Callie again and continued on. "I study mages. I know things… about how magic works. His magic, or pyro-based, psychic… all that shit. He has his connection, and he just kinda found a way to use it. I don't like the way he uses it, I've never liked the way he uses it, but he just used it to save our heads from getting blown off, so I'm going to swallow my pride and deal with it in therapy."

"Callie, it's not like I'm doing anything wrong."

The escort tossed her water bottle onto the floor and crossed her arms. "I think you *ate* a human *soul*. Tell me how that isn't *wrong*. You *ate* his *soul*."

He didn't respond right away, and it was Katherine who sighed and gave both of them a knowing glance. "She's actually taking it better than I did."

"You nearly got me shot by your father," Anthony pointed out.

"He missed."

"Because I *ducked*," the necromancer whined. "Callie, listen. I'm having a hard enough time keeping this guy down as it is. I don't need an argument."

"That's not a vote for '*I didn't eat a soul, I promise*,' you know that, right?" Callie shot back.

Katherine felt her eyebrow lift. "Which of us is the formerly married couple in this car?" The escort started to reply, but the older woman cut her off. "I know. The *experience*. Well, this is a new one."

"Yes, I ate his soul, if you want to call it that," Anthony grumbled. "Or as close to a soul as what some people get."

A little nervous shadow flickered across Callie's eyes. "That doesn't sound…"

"You, drive," Katherine interrupted as she turned her attention to the other passenger, "and you. Believe me when I say that I *don't* like the fact that the man I said my vows to is capable of taking 'til death do us part' to a whole other level just by waving his fingers in the air. Playing with the dead takes a lot out of him, but it's not something either one of us can change. People die; their souls go away, but Anthony can make them hang around for a little bit. That's all."

"Legally they're not classified souls," the necromancer muttered. "But yeah, they're souls. So what she said."

Callie took the outburst like a champ and held her tongue until his ex was done. Slowly, firmly, she finally asked a simple question. "Is that true?"

True was a loaded question.

"I don't keep them. I just borrow them," he admitted after the silence stretched onward for more than a city block. "There isn't a nice way to say it. Trust me, I've tried. To say it nicely, I mean. Not to keep them. Yes, I can take a soul from someone that's recently died, or call one back to an older corpse. I've got control over biological tissue that's quit working. Yes, it's a mess. No, I don't destroy souls. They go off to wherever they're supposed to go once I'm done with them. I'm not a monster, just…"

"It's more like a catch-and-release for your spirit," Katherine quipped.

When that particular analogy didn't do a damn thing to calm Callie down, Anthony took another stab at it. "I can't bring people back to life in the way you hope. I can't stop a body from decaying. I can't keep a soul from moving on for more than a few hours, but I can talk to one if there's enough of a connection left to its crydasta. I can make a body get up and move. But none of it is easy."

"Crydasta? What's that?"

Kath pursed her lips and answered for him. "It's… part of the body. But it isn't. You die, your soul goes elsewhere. If you haven't been gone for long, he can call it back into the body for a little bit if the… shit. Even I don't have a good way to describe it."

"A-Int always said to think of it like a balloon with a hole in it. You can stuff some air back into it but it's still gonna deflate even if you patch it."

Callie blanched. "So, there's really such a thing as life after death? You… you understand that this is a big deal, right? Why don't more people…?"

Another question without an easy answer. "Because we don't know what's after death, exactly. Just that for a little bit, death can be… temporary," Katherine answered.

"We have some ideas," the necromancer muttered under his breath. "Ultimately, though, no. We don't know. We know the Five came from somewhere and that souls go somewhere, and that I can talk to them. That's… the extent of it. Or at least, as far as I know."

Callie's look conveyed concern in quiet volumes, but Katherine's frustrated look cast it in stark relief. "Not. Helping," the escort growled.

"He's also leaving out the parts about how hard it is on the human body, how much it damages the natural flow of nth around people that are attuned to it, what the moral implications are…" Katherine growled.

"Don't forget legal. I'll fuck with souls before I fuck with the IRS," he added with a grimace before he continued on by adding, "But it's all true. I'm not lying to you, Callie. I don't know what happens after you die. I just… I can do something with the nth left behind. Call it magic, call it occult, call it demonic or divine, I don't know, and honestly, I don't give a shit. I can do it, and I'd rather focus on what I *can* do than what I can't."

The shadow in her eyes fell back across her full face as they slowed down for a stoplight and some asshole in a semi leered down at her from the next lane over. "The Army taught you how to raise the dead?"

"Yep."

The withering stare she gave him could've burned a hole through the ripped-up headrest on his seat. "The fucking *Department of Defense* employs *necromancers* as what? Spies? No. You *can't* be serious."

"Spies?" he asked. "Absolutely not."

"Thank God because —"

"The CIA has their own. The Army has us working for a sub-div of INSCOM. Two entirely different groups. Hoover Plaza has a sect of necros practically enslaved down in the Vaults. An actual fucking *sect*. They're a friggin' cult."

"You're bullshitting me."

"He's really not," Katherine interrupted. "You two can talk down to me about the bullshit on the streets all you want but when it comes to *this* shit, pull up a damn chair because class is in session. It's not news that necromancy is one of the tentpoles of modern nth-manipulation. The feds don't like to discuss it publicly, and the corps don't brag about it, but we all know it exists."

"Yes, but *this* magic *shouldn't*," she whined. "Call it nth whatever, it just feels wrong."

Katherine nodded her head. "Plenty of people agree with you."

Anthony shrugged his shoulders as he changed lanes again and flipped off an asshole in a 'vette who had gone all-out with headlight mods that equated to *'Screw you and your eyeballs, I'm a pretty rainbow, see?!'* Even for the start of a weekend, traffic around the city was just unreal. "It's just nth shit. That's all there is to it."

"Yeah well, there's playing in the Pyro-Bowl and throwin' fireballs across the damn field and doing some illusion bullshit you can do with a holo-broadcaster and then there's making a dead guy get up and walk. My dad used to take me to the *Circ de Lune* for my birthdays, so I get it. I'm not a complete dumbass," Callie argued before her shoulders sagged in defeat. "But it's not... none of it's..."

"But it's not fucking with a corpse," the necromancer finished for her.

"Yeah."

Katherine looked out the window as a brief silence stretched on for another mile. The concrete barriers were covered in ads from exit to exit, including a handful of repetitive, *All Sapiens Deserve Rights*, and *We all come from Adam's Home*. A brutal picture of a young, blonde-haired girl with a broken horn sticking out of the side of her forehead with the right side of her face covered in old bruises and fresh cuts added, *Daem Rights are Human Rights*.

All three advert-plaques were dwarfed by a giant billboard across the other side of the highway that read simply, *Your Jobs. Your Souls. Daems belong in Hell – Not Your Home.* She watched the various signs repeat until a new tremor coursed through Anthony's arms and made the car swerve back and forth. "You're going to get us pulled over," she warned. "Want me to drive?"

"You don't know where we're going."

"I'm not sure you can get us anywhere intact," she chided. "You know you can tell me where to point the car. I'm guessing you're doing the 'I don't trust the cops' routine?"

Anthony grunted and glanced over at her. "Unless you're in deeper shit than I know, they told you the wrong gang killed your brother and told you that you'd be safe a bit before the bullets started flying. No, I don't trust the cops."

"They're not all bad," Katherine countered.

"Yes, they are," Callie interrupted. "Listen, lady, he's got a point. Everyone has a price around here, LSPD included. Do you really want to hope for the best…?"

His ex-wife turned around and glared at the escort. "Oh, now you trust his judgment?"

She shrugged. "I trust that he doesn't want to get shot."

"And I just shot a bunch of motherfuckers," he argued as his vision started to blur around the edges. "I'd like to be able to explain why before we go get checked in."

Callie snorted. "It's Texas. You're allowed to shoot people here."

Katherine rolled her eyes and flipped on his emergency flashers. Reluctantly, he pulled over on the side of the highway. "Fine. But I'm driving us there. Wherever there is. Just tell me."

"Since when do you listen to directions?"

"Since I can see how hard you're struggling to keep that goon down."

Callie listened to the exchange and pulled herself up in a tight cringe. "Keep it… down? You know that's not helping me deal with any of this with him… you know. Looking like he's going to shit himself."

"I wish it were that simple," Anthony grumbled as he stumbled out of the passenger seat and switched seats with Katherine. Once back inside, he cradled his head in his hands and unleashed a shaking, anguished groan.

"Men are created equal — but souls? Not so much," Katherine mumbled. "At least, that's how I understand it."

"That idiot kid couldn't have been a day over nineteen. Are you telling me that some jerkoff with a gun is so evil he can… what? Poison you just by you eating him?"

When Katherine didn't answer, Anthony slowly unbuttoned his shirt and pressed his fingers against his chest. His skin felt hot one second and clammy the next, and a steady *crawling* feeling persisted just beneath his ribs. "Can we say 'absorbed' instead, maybe? Please? I didn't have time to do it right, and yeah — not all souls are right with the world. This one just…"

"He swallowed it raw, didn't take precautions, and whatever the kid was doing, this dumb-ass ended up with toxic exposure to it. Anthony, where am I going?"

"Maple and Christi. There's a fresh organic market there," he replied as he tried to spit something out from between his teeth. "You'll need… hell. Exit 115."

"Toxic exposure... from a soul?" Callie wondered aloud.

Katherine glanced over at her ex-husband and sighed softly. He wasn't the man she used to love. He wasn't the strong, firm, *driven* man she had fallen for. "You didn't know him before the DoD got their hands on him. You didn't have to put him back together after they threw him away, either."

"It helps that she works at U-Anth-Med," Anthony added. "Nth, anthenium, and other magical treatment is entirely their thing."

Callie saw the lost look in the nurse's eyes and decided to drop the subject. "Are you... are you going to be okay?"

"Dunno," the other woman answered for him. "He won't admit it, but the n-tox is plain as day. If I could drag him into my office, I imagine his heart is pounding on a dual-rhythm right now. He's taking double-gasps of breath, and... let me guess, your vision is all a mess?"

"You make it sound so bad," Anthony grumbled under his breath.

"N-tox. Necromantic toxicity," Katherine explained to the escort as she turned her focus back onto the road. "Bodies are only supposed to hold so much *alia naturalis* at any given time. Dumbass here took on a whole damn extra one, and it's trying to take over his body. Probably not even trying to."

"Alia...?"

"Exalted-nature," Anthony grumbled as he rubbed at his lips. "Some Army quack coined it after the Five started doing Their shit. They didn't like admitting that magic's existed since the dawn of all fuck, so the feds thought giving it a new name would make them appear less idiotic once they finally acknowledged it publicly."

His ex snorted and calmly jumped three lanes without even looking to see if she had clearance. "Because the Army knows best! Can't call it a *soul*, nooo. Can't imply there's a power greater than the Secretary of Defense. God and country, my ass."

Callie scrambled in her seat and frantically looked around for anything that might double as a weapon. "Wait! You're telling me the dead guy is trying to –"

"He's trying to make my heart beat."

"I happen to like your heart beating," she argued. "Why is that a bad thing?"

Katherine couldn't decide between a smirk and a sigh, so she settled for just tapping her fingers on the steering wheel. "It's trying to make it beat in the rhythm it was used to. You know how you can't load a Droid-OS onto a FlixBook?"

"Yeah, the operating systems aren't compat… oh. Ohhhh."

"Necromancy 101 in a nutshell," Anthony finally sighed.

"That doesn't explain if you're going to be okay. How do you get over… that… n-tox?"

"He's going to have to purge," the nurse replied before her ex could. "It won't be fun, nobody's going to like it, and he shouldn't do it outside of a medical facility. Which means he's going to do it on the curb in front of preschoolers, aren't you?"

Anthony flipped her off and pounded his fist on his ribs like he was trying to knock on someone's door. "Once we get to E-Ve's, she's going to have something for it. Just… drive a little faster, would you?"

For once, she didn't argue.

3. A QUICKER FIXXER
Sunday, May 27th, 10:33 PM

N-tox had a habit of being a little uglier than the clinical description that Katherine had offered. By the time they made it to *E-Ve's Produce Emporium*, Anthony was as green as the 'organic' cabbage that decorated the front of the greenhouse's stalls. The bile seeping from his mouth, on the other hand, was not – and the smell wafting from his skin was enough to make Callie gag alongside him.

If they'd expected a wait before being seen by the owner of the establishment, they were surprised, even if not pleasantly. A tall, lithe, and tan woman with glistening aqua eyes had the passenger side door open almost as soon as they parked. She gave one scathing look at Anthony and then spared the briefest of glances at his ex-wife through her platinum-blonde bangs.

"Did he have other options?"

"Other…?"

"Than to do this to himself," she snapped. "Did he?"

"Um, maybe? No?"

"Maybe. Maybe no," the woman retorted. She was more of a force of nature than she was anything else; that much was obvious to everyone. "Then maybe I'll do something about it, or maybe not. How long?"

Callie scooted to the far side of the rear cabin. "Shit's been bad for… I dunno. About… hour and a half? Two?"

Katherine took a steadying breath as the strange woman worked her ex over. She checked his pulse, eyes, and even peered in his throat without so much as unfastening his seat belt. "Our lives have turned inside out in two freaking hours. It's unreal."

"Yes, yes, your lives. Utter disaster. So sure. How long has *he* been like this?"

"Oh. Um. About an hour-thirty. Nothing more than that."

"Ninety minutes, toxic and non-grounded, I can tell," the blonde sighed before she hauled off and slapped the necromancer across his cheek. "Anthony. You arrogant child. He needs to down-shift in the worst possible way, and apparently nobody had a sedative on them?"

Anthony looked up at her with bloodshot eyes and smirked a little. "Good to see you too, Erica."

"The feeling should not be considered mutual," the older woman snapped. "Though there is very little point in giving it argument now. Should I further assume that men with guns are after your pretty little heads?"

"Not just ours," he grunted as he painfully swung his legs out of the junker. E-Ve – or Erica, as some people were lucky enough to know her as – gripped the collar of his shirt absentmindedly and helped pull him to his feet. "Ugly shit is going down tonight. I don't know why, but we're part of it."

She took a single step back and gave the two women with him such a withering, piercing stare that both of them felt they'd have been better off completely naked. "No, you know why. You just don't know the extent. How much of a price are you willing to pay?"

"A soul for safe passage?"

"Yours or theirs?"

"The soul or the passage?"

"I certainly don't want the one you swallowed," Erica chided. "I can smell it from here. Nor do I have a wish for hearts tainted by your love."

Callie bristled up a little at that, while Kath looked like she'd been slapped. "Excuse me, he doesn't love me. He's –"

"He's in shit shape and you're here with him. If that doesn't equate to 'love,' it equates to desperation or insanity and I know him well enough that any of the above are a taint on your soul," E-Ve countered. "Anthony: as we both know your soul isn't worth a damn, I imagine that this will be an offer made on credit and honor, yes?"

As his companions made aggressively louder complaints about Erica's attitude, Anthony's brow furrowed. "What's wrong with the one I have?"

"Come now," Erica retorted, "there are certain, shall we say, *international* gardens even I don't tend."

"That's bullshit, and you..." he began before his voice trailed off and he caught a mouthful of bile before it escaped his lips. "International gard...

Oh fuck, come on! I thought they were just local 'bangers! Why the shit do you think –"

"One can be in a gang and still worship in the cult. The two are not counter, and as of late, all of the local green-wearers have been pressed into service to the True Believers of Cultivation. They're not just guns, they're *faithful*."

"To Yelthid," he spat in disgust, "while the cops are out looking for the Grims. Well, that's freaking quaint."

"Faith and misdirection of government at the same time? You can't say that this isn't the first time it's ever happened."

"Yeah, but then it normally becomes some kind of 'historical event,' and I'm fucking tired of living through those. Fuck."

"Yes. Agreed. Now. Inside. All of you," Erica demanded as she guided him away from the car and deeper into the open market. Half of the stalls were covered by translucent solar panels that emitted a faint glow at night and dimmed the light of day. The other stalls had fresh plants of all shapes and rarity, waiting to head to a kitchen or botanical garden for a stay.

As she helped him through the maze of shifting flowery retail, two discretely-armed gentlemen in dark suit jackets and matching See-It-All wrap-around visors appeared seemingly out of nowhere and made a very polite suggestion that the pair should follow Anthony and his 'friend' through the brush. It wasn't the kind of suggestion you were allowed to ignore any more than it was the kind that you would be rewarded for resisting. When they tried, the older of the two made a casual display of the G-Locke at his hip and just offered the faintest of smiles.

Before long, everyone had been ushered into the back room of a neon-light-draped bodega in the back of the nursery. The first thought in Katherine's mind was 'drug den,' and the freaked-out escort had similar (if not more profane) thoughts to accompany it. By the time they arrived, Erica had Anthony half-undressed and his head dangling over a smoking crucible.

It smelled like a wad of burnt weed and patchouli – and that was being kind. "This shit? C'mon E, I've been good," he whined as she pushed his head down close to it.

"Are you certain that offering such a lie up in this chamber is worth the breath to speak it? The Mother N would assuredly wish me to make this as painful as possible, yet I suspect that you'll be offering dust to dust as part of your apologies?"

"Gonna have to if you won't accept this guy," Anthony grumbled as heavy, acrid smoke wafted up from the crucible and washed over his eyes. "You know my rules, though."

"Oh, I do," Erica replied. "An interesting mishmash of morality. Willing to kill but only within reason, and within reason must come with a *personal* reason. Not at all one to complain about ripping a soul from Mother N's embrace and despoiling the balance of life and death if you can earn a few greenbacks, however."

Katherine looked over at the escort and mouthed a quiet, "*Mother N?*" to which the escort just shook her head and shrugged. The walls were covered with paintings of a black-skinned woman draped in gold and a pale woman draped in flames… where the walls could even be seen. Alcoves and build-in bookcases surrounded them with an actual, open-to-air fireplace against the back wall across from where Anthony sat.

And everywhere else?

Blossoming grape vines covered almost every square inch of anything not claimed by books, crystals, or stacks of herb-filled bottles. Most of them were labeled in Greek, which exhausted the limits of what Katherine could identify. Callie, however, took note of a curved, serrated knife sitting on the fireplace mantle.

A curved, serrated knife with fresh blood along its teeth.

"They're dead," the necromancer argued. "They don't get a lot of say in it."

"If that was the case, you wouldn't be seeking a boon from Nyx, would you?"

He coughed and wiped spittle from his lips with the back of his hand. "I'm not here for Nyx. Here for you, E-Ve."

"You're here to have my help in bailing you out of a horrible situation even if you aren't aware of the full scope of it. Save the complaint and assume that Frank called before you arrived. Personally, I might add."

Anthony's face fell. "Oh. I assume he's in a mood."

Erica nodded and turned away from the table where she'd been standing. In her hands were a pair of fist-sized gemstones: a chunk of tiger's eye and a matching, roughly polished piece of tourmaline. "Almost as much as I am. I won't waste your time telling you what his concerns are other than he's miffed that you haven't called him yet."

Off to the side, Katherine made a semi-silent "EEP!" and grabbed Callie's shoulder in a panic when she got a little too close to one of the apothecary's pets. Of what or why, neither the necromancer nor the blonde-haired caretaker looked like they cared.

"I can't call him until you accept my offering," he answered as he took another breath of the fumes and smoke. "So do you want to hurry up and…"

Erica gave him a slight nod and carefully tilted his chin up with her fingertips before she peered down into his eyes. With a disgusted little 'tsch' noise from the back of her throat, she brought her other hand up and placed two fingers in the middle of his forehead. She said something under her breath so softly that nobody could hear it.

They didn't need to. A little ripple of air washed out from the point of her fingertips and made loose locks of Anthony's hair flutter away. Both of his companions felt it; it was like a faint spring breeze washed over their skin. Whatever she did, whatever the spell did at her request, visibly made him relax.

He sagged back in the chair and wiped a bead of sweat away from his eyes when she was done. "Thank you."

"Thank me for nothing. I can't have you pass out before you disgorge. It would be… inconvenient."

"Pass out? Disgorge? Disgorge… what? The soul? Okay, no. Anthony, who is this? Where did you have us take you?" Callie asked. "I… I don't think I like it here," she replied as she glanced around the room.

"Oh, you little *paidi*, do you not feel safe? Does the sight of non-Abramahic religion offend you so much? Or you, nursemaid to American medicine. Are you distressed by the sight of such holistic care, care that has existed before the time of the new Gods and the newer wishful-to-be?"

Katherine pointed a red fingernail at a skull sitting on a box and half-hidden in a corner. "No. It's because that skull just winked at me, and bones *aren't supposed to do that*."

Erica blinked as her righteous indignation was abruptly deflated. "Oh. Edgar. How did you get out of… well. It's of no matter. I assure you, he's perfectly safe. It's Vincent that's more of a worry."

"Vincent?"

Anthony's friend pointed to the top of the shelf where a skinless, mummified cat was curled up on its side. "Oh, that poor little kit-" Callie started.

Vincent opened a single cloudy eye, sniffed the air, and hissed at her. A little puff of dust followed out of its mouth and ears, much to Erica's amusement. "He doesn't like strangers," she non-nonchalantly remarked.

"FUCKING CHRI-"

Anthony lifted his hand and waved her back away from the shelf, not that she needed any prompting. "You two are perfectly safe," he croaked. "Promise."

"I REALLY fucking doubt that," Callie snapped. "I'll ask again: who the hell is this? Where are we?"

Anthony sighed and moved away from the crucible as the blonde carefully placed both gemstones inside it. "Callie, Katherine. This is Erica Veight. She's one of the very few um… unaffiliated cross-magi in the city."

Erica scoffed and pushed the stones closer together in the crucible as they began to spark of their own accord. "I am very much affiliated," she huffed. "Just neither with the Five nor the Feds."

"What about the Church?"

"I already said I wasn't affiliated with the Feds, did I not? I did, didn't I, Anthony?"

"Cross-magi?" Callie stammered. "Anthony, I swear to fuck. It's like you're speaking in Braille."

Katherine cleared her throat as Erica looked up with delighted mirth in her eyes. "Um, Braille isn't spoken, it's –"

"I *know* what I said, thank you," Callie seethed. "Get me the fu-"

"No," the necromancer interrupted. "Just no. You two are staying here until I find out who is trying to kill us and why. I gather the *why* is because you –"

Erica very lightly slapped him across his cheek. "Thine tongue, Anthony. Mind it. We do not speak of reasons to need my help in this chamber, nor others. Frank did not say, so I will not. Rules are rules. You need help, and you negotiate. A negotiation that has not been completed nor accepted as of yet."

"I still don't even know what you are," the escort huffed. "Why should I trust you? Dammit, at this point, why should I trust *any* of you?"

"The small, angry one does make a point, I suppose," Erica sighed to herself. "Fine, then listen, Miss Yippy-Dog Girl, I am –"

"A cross-magi is someone who can serve as a bridge or a conduit for necromancers and others who abuse the living shit out of anthenium and nth-essence," Katherine interrupted. "They claim to be grounded with the 'spirits of earth' or sometimes 'the old Gods,' and maybe, just maybe, they dick around with the Five. They don't blend types of magic, so much as they manage the functions of spellwork itself."

Erica looked at her with wide, almost glimmering eyes as a smile blossomed across her face. "My, my! The nursemaid seems to know a few things. Anthony, you taught her well."

"When the hell did you become some kind of encyclopedia of magic? I thought you were just some rich bitch from the north-end," Callie grumped with her arms crossed.

"Because she's a rich bitch that works at Anth-Med," Anthony replied, with what could almost be called a proud smile. "She's a cross-magi herself in nearly everything but name."

Katherine glowered in Anthony's direction. "I would not and do not bunk with whatever metaphysical crap you call *magic*. I am a scientist and a professional, and my *job* is to make sure that people who get exposed to metaphysics and nth-patterns don't *die* of metaphysics and nth-*abuse*."

"That is the essence of a cross-mage, my *agapitós*."

"I don't have a clue what that word is and don't even want to know," the nurse growled under her breath. "You're the equivalent of an ether-abusing chiropractor, and I want nothing to do with you. Anthony? I'm in agreement with your skank. I'm not staying here."

Erica rolled her eyes and huffed as Callie turned her death-glare from the necromancer to his ex-wife. "That's too damn bad," Anthony retorted, "because you are. Until I can get whoever is trying to shoot you to stop, you're stuck with me… or better yet, E-Ve."

"Are you going to stop us from leaving?" the escort countered. "Adding *kidnapping* to *murder* and… and… *defiling a corpse*?"

"No, my *agapitós*, no, dearies, there is nothing at all stopping any of you from leaving," Erica countered with her accent rolling over the Grecian words, "though I do expect you to understand that the grave is both the danger you are in and the place for which Anthony will ask me to send flowers to, should you choose to abscond from my care."

"Listen, girls, I'm serious," Anthony interrupted. "There are only a handful of safe harbors I can think of to hide you two in, and Erica is the only one that I can be certain isn't playing with whoever was taking shots at us. Give me a day. That's all."

Katherine looked the Grecian woman over and shuddered at the smile she offered in return. "You're serious, aren't you? Why do you…?"

"Because E-Ve doesn't deal with the corps, won't touch the Churchers, and the only time she deals with the feds is when she cheats on her taxes," her ex answered honestly.

"I can always call Alara and —"

"From the news, she's working your brother's case, so no, you can't," the necromancer argued as E-Ve's magic started to wear off. "Either her office fucked up or someone deliberately fed you bad info. Can you please just let me work this?"

"And can you please be quiet so I can work?" Erica added. "I do understand the concern of a law-abiding pair of citizens like yourselves, but is this really the time to argue…?"

Katherine caved and stepped back. "No. It's not."

"Good. Thank you. Now, if you two will be so kind…" she began as she turned around, and a small little fleshy stump peeked out from her hair on the side of her head.

"Hold… hold on a minute," Katherine interrupted as she became transfixed by a spot on Erica's head. "Anthony… she's…"

Erica smiled and brushed her hand across her own face. The gesture parted her hair to display a small, rounded bump. It was a hard callous, almost bone, that had been surgically shaved down to just a stub. "Beautiful? Kind? Talented?" she asked in quick succession. "Or am I the one your former love is entrusting with your safety at great personal risk and cost?"

Callie's jaw dropped. "A Daem? You're sticking us with a crack-"

"*Don't* finish that," Anthony interrupted with a growl that stunned her into submission. "E-Ve is the exception. If *any* of us gets to set the damn rules on that, *I* do."

Erica sighed and placed her hand on the necromancer's cybernetic shoulder. "I do understand the hesitation. 'Oh no, she has blood that doesn't look like ours! It's slightly less red! Her distant-and-only-by-genus-related-kin were involved in…"

"And *you* stop too," he snapped as he looked up at her with tired, yellow-tinted eyes. "I wouldn't be here if I didn't trust you. I wouldn't have brought them here if I didn't like you. I don't want to fucking hear it from *anyone*," he growled a little louder. "As far as you two are concerned, she's safe," Anthony stressed, "and more or less neutral. Some of her clients have bosses that would be angry if she came to harm. She's like the Swiss before the Ru's got their dicks chopped off by the Ukies and Europe ass-pounded them as a unit."

Katherine and Callie gave each other a long look. Daems made up a whopping two-percent of the population of the US, and of that eight million some odd souls, you could find about a quarter of them living in the Gulf. It didn't matter if you thought they were nth-born mutants, a natural genetic offshoot of humanity, or living and breathing Hellspawn, they *existed,* and at the end of the day it didn't matter what you thought about it.

Unfortunately, a lot of people had a lot of thoughts about it. Daems didn't appear on anyone's radar until after the rise of the Pentaship, and were first spotted in areas rich in deposits of natural nth – places like Florida, Turkey, and the Iranistan Confederation. Like magic, they'd always existed in the world; the world had just gone out of its way not to notice. Like everything else, that changed when the Pentaship rose to power.

They got along in some places better than in others.

The Gulf was one of the better. Not the greatest, but one of the better. When Mother Nature's will and Uncle Sam's combined foolishness decided that Florida had existed long enough on the surface of the planet, anyone that *could* flee the ruins that made up the south-of-Tampa peninsula *did*, and a lot of them ended up in and around Los San. Texas wasn't where anyone wanted to go, but Texas had a long list of sins to make up for, and this was one way Texas had decided to try to make things right.

It didn't always work, but Texas tried.

His charges weren't necessarily in the wrong for having concerns, but now was simply neither the time nor the place. "I will note that staying here is not staying *here*," Erica clarified after a few moments of pained silence in her study. "Boys? Come take this man-child's playthings and go find them a room. The Tabletop next to Oidou's Market will do. A shipment leaves for there in an hour."

At her call, the same two well-dressed and well-armed men from earlier appeared as if by magic and flanked both of Anthony's companions. "What do you mean, we're not staying here?" Callie demanded.

The cross-mage gestured her hands wildly and made a show of walking to the exit. "Short and angry one, do listen. This is my place of business. It is not a hostel for the lost. This? This is a storefront. I have other places that are hostels. What, you think I keep a stock of RPGs and AK-91s hidden beneath the begonias?"

"Yes," muttered Anthony under his breath.

Erica ignored him. "Today, I am willing to accept – and *without* negotiation from you, my Anthony – delivery of your women and to give you a… healthy exit of your current possessions."

"His *women*?" Callie exclaimed, a little louder and sharper than she meant to.

As Katherine raised an eyebrow and glared at the Grecian daem, the necromancer lifted his head and pulled away from Erica's hand. "Wait, *without* negotiation? Why?"

"Because a deal was already made to fix what ails you."

Anthony groaned. "Oh no. He got to you?"

"Without my express request," Erica snarled through clenched teeth. "I'm not negotiating because you've already agreed on services to be rendered. Presumably, you will be told what these services are – later."

"Fuck."

She ignored the outburst and turned her attention back to the two women. "Once he is resolved, I expect that he will work with his *contractor* to ensure that your time with me will be brief. Treat it as a vacation."

"I'm not working for him! I mean, I have an account with…" Anthony began before his bloodshot eyes went wide. "What the hell did Frank tell you? He's not calling in the chits I owe is –"

"The thing he always says. To do it quicker."

"Trice-fucking-dammit," he groaned as he gripped his chest with one hand. His heart skipped a beat, and he sagged back against the chair. "Kath, Callie. Please. As bad as tonight is it just got worse. Don't add to it."

Callie shot him a hateful glare, and then stomped across the room. Before he could stop her, she grabbed him by the jaw, tilted his head up, and planted a violent kiss on his lips that stole his breath away and made Kath's jaw drop to the floor. "She got me into this mess, and you're keeping me in it. Understand *me* for a change when I say that when this is over, you two are going to owe me so much that I'm going to get to retire. You got that, *Tony*?"

Any other day, the violent edge to her voice would've been the hottest thing she could've done. Right now? The threat carried enough weight that Anthony had no room to doubt its validity. It was still hot, it just didn't seem like he was going to enjoy the outcome for some reason.

In the silence that followed, Katherine found her voice again. "Why do we have to leave right now though? If it's going to be an hour before we get in a truck?"

"Because I need to do things with your toy of a man here that neither of you wish to see. No, not those things," the cross-mage added before either could even think to suggest it. "But even so."

"You're gonna purge him?" Katherine asked as she put her hand on Anthony's shoulder.

"Ah, yes. In a sense. Though I suspect he has a second task to do once he is emptied of soul."

"Emptied of the other soul," he muttered. "I'm keeping mine."

"One could debate."

Katherine nodded once and put her hand on Callie's neck and steered the younger woman out the door as she protested. "Should've just led with that. It's bad enough when it's done in containment. I am *not* watching it in here." Katherine glanced over her shoulder, giving Erica and Anthony one final look over and a goodbye loaded with enough sarcasm to melt his liver. "Have fun, sweetie," she called, as they marched out of the room and were escorted down the hall.

Erica sauntered back over and put a hand on top of Anthony's head. "Always the spicy ones, you. Always."

He ignored her and sighed as he turned his gaze to the graphite crucible and the gems inside it. He hadn't noticed them until the herbs burned off. His heart was pounding in his ears with alternating beats in opposite sides of his head. It was enough to drive a man mad, if her earlier herbal concoction hadn't slowed the process down. "All of it or part of it?"

"You're the necromancer; you tell me."

"What are you going to do with it?"

"You both reek," Erica replied quickly, "so there is not much that I can do. This soul belongs to a cretin unwelcome in my oasis of greenery, but there are other places for it. Unless you think you need to traffic it elsewhere."

He glanced up at her and coughed painfully. "Gonna flush him down the sewer?"

"Los-San Sanitation and Reclamation could not be so lucky."

Anthony chortled at the thought of some random sewer worker finding the remnants of a sludge-covered *storin-stone* and then braced himself for the inevitable. "E? I'm sorry to drag you into this. And thank you."

She smiled gingerly and gently slid her hand from the top of his head down to the back of his neck. "I wish I could say this will be pleasant."

"But it's better than dead."

"Much," she agreed.

Without another word, he took a deep breath, traced his fingers down the scar over his chest, and simply *willed* the runes to activate. One by one, glowing chartreuse cracks began to open across his flesh and around his myriad scars. No words were needed to activate the spell; no rhymes or muttered muck. The DoD had made it clear: if you had time to talk, you had time to do something more productive. You just needed good-old-fashioned force of will to get the job done.

Be an army of one or whatever that motto was.

Just get it done.

A rush of pain welled in his gut as a face briefly flickered under the cracks of his skin. His head shot back as a gout of etheric, unchained power erupted from his eyes and nostrils. A cloud of green and white vapor manifested in his throat and rushed out into the air, unobstructed as a skull-like shape took form in the center.

The vapor and the necromancer both screamed.

Erica just patiently waited and watched.

Anthony inhaled sharply and sucked the entity back inside his mouth even as it struggled to break free. He doubled over in pain as his shaking hands clutched the crucible. His cheeks billowed out and his eyes began to swell with pressure as he placed his full focus on the writhing mass raging around his heart. The spell didn't need words, but it did need a thought.

This time, it was a simple one. One word. One meaning. *Go.*

He opened his mouth a second time and *vomited* a cloud from his body. It sparked as it washed over the gemstones. Twisted, skeletal fingers and a vaguely human face that was contorted in pain and fear writhed in the toxic gloom as it pushed away from Anthony's chest. The cloud twisted and tried to speed away to freedom.

Tried, but failed.

The sparks from the gemstones intensified as a storm of electricity arced from them. Dark shadows whipped out from the tourmaline and encased the gaseous soul in a spreading black shell that compressed and pulled it together. The tiger's eye sent shards of amber light into the midst of the agonized green mass. Wherever it touched, the cloud slowed and settled.

Tourmaline to protect, to shield, and to control the toxicity.

Tiger's eye to relieve fear and anxiety.

Together, they were enough to soothe the dead man's soul.

As the seconds flew by, the cloud collapsed in on itself until it was little more than a glowing green and black-speckled rock nestled between the gemstones. It emitted a few cracks and pops as it shrank to the size of a thumb. By the time five minutes had passed, the sounds were gone, the gem was silent, and the other stones lay still.

One soul. Condensed down into a single rock — a storin. An intangible mass of energy inexplicably turned into a solid chuck of stone. In due time, it would disintegrate back into nothingness without so much of an atom-sized chunk of dust behind. You could use it to enhance someone's natural nth-abilities or power nth-consuming spells before it deteriorated.

Some people even called it 'natural anthenium.'

And if you hit it with a hammer, it'd put off enough anth-rads to set off every nuke-detector and x-ray machine in a one-mile radius. There were reasons the Feds regulated necromancers, and not just because they were *icky*. The Department of Energy alone hated how Anthony's type violated the laws of 'normal' physics.

Not as much as he did, but close.

There were other, more fundamental concerns about using a soul like it was a US-subsphere. Reasonable ones. Ones he tried very hard not to think about. Even the Church (several different churches, at that) had a reason to be irritated by the general idea.

Erica was by his side with a wet washcloth and a bottle of water almost as soon as the gunk was out of his mouth. The glow on his chest subsided as the essence left, although cold steam continued to roll off his back into the humid nursery's air. Shaking, gagging and swearing, it was all he could do to hold his head up by the time that the storin-stone had finished forming. When he finally let her lift his head up, a single red streak appeared in his left iris before it faded away to nothing.

"Another mark on your heart, Anthony. How many does that make now?"

"Probably too many."

"Those that claim to define themselves by defending the world never do fully explain the costs of what dabbling with the dead does to a man, do they?"

"Serving the greater good and all that, I guess," Anthony sighed painfully as a fresh spasm and an ugly, mucus-filled cough wracked his body. "Born with it. Gotta assume we won't burn for using the gifts God gave us."

She tapped her finger on his nose and shook her head slowly. "Was it God? And if it was – which one?"

That was a question that had been pondered for centuries by churchers, philosophers, and bottom-feeders alike. It was, with all certainty, one that was outside of his pay grade, and he didn't bother to hide it. "One that doesn't like stories to end at the end, I guess."

"Few truly do. Even when the story is monstrous, an ending implies that there is a cessation of all things known and unknown. To delve into that is to ponder the very existence of no existence." E-Ve tapped at the rock and gave a sad little bob of her head. "Even when we know of the existence to follow, we do not yet know what exactly it is, or how accurate it is we perceive it from where we are now – and if our perception of alternate planes as lower beings is correct. There are so few of us are capable of discerning that truth; fewer still seem to want to share what little they learn."

The necromancer wiped a sheen of sweat from his forehead along with some kind of grime that hadn't been there the minute before. "Well. Now he gets to talk about it. Do you want to be here for it or…?"

"How much do you expect the fool to speak?"

Anthony picked up the storin-stone and looked into it. With just the right training and just the right gifts, you could figure out what wasn't supposed to be seen…or rather, what couldn't. The figure within was lost in a maelstrom of dank fog and sickly green gas that swirled around a vaguely humanoid form. It was said – or believed, or maybe just naively hoped for – that even if you saw a ghost left behind in the real world, you had no idea of knowing what it really felt or what it could possibly be experiencing in the moment.

Those same people said that ghosts writhing in torment were just distressed over memories of their lives. Or fear of what lay beyond. Or some kind of meta-magical interference from the next realm over. By order of the President back in the early 60's, they weren't souls.

Legally. Realistically? Anybody's guess.

And the thing was – the real bitch of it when you thought about it? You didn't have to be a genius to realize that since *demons* existed, the myths of the places they ruled over probably weren't just *myths* like the old-timers liked to imply. For all intents and purposes, the afterlife had been scientifically *proven*. So, what if you dropped dead after pledging allegiance to one of those demons?

Mundanes didn't like to think about it. Metaphysics hated the word 'soul' for just that reason. It implied… connotations… that the scientific and philosophical communities didn't like. You'd think the idea would serve as a deterrent to encourage people to be nicer to each other.

It never did.

"I think it's just going to be a mem-tap. I don't have it in me to force a conversation."

"You haven't talked to him already? I'm surprised. Since when do you need to eject them first?"

"Since this one tastes like the underside of a plunger in a gym bathroom," he answered with a gag. "Not like I could at the time. Had to keep those two from shitting themselves and find somewhere safe to drag their asses to."

E-Ve gave him a bemused little smirk and patted his cheek gently. "It seemed to me as if they were doing the dragging. Is this one such poison you could not just remove from his mind what you needed? I have seen you work before."

He carefully picked up the stone with his metal hand and rolled it back and forth between his fingertips. "You ever start a job for someone, it seems about par for the course, and then you realize they haven't told you everything? And then you end up in the ICU with a limb missing? I'm getting that kinda vibe from this asshole."

"Then I'll stay," Erica replied as she poured herself a drink of something that looked like whiskey but smelled like apples. "Just don't think too loud in my direction. Please?"

It was so cute that she thought he had enough control left in his body for that to even be a choice. "I'll focus my thoughts if you get me every can of Red Monster you have stashed away. I'm exhausted and I can't think, and I have this horrible feeling that I am going to get shot at again tonight."

She replied with a visible shudder. "You… you just asked *me* for a can of that… *me…*?" The botanist looked down at her drink and sneered. "If you suggest that I consume that chemical garbage, then your idea of being shot may be self-fulfilling."

"You? No. Your grunts? The produce packers do ten-hour shifts five days a week and you only let them piss in the compost hut. We both know they drink it to spite you."

Erica turned up her nose and unleashed a plethora of comments in Greek that Anthony, gratefully, could not understand. She ended her diatribe with a short, succinct: "If you intend to poison your body, you ought to have just kept his soul," as she stormed out of the room.

The exchange wasn't wise.

But somehow, it felt like it was worth it.

That just left the soul – twisted and panicked – by what (other than the immediate, obvious circumstances), Anthony didn't know. There were several ways to talk to a dead guy, though usually it was easier if you still had their corpse on hand. When you didn't, the biggest question to answer was, "Does it want to talk?" or, "Does it want to run the fuck away and never be seen again?"

Most of them usually fit the latter.

Anthony ran his fingers over the stone and watched as green bolts of lightning spat from the imprisoned cloud and at his skin. He could only assume that the metaphysical plane wasn't interested in making his life any easier tonight. That left three options to query the asshole, and the idea of doing a forceful, full manifestation of a spirit and all of the prep work that would take didn't sound like fun. The second option would work a bit faster, but only if the soul was willing to talk – otherwise, it'd take just as long, and he'd have to eat the idiot whole all over again.

That just left one possibility to entertain:

A memory tap.

Or as people who didn't drink the Department of Defense's tea called it: "*A memory/sensory astral observation of a prime-plane unbound remnant.*"

Which just meant it was a memory-tap done by a pretentious medium.

It didn't take a lot of effort to prepare for one, but the steps to get there were pretty damn important. It wasn't unheard of for an untrained or overworked necromancer to get lost in the memories of whatever soul he was playing with – and that opened up a whole new set of problems Anthony absolutely did not want to deal with. E-Ve, apparently, had already assumed he was going to have to prod the dead man's mind and had left a box full of reagents on the table for him.

Mirror, mirror. Anthony sighed as he propped the little lipstick box up and made sure the pane was big enough to clearly view from his chair. A few minutes later, he had transcribed a small series of runes on his forehead, with a dye meticulously crafted from what he was sure was the *finest* vial of rat blood Erica could find.

Organically, humanely, and ethically sourced, knowing her.

Once he was done decorating his skin in a way that'd make a henna artist proud, the necromancer picked up the stone and peered into the confines of the crystal again. Carlos was absolutely *not* having a good time in there, and for both of their sakes, he hoped that didn't translate into the next step. It didn't normally happen, but it wasn't entirely unheard of.

With a deep breath and a steady hand, Anthony looked into the mirror and carefully placed the bottom of the crystal over his reflection. A sharp pressure sank into his forehead as he pressed down on the glass until a single drop of blood blossomed on his skin. When the bead ran into the runes, they pulsed once and sucked a steady trickle down into the spellwork.

Anthony felt his eyes roll up into his head and...

***

E-Ve's Produce Emporium
The Grass is Always Greener – When it's Organic.
***

He stood in a hallway. The floor was damp, and the carpet squished underfoot. An omnipresent golden-green glow bathed everything in putrid light, from the peeling paint to the cracked ceilings overhead. To the left, the hallway stretched further than Anthony could see. Doors of various shapes and sizes decorated the walls at equal intervals.

This punk was rotten.

This wasn't just a case of a dead man's brain giving way to decay. This was the mind of a man that had let poison into his heart and mind. Worse, it was a soul steeped in actual rot, the kind you felt if and only if you'd thrown your lot in with one of the Five: specifically Yelthid, the Lord of Sustained Entropy. The Grand Cultivator. The Farmer. The Source of Living Reclamation.

Otherwise known as the Daemon of Decay.

The day just kept getting better by the minute.

His green jacket wasn't just for show. At some point, this idiot had decided to make a deal with Yelthid's signature scrawled all over the bottom. If the mess that ravaged his storin-stone hadn't given that away, the filth covering his memories absolutely did.

If nothing else, that meant Anthony wasn't going to linger.

To his right, a heavy, multi-faceted crystal wall blocked him from seeing much more than an ever-changing landscape of... something rancid and unearthly. Walls broke and reformed; doors vanished and reappeared. The wall moved an inch as he touched it, and fresh carpeting appeared, only to instantly dissolve into mold. A shroud-covered figure flickered into existence just at the edge of the undulating door frames. It shook its hooded head and made sure that Anthony was watching before it snapped its fingers for effect.

The distorted hallway beyond the crystal vanished and was replaced with Anthony's own reflection from E-Ve's back room. Apparently, the kid still had something of a future ahead of him. Judging by the figure beyond, Carlos probably wouldn't like it.

It was also a warning not to look deeper into whatever the afterlife had planned for the punk. It was one of those rare occasions that metaphysical practitioners received a heads-up. Time liked to be fucked with even less so than Hell did, and that was saying a lot.

At any rate, the warning was noted.

Anthony turned to his left and peered into the first door. It opened into another hallway; a clean-ish one. Blood was splattered across the walls and the carpet. Carlos lay propped up on the floor with a golden shimmer cast around him. A giant hole consumed his leg, and he struggled to breathe.

The door opposite the idiot opened and a comically-large shotgun barrel poked through. A giant, static-covered, horned figure in all black with red lightning for eyes stepped through and drew a dagger the size of a claymore out of his pants.

The necromancer rolled his eyes and stepped back into the moldy hallway and let the door slam shut without a second glance. Nobody liked seeing the person that killed them. Couldn't really blame him for how he processed those last few minutes.

That wasn't the memory he cared about, anyway.

A mem-tap wouldn't last forever. It couldn't. But if you didn't know what you were looking for… you had to go on instinct. Some doors vibrated as Anthony passed them; others sunk deeper into the wall. The carpet crusted over the further in he walked; the more distant the memory from 'now,' the more entrenched it was in time. A few emitted noises – a hum from one, a rancorous scream from another. The sound of a woman moaning from a third; the same woman crying two doors down from that.

The nature of the tap itself provided only access to memories with a sharp resonance in the soul. Some doors would open to other hallways as memories branched and entwined with each other. It'd be easy enough to get lost if you weren't paying attention. You stayed on the main drag if you wanted to come out of the tap.

That was the rule. He'd seen too many people ignore it.

Guessing how far he was into Carlos's mind was next to impossible. The doors didn't have dates on them. The corridor changed the further he went, though even it was distorted by the emotions that pulsed from one doorframe to the next.

Most of the memories had a feel to them. Sex and lust from one. Altered feelings from another; it felt like the kid enjoyed a good line of coke – and not the diet kind. Rage was an interesting one. He was full of it, and about half of it was aimed inward.

He wasn't a man that had been happy with his lot in life.

A blast of gunfire rang out down the hallway. Instinctively, Anthony dropped his shoulder and slammed through the closest door he could find before he could stop himself. Fourteen years in the Army made you jumpy. Nature of the beast, but not of the mind.

The closest door wasn't the right door. Instead of safety, he was met with a memory of a kid facing a cooking pot in a well-lit kitchen. Flasks, burners, and other equipment covered the counters, and the whole room reeked of cat piss and ether.

In here, you went by sight – which made the effigy to the Lord of the Entropic all the worse. Exponentially so as the kid nervously approached the commercial-sized cauldron and peered in. Little Carlos screamed as the necromancer stumbled out the door before he was forced to see what was cooking, too.

Nothing like a shrine to Yelthid to scar your childhood.

As E-Ve had alluded to – and Anthony had already guessed – Carlos had been in bed with a green-clad street gang that went by the name of 'The Gardeners.' Their full name was something like 'Gardeners of the Urban Harvest' or some shit, but honestly, nobody cared. It simply drove home old news that the LSPD were a bunch of idiots (not new) and threw a wrench into whatever the hell Katherine had gotten herself mixed up in.

At least it established a baseline – and, just as importantly, a guidepost. Anthony closed his eyes, focused on his body, and made it take a long, deep breath before he returned his focus to the task at hand.

Another burst of gunfire erupted and a chunk of doorway blew out a few feet ahead. The sound made Anthony flinch, but this time, he held his ground. It wouldn't hurt him even if it was pressed against his head, though it wasn't a great sign. Carlos's mind was either rejecting his presence entirely, or he was hung up on the last few minutes of his life in a desperate attempt to stove off whatever awaited him next.

Neither situation was ideal.

He had to take a moment to feel sorry for the asshole.

It passed quickly. Anthony reached down and sank his fingers into the repulsive carpet without a second thought and sent a jolt of pure willpower through it with the general 'concept' of Yelthid and the Gardeners in mind. Glowing black cracks laced through the mold like the Lichtenberg figures left behind from a lightning strike.

Some of the geometric fractures shot into doors at odd intervals down the corridor, but the strongest ones split the floor behind him and went back the way he'd come. Either direction was going to be a gamble, but it made more sense that the memories he wanted would be closer to the surface.

God only knew what horrors awaited the closer he got to the back of the punk's mind, too. Memories had a way of becoming distorted the closer to childhood you went. It was all about how the mind could recall things, or at least, how the soul could decipher them.

The next few memories yielded little. A fleeting memory of a meth sale here. A brief recollection of a traffic stop and a police officer bribed there (though he made a note of the name – a cop-for-sale wasn't a bad thing). It wasn't until he hit a door that positively vibrated with toxicity that he found something worthwhile.

Anthony stopped and opened a door that lead to a ruined bathroom in some shithole of a club. Loud Sub-Am rock pumped through the memory. Broken English and twisted Spanish pulsed in his ears as he watched Carlos lean over a filthy sink and stare into a broken mirror.

The punk had a split lip and some serious swelling around his left eye. His wife-beater tank top was torn and stained while his fists were wrapped up in gauze. "I ain't being the bottom bitch for Galvani's jackboots no more. Not no more," he swore.

Galvani. That wasn't a name Anthony recognized. He filed it away for later as the moldy green light from outside seeped into the room and saturated everything in the same awful color.

Another man's reflection appeared in the mirror. An older man; some jerk that looked just a little bit rougher. He had a telltale horn stump jutting from the side of his left temple, though if he was actually a daem or the memory was just distorting him, it was hard to tell. His face was covered in gang tats, and a scar traced the line from temple to jawbone. "Two more, Carl. You do two more, and Galv'll trust you."

"Beatin' people to death ain't what I signed up for, Alvin," the punk spat. "You promised me that if I get in good with these shits, I'd get out from Tina's thumb."

Tina's name didn't ring a bell either. Probably just some block-level hustler, Anthony assumed. "And you will," Alvin answered. "These people don't fuck around, Carl. When you see what's comin', you'll understand. There's a right side and a wrong side to be on when the future gets here. They've got new tech, man. Beyond life tech."

Beyond life? Anthony mused. *Necromancy? No. More than that.* That was bad. *What the hell is this dumbass involved with?*

"How in the *fuck* is watching a man get his chest bashed in being on the *right side*, huh? There ain't been any kind of fucking future in Corpi that don't involve pushing *azul* to the north, and then these green-shirted shits roll in and suddenly –"

The older man forced Carlos to turn around and gave him a sharp shake by his shoulders. "Azul won't matter. The mom-and-pop-corp-shops won't matter. The shit kids sniffing snow off of white-bitches asses ain't gonna matter. It's gonna be a new corp world for all of us." As Alvin talked, his face distorted around the next few words he said. "What *m@tt3rZ* is gonna be proving *y0ur worzzth* to *t3-e-3-3 bnl-bana1-caAB*."

*The **what**?* Anthony wondered as the memory started to fracture. Cracks appeared across Alvin's face, and even more so around Carlos's. More little horns appeared along the side of the elder gangbanger's skull, and his smile turned twisted. The entire memory started to crumble, and the door behind the necromancer slammed shut.

Before he even had a chance to panic, *everything* went dark.

Except for the broken mirror.

It expanded to the size of a door – and kept growing. It swelled over Anthony's head and filled the black void with such speed and intensity that it was impossible to tell if it was expanding, or if the necromancer was shrinking. Either way, the aura that radiated from the metal-framed broken glass doorway was one of utter, raw regret.

It blossomed to the size of a bus and spun in the darkness. Glass shattered and reformed in the shape of a two-tiered train that shot past Anthony's head with a thundering roar, louder than any mag-lev or an anth-fuzi bullet could've put out. That was the problem with mem-taps; half the shit was so distorted or misrepresented that getting anything solid took talent.

Except for a number emblazoned on the side: SBAL-131718.

Anthony had talent, but talent made you susceptible to the things in the memory – and the racket from the train hallucination was enough to knock him down with his hands over his ears. When the noise died down, it was replaced with *emotion*. Painful, intense, awful *emotion*.

A fresh wave of regret spilled out like a tidal wave, and if gravity had been a real concept, it would've knocked Anthony straight on his ass. It was damn near impossible to breathe through it – and in here, you didn't even *need* to breathe. It was regret and nothing but, and it was so strong that the words from all sides answered nearly every question he had.

"Why the *fuck* did I listen to that man?"

The bottom of the doorway opened just a crack and Anthony felt his mind get sucked through it and into the other side. The bathroom and moldy carpet was gone, the moldy hallway was gone, and the only thing he could see was the inside of a dank industrial complex. It looked like any other factory you'd expect to see in the city, but there was something intangibly off about it, or rather, the memory itself.

That was easier to recognize.

It was grief. Grief and terror. If Carlos hadn't been shitting his pants while going through whatever this experience was, the punk had remarkable self-control. Anthony hadn't felt anything like it since he'd had to tap into the bullet-riddled corpse of one of the New Persian Caliphate's executioners in the middle of Operation Dustup.

A moment later, the necromancer was standing on cold steel grating that quickly gave way to a full-length catwalk so old and riddled with so much rust it would've given an OSHA inspector apoplectic fits. A series of chemical vats covered with clear lids were lined up on the ground along either side of the walkway, and all of them were at least twenty feet tall and ten feet wide.

It was next to impossible to tell what was in them, and most of them just looked like some kind of foggy red stew. Each lid had a hole in the center, and red-stained claw-hooked hydraulic cranes hovered over the openings. One of them had little white and red lights alternating on and off along the side, while the others were seemingly content to dangle quietly and calmly.

The sound of two men dragging a corpse across the grate stole his attention from their surroundings. As they walked closer in the dim light, Anthony took a moment to crack the knuckles on his flesh-and-blood hand. Everything about it – the feel of the fingers rubbing against each other, the noise it made, the popping relief in his joints – was entirely a construct of his mind. A grounding mechanism to make sure his essence remembered that it *was* real and that he wasn't an intractable part of *this* experience.

As the two assholes drew closer, the first thing he recognized was that this was a much older memory than the last one – and a far more recent one. The dumbass punk looked exactly like he had just before Anthony had put a shotgun shell into his face, although his companion from earlier didn't look great. To be more specific, he looked positively *fucked up*.

And very, very, dead.

The punk, his companion, and Alvin's corpse were greeted by a figure that manifested right by Anthony's side – a corporate-looking asshole with an ancient trilby-style hat and large round sunglasses that almost covered the entire upper half of his face. "Gentlemen," he began in a voice that instantly sent a chill down the necromancer's spine, "vat 6B, please."

That was the same voice that had sent the goons to his apartment.

He'd been right about him being a corporate son of a bitch.

Carlos and his associate answered with a pair of curt, 'Yes sirs,' that established the pecking order faster than anything that Anthony could've hoped for. The pair made their way down the metal walkway and approached another disgusting cistern with an open lid and a frothing, bubbling mass inside.

As the thug-turned-sec guard made his way past, a symbol stood out on his shoulder epaulet – a round white patch with a jet-black wave on it. Below that, a name: 'Blackwash.' It didn't ring any bells, but it wouldn't take long to find out: just a phone call to Anthony's number one least-favorite problem… fixer.

The catwalk started to shake the closer they got to their delivery. When none of the memory personas reacted, Anthony swore under his breath. When the catwalk and the walls around it suddenly *lurched* and expanded three times their length, he cursed even louder.

As Carlos started to drip green slime out of his eyes, it only served to cinch the deal: the mem-tap was coming to an end, regardless of whether Anthony wanted it to or not – and he didn't. The grief was understandable. The fear, however, was not.

As the guards picked Alvin up, the memory *shuddered* and sent shock waves through the air. The older goon wasn't wearing a shirt, and from the look of it, someone had done their best to cave in his rib cage with something the size of a pumpkin. His pants and boots were the same wannabe-tactical type that the security guards had on, though it was his face that really left an impression.

It was a face forever frozen in terror.

His eyes bulged, trickles of dried blood coursing out of his ears. It wasn't the messiest murder Anthony had witnessed, but it was far from the cleanest. As they lifted him up to his feet and let him teeter on the edge of the catwalk, the dead man turned, looked Anthony straight in his eyes, and spoke just once before he was pitched in.

"Thanks for shooting me, motherfucker."

Carlos and the other guard dropped Alvin into the frothing mess without further pause. As he fell, the red gunk turned clear, and a mechanized *thing* lunged up from the vat to grab the old dead ganger in a pair of tube-wrapped metal claws. Alvin's corpse was ripped into shreds instantaneously in a burst of cloudy nth, which Anthony shouldn't have been able to see. It flowed from the corpse directly into the nightmarish, robotic creature.

A creature covered from head to toe in ancient Latin runes.

Did that just… no. It didn't. That… did that just siphon off what was left of that dude's soul? Anthony wondered, head spinning in distress. *What the fu-*

Carlos recoiled in fear and nearly fell off of the catwalk as the creature kept growing, and growing, and growing. Standing next to Anthony, the corporate handler began to expand right along with him. The prick's hat swelled up and swallowed everything that the necromancer could see, and after a moment, the void gave way to the real world.

All Anthony could think while the memory broke up around him was that the asshole needed a makeover… while he still could get one. He had no question that the puke had tried to murder half the people Anthony loved. Or at least, liked a lot. Or maybe just tolerated. It really depended on when he'd written his last alimony check. Regardless…

E-Ve rested her hand on the back of Anthony's neck as he came to. Her touch was calm, cool, soothing, and she smelled faintly like a mix of aloe and cinnamon. One deep breath was all it took to feel her personal magic worm its way into his senses (and sinuses) to push the aftertaste of the mem-tap and Carlo's essence out of the necromancer's head.

"Eventful trip?"

He choked back the first answer he had and settled instead on the soothing scents coming from a damp cloth Erica had draped across his forehead.

"I have questions and a target. And enough nightmare fuel to last the rest of my life. So…maybe."

She nodded sagely and patted his cheek gently. "For one such as you, yes, that is eventful. I can see the nature of some of those questions that are percolating in your mind, I fear, and I think you have seen things you'd rather not."

Anthony nodded in agreement. "Someone's fucking with shit they shouldn't, E. It's bad. Really bad. As in, 'a lot of people are going to die,' bad."

"Some problems must be solved by violence, I am most afraid to admit," Erica lamented, "and you, my dear paidí, are a tool to do just that. One that, I may add, is filthy."

Anthony scoffed at being called a child and looked down at the sweat, bile, and *gunk* covering his chest and pants. "And we both know how you feel about that."

"We do. The shower is where you remember it. Get clean and then… well. You know who you need to call. Quite surprised he isn't blowing up your phone."

"I turned it off."

"Do you suspect that was wise? You know he'll be upset you haven't followed his rules as it is, and to cut off contact after borrowing one of his toys? Shame. What is it you're supposed to do? In case of trouble?"

"I know, I know," he sighed as he stood up. "In case of trouble, you need a Quicker Fixxer-Upper."

***

Los San Water Harvesters
What's Below the Earth will Slake Your Thirst
***

Even at three minutes to midnight, 'secluded,' and 'edge of the outskirts,' were not words that paired well in Los Santuario. Still, if you knew exactly where to drive, you had a chance. The late hour helped, too, though those who wished to be in secluded areas at such an hour were not the ones you wanted to meet.

With his headache, Anthony was included in that list.

The foul concoctions E-Ve had poured down his throat after he got out of the shower were enough to stop the shakes and settle his stomach. Purging the soul helped, too, although there was more than enough residue left behind to leave the necromancer feeling like he'd been sleeping under a bus. At least it gave him some juice for later if he needed it.

Or rather, when. *When* felt much more likely.

Sadly, none of that mattered in terms of what he had to do next.

Most of the metro area drew its water from the desalination plants out in Wharton Bay, nestled along the Gulf of Mexico. The rest of the region siphoned it from pump stations and water towers that dotted the hillsides leading away into the upper valley. You had to filter out ungodly levels of pollution from it (both magical and man-made) but that was humanity for you.

The shadows cast by those towers offered both shitty cell service and enough privacy to avoid the prying eyes of countless security cameras and their minders. The former was great. The seclusion kept nosy script-kiddies from sniffing signals off phones being used for 'animated' conversations. If nothing else, it cut down on the constant ruckus from the crowds.

As for the watchers of those cameras?

The last thirty years had generated no shortage of ex-armed personnel. By and large, they were a lot like Anthony: underpaid and bored out of

94

their damn minds. Plus, they had something of a network for respectable retirees making ends meet, particularly those willing to scratch each other's backs.

Not every post-DoD-employment perk had an official name.

The last three decades of on-and-off warfare had inadvertently generated one of the most annoying yet incredibly helpful personalities to grace the twenty-first century – a man known by many names, not the least of which was Frank. Although, unfortunately, he had another he preferred to be called by, but only if you knew his direct number.

A Pyro-Bowl ad flickered from a blimp in the distance as Anthony picked up his phone and made the call he was dreading with almost every ounce of his body. "Operator. Please hold, Mr. Pierson."

That never ceased to set Anthony on edge. *Never*. It was a burner phone he hadn't even owned until thirty minutes ago and they *still* knew who was calling. Every. Freaking. Time. Worse? This time they didn't even give him shit about calling in from an unregistered number, nor did they put him through a dozen different questions. Clues which promised, above anything else, that Anthony's headache would soon become a migraine.

It started with an all-too-familiar chime, followed by the sound of an ancient modem being powered on and shoved down a garbage disposal. When the call finally connected, his screen flashed and scrolling scan lines appeared, accompanied by snowy static and a faint hiss. It made the display look like someone's pixelated bad idea of a pre-Anth 80's telecast.

A display that wasted no time before it showed off a perky, always-smiling, pale-faced jackass of a man with shiny white teeth and black-rimmed sunglasses. He always looked the same. He never aged. His voice hadn't changed in the last ten years, and presumably, it never would.

Much like the tortured digital noise that had preceded his arrival, his voice had a distorted digital reverb that was just irritating enough to make you grind your teeth. Anthony swore the prick did it on purpose because he knew, he *knew* if you were calling in, Frank could irritate you to no end because you needed what he had to offer.

A fact the jackass bragged about with Every. Single. Call.

"We-we-well now! Has li-li-life gotten you down? Have-have-have you picked up the check – and found it's past due? Then when you-you-you need a professional fixxxxxer upper, you know to call-call-call the one man that can make problem go-go-go away: the quicker fixxxxxer upper, Mr. Fixxer!"

Anthony groaned. Loudly, passionately, and profoundly. "Why are you like this?"

The smile never flickered, but the fake glint in the avatar's sunglasses flashed briefly out of frame. "Be-be-because we've all gotta be *somebody*. And you, you, yes, you – Mister Anthony Pierson, Captain – *ParaPsy*-Intelligence, Army, you – oh, you became some-some-*somebody* tonight."

The way that Fixxer stressed the *ParaPsy* part of Anthony's job curdled what remained of his stomach. The rest of the comment ruined any hope he had to eat for the rest of the night. If there was something to know, Frank the Fixxer knew it. If he knew and was gloating to boot, that could only mean one thing.

It wouldn't end well. *Ever.*

Fixxer's face popped on and off the screen as the background behind him changed from swirling geometrical designs to an awards podium that reached the top of a cloudy, lightning-filled sky. "Well, you aren't number one, and you aren't number two, but you are the-the-the *third* most wanted man in *ALL* of Los Santuario! Mul-mul-multiple hom-hom-homicide ring a bell?"

"That was quick. I guess the cops are really pissed this time?"

"Th-th-they ab-ab-absolutely do not care!"

LSPD was an absolute shitshow of an organization on the very best of days, but the idea that they wouldn't give a damn about a couple of dead gangers? A hard sell, to say the least. "If they don't, then who does?"

"Their boss – and their anti-boss!"

"The cops answer to three people," Anthony replied slowly, as the realization crept up his throat with all the bile he had left in his gut. "His Grace and Honor, Mayor Sotomos, and then Shelby Autoscis – the bitch that calls herself the local DA. I doubt they're happy about bodies dropping, but not enough to put me on their immediate to-do list. So… shit. Please don't tell me the Church is on the warpath. Or any path remotely near mine."

Fixxer's face popped back on the screen as he nodded emphatically. "The Si-si-sine-Pastor himself, Charlie El-Rhodes! He's very unhappy that one of their shepherds got splattered."

"C'mon Fix. Don't drag this out," Anthony whined. "I've got a splitting headache."

"Gettin' a bit crowded up there? Bit of a crack in your skull? Pulling in more souls than your body was made-made-made for?"

"So, I drop two assholes at my apartment in what was *clearly* a case of self-defense, and I'm a wanted fucking man? I mean, *that* level of wanted?"

"F-f-four bodies and a bomb!"

Anthony blinked in surprise. "Four? My ghast got that lucky?"

The screen cracked with a bullet hole in the center of the digital display as Fixxer laughed at him. "No but a bo-bo-bomb did! And yo-yo-you get the credit!"

"Oh, for fuc-"

"Not just what you di-di-did, Mr. Pierson! It's what they thi-thi-think you did! You pissed off both sides of the sa-sa-same coin!"

The necromancer's Adam's apple bobbed nervously. "Both sides? And wait – the fuck you mean 'anti-boss'? Someone flip a proton or some shit?"

"You turned Gardeners into fert-fert-fertilizer!" the digital face crooned. "Now the Ang-Ang-Angelic think you kid-kid-kidnapped the sister of one of their-their-their former preachers!" Fixxer's background flicked from cloudy skies to a wall of orange flames that wreathed his disembodied head in smoke as he dropped the other shoe. "Only a matter of ti-ti-time before both the Sine an-an-and Susan Sands herself wants a word."

The Farmer's Daughter. A woman that Anthony was not now, nor had ever been, a fan of. As both the media mouthpiece for Eden Farms and the (alleged) behind-the-scenes corporate contractor for anything above petty street crime by the Gardeners, she was the embodiment of damn-near everything wrong with the world these days. Which was saying quite a lot.

It also implied that there was no chance she was issuing the 'overzealous staffers,' statement he'd been hoping for. That meant – coupled with Fixxer's observations – that the Gardeners *did* have full permission to go ahead with the hit, current black-book treaties and agreements be damned.

Amazing how he figured that out faster than LSPD...

...which probably meant that they knew and didn't *care*.

Anthony slumped back in the junker's seat and stared at the console-docked phone with his jaw hanging loosely in the air. There were many ramifications to that revelation, almost too many to process. The Gardeners, he'd assumed; regardless of *why* their boys were at his apartment, they were dead now. Some kind of peace would have to be brokered eventually, which wasn't going to be a delightful experience.

They'd want money (which he didn't have), favors (which he didn't want to give), or worst of all and most likely, both.

Joy, he whined to himself.

Whining to Fixxer would get him mocked out of the car.

That was, of course, assuming they'd get over their desire to see Katherine dead. Big if. Bigger 'why.' The only real thing he had to go on was the message she'd gotten from Jordan, and without knowing why *he* got killed, it was going to be a monster of a bitch to sort out.

The Church, on the other hand? They were known to be forgiving…

…if they didn't have to hunt you down to make you repent. That was a different story entirely. "You can get word to the Sine that I'm hiding Katherine for her own safety, right?"

Fixxer didn't answer at first. He just flicked from one ominous background to the next for a couple of minutes before finally answering. "Are you su-su-sure you want me to?"

That was not the response Anthony was expecting.

"Um. Why would you ask me that?"

"For o-o-one: because it might make the CoAA concerned what state a nec-nec-necromancer is keeping her in," Fixxer remarked with a little laugh. "Dead? Alive? Dead masquerading as alive? How much faith do you have that they'll extend that faith to you-you-you? Do you really want me to veri-veri-verify you're the man they're after?"

The same sick feeling he'd had from eating that jackass's soul dropped right back into his gut. The CoAA despised his type, and Anthony was no exception to the rule on both a personal and a professional basis. It was practically written in stone that mages were equal to heretics, but mages who could manipulate the dead were on a special level of 'Satan-sucking heathen'.

"How the absolute cast-iron *fuck* did they zero in on me so fast?"

"You left a corpse in your apartment and a trio scat-scat-scattered across a parking lot, mi-mi-minus a soul," Fixxer pointed out. "You aren't a sub-sub-subtle man."

"I'm not the only necromancer in Los San!"

"You're the on-on-only one in Aldour Estates."

Anthony slumped back in his seat and slowly rubbed the back of his neck. "That's circumstantial and you fucking know it," he sighed. "Okay. So, the first thing I need to do is convince the Church that I'm not the bad guy. I'm sure that'll be a breeze while a hoard of random gangbangers are out hunting me down."

Fixer didn't so much as twitch.

"Wait. You said *'for one'*. What's the other shoe you're holding over me?"

"That you-you-you should ask me a different question. One that doesn't start with the Ch-Ch-Church."

If there was a mid-point between 'slumping' in your seat and 'sinking to the floorboard,' the necromancer tried to hit it. "I'm getting shot at because someone tried to kill Kath, and she's getting shot at two days after her brother got deaded. The cops think it's the Grims, but the guys who actually did it are Yelthid assmunchers."

"Bit-bit-bit of a *conundrum*," the irritating, disembodied voice replied. "I know some thi-thi-things that you need to know – if you're willing to tra-tra-trade," Fixxer offered.

Of course, that wasn't an offer. It was an order, plain and simple.

Work with Fixxer long enough, and you knew that his suggestions were actually statements. "Shit. You know something, don't you? What is it?"

The phone began to chime, and a waterfall of gold coins flashed across the entire screen. "Ah-ah-ah! First bite-byte-bite of a byte is free. Second bite?"

The necromancer cupped his face in his hands and groaned in not-entirely mock pain. "Please don't make me say it."

"*Second* byte-bite?" Fixxer pressed.

Anthony groaned again and gave up trying to fight the bastard. "The *second* byte-bite comes with all the fixin's."

"An-an-and *you* don't have the money to pay for a ham-ham-hammer, let alone the whole to-to-toolbox," the damnable voice countered.

"But if I didn't have something you wanted, you wouldn't have wasted time talking to me," Anthony argued. "You're pragmatic, Fixxer, and you don't waste your time. My time, sure, but not yours."

Smiling and laughing yellow emojis fell like rain behind the techno-twerp's head. "That means the fix is *in,* Mr. Pier-Pier-Pierson! We have inter-inter-intersecting interests!"

On a good day, the digital repetition would fray your nerves. On a night like tonight? Looking out across the dipping plain of Los Santuario and the neigh-infinite number of sparkling lights that dotted the cityscape as far as you could see? "Fixxer, I swear to God..."

"I'm a ma-ma-man in the machine," the avatar quickly interrupted. "Only Go-Go-God here is *me.*"

The simple retort shut Anthony up on the spot. He spared a moment to drum his fingers on the tattered steering wheel, until he could level the tone in his voice. "What's the offer?"

Almost immediately, Fixxer's face vanished and a mind-boggling data-dump filled the phone. Over top a map of downtown Santuario, boxes flickered to life, all of which were filled up with names. More boxes appeared filled with weapons, marked with initials that matched most of those names – along with brief descriptions to match – and then a list of affiliations. Those lists were shorter; most belonged either to the Grimshanks or their corporate overlords at the Heart and Spade Foundation. There were exactly two names he recognized – Clarence Abberdine and his sister, Clare Abberdine.

"Meet mo-mo-most wanted Numbers One and Two. Wanted by the cops and of direct interest to you."

He forgot to add that they were wanted by the fashion police, too. This was one of their better photos, Anthony mused. Both had black hair with strands of silver and gold, gray eyes utterly devoid of warmth, and outfits that had never met a tailor who didn't deserve to be shot. Impressively unimpressive, the twins made up for it with their nicknames – the Blood and Bitch Twins of Los Santuario.

Aliases that were very well deserved.

It was amazing how fast the digital broker could make a sick stomach *worse*. He never failed to find a way. "No they're not," Anthony countered, "I worked for them *three times* and that was *enough*. Seriously Fixx, if you're asking me to take a shot at the Blood and Bitch Twins, I'm just gonna fucking hang up now and go jump off a cliff," the necromancer grunted.

The sad thing was that he wasn't kidding. His occasional employer knew it, too, and that's when the screen wiped itself clean and a new set of names popped up. Anthony let out a low whistle because *this* set of people he recognized right away. He didn't even have to look at their stats. If you didn't know who Enrique Robertson-Yers was, you didn't live in Santuario. Or anywhere else in the US, for that matter.

In the same vein, if you didn't know what the Gang in Black was, you didn't work the streets. Of course, they didn't call themselves that – not on the public paperwork. The press called them that. The Grims called them that. So did the Gardeners, so did the Aphonse Sisterhood and the Sub-Soua Carties.

They called them that, but never to their faces.

But their actual name? Not necessarily God-given, but close enough?

Enrique Robertson-Yers was the Captain of the LSPD's Anti-Gang Unit. They were the shock-troops of the city; the real 'beat them with a stick' type. They were corrupt to the core but managed to be *legally* corrupt; they didn't take bribes from the gangs, but they took their money.

And their guns, and their drugs, and any of their other possessions.

If they were feeling kind, they wouldn't take your life.

They didn't usually feel kind. The AGU was the organization that the terms 'police brutality' and 'extra-judicial' were coined to describe. There weren't a lot of nice things you could say about Ab/Psy or the CultBuster divisions that worked under the giant golden badge of the city's 'protect and serve' mantra, but Yers and his goons in black took the cake for their 'keep the peace at any cost' slogan.

The boxes faded off the screen and the map flashed up again. This time, a city block outlined in red lay overlapped by a larger one, slashed out sections highlighting a warehouse and metro section. A pair of red-and-white crosses popped up on the corners, flanked by little red hats with flame icons just below them.

"Holy. Shit. Fixx. You can't mean…"

"Re-re-read on!"

He did. As he stared at the map of doom-to-come, the screen changed again and one more picture popped up: an officially-signed arrest warrant for both Abberdines. The charges ranged in everything from drug smuggling to unlicensed sex trafficking, and a sub-charge of Enhanced Weapon Possession. That last bit ensured a death penalty addition to every other charge on the docket. The document was complete with their photos, current location, and a check mark in the box that read *PMI Approval.*

A second mark below that was self-explanatory. *Headshot.* It was marked with an 'x' in the 'no' column. A simple request from the Powers-That-Be in the LSPD to aim for anything other than the face.

PMI. The lifeblood of his non-Department of Defense paychecks.

Postmortem Interrogation.

It even included a sworn statement from the D.A. for good measure.

'In the event of circumstances beyond the control of the Anti-Gang Unit, it has been deemed acceptable for the Service of Public Good for alternate arrangements counter to biological functionality to be considered.'

In other words? Shoot them, don't shoot them, it doesn't matter.

Just absolutely not in the head.

That order was coupled with a date, a time, and a second set of signatures that carved it into stone. The timestamp was particularly important: if a non-emergent arrest warrant was expected to end in the death of a subject, the police had to file it up to forty-eight hours in advance to ensure that the right person was being targeted and that all reasonable methods to negotiate a peaceful surrender were undertaken.

If the situation became 'urgent,' that requirement was thrown out the window. The cops liked to add it as a rider for particular subjects of investigation who might not cooperate. It took a lot of stress out when you could talk to the corpse after the fact. Helped with counter-terrorism actions, too.

Anthony knew that much a little too well...

...and the police loved the practice a little more than they should.

It was yet another reason why necromancers were licensed and their usage regulated. If you thought that any of those words mattered, you watched too much news. If the cops wanted to know badly enough, they would, and your right to complain ended with the flatlining of your pulse.

As he watched, a timer popped over the warrant – one hour, fifty minutes. Below that, a name flashed onto the screen: The Handed Down. A trading hub of sorts. Part black market, part D/s sex club, part shrine to Lady Helesiki. Everyone in the city knew where it was; you couldn't miss it even if you tried.

"Are you-you-you getting the idea?" Fixxer's disembodied voice asked.

"That comparatively speaking, Hell's not a bad place to be tonight?"

"We-we-we need to speak to the Abb-Abb-Abberdines. Bo-bo-both of us," the digital voice droned out.

Anthony couldn't even hide his snort of derision. "I'm assuming you want me to get shot, then. Kath told me that Anth-Med is running on red with the expectation of a full-on mass-cas event tonight. I know you know that, so I'm guessing that it's because of *this*. Am I right?"

"In one!" Fixxer replied with a sense of eager joy. "Bitch and Blood about to be spilled. And yo-yo-you know *why*."

"I swear to God I have no idea."

Fixxer's face vanished and was replaced with a familiar, corporate visage that made Anthony's stomach turn just to look at it. A painfully slow realization crept into his mind as he studied the unnamed figure. "Hang on. I know this shitbag."

"Do-do-do you now? Meet the man that paid for your lawn-lawn-lawnscaping," the digital voice replied through the photo's lips.

"I pulled a mem-tap on one of the assholes that came for Kath and saw him in it. Heard his voice on Callie's phone right before the shooting started, too." Anthony's lips narrowed down into a razor-thin, predatory smile. No reason to give away the data-sphere just yet. Fixx was handing out information piecemeal. Two could play at that game.

"Then your mem-mem-memory work was top no-no-notch as always!" Fixxer stuttered. "When Pastor Fisher pushed up daisies, word spread fast about the maybe *who* but not-not-not the maybe *why*. LSPD got evidence for their reason, but after your en-en-encounter? I think other-other-otherwise."

Anthony pursed his lips and ran his fingers over the screen, as if to gain a tangible feel for the cretin. "Well. If you're asking me whether I trust the Gang in Black or my favorite hardware salesman, I'm going with you."

"I thank-thank-thank you! Meet Harold Vincetti. Ak-ak-a-k-a Harry V, aka Mister-Mister-Mister Slash. Free-free-freelance wetworker and-and-and gray-corporate sub-contractor, West Coast. Oregon."

"Oregon is the Grower State and Yelthid's backyard, so I get the link to the Gardeners for Slash here, but what in the fuck would a street preacher do in *Los fucking Santuario* to get the attention of a corp/gang co-op from that field of dreams?"

"Hitter, not-not-not farmer," Fixxer was quick to clarify. "He sows but has not yet-yet-yet reaped. Takes greenbacks; doesn't wear green on his back."

The necromancer tapped his finger on the screen and the picture was promptly saved to memory. "Okay, fine. What the fuck did Jordan do to get a hitman from Oregon to fly all the way to Texas?"

"He was al-al-already here," Fixxer intoned as the background changed to a dark field of gravestones and dead grass. "Has his hands in muck south of Sub-Am border and-and-and his dick in *more* muck in West-Corpus. Plowing fields left and-and-and right all around the city."

"That doesn't exactly fill me with joy and —"

The low-poly avatar jumped around on the screen as his voice took on an absolute shrill octave. "E-e-even better: he's the regional ops officer for a gun-for-hire firm – Blackwash!"

That tied into the snippets he'd seen in Carlos's memories, but not in a good way. A few taps on his phone later, and a quick summary popped up on the screen. There wasn't much to them on a public overview; they were corporate muscle and not your average rent-a-cop. A quick glance through some of their past employers said all that needed to be said:

These guys were barely-legal inner-city mercs.

And they were effectively a subsidiary of Eden Farms, at that.

"Gray-corporate contractor is right," Anthony muttered. "So. He provides security for a security firm. I'm guessing that means he's a cut above the rest?"

The screen went black for nearly twenty seconds. "You did-did-didn't just say-say-say that, did you?"

The necromancer flashed a smirk that downplayed the feeling of dread that had just landed in his stomach. "So, Jordan's trouble was local, but the hitter imported on other business. Not sure why they felt they needed to go out-of-state on a job that could've been handled with a dark alley, a butterfly knife, and someone with a hand tremor, but okay. Still don't see the connection. ANY connection."

"You may-may-may not know that the weed-eaters in Los San are just mu-mu-muscle for hire," Fixxer clarified. "No brains. Just bullets. No ter-ter-territory here of no-no-note."

Anthony nodded along. "I'd heard. They're here because it's *here*, but they don't run any major operations. None that I know of, anyway. More facilitators for the shit that the national leadership wants to be moved up from Sub-Am, right?"

"Rightio! Now. The ass in the hat? That's the one that need-need-needs hammered. He has corp-corp-corporate ties. Big ones. Unsure whi-whi-which; but li-li-linked to Eden Farms."

"Oh I don't like where this is going. The Grims and the Gardeners don't get along, and since one of the only thing that keeps the peace is that their corporate overlords are at each other's throats. Nobody wants to get into a ground war when it might affect the bottom line."

Fixxer's faux-face popped back onto the screen with an unwelcome answer. "Except it fe-fe-feels like a turf fight. A set-set-setup to push the Grimshanks out of to-to-town, maybe?"

"Which would normally be next to impossible since the HaS uses Los San as their personal corporate playpen. On the other hand, if the Grims can be removed by the cops..." Anthony mused before he let the idea dangle in the wind. "Going back to Mr. Verb here – you think he's the one that offed Kath's brother? Again, I'm going to ask this as simple as I can: the fuck why?"

A giant question mark appeared on the screen, followed immediately by Fixxer's not-so-welcome response. "'Why' is the question we bo-bo-both want to know. He doesn't do business for him-him-himself. He contracts out."

"Oh, so he's a fix-"

The screen exploded with the number one in dozens of different iterations, fonts, and symbols. "There's only ONE Fix-Fix-*Fixxxxxer* in this city!"

Anthony turned the car on and fired up the AC while he was at it. "This still doesn't tell me why I need to talk to the Abberdines. Shit, Fixx, it doesn't even explain why the *cops* think the Abberdines have anything to do with it. Please tell me you're sending me over there on more than just a hunch."

The phone went completely blank and silent, save a little hourglass and the faint hiss of running sand. It didn't come back on until he was well onto the highway, though he damn near wished it hadn't. The new stream was seventy-five percent shitty security video marked as the day before Jordan's death. The rest was a focused, zoomed-in shot of a trio of people as they climbed into an SU-Limo. Jordan was the first one in, and he looked absolutely terrible; exhausted might have been a good word. Defeated would also do. The other two?

"Does this answer your qu-qu-question?"

Anthony's eyes went wide and his stomach dropped into the seat. "Why the *fuck* did Kath's brother get into their fucking car?"

"Now-now-now you see why LSPD wants to talk to the B&B Twins," Fixxer replied as the question mark popped back up on the screen. "As be-be-best as anyone can tell, that's the last meeting Pastor Fisher had with any-any-anyone of note before he was pummeled to a pulp! The CoAA is piss-piss-pissed, so C'pn Yers decided it was time to hold the twins ac-ac-accountable. Just to show go-go-good faith for the city."

There wasn't a damn thing about the revelation that made sense, other than the way that Anthony slammed his foot on the gas and sped down the highway. "If those two get dead *and* it turns out the Grimshanks had nothing to do with it – there's gonna be open war between the AGU and the *Heart and Spade Foundation*. Outright war between the cops and the fucking corps. You know that, right?"

Fixxer's face popped up on the screen with a conical wizard's cap and five gold stars appeared under his newly-bearded chin. "Rightio! To quote the old kiddie-bookies, fi-fi-five points to-"

"Followed immediately by the Gardeners moving in to capitalize on it. Fucking slick move. But... okay, I still don't get it."

"Wh-wh-what's n-n-not to get? Seems pretty cut-n-dry."

"Well," he began, "Clarence and Clare don't shit without either Heleski's direct approval or a sign-off from her VP of Corporate Sec.

What's her name? Lina Lohas? Lives at the tippy-top of their tower at *Spade Down* and is rumored to never leave it?"

Fixxer paused as his screen went black. "Then the question is: do you think that Heart and Spade would?"

"Give the greenlight to flatten a priest? Absolutely not. That's an all-bets-are-off-and-the-Apocalypse-is-on move, and we'd have more bodies than just Jordan on the slab," Anthony shot back. "But the AGU being willing to risk it? Someone's either paid them off or put a tanker full of bullshit in their lap."

"Or you're mi-mi-missing the obvious."

"Not the first time."

"They're cri-cri-criminals. What if Yers has just been waiting for an excuse? And no-no-now the Church wants what the Church wants, Mister Pierson! What do you suppose all of tha-tha-that means?"

"With my luck? It means that they had absolutely nothing to do with it, video footage and the rest of us be damned," the necromancer grunted. Before Fixxer could come up with another quip, he hauled off and punched the steering wheel hard enough to make his car swerve into the next lane. "So, what about that Slash asshole? What's his tie-in?"

Fixxer shook his head so fast that pixels bounced off his scalp toward the edges of the screen. "Un-un-unknown third party interest! Which is why we need to know what the Ab-Ab-Abberdines were doing talking to your brother-in-law."

"I get the feeling he's good at his job."

"Not good-good-good enough," the digital avatar countered. "You're still able to ta-ta-talk."

"Yeah. Because chats like this are the delight of my day," the necromancer muttered under his breath. "So we're left with a big freaking question mark about why Jordan is dead, but we know it's tied to gang activity, and honestly, it looks like either Eden or the Gardeners are getting ready to have a hell of a fight with the HaS. Guess that leaves me with one giant question to ask."

An emoji with a raised eyebrow popped up on his phone. "Only one?"

"What the hell am I supposed to offer the twins to get them to talk to me when their lifespan is being measured in minutes? I'm not going to help them shoot their way out of a siege by the damn cops."

"The truth. Tell them wh-wh-who set them up."

Anthony snorted in absolute derision as he answered coolly, "How's that conversation supposed to go? 'Sorry to interrupt the last ten heartbeats you have, but you should know, some jackass from Oregon wanted your heads and decided that death-by-raid was the best choice.' You think that's going to go over well?"

"It might if you help them get out of it. If you tapped a Gard-Gard-Gardener that went for the hit then…"

"…then I've got Dead Man's Testimony I can offer the cops. That was going to be *my* get-out-of-jail pass."

"Gets you *and* them out."

"Or at least sends the warrant for reconsideration. You have a point."

"Nor-nor-normally you'd have thought of that by now."

Anthony ran his hand through his sweaty, slick hair and sighed to himself. "Really had a hard time with the corpse earlier, okay? So why are you telling *me* of all damn people? Why do you even care? Like you said, I'm broke, and much as we put up with each other, you don't let me run on credit."

"Because your cred-cred-credit is terrible. The tru-tru-truth? You have a vest-vest-vested interest in not being shot, and I-I-I would like a bullet of my own to direct!" the digital voice cheerfully exclaimed. "You get what you-you-you need and I get what I-I-I want without paying a dime!"

Anthony glanced away from the road long enough to spare a frown at the screen before him. "I love how succinctly you put it. I don't object to shooting an asshole that shoots at me first, but I'm not your private assassin, Fixx, my other intentions be damned. Why do you want him dead?"

The screen flickered again and when it came back, Fixxer was wearing a hard hat, and caution tape was stretched across the background. "Why, this here is a U-U-Union town! We don't like scabs taking jobs from hard-working local workers."

"You're saving my ass and putting me on the trail of this guy just because you don't like the fact that he's… *hiring*?"

"He-he-he doesn't care for his employees like I-I-I do. Hard to employ people once they've been sho-sho-shot," the digital head complained. "Besides," he added as the clock appeared back on the phone's bright screen. One hour, forty-seven minutes… and counting down. "It's also be-be-because you can still get answers from the *Abber-d's* after the clock strikes ze-ze-zero!"

"Shit." Silence reigned between the two of them for several long seconds – a rarity when dealing with the technological avatar – until Anthony offered up a deal of his own. "This Slash asshole; what aren't you telling me?"

The response was uncharacteristically short.

"A lot."

"You aren't the jealous type, but you're just going to sit there and tell me you want him dead just because you don't like him writing contracts?"

A red 'X' flashed on the screen as an obscene fart noise railed the speakers. "I-I-I am not one to try an-an-and make the world a necessarily bet-bet-better place," the avatar replied after Anthony gave him a silent and dirty look, "but Slash's knives getting *dulled* would be a go-go-good *start.*"

It was so unexpectedly absurd that it made the necromancer laugh, even as he swerved to avoid oncoming traffic. "Fine. I'll go deal with the Abberdines; see what they wanted with him. Probably means I'm about to take a stun-shot in the nuts from the PD because I *know* those two are gonna want to run once they see the warrant, but why not? Could be fun. Or I could eat a bullet and not have to worry about it."

"That's a go-go-good man! Keeping your head on your shoulders!"

"On two conditions."

A crude image of Anthony's head being sliced off by a guillotine popped onto his phone in response. "Is helping you find your wife's attempted murderer not e-e-enough?"

"*Ex*-wife," Anthony stressed. "You want Slash gone, but I need to make sure whoever is paying for her to go tits-up gets off her ass. *You* aren't the jealous type, but sometimes *I* am."

"Are-are-aren't you seeing that young..."

"She hates me at the moment. I need your help getting that contract canceled. And yes, I can pay – I told you I mem-tapped that ganger, Fixx," he replied with a smug grin. "Which means I'm not as broke as you think I am."

"In the age of anth, information is just as val-val-valuable as a fat bank account number," Fixxer replied with a faint tremor of what almost felt like raw lust. It was... distressing.

So distressing that the necromancer nearly drove off the road. "It's a trade – I'll toss what I have for you and you stick with me until Kath is in the clear. *Plus*, if you're sending me into a showdown between Yers and the B&B Express, I'm going to need an exit that doesn't involve me shooting up the place. I want everything you have on the *Handed Down* – blueprints, conduits, tunnels, whatever. I know it's a big ask, but you can't skull-fuck me like I can skull-fuck *them,* so don't even try to complain. Take it or leave it."

"Lea-lea-leave it? You aren't that dumb, Mister Pierson! And you-you-you're already driving to the twins!"

"I can drive to a canni-shop instead and have a lot more fucking fun than this," Anthony retorted. "Your choice."

His phone's screen flickered on and off for a heartbeat. "Abandon your ex-wi-wi-"

Anthony cut him off before he could even continue the remark. "I know why Kath's being shot at. Kinda."

"You do-do-do?!" Fixxer replied eagerly before his pale face darkened with little thundercloud emojis that surrounded his head. "You did-did-didn't *share*."

Anthony nearly lost the chance to as some asshole in a 4×4 nearly ran him off the road. It took *everything* in his limited patience not to chase after the trucker and give him something *serious* to dodge, but he restrained himself. Himself, yes. His horn, no. By the time he was finished, Fixxer had earmuffs on.

"Take those off and listen," Anthony scolded. "I put one of those dead guys to work. Got an extra name for you — someone called Galvani and something I'm guessing that's a corp-codename, too — Wetshell."

His phone pulsed with lights that would've made a 1970's disco joint proud as the digital avatar — or whatever he *really* was — performed a few standing flips on the screen. "Names! I do-do-do like names. Let me sear-sear-"

"Search on your own time, Fixx," the necromancer retorted as he blinked away the glare from oncoming headlights. "Don't think I can talk and drive much longer tonight. I've got a feeling they're one and the same, and they've got an 'in' somehow with those green-jacket fucks. Your out-of-state contractor made an appearance on that call, too."

Fixxer's face bounced on and off as the lights dimmed. "Names are go-go-good news. I got ex-ex-*excited*," he replied with a not-quite-sensual hiss.

It sounded more like someone strangled a balloon giraffe.

"You're about to feel worse," Anthony muttered as he fished Katherine's 10/9 out of his jacket pocket and plopped it on the screen. "Whatever the Gardeners and this Slash jackass are doing? This isn't just corp-op/gang-bang bullshit. Memories are fickle things and can't always be trusted, but..."

"But? You aren't one to deal-deal-deal in pointless conjectures, Mr. Pier-Pier-Pierson."

"What looks like ground beef wired to an exo-skel, sounds like a thousand pounds of squealing hydraulics, and wears more nth-marks than a meth-a-magic addict? Caught a visual of it in a dead man's brain."

A swath of question marks appeared on the phone, and an old quiz show's theme played in the background until the face appeared again. "Wha-wha-what?"

As the file transferred, Fixxer's pale face warped with corrupted pixels and the backdrop turned cloudy with thunderstorms all over again. "Not a damn clue. When you find out, let me know."

The phone shut itself off in lieu of a goodbye.

4. WARRANTED BONDAGE
Monday, May 28th, 1:03 AM

One in the morning – on what was now technically Monday, of all damn things – wasn't when you'd think a lot of people would be out and about. You'd be wrong. Just because the weekend was over didn't mean the party was.

It was Los San. The party never was.

And the perky tits were always out on display.

The blonde who answered his call was no exception to that rule. She wasn't wearing clothes; as far as Anthony knew, she never did. Presumably, she had to put on pants to get groceries; but just as presumably, she had underlings to do that for her. Emiline was a lot to take in – both in attitude, looks, and her mind. She hid the latter behind the looks, and God help you if you ended up on the wrong side of her attitude.

"Monsieur, I gave you this number as a sign of respect for jobs before; you are not on one now, and you know better than to call without invit-"

He quietly waved hello and flipped the phone's cam to the reverse side. The streets of Los San were bustling with human, mutant, and Daem life alike, without a single soul down there aware of the LSPD units circling the block. He looked down at all of it from a vantage point he'd found in a nearby parking garage that had a perfect line of sight to Emiline's office – the world-renowned hedonistic playground known as the Handed Down.

The garage was probably built with just that idea in mind. Either by the club's owners or one of their detractors; that was anyone's guess. You could see anyone walking in through the front door, and you might even catch a glimpse of people as they tried to hide their faces when they ducked in through a side entrance.

Anthony tapped a command on his phone, and a picture of Fixxer's warrant popped up. "They're not negotiating in good faith, and your bosses have fifty-seven minutes before the AGU has authorization to redefine the phrase 'heart attack.' Didn't think you'd want that over a text."

Dead silence rang out until he flipped his camera back around so she could see his face. Finally, the beautiful young woman gave a flat, emotionless reply of, "I never knew you had a sense of humor."

He shrugged in lieu of a verbal reply. "I didn't know I'd spend the night being shot at by Gardeners and that I'd end up trying to beat the cops to your bosses for info; that makes us even."

Even more silence reigned as her brilliant green eyes bored into his face. "You're not fishing for a hand-job tonight, are you."

It wasn't a question and his shoulders slumped as he made his resigned answer of, "You have no idea how bad I wish I was."

"Fifty-seven?"

"Down to fifty-five. How many funerals do you want to go to this week?"

"Yours, if you're wrong."

She absolutely, one-hundred-percent, was not kidding. He tapped the screen and the full file popped across the cloud. "Read it yourself if you don't believe me."

You could barely tell she even glanced at it. One of her eyes took on a glint for a fraction of a second; if his own tech hadn't noted it, he'd have never known. "Are you the interrogation part of it?"

"No. I got this info second… um… hand, I guess. Your bosses know some important shit. I know they know that shit. The cops apparently think they know some shit too, but I'm not sure if it's the same shit or if they can be trusted to have the shit."

"The AGU is, of course, also shit," she remarked idly as she reached up to twirl a long finger through her golden locks. "So, what do you want for this?"

"Not going to hang up on me and tell them to get the fuck outta the Alamo?" he asked with a faint smirk. "I'm shocked."

Emiline leaned in and put her remarkable assets on remarkable display. The night may have been a bloody mess but he wasn't blind, and she knew how to disarm someone when she really wanted to. Literally and figuratively both. "Who says I haven't already flashed them?"

"Because they haven't started shooting out the windows yet," he answered honestly.

"Fine. You know the drill – the rules of Desire's Lexicon demand a trade. Make your offer."

He did. He hated that he did, but he did. If you ever, ever had to work for the twins, you knew the important parts by heart. A favor for a favor; a trade for a trade. Desire never gives without getting something in return. It didn't make it any less frustrating to negotiate over. "C'mon Em, I just did."

"In return, I notified the doorman to let you in. What do you want once you're inside? There is *non* time for you to enjoy the city's special playground, if you have not been mislead."

She was good at what she did – and she did damn near everything – but he knew her well enough to dodge the question. "Do you want to know the answer to that question when you're arrested? Or are you going to be happier not knowing why I'm here after they raid the club?" he asked as he glanced at a countdown clock on top of his display. "In fifty-one minutes?"

Emiline paused and pursed her lips. "Happier not knowing; you are not wrong, Monsieur. But I do need to know – why are you here?"

He tapped his phone twice and a file flashed across the screen. "Same reason the cops are but I've got better intel, apparently. Pastor Jordan Fisher. You know him?"

"The name. I saw it on the news recently."

"Know it from anywhere else?"

Her eyes narrowed slightly. "A question better suited for my employers, I would say."

"Maybe. That's what the warrant is for, but I've got evidence that shows they probably didn't curb-stomp his ass. Should be enough to ease the heat, though I wouldn't count on the entire raid getting canceled."

"Probably didn't or didn't? Those are two different things."

"So are postmortem interrogations and regular interrogations," Anthony countered. "I've got DMT that should muddy the waters enough to move the slider until someone can tell the difference."

The thing about Emiline was that she didn't take a lot of effort to convince her to work with you – as long as you treated her with respect and didn't insult her intelligence. It was almost refreshing. "Noted. I cannot promise they'll accept, but despite how much they'll argue otherwise, I don't doubt that they'll need it. You'll trade the full once they accept your terms?"

"I don't think they're going to get time to argue the point with me."

"No. No, I don't think they will. And I appreciate you looking after me and what I may or may not know for the sake of legal concerns, Monsieur Anthony; more than you realize. Fire door – west side."

"Front door. They gotta see me coming."

"They won't see you at the fire door?"

He flipped the camera around again and panned across the street. LSPD was there; they just weren't in marked cars and uniforms. She didn't have to see everything he did to get the point, but it helped. "They'll see me at the fire door and they've got officers close enough to grab me before I can get through it. However, I've got eyes on two units of under-c's trying to blend in with the crowd watching the front and nobody handy to intercept without breaking cover. So, your front door will actually give me a chance to get inside."

The twin's 'personal attaché' (as they liked to call her) gave him a thoughtful look through the screen. "Remind me why you quit coming here for work?"

"Because Clarence and Clare are two of the biggest sociopaths in the city and their 'I wish I lived in Paris' bullshit is worse torture than the sex, drugs, and rock-your-roll they traffic in on a good day."

Her laugh was music to his ears and brought a smile to his face. He was pretty sure she'd had her voicebox modded to elicit that response, too. "Ah. Yes. Yes, that's a reason. The door will be cleared."

"Make sure they let me bring my kit in."

"Your kit? Do you promise you're not...?"

"Em, the day I can get away with lying to you is the day that I figure out how to hack the tech in that head of yours, and we both know I didn't get paid enough in the Army to learn how to do that," he answered. "But if it makes you feel better, have your watchers watch the people watching me when I come in. They'll know."

She leaned back in her chair and allowed the leather back to practically swallow her short and athletic frame. "Accepted. You're tense tonight; you know, we do offer various stress relief -"

"Forty-eight."

"Can't blame me for trying," she countered before the screen went black.

Off to the side – and well away from Emiline's view – a phantom form stepped up to the necromancer and glared down at the phone. "*I can blame her. Boy, I do not know what you see in her, but –*"

Anthony pocketed his tech and made a show of buttoning up his coat. "You know exactly what I see in her *and* you know it's because of anyone who I know who has connections to the Grimshanks, she's the brightest of the damn bunch. Don't blame me for having eyes, and besides, we've never… you know. I'm not that stupid."

"Yes, you are, and if she were that bright, I'd assume she'd be leadin' them and not just taking their calls," Blackburn countered.

"Okay, yes, I am, *but she's* bright enough *not* to lead them and that takes a certain level of self-awareness that I happen to admire. Speaking of awareness, how bad is it?"

His phantom familiar would've taken a deep breath if he could've, but he didn't skimp on the theatrics for the rest of his display. He gestured down at the street and the buildings around with a wide-open sweep of his arms. *"I can't tell which of 'em has more watchers loose – the sinners or the saints."*

"Which ones are the sinners?"

"Both groups you know about."

That didn't bode well. "And the saints?"

The ghost pointed to a building across the street and down half a block from the *Handed Down* and called them out with a simple, *"I spy an Inquisi from the Church. They've got their own eyes on the goings-on."*

"And probably not just to catch glimpses of the straying faithful," Anthony mused as he turned away from his perch and started a fast walk through the concrete structure. "Guess that definitively answers who talked Yers and his goons into raiding the wrong gang."

Blackburn blanched and agreed with an unhappy, *"I do despise police corruption, no matter how well-intended. Speaking of, I'd advise being too noticeable on the next two floors down."*

He took the warning seriously and didn't even bother to ask why. LSPD, feds, a car full of Grimshanks waiting to get in on the celebrations; any or all of the above wouldn't surprise him. "Since when has the CoAA done anything with the cops with a good intent?"

"Well, we used to believe in a document that said 'separation of' as if it was important."

"We used to put 'don't remove me under penalty of law' stickers on mattresses, too," Anthony grunted as he adjusted the gun at his waist. "Nobody ever cared about that, either."

***

The Heart & Spade Foundation.

The Handed Down.

It wasn't the kind of club you took a first date to. Probably not even a great idea to take a second date. *Hell, taking Callie here might get me castrated*, the necromancer muttered somewhere in the back of his head. *Taking Kath here absolutely would've…*

If you envisioned what a BDSM-themed sex club *might* look like and then you decided to add neon lights and someone playing low-tempo EDM, you had a good idea of what the Down was. A good idea – but not an exact one. Sure, it had black tile floors and a smattering of hardwood stages across the club. Yes, it had red leather single seats and couches along those stages and plenty more tucked away in half-hidden alcoves.

It also had rules. Rules enforced by pretty boys and girls that didn't look like they would be a threat to a flea. Rules enforced by pretty boys and girls that had enough cybernetics under their skin to either fight an army – or fuck one. There were national banks in the city that had less security than what the Down used, and all of the perky little playthings made sure that their clients could pretend to be as unsafe as they wanted while being fully protected.

Fully. Protected.

Emiline greeted him without any semblance of her normal charm the moment he made it through the blacklight-saturated lobby and past an obligatory weapons check. She was still sans clothes, but she was also sans any semblance of humor. All she said was, "Time?"

His answer of, "Thirty-seven," didn't mollify her at all.

Even as the clock ticked down, just being in her presence made it damn hard to focus on anything except for the way that she pushed her skin on his. Or the way she smelled. Or the tempting lilt to her voice. Or the way her hair brushed against his arm seemingly of its own accord.

Some of it was being mitigated by a hex he'd put on himself; an anti-magic ward, of sorts. Wouldn't keep him entirely off of anyone's magical radar, but it'd piss off the metaphysical trackers lingering in the air outside. It'd also disrupt any low-key attempts to tweak the senses – a trick that the Grimshanks were well known to use for a variety of illicit reasons.

He was willing to lie to himself that it was mostly because of the pheromone enhancements he knew she had implanted. They used the same shit for therapists in the VA clinics, and knowing why she had them installed managed to piss him off just a little bit. "In twenty, the guests will be set to leave. In twenty-five, I have been told to inform the police that twins are done with negotiations. I will step outside and hand a pile of evidence the AGU may use to understand that nobody in this building has culpability in any alleged crime that the LSPD may have an interest in. I am then to tell them to stand down and go home."

"Em… I'm no fan of theirs, and you know it. Sure as fuck not a fan of most of what the Grims do and what the Twins *specifically* are accused of in this warrant. I am not even remotely sad about this and I'd much rather be back at my place eating popcorn while watching the news."

"Allegedly do, you mean," she countered.

"I meant what I said. You, I respect. Them, not so much."

"I suppose that means that on any other day, you'd ask for the contract to do the work for them, true?"

He couldn't deny the accusation. Nor did he want to agree to it. "I'm licensed. If I'm given a mandate, I have to. Honestly? I don't want to be anywhere near a point you could call 'involvement,' but here I am. Joy."

She paused in the middle of one of the "show" floors. Naked men and women paraded themselves about while leashed to chest-high poles scattered across the room. Interested parties lounged on couches and chaises in various states of undress while they watched; it gave the club floor a kind of 'meat market' auction feel. It never ceased to make him feel uncomfortable, and never more so than when he was standing in the middle of it.

"Of course. I do understand, you know. Right now very angry calls are being had between legal representatives of both parties to avoid just that. There are parties involved that have no intention to see tonight end in violence. And parties that I am sure do."

"Em…" Anthony cautioned.

She cut him off with a curt nod, "I know, Monsieur Anthony. I think I will owe you a private thanks for the warning when all is said and done. To ease your own mind, should it be worried in my direction, once I am outside per the request of the Management, I shall stay there."

As she spoke, she made sure to sway her hips with every step – and she made damn sure that he paid attention to the way she moved, too. Someone screamed in pain from the far side of the club, followed immediately by excited laughter and catcalls. He twitched and couldn't stop his hand from dropping to his gun, though she had her hand on his before he even realized she had turned back around.

Her grip was a comfort. A brief one, an almost magical one, but a comfort. A pleasurable jolt danced up his arm and he knew it had nothing to do with *her*, but whatever hardwired tech she was loaded with. "Not every pain is pain. Don't forget."

"I can't even imagine how you manage to work here…" he grumbled as he took a step back and tried to focus on her and not the PTSD-inducing noises all around his head.

All she did was reach up to her throat and pushed a little piece of fake skin to the side. A thin ring popped out from under the synthetic flesh, followed immediately by a gold chain. "We all seek to have a place to belong. Membership and ownership have perks."

"So do bathrooms," he grumbled as he tried not to watch her fiddle with the end of her leash even as she continued to walk – backward, at that – into a hallway at the back of the club. "Speaking of which, is there one?"

"You don't have time."

"I'm not putting my life at risk with a full bladder."

She rolled her eyes and impatiently leaned against the wall. A curt nod pointed him in the direction of a pisser, and he more than eagerly took off without another word. It was only a minor miracle that the bathroom wasn't a stage in and of itself, though one lone glory-hole suggested it might be at the right time with the right (or wrong) person.

By the time he was done, the clock had burned another twelve minutes since he'd stepped foot in the club. If Carlos hadn't been such a bastard, his stomach would've probably been kinder and the shitter would've smelled better. But no, everything about the night had to be unpleasant.

Down from the opposite end of the bathrooms, the hallway split into two – and once they were beyond a set of 'Employees Only' double doors and a grumpy jerk with a suit and an openly-carried SMG, a pair of stairwells greeted them. Little signs denoted them with a promise to Heaven in one direction and a promise to Hell in the other. Either one would get you closer to God, he surmised.

The question was 'which.'

"Em? I've got a bad feeling that I'm going to need another way out. Where's the exit down there?"

"I can't tell you. Your way out will have to be the way you came in."

"That may not work, and you know it," he countered. "Can you at least give me a hint?"

She lingered two steps down the spiral staircase. "There are two doors that lead to discrete exits to the buildings beside this, and I am aware that the owners have placed guards at each. I expect that many of my coworkers intend to depart that direction if the police do not agree to the terms presented."

The way she tilted her head when she spoke gave him pause. "That's not a recommendation."

"Mr. Pierson, I know you too well. You would have had a plan for an exit before you even stepped foot on this street. Why ask me?"

Anthony leaned against the old oak door and took a deep breath that turned into a deeper sigh. "So I'd know if it was the right one. And I know that you know where the twins bury their bodies."

"That's not what you should know."

"What should I know?"

Emiline glanced over her shoulder and smiled. Her left eye flashed with cold LED light and he felt a subtle 'ping' go off in his own hardware. A floorplan popped up in his head almost immediately with a mark indicating a highlighted staircase behind a false wall. "You should know that you're the only person I'm advising to steer clear of those exits."

She didn't say another word until after they entered the basement.

***

'Basement' was a word that didn't quite do the short maze of hallways, storage rooms, and assorted hubs justice. Los San wasn't an 'old' city by any definition, though a lot of the early structures had been built in a rush and then rebuilt to handle new city codes a few decades later. Get below ground level of just about any greater-than-three-story structure and you'd find labyrinths that combined old style with new tech.

Though – if he was being honest – the floor plan didn't match up with the reality from what he could see. Sure, there were adult-entertainment devices scattered throughout the concrete basement, but between the half-walls and full-stocks sat dozens of unmarked wood crates and thick plastic shipping containers. It was anyone's guess what might be in those boxes... but you could start and end each guess with the word 'illegal' or 'smuggled'. It was what they did. It was their bread and butter.

When they weren't fucking like wild dogs.

When Emiline brought him into a larger warehouse-shaped room, he finally laid eyes on Clarence and Clare Abberdine. You could more or less

119

tell which one their mother loved more just by looking them over – which was to say – neither. They weren't particularly ugly or unattractive, it was more in the way that they carried themselves. Their shoulders slumped, their heads hanged, and their eyes darted around the room in a state of near-constant paranoia.

How the ever-loving *fuck* they'd ascended to the regional leadership role of the 'Shanks was a question for the ages, one likely too nuanced to be answered. Anthony braced for the worst as he came face to face with a gang of goons surrounding an antique wooden table under a single hanging lamp. The Bitch and the Blood sat side by side atop the desk like they were trying to imitate the cover of some old vampires-go-gang movie from the early 90's.

They weren't alone, either.

There were just short of a dozen Grimshanks that Anthony could see, with two manning a doorway in the far back of the basement and two more who flanked the hallway leading to the ground floor. The rest were scattered about, either taking up supporting positions or stuffing piles of cash and meth into duffle bags. All of them were very well armed, and if he had to guess, armored with the finest in sub-derm defensive plates and cermimax-lined jackets to boot.

If the situation wasn't so damn dire and their guards not armed to the teeth, it might have been funny. As it was, not a single one batted an eye at the sight of a naked woman leading a man into their heated argument by her own leash. Three of the armed goons bowed their head in greeting, while Clarence flung his arms wide to welcome her.

Clare didn't move. Like her brother, she was adorned in red and black – while he wore a red fancy silk button-down shirt and black slacks, she'd gone the route of a long red dress and a black coat. It might've looked halfway decent if anyone else in the world had been wearing it.

As much as 'green' defined with the Gardeners, red and black were the marks of a 'Shanker. The pair also liked to speak French every chance they got, but they weren't good at it and it was a nightmare to deal with them when they were in one of their 'moods.' They felt that it made them sound 'classy' and 'better' than the southern suburbs they'd been born in.

Anthony's escort stepped back and dropped to one knee on the cold concrete floor. It had to hurt, but she did it without flinching. "Owner Clare. Owner Clarence. Accept my apologies. This guest is known to the club, and –"

"*Oi, oi*, I know who this *le con* is," Clare interrupted. "An asshole who speaks to the dead. We have done business before, though he is not one who shares the proclivities of our establishment. Thus, he is here without invitation, and even if he weren't, now is not the time for a meeting. So, Monsieur Pierson, do take an exit. Now."

The Grimshank's leader glanced away from the necromancer and back to the tablet in her hand, before the club's pet spoke up again. "Owner Clare, I must again apologize from the depths of my *âme*. Monsieur Pierson offered information that I had to immediately disseminate to the Property Management."

"Can we hurry up? None of you have any time here to dick ar-"

Emiline whipped her head around and gave Anthony such a withering, furious glare that he shut up and bit his tongue. "There. Are. *Protocols*. In this house. You wait your turn to speak and do so when your hosts are ready."

"Well, *le chein* does seem eager enough to have a place at our table," Clarence quipped. "Maybe there's room for the trained dog to sit and speak?"

"Owner Clare, there should be. Time is short, and he has offered information we can use to prevent an inconvenience."

"I love how you phrase 'imminent death,' but sure. Inconvenience," Anthony added. "I have a question. You can't answer it in LSPD custody. Can we skip the bullshit?"

Clare sized Anthony up and smirked as she imagined what would've made him look like he'd been on the wrong side of a hit-and-run. "How misinformed he is to think we'd ever be in their custody. How cute that you are interested in speaking on his behalf."

Emiline defiantly stuck her chin out at her 'owner' and addressed her succinctly. "It would be extra PR to handle were the club to be damaged."

"Ah yes," Clarence replied, "always our *pratique* little girl. Yet, she is right, and time does seem to be of the essence. Walker of dead men, whatever you have offered to the Manager of the Property had best be true."

The way he phrased that made Anthony clench his jaw, and damned if he knew why. He was also reasonably sure that wasn't the right use of 'pratique,' but he let it slide as he reached for his phone. The move made two of the other goons in the room dropped their hands under their suit jackets or to the holsters on his hips and their hands stayed there until he waved the device in the air.

"A guy I know got killed; a preacher. I'm more or less certain the Gardeners did it, but for some fucking reason, the CoAA has aimed the AGU at you for it," he replied as the timer on his screen clicked from eighteen to seventeen. "I can't stop the raid but I can gum up the worst part of that warrant for you."

"The Church is interfering with police?" the Blood marveled as his sister crossed her arms. "This is not new. But after seeking our help? Interesting."

The Bitch had her own thoughts and didn't hesitate to share any of them. "Oh I do hate being moved about on a chessboard. So tasteless. We have done nothing wrong; surely the AGU is not so blind…?"

There were words that made sense when put together, and 'the church wanted help from the Grimshanks,' didn't qualify. Neither did their feigned ignorance – and the stockpile of weapons in the storeroom was enough evidence of that alone. "You two run the fucking *Grimshanks*. One of the largest criminal organizations on and in the Gulf, for shit's sake. I've *worked* for you. You haven't done anything illegal? Really? *Really*?"

"Eh," Clarence countered with a wave of his hand. "*Non* more than the usual that is permitted by matters of nature. We… are of criminals. They are of not. We do what we do, they do what they do. Nature is what nature is."

"One can see how someone may have doubts – though why you would, of all souls, does seem odd," Clare spoke slowly, as if addressing a lost child. "Yet this is not new to the AGU. There are lines we do not cross and they tolerate us so long as we do not cross them. To do otherwise would be detrimental. We provide things they desire, and they –"

"– and they don't care," he interrupted. "I'm willing to provide DMT on your behalf but not until you explain what kind of *help* the CoAA wanted from you *and* why in the innumerable *Hells* that Jordan was last seen alive with you two."

"Jordan…?" the Bitch asked as she tilted her head.

"He means the man of the cloth that you were drooling over a few days ago," her brother clarified. "I presume, at least. That is the only Jordan to have crossed our paths over the last week."

"Yeah, Jordan. Pastor Jordan Fisher," Anthony added as he pressed a couple buttons on his phone and a digitally-hazy, green and black recording of Carlos's memories started to play underneath the ticking clock. "This is a conversation with a shitbag that links the guy that did Jordan's hit with the Gardeners. If you two weren't responsible for it, the 'postmortem' part of this PMI loses teeth."

Emiline cleared her throat from the floor. "As it is, he has shown to us that the police are negotiating in bad faith – a note our lawyers *sincerely* do appreciate. To add this? It may save lives."

"As long as nobody does anything stupid," he added. "I think we'd all prefer to leave the building without getting shot."

The twins shared a silent and unhappy look back and forth before Clare jumped off of the desk and swiped Anthony's phone out of his hands. She passed both hers and his down to Emiline before he could do more than curse at her. "Manager. Copy the file and deliver it to the Gang in Black posthaste. You. *Nécromancien.* Speak your question quickly and leave us."

"For one, you're welcome," he grumbled as the blonde on the floor synced the files. Her eyes pulsed with rapid flickers from the dead center of her irises. "You better not put any malware on that or I –"

Emiline reached back and grabbed his pants-leg before he could finish the remark. A moment later, and she was on her feet with his phone pressed against his chest. "Of all the things we give in this place, a virus is not one."

As he fumbled to take it back, he managed to mumble a, "You better not."

"I only give gifts. I promise," she said with her voice back in that same calm, tech-enhanced reassuring tone she was known for. Then with her voice just barely above a whisper, she added, "Your eye for the reprehensible will serve you well."

The exchange – as pleasantly uncomfortable as Anthony found it – didn't do anything to improve Clare's mood. "If all you want is her, you may have her at another time. Otherwise, property? *Manage* elsewhere."

The blonde made a quiet 'eep' and nearly sprinted out of the basement. The noise was for show, but the irritated look on her face that the twins couldn't see was that of a woman that was beyond *done* with their shit. When she was gone, the Blood turned around and puts his efforts into emptying his desk drawer.

"Not to burst your bubble," Anthony started, "but I want the same thing the cops do. You are the last people of note that might've seen Jordan alive. Why? What in the actual fuck kind of business could *he* have had with *you*?"

"The same kind of business all devout men of the cloth have with procurers such as us," Clare retorted with a bored shrug.

"Yeah. No."

"What makes you so sure of that, hm?"

The answer was 'everything,' but he knew she wouldn't accept it. "Look. I knew him. I didn't like him but I knew him, and whatever happened to him he probably didn't deserve it. Because I know *him*, I know there is absolutely no fucking chance the man sought either one of you out willingly."

"You make that sound almost insulting," Clarence snapped, as he rustled around in the drawers of their desk.

"Because Jordan wouldn't spit on a sidewalk unless God told him to by certified letter. Getting into a car with you two? I'd really like to know *why*."

Clare patted down her vest and glanced up in his direction. "Made him? He contacted *us*."

"I'm sorry, what?"

"Yes, it was his pleasure to have our company," the pint-sized sociopath clarified. "He was given his orders, and we had our own."

None of that made a damn inch of sense – especially when coupled with his recent trip to Northern Italy. In turn, it suggested that his trip to the Canuck Pope might've been weirder than anyone could have guessed. "Orders to do *what*?"

Clare shook her head and calmly slipped a spare magazine into one of her pockets. "*Non*. You do not need to know more than this. His peers sent him to us – ask it of them."

As much as he wanted to agree, he couldn't. The small swarm of Grimshanks around him with their weapons cocked didn't help, either. "There's a less than zero chance that they'll tell me. It's literally why I'm here. What did he want from you two?"

Clare sighed and stormed over to him and pulled his watchband up where she could see the timer clicking down on it. "At best, *Monsieur nécromancien*, matters of demons and devils should be handled by those who spend their lives in service to them. The High and Mighties found an issue; we were thought to be able to lend a hand."

"You're telling me that the freaking *Church of Angelic America* gave Jordan orders to bring his ass down here and tell the *murderers employed by the Daemoness of Desire* to clean up a mess," Anthony pointed out. "You understand that it's really hard for me to swallow?"

"I do. As much as it is hard for us to *comprendre* why you think the green-cloaks would have an issue with us, we have not done a thing to them as of yet."

Anthony started to have a reply to that, and then her phrasing caught up to his thought. "As of yet? That implies there's a future plan."

"A future for some, yes."

"You know, dear sister, maybe there is a thing that this man can explain for us," Clarence interrupted with a thoughtful look. "I know you know of our reputations; the things we do, the things we don't."

"Pay taxes?"

"*Non*. We pay taxes. We are not crazy. Magic, *Monsieur*. It is not our dabble. A thing that we have respect for, *oui*. A thing we dabble? No."

Clare shuddered and a lock of her hair drifted down across her eyes. "I understand that some of our methods and manners do bring you distress. What you do? Makes us feel the same. We will do business with it, of course; business is business."

They weren't exactly the first to share that sentiment, but it was surprising to hear them actually admit it. "Business is business. What about it?"

"If one were to use... what you do..."

"Necromancy?"

"*Oui*," the Blood replied. "If one where to do that to... shall we say, *empower* a body to do harm? To... give it an agency that would not be... typical? Be more... metallic than man."

Anthony blinked. "Like a drone?"

"Like a drone, maybe. Or... like you and your arm. Without your... selfness attached, as it were. Would that be a difficult thing?"

The question made him take an involuntary step back. That matched up *way* too close to what he'd seen in Carlos's head for comfort. "I mean... I can resurrect a guy with tech for a bit. But that's not what you mean, is it?"

"*Non. Non*, it is not. Think... broader?"

"Shit. What *the fuck* did Jordan tell you?"

The twins exchanged glances. "He suggested things we do not understand that are being used for, shall we say, offensive interests. They seemed obscene, obscene in a manner not conducive to a weekend's entertainment. We have been wondering about how... likely... it could be."

"Not. Not likely. It'd be weapon-grade stupid and probably easier to build a fucking ICBM than to pull it off. Tech is tech and magic is magic. It's one of the few things that the Pentas and the Feds agree on."

"But you could."

"Right amount of funding you can do anything but..."

"...but I think now you should have a better understanding of the depths of the waters that the Pastor was treading in before he sank," Clare replied slowly as the color drained from Anthony's cheeks.

Weapon-grade stupid. Weapon-grade magic. Two great tastes that never tasted great together. Two great tastes that matched up with the abomination he'd seen in Carlos's skull. "I really – I *really* – cannot begin to stress that if you know someone is using necromancy to build or power some kind of… I don't know, something tells me that calling it a 'weapons platform' isn't doing it justice… but if you two *know something* then you need to tell *everyone* about it."

"Everyone? Everyone seems like an exag-"

"*Everyone* means the bitch that dry-cleans your suits to whoever your Goddamn Congressman is. You *tell them*, and you don't stop telling them until someone shows up with a tank to shoot whoever came up with the idea. I know who your bosses are, and I *know* they don't like statements that start and end with the phrase 'international incident.' Do they? Did I miss a memo where they'd be okay with that?"

Clarence's jaw dropped and damned if Anthony had any idea if it was because someone actually had the balls to interrupt him or if it was because of the way spittle was flying out of the necromancer's mouth. "Such hostility. I didn't expect it. You do… speak with urgency, at that. The Pastor said something about EBR…?"

"Oh if he did I understand why you two are about to be paste," Anthony groaned. "Okay. I get it; you two don't give a shit about the law. Fine. But even you two have to know that there are laws you break and go to jail for and laws you break and go into a woodchipper for. The EBR laws firmly fit in the latter."

"That is true, good brother," his sister added with a faintly reassuring tilt to her voice. "I know you know better than to come to this house with disrespect but it is your… vehemence… on the subject? I think that offers enough to answer our question as to how serious to take the Pastor's words. To assure you – in good faith – that we are not dabbling in such… concerns… as he expressed, we will answer another question. One more pressing to you, if we heard correctly."

They never offered anything for free. Ever. Which meant that whatever Jordan had told them had them freaked out on a level he hadn't been expecting – and they were afraid of being held accountable for knowing about it. More than they were afraid of the cops.

All he could think was a simple, succinct, '*Shit*' that he kept to himself.

"A pack of Gardeners just tried to blow my head off, and their handler isn't local – some asshole named Slash. That's where the DMT I gave you came from – the dead guy was one of the fuckers that turned my apartment into 9mm Swiss cheese."

The Blood blinked in confusion. "A man is named as an action?"

Anthony shrugged. "Maybe his dad was named 'Hack.' I dunno. Fucker is trying to butcher me; guess he started with the English language."

"*Hommes*," Clare sighed, "always with the aggrandizing."

"I have heard this name, yes," her brother replied. "A *mercenarie*, of sorts? More of gun than man, mayhaps? More metal than flesh; more care for currency than for concubines."

"I don't know," Anthony admitted. "All I know is that he killed Jordan, then he tried to kill my ex-wife, then he tried to kill me and I ended up with a serious case of indigestion after eating his help. I'm a little irked about it."

Clare batted her eyes at him before she bent down and picked up a small pistol. "Aww, my dear *nécromancien.* Are we not good company?"

He bit his tongue to avoid the honest and obvious answer. "Well, since you're being blamed for murders *he* committed maybe you can tell me if the name of his boss means anything to you. Blackwash, maybe? Or Sojourn?"

Clarence stopped rummaging through one desk drawer after after another and gave Anthony a piercing glare. "We are not fools, Monsieur Pierson; do not take us for such. Knowing who did what to whom tells us whom we need to have visits sent to once this night is done; some of your problems have potential to be resolved as we resolve our own. Do not assume that handing over some tidbits makes us equal partners."

"I don't. I just need answers. However you two decide to clean up is your call," Anthony shot back as he glanced at his phone. There were less than five minutes to go before the LSPD flipped the switch, and that was three minutes less than he wanted.

"Free advice, Monsieur Pierson. There is a saying in this country – a dog chases a cat into a bush when he is meant to go in the hedge"

If their crimes against the federal government weren't enough to make him root for the AGU, the way Clarence just butchered the phrase was. "Um. You mean barking up the wrong tree?"

"If one must, I suppose. I like it as I say it better. Blackwash is not a tree you should risk pissing on, regardless of... doggedness."

That wasn't much, but it was something. "A bunch of assholes big enough to rankle your skin? Duly noted. But what are they?"

"Private security; but it is who owns *le* store that is of interest to you more than not, one would suspect," Clare interrupted. "But of Sojourn? Actually, we do know much of them. It is why *le* Pasteur asked for us, specifically."

That was interesting. Even better, that was *actionable.* It did not, however, come without complications. "Finally. What are they – what do they do?"

"And not what our interests are in them?"

"Your interests are in tits and cocaine," Anthony countered. "If you were doing anything more than that, I doubt you'd tell me." As he replied, his phone buzzed in his pocket.

"Oh, we do much, much more than that," Clarence answered. "The next time you have cause to visit our *établissement*, take a closer look at the good little girls and boys. You'll find that their parts are not exactly... how to say? *Spécification d'usine d'origine?*"

The necromancer gave him a silent, blank stare before Clare patted him on his metal wrist. "Factory spec, I believe, is how you Americans say it. Sojourn is very good at giving the body exactly what it needs to be the best it can be."

The phrase had multiple meanings coming from Clare, and every one of them made Anthony's skin crawl. "Sojourn is bio-med, and Blackwash is their corp-sec?"

She corrected him as shouting erupted from upstairs. "Bio-med? It is... a stretch. Soj is bio-*mécanique*. One can hardly call all that they do to be of medicinal value to life."

Anthony couldn't stop himself from blurting out his response. "Then those vats I saw. That shit was real and not –"

"Vats? You saw vats? What was in them?" Clarence demanded.

The necromancer caught himself before he gave up anything else. "Nothing... nothing important."

"There are many things that the Lady of Desire tolerates and encourages, Monsieur Pierson. A lie is not one of them," Clare cautioned, "especially in this house."

"Noted. Now, we can't stop the AGU from pulling a raid, but..."

Clare smirked. "But? There is no but. Our lawyers have been in a call with them since you began speaking to us. They – as you said – did not decide to operate in faith good, so neither shall we. All fun and games have their end; there are other cities we can play in."

"Once you get out of this one."

"Yes. Once."

The words were barely out of her mouth before her brother pressed his finger to the back of his ear and uttered something under his breath. On cue, gunshots erupted out from the back hallways. Two of the 'shanks in the room with them took immediate flanking positions by the door, and half of the lights went out.

His left hand went right for the shotty under his coat, and he quickly started to work the fingers on his right like he was gripping at a phantom stress ball. Little flickers of greenish-yellow light pulsed between his fingertips each time he curled them together into his palm. Clare sat still with a smile, though Clarence made a show of stretching his neck and shoulders.

"Did you just – are you out of your *Goddamned minds*?! Was that you or them?!"

"Our *informateurs en noir* with the police made it clear there was nothing we could do to change the course of this ride, once you informed us which one we were on," Clare answered with a helpful little smile. "We advise that you follow; through the front will not be an option."

Anthony started to reply to her, but a little chat icon flashed under his vision. He glanced at it, and a quick message popped up overlaid against the room that said simply, *'Don't. - Em.'* Sometimes, the simplest messages were the important ones. Moreso because he hadn't actually given her the contact ID for his HUD-OverLife™ system...

...which implied she wasn't as honest about the 'no virus' statement as she'd said. Or she didn't need a virus to get into his headware. Either way, it made her more dangerous than he'd given her credit for, and he'd given her credit for a lot.

"I came here to keep you two from getting shot and..."

"...and it is by that we knew we needed to clear the exit. We have one piece of business left to do, and then we're leaving. Follow if you wish; explain yourself to them if not."

He had a witty comeback. He did.

It was funny, and it was profane, and he wanted nothing more than to say it. But before it could leave his lips or escape the rough stubble of his graying goatee, her brother very calmly pulled one of the biggest revolvers the necromancer had ever seen from the back of his belt. Without another word and in a single fluid motion, he placed it to the head of one of the thugs in the basement.

No muss, no fuss, no fanfare. Just a simple practiced move that preceded an ear-shattering *crack* that exploded through the basement and surrounding conversation. The bullet exited the Grim's skull with an arcing shower of blood and brain matter that decorated a nearby woman's face. "As my sister said. Lies," Clarence added, "are not permitted in a Den of Helesiki. The Gang in Black should know that by now."

The rest of the gang didn't react aside from a few flinches and startled glances. They knew better. Anthony did, too; he just didn't care. His shotgun was drawn and pumped before the body hit the floor, much to Clare's bemused delight. "Oh, for *fucks* sake, tell me you didn't just…"

"Did I know that those in the AGU have been listening to this? They wished information; you wished information. You offered by trade, they by theft. You, one does assume, also wished for them to know of your plight, so I let you speak so they could hear what tale you had to spin. Now the police know of your story, and you did not have to be arrested for them to hear it. *La victoire, oui*?"

"You just shot a fucking cop in front of me!" the necromancer screamed as he chambered a round and pumped the shaft with his metal hand. "How in the *fuck* do you think that gets me a safe trip out?"

"Ah," Clare interrupted before her brother could, "because that one was not one of the *Unité* Anti-Gang. That one was an employee of a rival group to ours."

There was an obvious answer to that question, but if he gave it, he'd probably be next on the floor. Anthony stared at her like she'd grown a second head and tried to hold back the strangled cry of frustration building in his heart, even as his palms started to sweat. The gunshot had only exacerbated the shouts and screams of orders being thrown overhead. "Then we need to get the f-"

The Bitch pulled her own gun out: a dinky G-Locke 12 that looked small even in her tiny hands and took aim at one of the two Grimshanks standing by the hallway. "But this one is, and the punishment for a lie of being a tool of the police is the same as the punishment as a lie of belonging to a rival."

Maybe her target was.

Maybe they weren't.

The gangster beside the accused LSPD informant went pale and pulled her own gun up and aimed right at the Bitch herself. Anthony had time to fling himself behind a short stack of crates before the first burst of gunfire shattered the air, right along with everyone's eardrums. Tri-fiber carbon cerimax worked wonders to protect you. An entire global marketplace had been built around the idea. Extra ceramic plates or steel sheets could be slipped inside the armor if you really felt the need, but the ballistic fibers themselves worked to save lives in conflict zones and supermarket shootouts across the country...

…when your assailant had the manners to aim for it.

The turncoat Grimshank loosed five rounds on one single pull of her trigger. The first two went chest-level into the Bitch and failed to puncture the ballistic plates. The last one went wide and punched into a support beam overhead. Rounds three and four tore through Clare's collarbone and shattered the short woman's porcelain-white jaw.

While the other gangsters moved to take cover, Clarence returned fire. His revolver barked twice. His victim — be she LSPD or maybe just someone that decided that the Twins weren't being picky enough to think past the then and now — didn't get the opportunity to take another shot.

That was the thing about 'big' guns. They usually had big bullets.

As firefights went, it was short and terrible and promised to make the immediate future immensely worse. For a moment, nobody knew who was shooting at who; the room was way too cramped to avoid losing your hearing and the cover was questionable at best. The exchange promised that the cops would be sticklers on enforcing the 'shoot first' part of the 'ask questions later' warrant, and Anthony didn't want to be downstairs when they came to enforce it.

The Blood wasn't of mind to care.

Clare made one final, wet gurgle as she tried to breathe through the shattered mess that was left of her face. As she died, her brother went through the fastest five stages of grief Anthony had ever seen in his life. When he hit 'bargaining,' he focused his eyes and then his gun on the necromancer's head.

He didn't make a demand to bring her back or try to keep her alive. It was, shockingly enough, something far more criminally-minded. "Take her."

"Take her…?"

"Take her soul, you fucking *connard*," Clarence snarled. "Take, and we leave. Molest her essence, and you won't… you won't…"

The way the end of his over-sized revolver shook explained the 'or else' that came attached to that. "There isn't time. We gotta go *now*," Anthony shot back even as he scooted closer to her body.

"The Gang in Black cannot have access to her mind. Remove her. Now."

The gun didn't move. Clarence's remaining bodyguards did; they flanked the entrance into the storage room as shouts and commands from the cops upstairs reverberated down into the club's basement. All Anthony could do was slide over to Clare's body and place a hand on her chest to make sure she was actually dead before he got to work.

There was a zero-percent chance Anthony would be done before the LSPD breached the stronghold. He knew it. Her brother had to know it. Her brother also did not give a flying fuck, and the way he tightened his grip on his pistol made it clear that if Anthony refused, he'd take a bullet to his own face.

The choice pretty much made itself.

There was a guideline that suggested you shouldn't do more than one 'dry' transfer per week. The DoD brass insisted on it. ParaPsy didn't give a shit and told you to suck it up and deal with it if you had to, which was a choice someone else would make for you over any personal objections.

Clarence must've studied with them.

The process almost went the same way as it had at his apartment. As heavy *thumps* of con-cuss grenades going off on the first floor made the ceiling vibrate, Anthony skipped the 'protection' part of the 'protection' runes and charged directly into the 'storage' part. The only knife in his jacket quickly found itself buried in her chest and the etched runes across his skin lit up like a bunch of glow-sticks.

Clare's blood left his hands slick, but what made it difficult was the raw *disgust* that radiated out of every inch of her soul. She was so full of pent-up *rage* over being shot that her essence actively recoiled from his touch. It wasn't something he couldn't deal with, however, and she was neither the first nor the last that would argue the point.

Then again, she might be the last, if the freaking AGU had anything to say about it. They were trying, too. A bloodied Grimshank stumbled into the storage room with blood dripping out of his ears, and then he shouted out a warning that they had almost breached the stairs.

He almost wished he could pay attention to the rest of the details.

Instead, Clare's dead eyes flung open as he pushed his hand into her neck and *squeezed* her splintered spine. A sharp breath escaped her lips; a gasped mix of equal parts pain and ecstasy as he pulled at the vestiges of her essence still trapped inside her flesh. Her entire body convulsed once as Clarence called out her name.

Her soul slammed into his head with a rush he could not have expected. The sheer force of her eagerness to escape her flesh knocked him on his ass and nearly broke his wrist in her ribs. Or at least, he thought it was the strength of her soul.

A burst of cryonic stun-gas washed over his face as an AGU drone ricocheted out of the hallway and landed in the storage room like a giant pinball. It was shaped like a basketball-sized caltrop and each leg ended in omnidirectional wheels. He recognized what it was just in time to bring his metal hand up over his eyes – and promptly saved his face from being peppered with debris.

The little robot popped up into the air and unleashed a concussive blast that wiped out every Grimshank who wasn't already laying prone or behind cover. It broke boxes, shattered the lights over their heads, and sent papers flying. Clarence must've seen it too, because he managed to make his revolver bark again before the drone could unleash a second blast to keep everyone down.

That was the thing about the AGU. They didn't believe in 'knocking gently at the door.' They preferred to kick the door in and hope for the best. And, like the good little shock-troopers they were, they came armored.

A pair of grunts wearing full-body, gunmetal-gray poly-carbon armor stormed into the room with their guns raised and embedded green LEDs on their faceplates lighting the way. They moved with purpose and opened fire on the closest two guards as they struggled to get back to their feet.

One of them tried to bring a pistol to bear as the cops stormed in. Three sharp, barking *pops* later and the ganger became a candidate for a PMI. Two more *pops* and that PMI was going to be harder to pull off unless you scooped up his brain from the floor and ran it through a strainer.

Their efficiency was on par with the DoD.

Their planning, however…

Five people dead in just under five minutes. *Necrosi* filled the air in their passing; dying released energy, and that energy came in the form of a particular flavor of nth that had a special name. At best, the mundanes in the room might feel a weight on their shoulders. For nth-sensitives, it had a slick, oily feeling.

For Anthony, and other necromancers?

He'd have felt better walking into the front wall of a hurricane.

The plan to get out of the basement had ended the second that Clare had decided to point her gun at a cop and the corpses that littered the floor made it perfectly clear that the AGU wasn't interested in *negotiations* for a peaceful resolution. The leading two officers trained their guns to Anthony's face in what felt like slow-mo.

The necromancer sucked in all of that wild energy like he was the mouth of a cave as high tide slammed in. It filled every inch of his body and threatened for one brief moment to overwhelm his soul and every ounce of himself that he could bring to bear. As it boiled inside him, the

AGU rushed through the room and violently worked to pacify it with punches and the unrestrained use of the butts of their rifles.

Like a flooded cave on the shore, the blowout was spectacular.

Three of the corpses bounced skyward, propelled by the rush of power that Anthony unleashed. They landed on their feet and attacked the closest people they could find. There was a zero-percent chance that the trio of dead gangsters would do anything more than slow the AGU troopers down, and he counted on that more than he wanted to admit.

Right now, slowing down the police was infinitely better than taking a charge of killing one. It was going to be a hell of an argument to make later, but there weren't very many ways to ensure there was going to be a later to be had. As the troopers lost themselves in sudden shouts of surprise and horror, Anthony pushed himself to his feet.

Clarence yelled something behind him.

He ignored it.

The ghasts jumped onto the officers and dug into their armor with fingers, teeth, and whatever else they could muster. There was something just innately satisfying in watching a pair of the AGU's grunts get their shit wrecked by a cadre of corpses, though it wasn't something Anthony had time to dwell on.

Sprinting, as a rule, was not his particular forte. Surviving a desperate sprint, however, was. He pumped enough juice into the leading ghasts to let them plow into the cops like the Los San Ramsicorn's defensive line, and the zombies kept at it even when concentrated bursts of gunfire ripped their arms and heads off of their bodies.

When they failed, Anthony's metal arm didn't. He thrust his left shoulder forward and did his absolute best to barrel his way through even as booming demands for him to stop, surrender, and the like thundered through the air. While he ran through them, the surviving Grimshanks – and their boss – went the other direction, but not before Clarence spat a thundering round that almost hit Anthony right in the middle of his back.

Almost.

Clare's corpse jumped off the ground at the necromancer's command and spoiled the shot. The slug hit her in her stomach and tore a hole through her body that sent blood, bone, and chunks of her bowels out across the concrete floor. Dead or not, shooting his sister made Clarence freeze in shock.

The human mind was weird that way.

Even when you knew better, sometimes it just made you pause.

Just beyond the hallway door, Anthony contorted his hands like a puppeteer and twisted Clare's corpse around. One of the two struggling AGU troopers turned the barrel of his SMG towards the Grimshank's exposed leader and depressed the trigger. The necromancer didn't even bother watching what happened next.

Anthony sucked in a wave of fresh necrosi and ran.

Clare's body followed. The two AGU officers and the remnants of the other ghasts didn't; they were too useful in keeping the cops busy. The necromancer almost made it back to the main stairwell before the next three shock-troopers made it down the steps, and they weren't happy to see him.

They didn't bother shouting commands. They just aimed their guns. Anthony slammed his back against the hallway wall and forced Clare's corpse to fly at them with the force of a small car. Their bullets ripped into her body, but they didn't slow her down. When she hit them, her corpse knocked all three of them on their asses. As a delay to clog up the stairs, it worked.

As a way to incapacitate them for more than a few seconds, it didn't. A few seconds was all he needed to pull what was left of her bullet-ridden corpse back as he followed Emiline's floor plans and dove into a side room with an 'employees only' ladder that went into the club's main kitchen.

Normally, the Handed Down had a full-service kitchen complete with a fully-stocked walk-in freezer that was tended to by servers who only wore suit ties and aprons to take care of the club's guests. Tonight, it was tended to by a cop armored with sleek black tactical gear and three unlucky clients who were down on their knees for all the wrong reasons (and at gunpoint, to boot). The cop looked up as Anthony burst out of a closet that doubled as an entry into a wine cellar and brought her gun to bear on his face.

He froze and put his hands up at her command. He flexed the fingers on his right hand as she ordered him to get down to his knees. Right on cue, a heavy *thunk* slammed into the freezer door beside her head. The officer paused and turned slightly to face the noise as the necromancer channeled nth into the fridge.

Corpses were corpses and dead was dead.

It didn't matter if it was a human or a squirrel.

Or in this case, USDA-approved ActuallyOrganic™ beef.

When he flexed his hand a second time, the freezer door slammed open and a frozen slab of Ready-to-Heat Cow™ slapped the cop across her helmet. The sucker-punch knocked her to her knees, and Anthony very quickly grabbed her by the face with his steel hand and pushed her back into the fridge before she could stop him. Her screams to let her out turned to screams of terror as several more heavy chunks of frozen meat jumped off of their shelves with every flex of his flesh-and-blood fingers. By the time the heavy thuds turned into the sound of harried shots from her sidearm, he was out of the kitchen with Clare's body in tow.

The list of charges he was accumulating by the second were being carefully tabulated by a very judgmental inner voice, though for now, that didn't matter. As soon as he was clear, he was able to look into the dining room and performance floor. Getting out the front hadn't been an option to begin with, but the sight of AGU troopers scattered through the club put the final nail in *that* particular coffin.

Thankfully, they didn't notice him as he ducked below a counter and made a beeline for the back hallway – and the restroom he needed to get to now. If these walls could talk, you'd want to take a bath in napalm by the time you got your dick put away. Often considered the wrong kind of magical by the wrong (or the right) kind of people, the Handed Down had three different pissers. Two were actual restrooms outfitted with functional plumbing.

The other was a 'rest' room with 'fun'-ctional plumbing.

Or whatever the kids were calling it these days.

The real restroom harbored a cowering local politician in one stall – Anthony had seen the fucker on the news extolling the virtues of a new 'public decency' law, so seeing him there wasn't a big shock – and a sweaty Grimshank that was trying to hide behind the door with a pistol at his side and blood on his cheek. The thug lifted his pissant little pistol up in ill-advised self-defense the moment that Anthony barged in.

He didn't get it past his ribs before the necromancer caught the weapon with his left hand and delivered a cheekbone-breaking punch with his flesh-and-blood right. The guard dropped like a sack of rotten potatoes without as much as a word of thanks for Anthony probably, ultimately, saving his life from the AGU and their 'he's got a gun!' policy. With that solved, Anthony gave one look at the city's elected finest and rolled his eyes.

Outside, things were a bit more heated.

Clare's corpse plastered itself against the doorframe and clung to both sides of it with all the might her little undead body could possibly manage. As a barrier, it wouldn't do much; there was only so much abuse a body could take, and even less so once it was dead—at least, without extensive preparation. Time wasn't on anyone's side, and honestly? It hadn't been since the moment Katherine crashed his damn date.

If Clare didn't have something worthwhile in her mind, Anthony's main concern would be booking a trip to a non-extradition country; maybe to Spain. Or maybe even Iceland. Iceland was always nice.

Extradition treaties weren't but...

"Callie, I'll miss you," Anthony sighed to himself as he pulled his shotgun free of its mag-holster. Carefully, he aimed straight at an intricate black and red etching carved into the wall. An etching with a small, fingertip-sized hole in the middle of it. A hole with a little sliver of Carlos's crydasta nestled inside.

A hole, a stone, and a rune he'd cut not even half an hour ago.

There was more to necromancy than just playing with the dead. Souls were great and all, though there was no shortage of men, both dumb and wise alike, who would gladly claim they were overrated. The key was to understand that if something had ever been a conduit for life, it had been a conduit for nth, too.

Maybe not much. Maybe not anything measurable.

Just as importantly, you didn't *have* to have been alive to *decay*.

That, in turn, held true for clay. Gypsum. Latex. Water.

Or in other words – painted drywall, and the wooden beams behind it. The only ingredient missing was the reason he'd pulled Clare up behind him. It would work well enough without her, but this was a certified promise that he'd get the job done right the first time. Anthony glanced back over his shoulder, clenched his fist, and *pulled* with all his might.

Shots barked in the hallway at his back. He felt his hold on Clare's corpse take a hit as bullets punctured her heart, broke her spine, and nearly tore off her knee. Her use as a wall was going to end in seconds no matter what, so Anthony shifted his focus and turned her into a bomb.

Her body stiffened up and the skin around her face peeled itself away as the cops watched. One of them pointed a shotgun at her head. The others started to back up. He couldn't exactly *see* out her eyes but he could *feel* where they were standing through his connection with her body. It didn't tell him much, but it gave him an idea of what to do.

Clare's skull ripped itself out of its fleshy prison and battered its way through the hall. The rest of her body launched itself in the opposite direction and detonated in a shower of blood, gore, and bones that effectively wiped out the cops and broke their will to follow. Her head flew like a missile through the elegant lavatory and crashed with an utterly impressive amount of force into the center of the rune.

Anthony ducked into a stall to shield himself from the blast when both the flying chunk of bone and the soul shard connected. The stone detonated and sent spiral-shaped glowing cracks across the wall that flickered with sickly green light three times. As the light faded from the third, the cracks dissolved and the wall fell apart in their passing. All it left behind was a pile of rubble and a hole just big enough to duck through.

If everything else had gone according to plan, Fixxer had arranged for a car in the alley as a backup. It was a worst-case scenario, but at this point, the only one available. As soon as the necromancer made it through the hole, he was presented with a new problem.

Yes, there was a car there.

There weren't supposed to be two of them.

One was the car he'd expected: a nondescript junker born from a generic car brand sometime in the early 2020s before the owner went batshit crazy and tanked the company. The other was a slim-line black Zoom-Zoom that could only be classified as a 'car' and not a 'low-altitude rocket' by the presence of wheels and a license barcode on the back. The lack of branding and presence of muted amber lights across the dash suggested that the owner was either an obscenely overpaid EMT (which never, ever happened), or…

The cold touch of a familiar, cobalt-coated muzzle was pressed to his temple before he could even finish the thought. He heard its owner pull back the hammer with a menacing *click*. There was just enough hesitation between the touch and the safety going off that he knew he had time to talk. Just not much.

"Anthony."

"Oh, shit," he sighed out loud as he felt his shoulders slump. "Hi, Alara."

The Turkish native smiled faintly and pushed his head a little harder with the pistol. She wasn't quite his height, but her boots made up the difference. One glance from the corner of his eye told Anthony all that he needed to know: she wasn't dressed for the raid, nor was she dressed to be out in the field.

That meant she was probably here for more personal reasons. The way the gunmetal dug into his temple made him lean towards the personal side of the coin. "Katherine. Alive or dead?" she asked.

"Alive, last I checked."

"Safe?"

"Safehouse."

"Where?"

"That negates the point of calling it a safehouse," he replied as he carefully reached up to nudge the gun away. She didn't even flinch when he touched her wrist, though she pushed the barrel a little harder to his skull. "Do you mind?" Anthony mumbled. "We can talk this out."

The gun trembled, but it didn't move. The rest of the LSPD wasn't on this side of the building yet, though the alley was otherwise full of dumpsters, trash bags, and the driver of said sports car. A few seconds more, and AGU would rush through the hole and start shooting without checking for IDs, and they both knew it. "In the car. Get in."

"I'd prefer not to if it's all the same."

"I know," she admitted, "and I don't care. In. Now."

No was the answer he wanted to give, but it wasn't the word he used. The muzzle of the pistol pushed his head until he was tilted slightly to the side, and as it did, Anthony let go of his shotgun. All he did – all he *had* to do – was just say the name out loud.

"Marshal."

Alara tensed up and tried to keep him from finishing the sentence. "Don't you *dare* –"

Anthony's left hand shot up before she could react and a gust of wind followed his voice and blew her hair into her pale-gold eyes with a shouted, "BLACKBURN."

Two words. One name.

The necromancer's gun never hit the ground. The pistol slid away from Anthony's forehead as he pushed her wrist up high, and the sound of the shotgun as it chambered a slug ended the immediate threat, then and there.

Or at least any immediate threat to him.

The shotty's barrel hovered just beneath the chin of one of LSPD's absolute bonafide finest (and not even said sarcastically; she was truly one of their best) as a pair of ethereal, translucent hands manifested first, followed by the rest of the entity holding it. "*Anthony, there a reason you left me all bound up while you were in the club? I could've helped.*"

It sounded like his voice came from just behind Anthony's ear. It was one of those weird nth things that served to play havoc in the field and was almost assured to make things even more confusing for people who didn't know the ropes. "Pulling out a familiar in the middle of a gunfight with LSPD would get us both on death row no matter how justified it might've been, and you know it."

"*True, but,*" the specter replied with his trademark southern drawl, "*I don't think it could've gone worse. On the other hand, 'ello there, Miss Dimir. Good to see your charmin' eyes again.*"

"I swear to God I hate you both," she snapped. "Lose the fucking ghost and get in the fucking car."

Blackburn pushed his gun up a little as Anthony slid away from the wall. "*A simple please goes a long way, you know. I do recognize that he's been a bit ill-behaved this evening, but surely we can come to a polite resolution between friends that don't involve either of us holdin' gunmetal? On our own friends, at that?*"

"We are friends here, right?" Anthony added.

Of everything and anything that Blackburn was, a simple 'ghost' wasn't it. He wasn't just Anthony's familiar or a soul bound to a relic. He was one whole, twisted manifestation of a centuries-old lawman, with a moral code bent as wide as the gash in his throat. He was the other things too, but the man had an aura that you just couldn't deny.

Alara glared at both of them. "I don't know yet."

"*Then maybe the guns should be put away?*"

She spared him a glance as her blue eyes sparked violently. "Blackburn. Not the time, not the night. Do me a favor and go die again. Quietly. Anthony, we both know that the Marshal isn't going to shoot me, and I can smell the soul on your breath. So, get in the fucking car already."

"To be fair, you pulled a gun on me first."

"To be fair, you fucking deserve it," she shot back before she gave Blackburn a withering glare from her golden eyes. "Do you mind?"

The spirit dropped his gun and stepped back with a wave of both of his hands. "*You opted to get his attention your way, I only opted to do the same to get yours. But we do need to leave; the hex you put on your head won't hide you from ghostly eyes for none too long.*"

Anthony looked through the hole in the wall and immediately moved to flatten himself against the brickwork. One look at Alara, and his stomach seemed to drop to his knees. The glint in her eyes seemed to ignite the night air. "We do, and not with you. Honestly, those are *your* friends that keep trying to shoot me. Can we just handle this through an email later?"

Alara made a strangled noise in the back of her throat before she quickly glanced around the alleyway. Before the necromancer could say anything else, the glow in her eyes took on an even brighter shimmer as she balled up her right hand into a fist. At the end of the alley, a rusty green dumpster started to rattle.

Anthony moved, Blackburn followed, and both made damn sure they were clear of the hole in the wall when Alara flexed her arm. The steel bin jumped up into the air and flew a dozen feet down the alley before it slammed into the broken brick and plaster he'd left behind. A few startled shouts from the other side poured out, and that was that.

The chunk of steel covered the hole nicely, and a second gesture shattered the rubber wheels under it and dropped it flat to the ground. The tree-shaped *'Eden Farms Reclamation Service'* logo in the center looked like someone had slammed a battering ram into the middle of it. Just for good measure, and not to prove a point or anything, he was sure.

That was Lieutenant Alara Dimir for you.

She was the commanding officer of the Southern Los Santuario Abnormal Para-Psychology Squad. Licensed, certified, and modified to be part of the small yet incredibly potent ranks of the LSPD's med-enhanced nth-users. All she had to do was take one hit off a little vial in her suit jacket and she transformed from a five-foot-seven cop into someone who could manipulate nth vibrations as easily as she could breathe.

In the service, they called it meth-a-magic.

To her face, you called her 'Ma'am.'

"Anthony."

"Alara…"

"I am not in the mood to fight my way through Captain Yers's goons to get to you in whatever med-lab you land in after they break your arms and legs into pieces for resisting arrest tonight. You are in the shadow of a mountain of pain, and that was *before* you pulled this shit. We *need* to talk. Now get in the fucking car."

Anthony looked at the dumpster. He didn't have to strain to make out the angry voices just behind it. "I just needed to talk to the Abberdines. They started getting all shooty. Wasn't my fault."

"I don't care," Alara spat back. "Yers declined my request to be involved in their investigation, so we're both stepping on some toes tonight."

"It's always about you, isn't it?" the necromancer grunted. "You're not the total package, you know."

"*I'm* not the total… are you…" she sputtered. "Anthony, I'm about to be your whole goddamn Christmas-in-July miracle if you're not lying about Kath. Now. Do I need to make you get into the car or are you willing to do it on your own accord?"

Anthony and Blackburn exchanged a brief, concerned look.

Then, as politely instructed, they got into the fucking car.

5. GANGLAND STATE OF MIND
Monday, May 29th, 2:23 AM

"I don't suppose there's any chance we can be civil about this, is there?"

"Gee Anthony, I don't know," Alara snipped back with enough sarcasm to fill a prime-time comedy special. "I just got done lying to my bosses about knowing your whereabouts and claiming to be off hunting down some informant I know after you attacked my coworkers. I think you've about used up all the civility I have to spare."

She raised a good point. You could make the argument that she was currently aiding and abetting, though Anthony wasn't stupid enough to bring that up. Blackburn was equally silent, though in his case, he was simply struggling to stay stable in the moving car. "Okay. Fine. Then cut the shit and tell me where you're taking me."

"Away from the crime scene before the rest of Ab/Psy or S/QRD shows up. Seriously, you bloody idiot. You dumped a ton of magic in there. Magic that the AGU wasn't expecting. Magic that has the AGU pissed as all fuck. The Grims don't use offensive magic, so I was supposed to have the night off and be tits deep in a stripper, but instead, I'm here with you."

Even just invoking the LSPD's so-called Splinter/Quasi-Religious Department was enough to make him gag. The night was bad enough without calling for the cult-busters. If they got involved, he was running. Period. He'd run across the Atlantic if he had to, but he'd be running.

The rest of her statement explained a lot, but it didn't really help. In fact, it made things worse, because not only did that mean that the Gang in Black was embarrassed, Captain Yers' boss back at Vox Magistratus Plaza was going to turn his asshole into a drive-through for not showing up prepared. So not only was Yers going to be pissed, he was going to be hellbent on revenge. "I've got a feeling I'm due for a broken jaw."

"Broken jaw? Broken jaw?" Alara countered as she looked away from the road to tap a standing screen on her dash. "Read that."

Anthony cringed. It was an incoming Spot-Med report, fresh off the press as they drove, and the injury list was concerning. "Two broken legs, a broken arm, one minor concuss... scratch that, *two* minor concussions... shit. I thought those idiots wore body armor?"

"They WERE!" she shouted. "How fucking juiced are you*?* And *how* did you get that fucking juiced without blowing your heart out of your ass*?"*

Anthony sunk down into his seat in a vain attempt to hide from her wrath. "Not that..."

"Bullshit. Shitty nth is radiating from you like you jammed your arm into the business end of a power relay coil. I could smell how damn loaded you were from the other side of that damn wall."

"Ifin' I may so interject, what our mutual friend means is that he has very much been the victim of circumstances and circumspect people beyond his control. Like it or not, short of jumping right into a holding cell, I do believe that he has made the best choices possible this evening. And you will note that he went to great lengths to keep the Gang in Black from turning into the Gang in Graves."

"That's not an argument that's going to save him from jail time," the Lieutenant countered. "Anthony, do you know how bad it's gotten lately?"

He took a slow breath and nodded. "I mean, yeah. Taxes are up. Can't spit on the sidewalk without a Cop-U-Drone slapping a ticket on your ass. I mean, damn. Did you see that the freaking Angel Cats made it into the playoffs?"

That wasn't what she meant and he knew it; he just wanted to make her a little angrier. An angry Alara was never good for your health, but it made her an informative one. To his surprise, the only thing she did was sag a little in her seat.

"Remember that Flyaway that got grounded because someone made a 'terroristic threat' last month? Yeah, no. A fucking *drae-don* crawled into the lev-engine. There are non-sentient ghasts digging themselves out of the ground and *walking* out of the Tex-Des-Waste for no other reason than because they *can*. There was an honest-to-God alt-dim *tear* down on the L-line back in January."

"Heard about that one," he muttered quietly.

"You hear what came out of it?"

"No?"

She rolled down her window and spit out into the highway. "You're fucking welcome," she snapped. "Hell, we've got some chip-dick net-pimp in lockup who swears up and down that there's some secret cabal of Elder Daems running City Council."

"Really. Elder Daems? Those ones that say that they're the first of their kind to walk the earth? Pretty much loaded to the horns with alt-world psych magic that doesn't play nice with the stuff on this side of Hell?"

"Oh, yeah. Didn't you know? There's one in the board room of every nati-corp."

Anthony snorted. "Same one?"

"Who the fuck knows. I mean, yeah, we've got five *actual* Daemons who act like they run the Goddamned planet, so why the fuck not? Maybe they've decided to just let their children do the paperwork. See how far it gets them."

"So, you're saying that Ab/Psy's been busy."

"I'm saying I can't tell the difference between 'a crackhead found a phone' and 'yeah this is gonna blow up a city block' anymore when people call in a potential MAE. Now, tonight, I've got you! And *you're* busy running a rousing round of 'hide-a-witness' with your ex-wife, *while* you're adding a side of 'let's fuck up a police raid in a sex club for kicks!' just because you can."

He blanched and tried to hide his head in his coat. "You know I didn't want to hurt anyone. I just wanted –"

"Anthony, of all the problems I have going on right now you are both the one I want to push in front of a bus and the one I know that if I *do* push you in front of a bus, then the problem goes away. That's not a good place to be in my head right now, so cut your shit because since you like playing the field so damn much tonight, we're going to play a game."

The necromancer looked out the passenger side window and directly at the incoming traffic as he wondered which would be the better option: her, or jumping onto the Sam Houston Boulevard at 55mph. "I've hated your games since college."

"Oh, you'll love this one," the Turkish woman promised. "I am going to give you three names. Get them right, and you get to sleep in a hotel with a shower. Get them wrong…"

"Jail?"

Alara shrugged. "Maybe. Or maybe I'll kick you outta the car and watch Gulf West News air footage of 'the aftermath of Anthony Pierson's daring escape from police custody' while drinking a beer."

"I… yeah. I don't think I like this game."

"Might just be in your best interest to play it," Blackburn warned. *"Just for good measure."*

"Aren't you supposed to be on my side?" Anthony whined.

The specter shook his head, and it made the decades-old gash in his throat open a bit deeper. *"I am a man of the law if you forgot. She is well within her rights to question a suspect, though I'm not sure what exactly you're a suspect of."*

"Everything. He's suspected of fucking everything. I'd charge him with Lincoln's assassination if I could."

"Ah, one of those chats. I do understand. Anthony? Play nice."

The necromancer grumbled and wiped away a trickle of blood seeping out of his nose. "Fine. Make it quick. I'm overburdened right now and it's not helping anyone."

"Overburdened with bullshit," she muttered as she changed lanes and blasted her horn at some moron in a truck. "Andrea Adams. Know her?"

The name didn't even come close to ringing a bell. "Nope. Should I?"

"That depends on your next answer. Sojourn Enterprises?"

Anthony perked up and nodded his head. "Yeah. Their name has come up twice now. The Bitch and Blood knew them."

"Where's the second time?"

"Trade secret," he countered, "but lemme be blunt – whatever they're doing, I don't like it. I don't know them, but I need to learn more. I don't want to, but I have to."

"You, the Church of Angelic America, and the Heart and Spade Foundation," Alara replied. "That's a very interesting sandbox to play in."

Anthony's eyes widened in spite of himself. "I'm starting to think you picked me up for more reasons than just Kath."

She didn't give him the dignity of a response. "Last one. Get it right and maybe we have a bonus round. How about Project Wetshell?"

Two words. That was all it took to completely, and utterly, ruin the rest of his day,… and it wasn't even three in the damn morning yet. "Just the name –"

"*[I do],*" a familiar and vaguely French voice interrupted.

To make it worse, it interrupted from Anthony's lips.

"Anthony? Did you just…?" the detective asked.

"*[He didn't],*" Clare's disembodied voice called out from the necromancer's mouth. "*[I didn't think that being dead would be so désagréable. Quite a pity,]*" she exclaimed before she went silent…

…and Anthony went stiff.

As he seized up, Alara nearly drove onto the sidewalk. As she happily ignored the angry screams and curses from random insomnia-prone pedestrians, she grabbed his shoulder and tried to shake him back to consciousness. If anything, it just made him drool *faster* as he sank into his own head for a quick chat with his personal guest. "By the God of the Holy Empire, what is wrong with this man tonight?"

"*Invoking the Euro-Church, are we?*" quipped Blackburn. "*I didn't think you gave care to any of them.*"

"Certainly don't give a shit about Angelic America. If I'm gonna curse one, may at least be the one I grew up with," she grumbled. "Do you have any idea what's wrong with him, or are you just going to sit back there and be your typical 'oh, I'm a mysterious spirit with a heart of gold and a shotgun' attitude tonight? You know it doesn't fool anyone that talks to you longer than two minutes?"

"*If I have to talk to them longer than two minutes, then my shotgun isn't doing the job,*" Blackburn huffed and crossed his arms. His long, spectral coat didn't make so much of a whisper worth of a rustle as he got comfortable – the phantom fabric was an old memory that was more for show than anything else.

"My point stands."

"*I'm afraid our mutual companion has already had a bit of a night. This makes his second soul in under six hours, and the first was befouled; worse than hers, I may add. Now that he's decided to play Hotel California with a second less-than-moral murderer, I suspect he's in for a migraine that I, for one, am glad that I am dead enough to not have to worry about.*"

"Two...? Are you... and who the hell did he suck off for *Clare fucking Abberdine* to be the *least* toxic he's pulled down?"

"*As you're well aware, Lieutenant, there is the toxicity of morals and sin, and then there is the toxicity of poisoned auras. The punk he chewed on earlier had more ties to the Great Green God than you'd find at your local Lawn Center Extra Plus,*" the deceased lawman drawled.

Her eyes darkened as she readjusted herself in her seat. "The two gangers he put down at his apartment? Report said they were Grim."

Blackburn silently shook his head. "*While I was only involved in the execution of their exit from the mortal plane, I can quite easily assure you that, no ma'am, they had no tuck with the Grimshanks. From our mutual and honest standpoint, that has entirely been the incorrect opinion of the fine folks in your uniform.*"

"It's not an opinion, you literally can't confuse the two unless you're… deliberately trying…"

"We've come to the conclusion that the trying is very deliberate though we're not entirely sure as to the why. But, he did rule out 'trust the cops' after the first five minutes of the problem landing in his lap."

A bit of her attitude mellowed out as she slumped down into her seat, but her eyes never left her rear-view mirror and the ghost in the reflection. "Well, now I know why he didn't call…"

Blackburn soundlessly tapped the phantom five-pointed badge on his coat and ran his thumb over the part that read 'Marshal.' *"I daresay that ah, 'accidentally' confusin' one gang for another has been a long-standing procedure for Texas police when we needed an excuse to do one thing or another. Maybe it's changed since my time."*

If the dead man could've blushed, the expletives that fell from her mouth would've done the job. "It hasn't."

"I suspected as much. It's the thing that gets a quick check with 'find-and-replace' before the final report gets filed. So. While he's busy, any chance you have anythin' you'd be willin' to share with the rest of the class? Or was this just a less-than-social call on your part?"

Alara took a deep breath and ran her hands through her long, flowing hair. "When the call came in that someone had shot up her apartment, I went straight over. She was long gone by then. Then the shootout went down at Anthony's place an hour later and now…? Why the *fuck* did she go to *him* and not *me*?"

The specter sat in silence for a long minute as she watched Anthony twitch every few seconds. Just a few subtle little ticks here and there, nothing you'd really notice if you weren't looking for it. The nth around him though? It looked like someone had hooked up an oscilloscope to a garbage disposal.

"Because, like most of us in this cross-ways world we live in, he is an imperfect soul by the only rules that matter − the ones he places on himself. Ex in danger? He goes, and he bleeds. Girlfriend in danger? He goes, and he bleeds. Both in danger? Well. You see his ass now. I'd be a dumb dead man ifin' I was to daresay he'd not do the same for you."

"That didn't answer my question you old pile of −"

The Marshall cleared his throat and bits of gray flesh wobbled around the slice in his neck. *"I would assume that it is because he is not beholden to an institution that is known to not always be straight-laced as the people that work in it, your fine self included."*

"She'd trust his disloyal ass over mine *because* I'm a cop? Are you shitting me?"

"*When you need to lay low, you ask a rat.*"

Her mouth worked, but nothing came out of it until she finally cut loose with a heavy sigh. "I really hate it when you make sense," Alara sighed. "You know, I could shoot him right now and solve all our problems. Then you tell me where Kath is and we can all go out for breakfast."

"*Ya'll'd miss him, and you know it,*" Blackburn countered.

"Kath would miss the alimony."

"*Ma'am, I grew up in the middle of this fine, single-star state. Believe you me when I say that to many of us, missing the man and missing the money is the same damn thing. You can appreciate heart, dick, and wallet alike and miss any combination of the three when they're gone.*"

Alara stole a glance into the back seat and shot Blackburn a dirty glare. "Why do you always have to — no, no. Don't say it. It's because you've been dead longer than we've been alive. I've heard the line before."

Wisely, Anthony's familiar took the cue to shut up.

"Well, now, what the hell am I supposed to do with the two of you?"

Blackburn leaned forward and pointed at a glowing neon sign halfway down the road. "*Unless things have changed a great deal since my time with a functional stomach, you could pull up into that caffi spot over there. I guaran-damn-tee you that this is not the first police car — marked or otherwise — that's camped out in their lot with a passed-out perp and an' officer waitin' for them to sober up. Plus, all the same between us, we both could use a cup of caffi.*"

"You can't drink it."

"*Perhaps, but I do find myself able to live vicariously through the works of others. Do a favor for a dead man?*"

Alara started up the car again without a word, and they were halfway down the street before either of them said anything else. "So, you had a chance to pay attention to the outside world, lately?"

The specter made a show of stretching his arms out across the top of the back seat and smiled. Whether for her benefit or his own, Alara wasn't entirely sure. "*'Shamed to admit, I've spent most of my time ruminatin' on myself and the path that left me bound to this ol' judgment-stick. Haven't really been focused on the outside world too terrible.*"

"Oh? Then you don't know."

"*Know... what?*"

"T-Anth and Mech lost the cheerleading finals last week."

Blackburn sat up and leaned forward. *"Wait, they did what, now? After all the coachin' and…"* he started to rant before her half-hearted giggle cut him off mid-sentence. *"That's the kind of sass that gets cops like us killed, both on and off the line of duty. I do want you to know that."*

Alara let a smirk join the giggle as she pulled into a Daddi's Junior's lot. "Promises, promises. Now what flavor do you want to watch me drink?"

***

Daddi's Junior!
Because being good for Daddi means buying him Caffi!
***

One car replaced another. Marshal Blackburn and Lieutenant Dimir vanished as Clare and Clarence appeared. The police interceptor morphed into what appeared to be a mini-lim with actual, real-leather seats; a bit of illicitly earned comfort for the owners and a little bit of showmanship for their guest.

The view from Clare's head wasn't great, and a lot of what she saw was clouded in a twisting, pinkish-red fog. Clare herself looked perfect and pristine, almost like a supermodel. Her brother? A bit more like a clown with an ill-fitting suit and a distorted smile. Their guest, on the other hand?

She must've taken a liking to him. Having met the man – and been threatened by him with eternal hellfire at his wedding – Anthony knew damn well he didn't look like the Maximum Gene Model that she made him out to be. In real life, he looked like the kind of dumpy sad man you'd expect to see selling shoes at a discount foot shop on a Sunday afternoon.

In here, he looked like he was America's Next Shirtless Movie Star in the making. The sweat on his forehead and the Bible in his hand were true to form. From the way the Good Book trembled in his fingers, it was a bad form at that. "I… I uh, thank you. The Pope of the Americas understands that this is an unorthodox request to –"

"Monsieur Pastor," Clarence began, "do understand that to us, time is of value. The Man of the Pointy Hat has gone out of his way on more than one occasion to ensure that our *Matrone* has less of it at every opportunity. We are only obliged to offer ours now out of the absurdity that you would request it, but our generosity is limited."

"While we are respectful of all the world's religions – for without virtue, what good is vice? – we are not, one should say, trustful, of his nature. Nor, by relation, yours. To say that this is *inhabituelle* is to be an understatement," Clare finished.

Jordan cleared his throat and clutched at his Bible a little harder. "I'm always... rather cognizant... that our organizations are, as a rule, on opposing sides of most things. But I am here in good faith, and not to question its nature. I am authorized to engage in community outreach on the worst of days; I promise, this meeting is not one of the best of them."

"A priest who states he doesn't wish to argue faith? Now this is a true mystery. Then what is it, exactly, that you want?" Clarence chimed with a mocking smile as he swung one leg over the other and leaned back to listen.

"It has come to the attention of His Holiness that our organizations are under a... combined... threat of economic and legal exposure that neither of us wish to be. And I dare add, not just ours, but your handlers as well."

"*Les fonds*? Since when does the Pope of the Canuks care for how money is spent beyond what he pilfers away from collection plates?" Clare asked with a mirthful smirk. "Particularly in regards to those he finds beneath even the passing gaze of your God?"

The Church's representative slowly reached into his jacket and pulled a sub-sphere out of his breast pocket. "If only it were so that simple. You've had business with Sojourn Enterprises before, correct?"

"We conduct business with many places," Clare replied as she took the data-sphere and slotted it onto her phone. "What of this one?"

"I'll try and keep this brief: we have learned they're in violation of the EBR laws, and we have concerns that they may be... well, making weapons from unwitting donors. Weapons that could be turned on anyone; even you." He said it so simply, so calmly, that he could've been talking about walking a dog on a sunny day. The Twins just looked confused.

Between what he'd seen in Carlos's brain and the brief chat with the twins an hour ago, Jordan's frank admission of the problem made Anthony's stomach flop. The Expired Biological Reclamation laws and the Jump-Starter Act were the net result of more international political and legal bullshit than you could stick on a single sub-sphere. They made what he could do *legal*, and that was the extent that he cared.

It also made other things decidedly *not* legal.

Using bio-mechanical tech to keep a heart pumping? That was fine. Replacing an eye with a camera? That was fine. Using nth and nth-manipulation to tap into a decomposing brain or make a dead guy get up and walk again?

That was *fine,* but it was also *regulated* to obscene limits. Honestly, there were more laws about how necromancers could operate than there were laws for the usage of modern nuke reactors. It made sense, it was just annoying.

EBR laws boiled down to a single strict rule: if magic was involved, it had to be under the active control of a licensed practitioner. No remote tech and no secondary-user connections. No autonomous anything. No giving a corpse the ability to walk around and putting a receiver in its head for some drone-jockey to direct it with some souped-up arcade joystick.

Want to circumvent that? Tough.

It wasn't just a 'no,' it was a geopolitical 'fuck you for even thinking about it, now please face the wall' type of no. It was backed by a whole host of disparate entities – everyone from the Pentaship to the multi-nats to the Church and even the freaking Neo-Ag/Atheist movement. You could say it was the rare occasion where everyone agreed that something was a bad decision for thousands of reasons.

Even the Sub-Soua Carties agreed it should be off-limits. Nobody, absolutely nobody, wanted to live in a world where the dead could be brought back to life and left to their own autonomous devices. It would set *precedents*. Very, very, very problematic *precedents* around the concept of immortality, population density, potential designation of sentient life, cyborg/android shit... all of it.

Plus, it was downright icky.

And there was Jordan, sitting in a limo owned by the Bitch and the Blood, having a casual chat with them about it. "The shortest form is that we have learned that Sojourn has a program to develop bio-mechanicals in a worryingly obscene manner. Yet, our hands are tied."

"One would think that in matters as grave as, well, the grave, that the Church would be more open for discussion with the proper authorities," Clare slowly replied. "I suspect that you would have seen the police first, oui?"

"You would suspect," the priest answered as he started to fidget with his fingers "though the College of Eagles has determined that these concerns would be best off handled by other parties. For expediency."

Clarence leaned forward and planted his chin in his hand. "Oh, now I sincerely doubt that, Pastor Fisher. The Church is quite good at keeping her enemies at each other's throats. The only time your College of Balding Birds cares for laws is when they attempt to cover up their own transgressions, and the only time the Church makes an effort to care about our organization is when vows of chastity become too onerous to bear."

Jordan cringed. Knowing the pompous ass, that meant nothing good. "My… leadership… they did caution that you may not be as willing to do your civic duty as one would hope. I was advised to give you a name, though I was warned to assure you that I neither know him nor have any personal connections. To my knowledge, he is not someone myself or anyone in my Sanctuary have had dealings with."

"Ohhh!" Clarence perked up, his clown-like face alighting from a state of deathly boredom. "Names that come with a warning label? Dear sister. We have a priest who is terrified we'll hurt him, which of course we *wouldn't*, what with record of his entering our car and all. Plenty of cameras to see, and I know you told someone where you'd be."

Part of Anthony wondered if that was his actual response, or if Clare was trying to manipulate her memories to put her brother in the clear. She hadn't seen him go down, so it'd make sense. Probably it was just a bit of both, and it fit the Blood's former character in some way.

Clare snickered and patted the churcher on his knee. "Don't you worry dear boy. I won't let anything happen to you that you wouldn't like. My big bad brother wouldn't dare hurt you. In here. I promise."

The way she specified the location made the priest cringe. Anthony had a first-person view of where her eyes kept gravitating, and he fought the urge to vomit. "If our information is correct, Sojourn is being supplied with… ah… inventory… from a man named Galvani, and that the transactions are taking place here, in Los San."

The brief silence between the twins was punctuated by Clare tightening her grip on Jordan's leg – nails first. "I see why they cautioned you. Do you happen to know who Galvani is?"

"No," he admitted freely. "They said the less I knew, the better."

That was the second time his name had come up, and judging by the hackles raised in The Bitch's head, perhaps the Church was right for once. Fixxer hadn't put a face to it yet, or at least, none he had shared. Anthony's interest was piqued by the new details. "*Monsieur* Galvani is better known in our circles as 'The Industrial Organicist,' if that rings a bell."

It didn't for Jordan. But coupled with the name drop in Carlos's head? That was the worst link possible.

Anthony ended the memory-replay as soon as the words were uttered, and the scene blinked out of existence. When the fractured images disintegrated into nothingness, the necromancer faced the gangster down across an open, eternal void. He'd get the rest of the important bits later.

But first? "Did you have him killed?"

If Clare was shocked by the scene change, she didn't show it. She didn't show much, really. Her appearance closely matched how she'd looked just moments before her death—a bit smaller, perhaps, and not quite as stable. The edges of her body distorted and swirled, as if trying to diffuse into smoke.

"Non."

"This is my head. You're a guest. Don't lie to –"

"The Grimshanks did not have a hand in his death, *Monsieur* Pierson. I have no reason to lie at this juncture. It is my assumption, of course, that he chose the path which brought him to our doorstep—unless you think that le *Gang dans Noir* removed us from play purely as… *le hasard*? Mere coincidence?"

If the concept of 'rocking back on his heels' had any bearing in this particular mental construct, Anthony would've done it. "The fact that it rains every time I wax my arm is a coincidence. The fucking *Industrial Organicist*? I just… *fuck*, Clare. If you weren't dead, I'd probably shoot you myself for putting that name on him."

"Why? He did not know the relevance of what that name could do. The powers that guided him gave him no information to connect dots from one soul to another. A name is only a thing of power if one knows the power to be attached to the name."

Anthony cut her off with an absentminded wave of his hand that actually caused her lips to seal shut much to her equal parts surprise and terror. "Yeah, until he repeats that name in front of the wrong asshole who decides to shove him into an industrial shredder. Speaking of, did *you* give Jordan's name to anyone?"

"Non," she replied after he waved his hand back the other way and let her speak again. "We did inform our… benefactors elsewhere… of the message we received. We were instructed to, shall we say, *ask around*. We reached out to the Farmer's Daughter as a matter of occupational courtesy, to warn them against continuing on their chosen path. We said not how, just that we knew. The industrial aspects and legal concerns aside – all very concerning, but of course – there are *businesses* we cannot condone in our city."

"Businesses you can't condone if you aren't getting your cut?"

Clare shrugged. "A bit of yes, a bit of *non*. My brother and I did mention that we found the concept of what he broached to be uncomfortable."

There wasn't much more she needed to add. The Organicist was to the Gardeners as Clare was to the Grimshanks – and just as importantly, he was tied into your friendly-neighborhood international conglomerate, Eden Farms. The Farmer's Daughter did the speaking for the corporate side of their operations, while Galvani... was a bit more hands-on.

He had a lock on the anth-waste market that dominated the old ruins of Southern Florida, and he had as much control over the entire Penni as the Heart and Spades did over Los San. As far as conflict went, neither of their sponsor corporations got along very well, and that was in triplicate for the lower-tier gang-land functionaries, let alone the Daemons that ran both. Truthfully, the lines between the corps and the gangs were so blurry that they were all effectively one and the same.

And nobody cared, until the bullets or lawsuits started flying.

"Let me guess: you were told to ask around with a .50 cal, eh? The weapons stockpile I saw makes sense now; you and your brother couldn't abide by someone moving un-taxed goods through the city. Did your *benes* at the Heart and Spade even care about the carnage you were planning, or did they endorse it?"

Clare paused thoughtfully, shifting from one foot to the other. "You know how it is that corporate alliances are formed and worked with their, shall we say, sub-contractors. Sojourn Enterprises receives illicit cargo from a syndicate. Our syndicate does not appreciate the competition. Our benefactors do not appreciate complications that arise from competition in the realm of boardrooms and stock markets, and what your Pastor thought was that both the Gardeners and Sojourn were in the middle of making such complications. Either way, the nature of the cargo did no good. *For anyone*."

"What kind of cargo would that be, huh? C'mon Clare, the Grims move everything from tits to ass along with anything that can be inserted in a hole in either direction. You telling me that you have standards that I don't know about? The weapon system you two were suggesting?"

"Despite what it is you may think of us, our organization keeps more ill from the street than we provide to the masses. Yes, we bring in vice and verse, but they are *our* vices. *Regulated* vices. We treat everyone equally in our line of work – man, woman, Daem, or mutant alike. It *is* the 2050's. Equality is important. If it was only weapons, we would exact a fine and life would go on."

"So, what pissed you off? I saw the cache you had; anti-tank weapons? Drone-killers? You don't take that much to a negotiation over under-the-table tariffs."

Clare shifted again, a nervous tick that translated even into the void of eternity. "We are not against moving people. Workers are workers, places are needed, times are wanted. We do not lie to them, and we do not... abduct them. The Organicist has branched out to those of a more pointed variety with unethical promises and without intention to keep them."

"More pointed variety...?" Anthony repeated, as Clare drew a single protruding horn from her temple into the air. "Daems? They're smuggling Daems? You need anti-tank rockets to stop body trafficking? What the hell are they transporting them in – sub-orbitals?"

"Orbitals? No. It was a... suggestion... from our *benes*. A good offense is simply just a good offense, no? Truth, it was more the question of the entities involved in the transport. They possibly had the aid of... well..."

He felt his blood pressure spike with the way she let the statement dangle. It was the kind of feeling you got when you thought there might be a bomb on the side of the road, or a sniper ready to put your brains on a wall. "The aid of...? C'mon Clare, you're already fucking dead, tell me everything. It makes it easier."

"Monsieur, you should be able to come to the conclusion on your own," she challenged. "Has not the Church been involved in relocating the scaly disadvantaged as of late? And did you not pay attention – I said his superiors *in the north*, not the ones *local to town*."

The bomb went off. It may have been metaphorical, but the way her comment served as a punch in the gut, it might well have been literal. "You... can't..."

"Monsieur Pierson, I am dead. I am not aware yet of what I can and cannot do, but I know that your kind can compel the deceased to speak truth as easy as it is for you to draw breath. Do you smell a *mensonge* on my breath?"

He blinked. Slowly. Twice. "Sorry, I'm having a day here. Are you telling me that Sine-Pastor El-Rhode's Daem-relocation plan is being used as a carrier for a Daem-smuggling ring sponsored by one of the worst parts of the underworld in the south-eastern US?"

"That is not what I am telling you, *non,*" Clare replied earnestly. "What I am telling you? I am telling you that is what Pastor Fisher had come to believe. I have shown you what I have learned as a gesture of thanks."

"How is this a *possibly* a gesture of thanks? And for what?"

She pointed a phantom finger at him and suddenly appeared to stand right at his feet. The ghostly digit pressed against his chest as she looked up into his nth-tainted eyes. "Because I have died, and at no point this week was it *raining on my arm*, as you put it."

"Fuck. Tell Hell to keep a spot warm for me because at this rate, I'm going to see you there before the week is over," he grumbled.

"I would hope not to be in the position to pass such a message on. I have no expectations of going to Hell, as you say it; I have cast my service to..."

"...a literal Daemon who is probably pissed off She just had one of Her toyboxes dumped into the street," he snapped. "Accept the fact that you're fucked on this one while I try to think it through. Also, I want to add that if you'd told me all of this back in your damn club, maybe you and your idiot brother would still be alive."

Her face fell as he ran his hands through his metaphysical hair. "Wait, Clarence? He is...?"

"All but promise it, yeah. Sorry to be the one to tell you, but yeah."

Ghosts could cry. Or at least, they could remember what crying was like enough to come to a decent approximation of it. She got close enough for it to count. "Were you able to...?"

"He was shooting at me."

"Because you took me?"

Anthony raised a finger, but didn't raise his voice. His eyes took on a sparkle that they couldn't show in the real world, but in here? In here, he could do anything. "Because I went the other direction after taking you. I don't know if you understand how deep of a mountain of shit anyone else you may have cared for in your organization is in and whatever happens next *with you* and *who gets possession of you* is entirely up to how bad you piss me off right now."

The truth can set you free. The vehemence behind his words made her will crumble, and the honesty on his tongue did the rest. "Oh. It's... like that."

"It is. I'm sorry. It sucks, but I know you've had your way of doing this to other people and part of being dead is getting a taste of what it was like for others around you. Welcome to the appetizer of your afterlife."

The first remark had broken her will. This one paved over it. "I... oh. For... forgive me, Monsieur Pierson. I didn't... I didn't know you had this edge."

"Forgiven. Now. What – and I need you to be as accurate as you possibly can be – did Jordan tell you was going on? Give me a reason to let you keep talking."

"On this, he was vague. To be truthful, he began to sound like a speaker of conspiracies more than a man of the cloth," she started, "though it was his belief that some of the souls being smuggled were not surviving for long. He gave us addresses and names; we recognized one and others were sent to… other places."

Anthony raised his eyebrow and flexed his fists. "Other places?"

"There are those we work with that would have more use for names of engineers and companies than we do. We are not *enquêteurs*, Monsieur Pierson. Our job is not to be concerned over investigating misused technology or plots to move people against the grain. The intent for us is to ensure that those in our territories play by our rules; if the instructions came to pluck weeds from our garden, we would have."

"He told you where to look and you told the HaS lawyers."

She shrugged. "It seemed to be, how do you say it? Above our grade of pay? He gave us information that suggested weapons were being made in violation of laws both of government and of good conscience. We did not have time to do much with either except to begin to prepare to enforce the laws of the street."

As much as he wanted to be mad at her, there really wasn't any other way it could've gone. If their handlers had approved it, they would've rolled through the streets and flushed the Gardeners down the toilet. "What did he mean by them 'making weapons,' exactly?"

"He did not say, and we did not ask," Clare replied earnestly.

"I don't blame you," he grumbled, "though I've got a really bad idea on the 'what' he was thinking of. So let me get this straight: Jordan goes and talks to you, then a day later he gets flattened. Immediately after, El-Rhodes starts screaming on the net that you two did it. AGU decides that's good enough for them, and shit goes sideways without anyone in a green jacket getting blamed for it."

"Those are the short and the curly of it, *non*? I do feel quite that I have been set up," Clare huffed. "Does that answer your questions?"

"Mostly," he replied.

"Do tell. Please?"

Anthony stepped back from her and she shrank as he moved away. "I gathered his claim was that the Pope sent him. Did he say anything about anyone local? Did he name El-Rhodes directly, for example?"

"No," Clare answered immediately. "He did mention that the Church had involvement, but the involvement was to be resolved posthaste."

He frowned and absentmindedly wiggled his jaw. "Church cleans up Church shit, HaS cleans up corporate shit, you clean up gang shit. I'd ask why they went to everyone but the cops except…"

"Except that it is of the feeling that perhaps would the police become involved, we would all have worse days than better ones. Maybe even worse than this."

"The Grims wouldn't. If you aren't blowing smoke up my ass, your people aren't involved," Anthony pointed out.

She tilted her head to the side and he could almost watch the gears turn in her head. "There would be an… embarrassment… on our part. For failing to know what was going on in our *territoire*. That embarrassment, should it be broadcast by the local *Nouvelles*, as we French know the saying: heads would roll."

"You *aren't* French, but I take the point," he grumbled. "By the way, why *do* you two talk like that?"

"In French…? It is a beautiful lang…"

"When other people speak it," Anthony countered. "Why do *you* do it?"

Clare let her shoulders slump a little. Her presence managed to change entirely as she took her hair down and made a show of wiping away phantom makeup. Underneath the lipstick and overdone mascara, she looked like your average mom next door. "Branding," she admitted in an almost pleasant southern accent. "Callin' myself th' Bitch and I sound like this? Just makes me sound like some broad mad at a manager."

The necromancer rolled the end of his tongue around his cheek as he sized her up. With a flick of his hand, her ghost reset itself back into her gangland appearance. "I can't even lie. That's the most reasonable thing I think I've ever heard you say. Hell, that's the most reasonable thing I've heard anyone say all day. Alright. Fine. There's just one more thing…"

"And what thing might that be? I have given you all I know," she asked as her faux accent came back and her soul straightened back up in the empty construct of Anthony's mind.

"No, you haven't."

As confusion flickered across her fading facade, the void started to fracture into thin shards that morphed from sheets of opaque glass to reflections of objects that weren't present with them. Some appeared as envelopes, others as keys, but most of them took the form of monitors in a variety of shapes and sizes. "What is… what are…?"

Anthony caught one of the floating shards with a metal fingertip, spinning it like a child's toy top. "You're not long for this world. I can't keep you in here for the rest of my life. You know that, yeah?"

"Yes... I... I do feel the call of... other things," she agreed slowly. "I have given you the most of what I know about *Monsieur* Fisher. I do not know what more –"

"Clare Abberdine, you run... ran... the one street gang in all of LS that doesn't just know where the bodies are buried, but the one that's made other gangs pay for the rights to use a shovel. You're dead, and I'd like to avoid that same fate."

"I am not giving you information about my organization, my dear *nécromancien*. To do so would put my soul into greater, ah, risk of unpleasantness, when I am called upon by the Mistress to explain my –"

He looked over at her. Just looked. His face told the story. "Clare."

The ghost shut her mouth and shrank even more. "Ah... yes?"

"You're in my head. What you know, *I* know. When you decided to open your mouth, you made it a hell of a lot easier. This chat? We don't need to have it. It makes it easier to parse through your memories when you can help me link them together, and that makes it easier to record them," the necromancer replied simply as he touched his eye.

In the real world, there was a camera there.

In his brain, there was a single little sensor in the back of his neocortex. That sensor went right to a digital-sensory-recording device buried behind his right ear. A device with a slot for a chip, and a chip that had been very busy making notes of what he 'saw' with the dead woman's help.

Dead men do tell tales.

But you had to be able to bring them to court.

"Re... cord? For... others to view? You... know... everything?"

"Everything that you know," Anthony replied as he plucked another spinning shard out of the nothingness. "So, let's talk numbers." There was one that was oddly familiar: SBAL-131718. Confusing, but familiar.

In that very moment, Clare Abberdine, the ruthless, psychotic criminal mastermind of Los Santuario had one simple question. "What are... are these pieces my... is this my mind or... yours?"

"I can help you transition over, if you want. Comfortably, depending."

"On?"

"How easy you want to make my night," Anthony replied as he spun a shard her way. "So, are any of these bank accounts owned by people that might shoot me if they went missing? Plus the addresses you said Jordan

mentioned, and… did you say he gave you the name of an engineer? Oh –
and the Farmer's Daughter. I need Susan's number. Save us both the
trouble of me digging for it, would you?"

***

The void eventually turned back into a car.

A cursing woman a foot shorter than Anthony on a good day turned
into one his own height, and she cursed for entirely different reasons. A
passenger side door opened as the spinning world came back into full
view, and Anthony didn't even try to hold his stomach intact.

When he finished heaving, both Lieutenant Alara and Marshal
Blackburn hovered (literally and figuratively) over his sagging head. Alara
was 'kind' enough to hold his face up off the pavement by a leather-
gloved hand in his hair as he gasped for air. The ghost just watched,
though the gleam in his otherwise translucent eyes wasn't one to suggest
he was moved.

"Alara… I… I know."

Cup of coffee in one hand and hand full of hair in the other, she lifted
him up and helped him back into his seat. "You know if you throw up in
my car, I will beat the shi –"

"Someone beat you to it," he groaned through short, pain-filled gasps
of air. "Wetshell. What do you know?"

The detective looked into his bloodshot eyes and swore. "We know it's
some sub-legal biotech that Sojourn is working on, but they're a relatively
small corp. Nobody on our side would probably care, except…"

"*Except*?" Marshal asked with a long drawl. "*No cop ever says 'except'
unless there's somethin' hidin' behind it that they don't much like.*"

Alara took a deep breath. "Hoover Central sent it down to us. Part of
some civil rights investigation."

"Civil rights? Which one?"

"Trafficking."

"Human?"

"No," she answered quietly. "Daem."

The world shrank around Anthony as she asked, "What do you think
they're doing with them?"

"We don't know. Standard 'promise the world, bring them somewhere
quiet, sell an organ or a blowjob' shit, most likely. Supposedly it has to

160

deal with some kind of advanced AI research. Which makes little to no sense whatsoever."

Anthony managed to hold his own head up by pure willpower alone. "AI research?"

"That's the short form of what Sojourn informed TEC they were doing. They offered an overview of some kind of new chipset they were developing, and the drone-heads over there didn't see anything wrong. We didn't have authority to push further… until, well…" Alara trailed off and blanched as she glanced away, "until we picked out the project name for a routine data-sniff."

"Between who?"

Alara took another breath and ran her fingers through her hair. "Eden Farms, and…"

The pieces of the puzzle snapped into place with morbid finality. "… and the Industrial Organicist," Anthony finished for her. "Alara, they aren't working on AI. And they're not selling people… selling Daems… into slavery."

Both cops – living and dead alike – locked their eyes onto him. "That leaves a very short list of remaining options. Pick your words carefully and don't use any I'll have to shoot you over."

Anthony nodded painfully. Behind Alara's head, streetlights and advertisements twinkled like stars. A steady halo began to build around the edges of them as he felt his heart start to slow down. "We're fucked."

"How bad?"

"Wetshell is illegal necro-tech," he replied as he put a hand on his chest and winced. Clare wasn't happy, and she wasn't making any bones about it at this point. "Weapons-grade necro-tech. And I think El-Rhodes is running half the scam."

At that, he belched – and threw up black blood down his shirt.

***

The Expired Biological Reclamation Statutes
Ensuring that Every Working Man Retires in Peace
***

E-Ve had promised a safe house.

She'd said nothing about a resort.

Nor had she promised an easy, comfortable rest for either woman in her care. Clean towels? Debatable. A quiet hotel somewhere buried in the industrial district? As quiet as that kind of hotel got. But she did, at least, show them one small kindness:

An open case of Gulf Orchard wine. Not a bottle, a whole damn *case.*

That alone had moved her up significantly on Callie's list of favorite people. Katherine wasn't far behind her with the assessment, which had been one of very few things the wayward pair had managed to come to terms about. The other?

A heaping mix of concern and irritation at their missing partner.

Also, a bit of irritation that there was only one bed to share, and the nurse was adamant that she wasn't going to sleep in the same bed as *a hooker*. The argument both lost and gained wind when Callie, framed in the bathroom doorway with a towel wrapped around her torso, pointed out that since they'd already shared Katherine's husband, they may as well share the same faux-cotton bedding. A heated argument followed rivaling any past or future World War, but ultimately cooler heads prevailed.

Cooler heads and Gulf Orchard.

Gulf Orchard Winery: For Peace of Mind.

While both comprehended the reasoning behind that slogan, Cassie quietly braided her hair in the hotel's cuck-chair (that one chair that every hotel had that sat right across from the bed) while Katherine did her best to hide behind a pillow, a robe, and the bed's presumably clean sheet. "So, let me get this right. Two goons try to break into your house, shoot up the door, and that's not what you lead with when you barged in on us?"

"I mean, I should've — but honestly? I figured telling him Jordan was dead would make him happy enough that he'd be more interested in helping," Katherine admitted. "Anthony's petty like that."

"Oh, come on. You really don't think your brother being the dead guy would make him more amiable to help, do you?"

Kathrine blanched a little and took another long swig from her bottle, "Jordan, um… at our wedding, he threatened to personally drag Anthony's soul to hell when he found out what branch he was being sent to."

The escort paused mid-braid and bit her lower lip. "Okay, so I'm not saying that I wouldn't understand if Anthony threw a parade…"

"We haven't really talked a lot since the divorce was finalized," Katherine admitted with a defeated sigh. "Too angry. For all I knew, he was the one that had him killed."

"C'mon. He wouldn't do that, would he?"

"No, but… you know how it goes."

Callie shrugged. "So why come to him for help?"

"You didn't hear what I heard on that call," Katherine replied. "Knowing him, you never will. If he was doing it, I was fucked either way. If he didn't, he's the only one I know that could…"

"And not the cops."

The older woman shook her head no with a defeated slump of her shoulders. The movement caused her robe to slip open, and she nearly dropped her bottle trying to close it. "Who said I didn't? I'm close to some people on the force. I mean, we both kinda are."

Callie leaned in on her elbows and raised a perfectly sculpted eyebrow. "But?"

"But I did," the nurse admitted after another swig. "Before I went to Anthony. They just wrote it off as gang violence and offered me a place at one of their witness apartments. Last night? The asshole they had on guard at the door went for a smoke. He didn't come back, but two shitheads with shotguns did."

"Maybe I'm mistaken, but I don't think you mentioned that to Anthony. Or if you did, I sure as hell didn't hear it."

Katherine gave another shrug in response. "And tell him what? 'I'm sorry, I've been hiding out for two days, and then the cops sold me out.' He ate a soul before I could tell him much more."

"Someone's trying to murder you, and you're trying to play that man like he's a synthesizer," Callie remarked. Disgust dripped off her every word. "I'm starting to see why you weren't sure if he'd help."

"Yeah, well, forgive me for not blurting everything out to his hooker of the week."

"Month. Six, actually."

"What?"

Callie smirked and stretched out in her chair as she very casually draped one leg over the armrest, which gave Katherine a better view of her thighs than she had any desire to see. "Six months last week. Listen, I don't know what your beef is with him, but he's a really awesome guy. Glad you two didn't work out because *shit*, lady. *Primo*. You know, if you told me that raising the dead was anything like raising his co-"

The nurse gagged on her drink as a coughing fit overtook her. "Makes sense. Of course, a whore would fall for his ass after all the shit he pulled. Birds of a damn feather."

"Ooof. Honey, you got some rage issues towards that man."

"Oh, like he didn't talk shit about me."

"Sometimes," the younger woman admitted. "Mostly if I've tried to hit him up but the alimony withdrawal beat me to it. You really raked his ass over the coals with that one."

"Yeah well. The judge wouldn't let me shoot him."

Callie pointed the tip of her bottle across the room at her. "Maybe he deserves a new deal after, you think?"

"Why, so he can pay you more?"

"You say that like I'm seeing the fucker again after this. Are you insane? I'm just sayin'; he saves your ass, he should pay a smidgen less."

Katherine snorted and took another gulp from her bottle. "Oh, please, he's like a golden retriever. You'll be able to hold a jar of peanut butter out in front of your crotch for him, and he'll come calling."

Callie erupted into a hysterical fit of laughter as Katherine's words sunk in. "My, my! I didn't know you had it in you. What, don't tell me I've been doing it wrong all this time? Is he just a good boy that comes when called?"

"Bloody wish," his ex sighed. "I doubt he even knows what 'good' is anymore." The remark was met by silence, and the longer it stretched, the more uncomfortable she felt. "I mean, he's..."

"Is he?" Callie asked quietly.

"Is he what?"

"Good?"

The question was so soft and so *unsure* that it set Katherine back for a few moments. "When I knew him? Really knew him? When he was just some dude chasing a gen-bus degree at Anth-U? Yeah. He was. Helped old ladies cross the street. Let me copy his notes in poli-sci and penta-histo. After he had to take a Magical Aptitude Test and got drafted?"

Callie wrinkled her nose and snuggled deeper into the chair's cushions. "Good man turned into good soldier, huh?"

"You know the type?"

"Yeah. My dad."

"I'm sorry."

"Eh, don't be. He got stuck in the fuckin' jungle. Nobody came back smiling after that."

"The Amazon Offensive?"

Callie took a drink and stared at the trace of grape pulp in the bottom of the bottle. "The other one. The Kim-Jong-Joke? Is that what your gen is calling it these days?"

"An age joke from someone that looks like she's so young that she's blowing her professor for an A behind the high school gym? Really?"

Callie flipped the nurse off and didn't bother saying anything else.

After a second, Katherine added, "Anthony got stuck with the NPC. Dustbowl III: Dust Harder."

"Thought so," her roommate replied. "Heard if you signed with the feds five to twenty back, that was your one and only destination. No avoidin' it. So. Good before, not so good after, huh?"

"No, no, that's… that's not it," Katherine reluctantly admitted. "He still tried to be good. He just didn't… after he got sent back, it was less a case of, 'Oh, let me help,' too, and more a case of 'Oh, sure, but what do I get from it?' and… it wasn't the same. Everything became… transactional."

The escort smirked and finished off the bottle. With a practiced overhand toss, she arced it through the air and curled her arm in victory as it bounced into the trash. "Guess that's why we get along so well, then. But the service… he came out an asshole, okay, that shit happens. You can't do what he does and… be a good person, can you?"

"Eats souls, raises the dead? That's kind of stuck in your craw a bit, hasn't it?" Katherine reached for the remote to turn on the television. Some newscast was on while talking heads blathered away about a police raid halfway across town.

"How can it fuckin' not? Didn't know I was sleeping with a freaking necrophiliac. Shit," the younger woman grunted as brilliant blues and greens from the Spade-Video's interactive media display viewer made her eyes shine.

It was Katherine's turn to smirk. "Oh, trust me honey, he likes his bitches with a pulse. He got straight-up tempted into the dark side of the cunt while he was rampaging across Ankara, New Babil, and Baghdad. Didn't even bother trying to excuse it when I found out. 'It was there. I needed it,' was all he'd say. Nothing marginalizes your Goddamned wedding vows like hearing your husband talking about pussy like it's a gas station service stop," she spat. "He's done a lot of things with bodies that I don't wanna know about, and I promise, he didn't have *any* problem getting women to spread for him on the other side of the damn planet."

"Ohhh. Am I sensing grounds for divorce?"

"That, and after losing his arm, he became downright insufferable. I tried to make it work, but between the sluts he boned and the way he pushed me out after the injury?" Katherine scowled, feeling her own blood pressure rise at the thought. "Listen. I'm not the uncaring ice queen you seem to think I am, but damn, it was all just too much. Too goddamn much."

Callie listened in uncharacteristic silence. Finally, she looked up at her unhappy companion. "So, the dead girls you were okay with, then. It was the live ones who broke your back?"

"I guess you could say that," the nurse admitted. "I mean, he didn't have a choice. He got drafted. He didn't wake up and go, 'Wow! I wanna rob a grave today!' or whatever. Then I swapped degrees and went from Anth-U to Anth-*Med* U. Anth/nth Para-physical. Thought if I was on the same page, I could help."

The escort shrunk back in on herself again and posed another question, with no hint of indignation. "Did you? Help?"

"Shit if I know," Kath replied. "Look. I took it about as well as you are, probably less so. Nobody wants to hear that their *boyfriend experience* spends his off-hours poking around in dead bodies and eating souls for a living. I mean, I've been working in this field for twelve years, and I don't have a single God-damned idea if what he actually does is demonic or human or divine or just… *psychotic*. I just know that he's good at it, which honestly, doesn't help. And I guess…"

"What? What do you *guess* about the man that has us stashed away in some dingy hostel in the middle of uptown, hosted by a broad who seems way closer to plant life than I personally wanna know about?"

Katherine pursed her lips, pointing toward the screen with a trembling hand. "I guess he's in a shitload of trouble trying to save our asses."

"Trouble?" Callie walked over to sit beside Katherine on the bed and her eyes widened with absolute dread. "Oh, hell."

Katherine flipped the volume up in time to hear the details of the report. "*If you or anyone you know recognize this man, Captain Yers of the Anti-Gang Unit has put out an urgent Special Social Notice: Do not approach and do not interact. Contact LSPD immediately. He is presumed armed and should be treated as a Magical Anomalous Event.*"

Callie's face went pale. "So, either he's gone crazy…"

"…or he's a good man."

"And a total dumbass."

"That part's not new."

***

The Armed Forces M. A. T.
Be more than you can be. Be more than you knew.
Just. Be. More.
***

Morning came.

Everyone involved wished it hadn't.

For Anthony, morning came when someone rudely ripped the curtains open and bathed his bleary, pale, and stubble-covered face in the light of day. Curtains that he didn't know existed pulled open by someone that he didn't expect, and light that was as offensive as the taste in his mouth.

"The fu –"

"If you dare finish that sentence before you spritz the mouthwash beside your bed, I will dose you with it myself," E-Ve interrupted harshly. "You have befouled the air with enough toxicity. Spray now, talk after."

The necromancer slowly sat up and blinked. The bed was nice, the room was nicer, and everything about it reeked 'vegan femme,' which meant that it was miles beyond his beat-up hovel on the South Side. "How did I get here… and where the hell *is* here…?"

"Spritz. Now," she repeated as she crossed her arms and *dared* him to do anything else.

He listened and he fumbled around, which resulted in him knocking over a vine-covered lamp and an open bottle of water before finally securing the bottle of wash she'd set out for him. Once he took a hit and gagged, he glared up at her.

"Better?"

"Three. No more, no less."

Wisely, Anthony did as he was told. Erica had the aura of a pissed-off drill sergeant, and she looked like she'd slept less than he had. Once E-Ve seemed satisfied with the blasts of mouthwash he'd endured, he rubbed his eyes and shuddered at the black gunk staining his fingers. "Okay. The last thing I remember, I was talking to a friend and… oh hell. Blackburn. Where is he? And where am I?"

"You're somewhere you'll forget, if you have any idea what's good for either of us," she chastised. "I'm assuming you don't remember…?"

"As it turns out, no." Anthony pulled back the white cotton sheet over his legs, relieved to find at least someone had given him underwear. He counted his blessings that they weren't frilly, given the state of the rest of the bedroom.

E-Ve sighed and stormed over to the open window. The city expanded before her, glistening and bright in the blue cloudless sky overhead. She wore an old, tea-stained sundress that contrasted perfectly against her slightly tanned skin. "It's come to my attention that the LSPD's Abby-Squad knows where I live. It has also been noted that my wards against spirits badly need to be reworked. Your *pet* barged into my living room at a quarter-after three this morning, begging for help. How stunned I was to find you in the arms of a blood-encrusted LSPD agent who, for some reason, hadn't put you under arrest."

"Oh, shit. I'm sorry, I didn't ask them to…"

"Yes well, as it was explained to me, the choice was either bring you to someone you knew, or have to, and I quote, 'exhume his corpse from Anth-Med once Captain Yers found out where you were.' That spiteful little woman made it quite clear that you would be safer here than there, and it hardly takes a genius to see why," she growled. "So, once I assessed that you are, and I mean this personally, a Gods-damned idiot – plural, I should stress the plural – I found it unwise to fling you back out into the street."

"No offense taken."

"It should've been. Two. You have done *dyo*, you arrogant child. In less than a day. *In less than a day*. The temptation to go and tell your wife is outstanding. Let you be her problem."

Anthony grunted and checked his chest. The runes inscribed in his flesh were red and inflamed, crusted over from where they'd been oozing overnight. "Is she safe? Kath?"

E-Ve nodded her head as she continued to look out the window at the city beyond. "Vastly more than you; and your little concubine is as well."

He prodded inside the back of his head and groaned when nothing but cold silence greeted him. "Where's my cargo?

"Cargo, you say. Of course, that's how you would refer to her," she growled. "She is in a box lined with lead, sulfur, and salt. I had to negotiate on your behalf to keep her. I do not care to do so again."

"So Alara doesn't have…? Thank God… no, thank *you*," he exclaimed as he felt a weight roll off of his back. "Probably just saved my damn life."

"Oh, there is no probably. You should be aware how angry the detective is that she was not allowed to keep that disgusting soul you harvested, but your little helper spirit reminded her that if she had taken that from you, she would have had to admit to her superiors that she had also had you at some point."

"Which wouldn't have gone over well when she didn't produce me right along with Cl-"

E-Ve grabbed his chin and forced him to stare into her burning, furious eyes. "Finish the name and I will chuck you from this window and send that *crystada* to be mounted to the next satellite launched from this accursed Gulf."

There was absolutely no chance that was an idle threat.

None.

"Alright. I'll make sure nobody knows and..."

She gave his head one more shake and pushed his head back like she was throwing away a piece of trash. "Anthony, you have either grown your balls tenfold since last week, or someone has removed your brain. My assistants would have told me the former when they had you cleaned, so I am of mind to believe the latter. What is *wrong* with you, you daft, stupid boy?"

He looked up from the scars and tried to peer past the open curtains. "That's a lot of sun for it to be morning."

"Who said anything about *proi*?" she said as she bristled up even more. "You nearly slept til damn-near noon."

"Noon? Oh, son of a —"

"And you've yet to answer my question. What in the name of the Hells is wrong with you? What you could have possibly decided is worth the mess you're in?"

Anthony cleared his throat and forced himself to stand. She wasn't lying about the time — and the city below was already well into the midday bustle. "From what I've pieced together? Someone's —"

E-Ve spun around and put her finger on his lip. "I have told you about details. I do not wish to know them. General speak only, child."

"Join the crowd, but you're gonna want to know."

"I have my sincere doubts. Give only the most glancing of remarks, or else, do not open your mouth again."

Anthony took a deep breath and decided to risk her wrath. Maybe she really would throw him out the window if he got lucky enough. "Someone's making weapons out of corpses. Not with tech; with nth."

"Gods *damn* you, I said I didn't —" E-Ve turned pale as the words died on her tongue. "That's... a violation of the natural. In every sense. Every... natural. You didn't know this going in, did you? Please, say you didn't."

Anthony pressed his head against the cool glass. "No, but I could tell something bad was up at the start. It reeks, E. This is the kind of shit that people go to war over."

"They could, yet you say it is worse. I caution —"

"Daem-Sapiens."

Her left hand flicked up to touch a little nodule on the side of her head. "Pardon?"

"You heard me," he replied slowly as he searched the cityscape for... something; anything. Some small clue amidst the swirling mass of humanity going about their daily lives uncaring, unconcerned, unfazed. "Everyone's getting their dick wet in this, E, and it's your people who are on a silver platter for it."

Her fingers moved away from her temple, and she carefully bit down on her thumbnail. If she'd had a tail, he expected it would've twitched. The air felt the same either way. "I... I know that you do not have... a profound reason to... be inherently trusting of... those that share my nature," she admitted after a long, drawn-out pause. "Not that I blame you for your... lack of tolerance."

Anthony nodded slowly and leisurely tapped the back of his hand on the pane of glass with a metallic *tink.* "I know. We've talked about it. I'm working on it."

"Better than some," she sighed, "worse still than others. But if anyone should understand 'imperfect humans,' I suppose it would be us."

"Nah E, you're perfect as you are. Don't let anyone tell you otherwise."

E-Ve let her guard down for just one, brief moment and answered with her voice trembling on the edge of a growl. "The whole world tells us otherwise. Now the world has... what? Found a new way to exploit those it does not like?"

"Well," he replied slowly, "if not the world, at least one gang and a corp. Maybe the Church... more than their usual," he added. "Understand that I really hope I'm wrong, but I'm pretty sure I'm not. *Someone* is crossing lines that don't get to be crossed."

"You intend to stop them, then? Playing hero?"

The necromancer shook his head as vigorously as his headache would allow. "Kath's brother isn't the only dude that's gotten turned into a meat-puddle over this. I'm not in the mood to give up my life and go into wit-sec, and I don't think running is an option."

"So it seems your choice is to be a pain in the ass until someone is shot or sent to jail," she deduced nonchalantly. "Anthony, being honest... this is not the kind of mess that goes away if you decide to ignore it. It also isn't the kind that goes away with a few quick calls."

"I know," he admitted after a minute. "I know who's trying to kill me, and I have a good idea who he's working for. They know that their secret is out in the wind or else they wouldn't have come gunning for me in the first place."

E-Ve simply nodded. "Knowledge is like energy. Once created, it's never destroyed. Not in this era."

"Right. Except I *don't* know what they're doing. A few flashes in a dead guy's head isn't enough to get the cops to do anything other than open a general inquisition."

"At best, I assume you can expose it. Let those with greater resources than yours disrupt and disable," she pointed out. "A risky proposition, but the only one you have?"

"Unless you can think of something better," Anthony replied forlornly as a cloud of thick black smoke erupted in the distance. Gunshots followed, and as if on cue, three different varieties of sirens erupted and echoed through the alleyways below. On a lark, he peered down to the street below. Mixed between canopies covered in advertisements and building-sized advertisements that competed with the sun, people scurried around like angry ants. "Ok. What's going on outside? It's mid-morning. I get it; not when I'm usually awake. Getting a really nasty vibe from the nth down there."

E-Ve rolled her eyes and walked away from the window. "Are… are you stupid? You were in the middle of it."

"E, c'mon. I'm not nth-psych, but even I can tell it stinks out there. You can feel it too, can't you?"

"Of course, I can. It is not a direct result of you, but you had a hand. The Grimshanks are weakened. A war erupted five minutes after you left the Down – war for territory, control, corners. Name it, and it is a mess."

"Fixxer warned last night that this was on the menu," he noted as the chaos in the distance was joined by the sound of a car accident a few blocks north of E's apartment. "Dunno if he's pissed, elated or both."

E-Ve wrinkled her nose and rolled up her flowing silk sleeves. "Giving any emotional credit to a man that you've never seen in the flesh is a brave statement in and of itself. I am unconvinced he is more man than machine."

That was a debate they'd had for years, and Anthony decided not to engage in it just then. "Still can't believe that the AGU pulled that shit. They had to know."

She shrugged and poured herself a cup of water from an old, worn clay pitcher. "When the dust settles, the streets will be calmer, the city safer. Be assured, it was a tactical decision. There's likely a judge or five who wished to take a vacation, and this is a way to clear the dockets."

"Oh it's planned," he mused after a moment. "Some new weapon is getting ready for the street and suddenly the streets are ready for a new weapon."

"I know you're thinking it, but Anthony – if weapons are the problem, then you need to find the source."

"Shit… no," the necromancer replied after a few seconds. "No. I know what I need. I need to know what the damn thing is they're cooking up."

E-Ve shot Anthony a look somewhere between disapproval and resignation as she reached the same conclusion that he had. "At least it's a plan. But until you do – what am I to do with your wayward women as you disregard all warnings and consume your third soul this week? Unlike you, I can't collect favors from a dead man."

"I'm not going to eat one, just talk to him."

"You are a necromancer. Your heart is greedy for more souls because *your* soul has a piece sliced off for each one you meddle with. You take, but you give and that cost always forces you to hunger for another. Do not think that I do not see you for the type of addict that you are," she scolded, "though I do not have a desire to see you dead. What more do you expect to get from a corpse than the police haven't already obtained?"

The idea blossomed to life like the 'breaking news' chyron at the bottom of a IMD-V newscast. "The cops *can't*. They'd have to have permission from his family to do it."

"Katherine would give that, wouldn't she?"

"Not willingly, but yes. Except back in '29, the Church lobbied DC to ban postmortem interrogations on their personnel. The cops can't touch a dead priest without thirteen different levels of permission."

"Ah, I forgot. Anthony Pierson: legal scholar."

Anthony glared at her and then lightly banged his head off the window. "It's my job, okay? The Army sent me home and said 'Hey, before you leave, here's a rulebook full of things you can't fucking do, so don't even try, or we'll come back and shoot you. Memorize it, or else!', and so I fucking memorized it."

"You know you are the most irritating type of man: one who claims to have answers for every question asked. Maybe, then, you can answer another."

"What?"

"Well, in the spirit of oversharing, as that is a thing we are currently doing – *despite* the rules to the contrary – there is more than petty gang warfare and corporate flexing going on," E-Ve told him with a frustrated sigh. "The Others have been talking, and they are not joyful."

He cringed and didn't bother to hide it. The 'Others,' as she put it, were known as unfocused spirits. Things that existed in the shadows, semi-conscious constructors, and, well, *other* entities. They weren't inherently malicious, or necessarily beneficent. They existed because they existed.

And when they started muttering, the magical community took it to heart, which meant he had to take it to heart. And if there was anything he didn't want to have to do in the middle of this utter disaster, it was to take whatever the Others had to say to heart.

"I'm going to guess that they're talking about bad mojo?"

"Mojo is such an insulting, dismissive word," his host spat, "but for lack of other words, yes. Someone has moved into our fair city from parts unknown with ill-intent. That someone that is dead-set with a desire to unbalance the local *nthome*."

That was another one of her favorite words that he hated. "Yeah, because we'd all hate to disrupt the local magical flora and fauna," he grunted.

"Yes. We would. You may live in the shadows of such disruption, but for the rest of us, balances are key. And a *lack* of balance breeds dangers; dangers which you're well aware of."

He took a deep breath and felt the squeeze of a pressure headache build up in the back of his neck. She was right, and he knew it. It also made a lot of sense. "Well, tell the Others to either cut me a paycheck or get in line, because I'm working on it and I *do not* need the local imps or faeries or whatever else that licks the gutters to poke their noses into it."

"Always so disrespectful," she chastised with a sigh. "One day, you'll learn, but today is not that day and you have too many questions that need answers – to start and end with one as simple to say as difficult to answer: Why?"

"Why what?"

"Why are they trying to kill you?" she asked. "As you said, the information is already out; Jordan already ran his mouth. Why should any of it matter?"

Anthony grimaced. The answer was simple, brutal, and more-or-less to the point. "Someone's in cleanup mode. Kath's a rounding error on someone's spreadsheet."

"And you," E-Ve added slowly, "deducted both employees and reputation from the people in charge of the project. There is a corporate officer in some tower much like this one that has made a calculation that whatever you *might* know may show them where a leak is. You know a thing, and they'd like to know from who."

"Funny part of that is that they already killed the leaker."

"No," she said with a firm shake of her head. "They killed who *their* leaker *leaked* to. Maybe they've taken care of the leak, maybe they haven't. Maybe since they had one, maybe they have more."

He lightly banged his forehead against the window just to make the throbbing stop. "Shit. Shit shit shit shit *shit*. This is the point where things don't end until everyone involved is in the ground."

"Anthony." The way she said his name brought his exclamations to a screeching halt and brought all his focus right to her aqua-blue eyes. "We are not close friends. I think you are often absurd and thoughtless, and I detest the very nature of what you do."

"Love you too, E," he grumbled, just loud enough for her to hear.

She tapped her finger on his forehead, and he felt a little sizzle of energy jolt into his skin. It was… peaceful. Calming. Energizing. "I also happen to like you. You fixate on what you feel is right, and you do what you can to correct things that are wrong. I do not like your methods, but I do find there is a solid lack of people in this world who still hold fast to such beliefs. The world gains a bit of peace should you find yourself bleeding in a gutter, but the world will also be at a loss for something more valuable than a reduction in chaos."

Anthony slowly worked through what she was saying as he rubbed at the warm spot left behind by her touch. "I think there's a compliment buried in there, somewhere."

"You're not sure if they still want you dead because you haven't asked. You expressed an assumption, but while you're concerned with your ex-wife and your pet Texan, you haven't even bothered to ask how the world currently sees you, and that means you are being thoughtless. Being thoughtless is what gets men like you killed, and leaves women like me to pick up the pieces."

"I… I don't know what to say," he finally replied. "So, fine. What does the world think of me?"

"At this immediate moment? That you'd be better off dead." E-Ve plucked a data pad seemingly out of thin air, and handed it to him.

Anthony touched the PDA and blinked slowly. It wasn't a shock that E-Ve had access to the regional Alt-Net, though it was a bit more shocking that she had admin-level access. It gave her the ability to see behind the curtain on many things your average back-data browser was simply barred from seeing.

As he read through the highlighted bits on her tablet, he very calmly flipped up a connection to his email and sub-line server in the back of his head. Right on top of a pile of flashing texts, emails, threats, and boner pills was a warning from Fixxer that matched the comments on Erica's pad. *Contract: Anthony Pierson. $50k. Payable: US T-Bonds or Neo-JPN JGBs. Service request: Live or 3hrs postmortem. Value decrease: 5k per 1hr postmortem +3.*

Fixxer had already taken the time to register an interest in the contract, though the job offer was from a typical Jane Doe service. The rest of the details on the request weren't important enough to look at, though it was notable that there were already seven pairs of eyes on it and a handful of questions from Active-Now users. As with any job posted on the Alt, some of those questions would be from poorly-disguised LEOs trying to be stealthy, while at least two or three of them would be from people genuinely interested in popping a bullet into his heart.

"What you're not asking, and you should, is the *why,*" Erica added as she took the pad out of his hand.

"I'm assuming you did?"

"Do you think I'd let you into my house if I didn't already know? There are standards I have to uphold. I am a pillar of the community, and all that."

Translation: if the hit was because he'd fucked someone's wife or flattened a kid, she wouldn't have let him cross the threshold. "I swear, E, I'm just trying…"

"The streets think you're on the Grimshanks payroll. They're denying that; double check that contract list."

He did. He grimaced.

The Grims had their seal of approval on an 'alive but wounded only' order. "Shit. Well. Can't be surprised. So that's the word from the streets. What's the word from the *alleys*?"

E-Ve's smug smile faded to nothing. "You're a person of interest in the corp-sec sphere. Blackwash isn't known for missing a target, and you managed to embarrass one of their top contractors. People want to know why."

"Oh. So not only am I fucked, I'm *valuable.*"

"You, and all those around you."

"Including you?"

"You wouldn't trust me if I said no."

The throbbing in his head turned into a full off-tempo band practice. "I'm already up to my ass with Fixxer, E. That Blackwash contractor? He's stepping on Fixx's toes."

"Bold of you to assume he has toes."

"Yeah, well, you know I don't do wetwork, so I'm having to be creative as it is. What do *you* want?"

Erica tapped him on his forehead with a single finger. "I want the same thing you're wanted for: blackmail. You are convinced that my people are being exploited?"

"It really looks that way. I'm just dicking around on the surface right now, but yeah," he admitted.

"Then I want to know the who, the when, and the where. Provide *that,* and my people will make *your* problems go away. I do not take kindly to my brothers and sisters being targeted."

Anthony looked at her – *really* looked at her. There wasn't a hint of dishonesty around her; she meant it. *How* she meant it? That was a different question, and one he wasn't sure he wanted an answer to, truthfully. "I don't know yet what the fuck I'm supposed to do about it."

E-Ve pulled a piece of paper from the front of her blouse and flicked it across the room like a playing card. "Well, you may thank the officer who dropped you at my doorstep for the dead man you have to speak with. She apparently knew what your next step needed to be before you did. Your step for her will be the same for me."

Anthony caught up the folded-up index card and peered inside. "Med-Reclamation for District Five?" he asked aloud, a split-second before recognition sunk in. "Alara told you where Jordan is being stored? Unbelievable. No, believable," he corrected himself before E-Ve had a chance to reply. "It'd be nice if she had just *asked,* but I get the point."

"As you have decided to make this my problem, then I suspect you'll have questions for me, beginning with if I know of any of my kind who have gone missing, correct?"

"Uh-huh. I know there's kind of public outcry in the Daem community lately, but honestly I don't know shit about it."

E-Ve took another uncharacteristic pause and slowly worked her fingers through her hair and down her neck. The movement showed off a faint line of ridged bone that followed the bump on her temple down the back of her neck. A handful of faint, gnarled spurs interrupted the flow of her form like small saw teeth.

"It is… hard… for us to find acceptance, even in a city like this. We do, of course. We try. But we don't… we don't talk much. Outside of our immediate circle."

The necromancer looked out the window again and watched a fight unfold on the sidewalk below. "Doesn't help that nobody is in a huge hurry to see a bunch of Daems all finding another public figure to rally around. Five's enough."

"No, it does not," she agreed. "We are not easy targets. Yet…"

"Yet you are convenient ones," Anthony finished.

"Very. Distant as we are, there have been rumblings. Men, mostly. A few dozen, in a city this size, a small number. To their families, incalculable. People come, they leave, they do not go where they were supposed to. Nobody cares."

Anthony sucked on air as he tried to find the thing she *wasn't* saying, "They're going missing when they're in transit somewhere? Is that what you've heard?"

Erica smiled slowly and shook her head, not out of denial, but rather, refusal, "What I have heard is that you plan to do something very dumb with someone neither of us has cause to like. What I suggest is that you get out of my house – if you would be so inclined – and ask *him*."

"Not like you to want to get involved."

"You are standing without pants in my home, Anthony," E-Ve countered, "and you did nothing to earn that privilege. At the same time, the mess you have stuck your dick in has all the hallmarks of being the same source of consternation families I personally know are now suffering through. Consider your payment to me a matter of community service."

"Specifically, your community. That you want me to service."

"My community is currently servicing you by providing safety for your loved ones. Can you not do the same for ours?"

She had a point.

A very good point, now that she mentioned it. "I'll get out of your hair once you can tell me where I can find pants. And where Blackburn is."

"In Hell, one can hope," Erica retorted. "Though presumably he's asleep in his anchor. Of all the entities you could have chosen as your familiar…"

"You presume I'm the one who did the choosing."

She took a drink of water and rolled her eyes again. "I presume that you won't leave until I am satisfied you can eat solid food and keep it down. And that, my dear friend, is not negotiable."

***

The streets were busy.

The streets were always busy. People walked; people ran. People drove. Most of them were utterly oblivious to the world around them. They ignored the constant signs advertising Anth-Med, whatever new product Heart and Spade wanted to tempt them with, and the frequent advertisements for all of the new rail and air lines that promised a way *out* of the city if you could only afford the fare.

The streets also watched.

Daylight did nothing to obscure the neon lights and LEDs that saturated every inch of every static structure; it just made the glare a little less. All it did was highlight the people that shouldn't belong in this neighborhood at this hour. The locals? They were average city folk. Business-casual types when there was business to be had. Business-as-a-service types in blue shirts and slacks.

Erica's apartment was just one of dozens of lower-middle class abodes that all nestled around an oasis of restaurants and chow-shops that the community somehow managed to sustain even when the menu prices were a little *too* high for the average income. It was the kind of neighborhood that someone had designed to be comfortable. Designed to be safe. Designed to be out of the way.

A perfectly camouflaged haven for people that didn't want to be noticed. If you knew that, you knew the lack of ease to notice the locals made it all the more important *to* notice them. Erica, and others like her – be it species or profession – had built the community out of sweat and blood for safety and privacy.

If a lady in a white faux-vinyl suit had anything to say about it, it'd be more blood than sweat. Anthony hadn't noticed her, but she'd noticed him. And when her phone rang, she answered it succinctly:

"He's on the move now."

If you weren't looking, you wouldn't have noticed that her brown eyes flashed yellow as she spoke. Even if you were looking, you wouldn't have known what it meant, or who she was. She liked it like that.

And she liked how easy she could disappear into E-Ve's crowd.

6. MORTALITY MORATORIUM
Monday, May 28th, 2:00 PM

It was weird the way you could just pull up to a morgue, park your car, and walk in like you belonged there. You didn't need to call or make an appointment. Or dress up. Or have a warrant. In Anthony's case, he had only to flash his ID and pray the disinterested wage-drone behind the desk didn't pay attention.

The receptionist saw him coming from a mile away, literally. Anthony stole a quick glance at the sec-cams and noted that they gave a clear shot of everything up 59th street and the alley in the back. If this guy had flipped on the news any time in the last couple days, Yers would probably be here in the next five minutes.

Mercifully the drone hadn't; and even better, Yers didn't.

That wasn't to say he didn't feel the eyeballs on him. Like every other street downtown, it was lined with parked cars and cargo vans of every shape and size. At least one of them had to have Alara sitting in it; she wasn't so stupid to tell him where to go without waiting to see what he'd find out. There was an odd scent of latent nth hanging around too, but there was probably a good reason for that.

Ghosts hung around graveyards, after all.

Honestly, a Med-Rec facility was just about as close to that as you got in the concrete jungle. There was always some scavenger hanging out in the shadows or lurking in the immediate sewers that you could gun down and get the city to pay up a bounty for around places like these; part of City Hall's 'no monsters, more tourists' policy. Today wasn't the day, but if the stench persisted, maybe next week.

If he got to have a next week.

The desk agent was little more than a surly gatekeeper who looked like he had as much interest in his job as he did in the overflowing trashcan behind the counter. The front end of the building bore all the trademark grime and gunk you'd expect from a third-rate bio-reproc-shop in the middle of downtown, and the bored-out-of-his-mind drone matched it perfectly.

There was another one of the glaring mini-billboards fastened to the story above it that advocated for *Honest ABE: Under Orion's Hand*. *The Master Chief that's Mastered Travel*! It was one of those advertisements that you saw it *everywhere,* and it was just so bloody garish you couldn't help but notice it every single damn time.

Walking into the morgue and it's the windowless lobby was a relief. Illuminated only by a flickering light overhead and a glowing faux-neon sign behind the front counter that cheerfully declared *Every Sunset Opens the Sky,* it served to be a stark contrast to the corporate sales-pitches that dominated the city proper. It was immediately countered by a placard on the counter that said, *NO SOLICITORS. PAPERS ONLY.* Papers which he presented without argument.

Document #1: a signed, sworn statement that he was present to collect, review, and provide secondary identification of the belongings of one Pastor Jordan Fisher. Nestled in that was document #1B, stating that yes, he was the registered agent of the next of kin, and this supplemental viewing was requested outside the jurisdiction of law enforcement to determine additional culpability and 'personal ease' of the family. The best part?

It wasn't even a lie.

Document #2 was a perk of having worked for the DoD. While his license was on hold — police actions, suspension pending investigation, and whatnot — having one opened certain doors. Necromancers and morgues were two peas in a pod. One glance at a fed-nec softened the attitude of the secretary-in-charge.

A trio of credit-stubs dangled below the piece of plasti-steel ident-badge. With a nod and a complimentary eye-roll, Marcus the Disinterested pressed a buzzer, and granted Anthony direct access to the viewing hall. It wasn't where he wanted to be or needed to be, but at least it was a start.

Anyone of a rational mind would've expected Jordan to be interred in a public friendly, discretely maintained morgue. In fact, it was just as likely that his former parishioners had been told to look for him at the Walnut Memorial Garden, or the Elysium-Cotton Fields uptown. From everything on the IMD-V, he was more beloved than the necromancer would've otherwise believed.

In a high-vis case like this one, though? LSPD policy maintained that the best security was secrecy. This wasn't the first corpse of public import to be shoved into a low-grade reproc-shop, and it wouldn't be the last. It made it easier to get in but significantly harder to find. Without Alara dropping the address, tracking the corpse down could've taken a month. Or more.

He didn't have to wait anywhere near that long before the lone forensic pathologist wandered into the waiting room. He, somehow, looked even more disinterested in his job than the receptionist. "I uh, yeah. Hi. Fisher, your note said? LSPD hasn't given me any —"

"LSPD doesn't schedule for the family."

"But I was told that his only family was his sister and... oh. Are you his sister?"

Anthony took a moment to delight in the idea of being mistaken for Katherine, but it was short-lived. "Gainsig, right?"

"Doctor, please."

Doctor, maybe, the necro muttered inwardly. "*Doctor* Gainsig. I'm here on behalf of his sister. I need the body, and I need privacy for ten minutes with it. No interruptions."

"Ah, no. I can't do that. I can do a viewing. Anything else has to be cleared by the officer in charge of the case," he responded with a smug little smile.

The smile wasn't bad. The fact that when he did the wires that slid into his skin around a synthetic ocular port in his forehead *also* bent into a smile was another story. The pathologist wasn't fully kitted out, but he'd clearly acquired some bonus appendages — a green-lit extra eye, a small metal sensor embedded on the right of his nostril, and a line of port-hubs installed along the top of his left forearm.

It was everything that a budding scientist might need.

"Alara Dimir, by chance?"

"Ah, no," the wiry, balding man replied as he scrolled through his records on a state-issued tab. His glasses reflected the screen with a soft sheen that was almost unnoticeable in the pathetic attempt for warm light the morgue offered. "The investigation is being handled by Captain Yers. Oh, and a secondary... a Detective Matthew Haythes?"

Anthony grimaced at the name drop. Yers was an obvious problem, but Mat? Also known as Matty Hat, he had a discrete reputation for being mad as one. What was really interesting was that Matty was usually assigned to the Ab/Psych squad; more Psych than Ab, but it signaled that not everyone in Vox Magi was as sold on the idea of 'gang violence' as Yers was.

It also made him wonder if Alara had been booted off the case as a lead officer because her past connections to Jordan's family. The LSPD was good at putting links together, even if it meant that they were too good at public surveillance for anyone's real comfort. Of course, that also implied that they had eyes on her and suddenly he felt less happy about not boarding one of ABE's trains to get the hell out of the city when he'd left E-Ve's condo-maximum.

"The front-desker told you I'm li-nec, right? Federal?"

Dr. Gainsig looked up from his pad and frowned. "I was unaware that this case had been handed to the Hoovers. You'll have to allow me to make a call, and —"

That was the magic word of the morning. "Okay. Let me cut you off there. I need to see Jordan's corpse, and I need some privacy. I am going to get it, and it's going to be easy. How easy is up to you."

"Well, I mean I can just call and I'm sure..."

He didn't get to make a call. The second that the pathologist's hand went into a pocket on his stale-blue lab coat, Anthony closed the distance between them and grabbed the doctor's wrist. "You don't need to make a call. You need to decide how 'easy' this is going to be. It's easy for me either way. It can be easy for you, too."

Gainsig's demeanor changed immediately, and shifted from mild annoyance to open disgust. "Oh, you're one of those. I'm aware that under Dr. Rietta's regime, things were more... open and available to the public, but since her retirement, that practice is no longer allowed here."

"That practice...?" the necro asked as he slowly let go of Gainsig's arm and took a step back.

"Well, yes. The... oh, how was it phrased... 'meat and greets,' I think? No, I can't speak for the other Medical Reclamation offices, but at this one, no. Marcus out front should have told you," the doctor scolded. "Oh, let me guess, you didn't *ask*, you just gave him stubs. There are no refunds."

"Meet and greets...?"

"*Meat* and greets," the pathologist repeated.

The way he said it made Anthony's skin crawl, and he failed to stifle a gag. "Doc, I will honestly tell you I don't know what the Hell you're talking about, and I'll even let you pick which Hell. I'm here because I need access to Pastor Fisher. Please."

Gainsig narrowed his eyes and carefully pushed his glasses up with a single finger. They had a faint white glow to the edges – aura scans, probably, or a news HUD. "You're here for access, but not for… prior services. You don't want me to call the police to verify you, and I suspect you're not opposed to making my life difficult if I choose not to allow you access."

"More or less."

"Interesting. I will warn you that he's in absolutely terrible condition, even for a murder victim. I know how *interested* men in your… hobby tend to be over high-profile events, but if you're lying to me, do understand that's a mistake."

"Not even on my worst day," Anthony promised. "The family sent me. They don't trust the cops and quite frankly, neither do I. I've got cred-stubs, I've got juice, and I've got a gun," he added as Gainsig's ocular scanned him over.

"No, you don't."

The necromancer rolled his eyes and sighed. "It's in the car. You really gonna make me go get it, or can we work out an arrangement that doesn't involve you ever saying the word 'meat' to me again? Ever?"

The pathologist slowly looked him up and down and made every moment of it feel horrifically uncomfortable. "I wouldn't trust them either," he muttered, finally. "Fine, then. Come along."

"Going to show me where he is for free? That simple?"

"Nothing simple about it," the examiner replied as he opened a door in the back of the room and marched Anthony through a short hallway. "With federal training, so maybe you can make something out of this that the PD's necro-corps couldn't."

A helpful morgue worker was both a blessing and a curse. A blessing, because it made his life easier. A curse, because in a city like this one, a doc who didn't know the details around someone's death was a rarity. A few minutes later, they were standing in front of a wall of mixed C/D Store/Process units. Cold for corpses, D for disposal. Thinner slots beside each door were for set aside for post-autopsy implant storage.

Unlike a funeral home, city services followed separate protocols. Once the body was dissected, and anything reusable had been salvaged, it went back into the slot with a dose of decomp-spray if the family couldn't afford a proper burial. The residue was prepared for home-garden use, and the drawers were repurposed next morning.

Santuario County Bio-Medical Reclamation Stations: Your One-Stop Shop for All-Things Chop.

When Dr. Gainsig popped open the steel door and wheeled what was left of Jordan out, Anthony doubted anyone would find a use for him ever again. "So, I'll be honest," the doc began, "Cybernetics? Implants? Fine. We get a flesh-drone in or a bod-mod? Weird, but whatever. People do people shit, and people shit's dumb shit."

The necromancer ran his thumb over the lump that remained on Jordan's neck. If you didn't know it was supposed to *be* a neck, you'd be forgiven. The staff had done a great job at keeping his corpse chilled after cleaning up the bloody mess, but when someone's head is in a plastic bag, it looked more like a chunk of dragonfruit.

"But there's levels of dumb shit that you're willing to deal with."

"Willing isn't the question. I get paid enough not to care. The runes, though? I do not care for nth-abuse, and that, my friend, is nth-abuse. Preacher should've known better."

"If he was the one who did it," Anthony muttered as he looked down at Jordan's torso. It was covered in mottled bruises and marks, along with a series of evenly-spaced burns along his ribs, collarbone, and left arm. "These don't look very old. Why are they spaced like fingerprints?"

"I don't know, and they aren't," the examiner replied as he touched one. "A R/N/SCI scan was carried out, per norm. No elevated levels of radiation, limited latent-nth reverberations, and no sub-dermal or cybernetic implants that could've gone wrong. Most of the wounds are surface only, deep enough to break a few ribs, not kill him. He'd be in ICU if they hadn't worked his head. The branding had to hurt, but again, not fatal."

Anthony ran his fingers over the lettering. It was impossible to say what language it was, and he didn't carry around a translation guide in his pocket. It wasn't anything in Latin or from the Middle East, and sure as fuck wasn't in English. "They don't look postmortem."

Gainsig picked up the bag holding Jordan's pulped head. "Presumably because they weren't. As far as his head goes, I had to amputate what was left from the C2 verti on up. Went ahead and peeled his neck off down to C6 just so the stump'd quit flopping."

"So, he got pummeled, branded, and to finish it off, he had his head turned into cat food. Jordan, you absolute idiot."

"Ah, so you do know him?"

"Unfortunately. He was a prick, but even so... this is a bit much."

The pathologist adjusted his glasses. "I thought he was a priest."

"You can be both."

With a short, cold laugh, the doc placed Jordan's head back into the drawer and stepped back. "You're not getting my workup, if you're thinking of asking for it. Only reason I'm letting you see this much is because if I didn't know better, I'd say he had an accident with an industrial press, 'cept he didn't, and I don't want to see anyone else cross my table looking like this."

Anthony reached into his jacket and pulled out a wooden kit box he had squirreled away inside a protected pocket. "I just need to talk to him."

"Talk to him?" Gainsig replied, bemused. "What, you think you're gonna bring him back from… oh. You… are. You're aware that's uh, an invasion of personal… I am pretty sure his chart is going to say no –"

"I don't care what his chart says, and I've got a credit stub that'll help you not to care, either, if you want it," the necromancer retorted. Clare, for all of her faults, knew of several discrete holding accounts and digi-stashes stored away with funds that would be lost to the ether after her death. Blood money, sure, but it was still money.

At least now, it would be used for a good cause. Anthony pulled out a small pile of credit stubs and laid them on top of his kit. "You don't want to see anyone else crushed like a juice box, and I don't wanna leave without knowing what did it. Can we cut the bullshit and deal?"

Gainsig stared at the stack of cash. "You get this one, and later you do one for me. We have a deal?"

"Absolutely no kids, and I do not raise bodies for fucking."

"At least you have limits," the doc replied after a second. "Deal. What do you need me to do?"

"Leave," Anthony replied curtly. "What I gotta do you don't wanna see, and honestly I don't need the audience."

The pathologist swiped the pile of stubs and stuffed them into his lab coat. "You make a mess; you clean it up. You've got thirty min. *Max.*"

"Shouldn't need more than twenty," he countered earnestly. "Not exactly a lot to talk to."

"No, no… no, don't suppose there is," Gainsig replied as he made his way out of the locker. "Just… be quick about it."

Anthony barely even registered the doc's response as he stared down at the corpse. Once the door slammed shut, he popped the lid on the wooden box and went to work. It would be harder without Marshal on hand to assist, but it wasn't like he could stroll into the morgue with a shotty on his hip.

"Well, Jordan, you're gonna be pissed but… perk of the job."

***

Alara flicked the phone off with a quick press of her thumb and breathed a sigh of relief. A city-ordinance-defying, overly-bright sign flashed down from above across her sunglasses with the words, *The Pentaship: You've Got Friends In Warm Places,* much to Detective Haythes' amusement.

"That was Gainsig. No arguments, no problems," she said as she pressed a button behind her ear and disconnected a call. "Anthony was so busy handing out stubs, he didn't even think to ask why the doc wasn't giving him a hard time."

"That's a blessing in disguise," her companion replied. He wasn't a big guy, but like her, he wore a dark blue neo-vinyl suit and sported a pair of Actually-Leather™ gloves and a pair of green-tinted visor shades. "From what I've heard about him, he's usually more cautious."

"He's not usually being hunted by half the county, either," Alara countered. "Either way, it'll be a payoff. Thank you for backing me on this bullshit, Matt."

Matthew smiled and stretched back in his seat. Depending on who you asked, his Ab/Psy affiliation was either 'psychic' or 'psychotic,' and on any given day, it was arguably interchangeable. "Hey, what can I say? Both of us think that Yers is full of shit, and if this gets the bad guys, it seems like a fun day to me."

"You have a strange opinion of fun, you know that, right?"

"They don't call me the Hatter for nothin'," he retorted with a boyish giggle. "Besides, he's a necromancer in a morgue. This either works and we bypass the Church's 'don't dick with our dead' order, or it goes horribly wrong. Either way, it's fun."

"You are a sick man," she muttered as she peered into her side mirror and frowned. Middle of the day or not, the entirety of 59th was cast in an omnipresent shadow from the high-rises that lined both sides of the thoroughfare. In some places, the only light that made it came from flickering signs or flashing 'STORE OPEN' displays. "Hang on. Five cars up. That van that just pulled in. Does it look familiar to you?"

The detective flipped a switch on the dashboard and a rear cam powered on. Another quick tap, and the lens focused on the van along with a line of city-stats beside the license plate and the truck's WIF-ID transponder. "According to the database, there's no less than six-hundred thirty-five black 2039 M-Bez vans in the city. Three-hundred and nine of them are painted white. One-hundred and twelve are rolling billboards. Two-hundred and fourteen have been done in black."

"Popular style," Alara replied under her breath.

"Quite. They're rated for enhanced cargo weight."

The Lieutenant pursed her lips and reached into her jacket for a bit of her own personal special blend of magical helper. "Two and a half million registered vehicles in Los San. Couple hundred of that make and model are black. What are the odds that that the one we have on cam from Allenway is the same one that just pulled in behind us?"

"You'd have to ask TEC, L-T. If I could do numbers, I wouldn't be in the field." Matthew tapped on the screen a few more times until the clear picture was replaced with a fuzzy, opaque outline. "X/R blocking in the panels on that thing. Whatever they're hauling, they want it kept private."

"Well, that's something we can write a ticket for," Alara mused as she slid her sunglasses up her face and tilted her head back. With her other hand, she pressed a small injector to her tear duct – nothing bigger than a clear lighter with a glowing blue substrate inside. She winced as it made contact, and then repeated the process in the other eye.

The dark-haired cop glanced over at her and watched as a familiar blue tint settled around her irises. "Call for unis?"

"Flag for AGU. Gang activity; 51st. Green-57W+2 it."

Matthew nodded in response and quickly hit a button embedded just below his ear. The call would do two things – send a response team to 51st, and order them go quiet. The code? Part of a rotating password system intended to confuse anyone with a scanner. Today, that mean no gang activity present, but the risk for antisocial activity remained – and the plus two added an extra two blocks for the preferred staging point. Their distance would help provide cover, should some asshole be listening in on a scanner.

And if there was *anyone* who could cause antisocial activity...

***

"Before you even open your mouth to bitch, I want you to know how much of a pain in the ass this was," Anthony complained. "Where the hell were you? I've met souls literally bound to Hell who were easier to wake up than you were."

Jordan didn't answer. He couldn't, not yet. Getting brought back from the other side took time, and when the other side didn't want to let you go, it took longer.

The other side really, really hadn't wanted to let him go.

Unlike Clare or Carlos, Jordan was… special. You didn't need to have an intact head to have a soul walk and talk, but it made it easier to hold a conversation when the resurrectee had a familiar medium to be anchored to. Blackburn, for example, had bonded with the shotgun he had died holding, whereas Clare *couldn't* stay in this world because Anthony didn't give her more than a brief hold.

For the priest? Having his body helped. The fact that he *resisted* the callback didn't. At all. Anthony had his shirt off and folded in the corner, and he'd cut open nearly a dozen spots up and down his ribs to get enough blood-nth flowing to pull Jordan's soul from… wherever. They were painful cuts, ones which would take a full tube of Silver-Honey Squeeze to heal, and there was no chance of getting his hands on any at the rate the week had been going.

"Ground rules: we have maybe fifteen minutes, and you look like you're in a hurry to go back to wherever exactly you were hiding. We agree we don't like each other; we agree that you were right that Kath shouldn't have married me; and I presume you'd like to trade spaces on the slab. That's not happening, but we can also agree that whatever did this to you doesn't deserve to pass Go! or collect two c100-stubs. Deal? We can work this out."

Jordan's spirit clenched his fists as he tried to move out of the circle that the necromancer had drawn onto the ground. On its own, it was just a shape scrawled with sulfur and filled with a lazy infinity mark scribbled in the middle. Adding a mix of spit, blood, the crushed remnants of a year old storin-stone, and a bottle of classically-chem'd silver nitrate?

It was going to leave a stain.

When Anthony dropped Jordan's freshly-dismembered right hand into the middle of it (which was *going* to piss off the doc, he just *knew* it) and activated the nth-channels the DoD had carved into his chest, the circle became both a prison and an anchor. The hand served as a magnet and a base; the ground-up storin-stone a way to entrap the radiant nth that was going to be required and emitted, and the silver served to purify the immediate area. All that was missing was enough of the necromancer's own essence to serve as a catalyst.

Essence that had to be reapplied every time his asshole of an ex-brother-in-law resisted the call. Although, it was entirely possible, he wasn't resisting as much as he was being *forbidden*. The chains wrapped around the ex-priest's naked body lead some credence to that possibility. After three minutes of simply floating in morbid silence, he finally spoke up.

"Where am I? This isn't Heaven."

"What gave it away?"

"You're here."

"You woke up on the wrong side of the coffin, I see. Hi to you, too. We need to talk."

Jordan scoffed at him. It was a wordless little noise and might've been funny in the right context. *"I'm dead?"*

"Yep."

"Oh. Then no."

"Too bad. We don't have time. Listen to me: whoever killed you is gunning for your sister," Anthony bluntly informed him. "I get it. You're pissed you're dead and you're confused about being dead, but I do not want to have to compel you to talk to me. Do it on your own accord, please."

That got a reaction — an instantly visible, easily notable one. Jordan shook, and the chains holding his arms behind his back quaked as he struggled to break free. Specters had a flaw of being more emotional than the living. All Anthony knew about it was that it was some metaphysical, meta-psychological bullshit.

"Katherine…? Is she… is she safe?"

"For now, but there are a lot of moving parts working to try and change that. I'm running short on ideas about what to do to get the hit called off and honestly, I never got a chance to tell you to go fuck yourself."

Jordan seemed to calm a bit, though he fidgeted as the runes at his feet struggled to hold him in place. *"Chains… wounds. Why am I here and not… was I wrong? Was the Pope wrong?"*

The necromancer made a vague gesture with his steel hand and little servos *whirred* quietly behind his fingers. "I think the Church is wrong all the time, but no, I have no idea what happened to you. That's kind of why we're here."

*"I'm dead but not… what is this… am I… am I in a **city** morgue? Why am I not in the one which the Church maintains?"*

"Police investigation. Church got cock-blocked on storage and processing. Honestly, just give it a minute. You're fuzzy. You don't want to know how you died, so be happy about it."

"Oh."

"Sorry. I mean that, really. I mean, not that sorry you're dead, but… listen, it was kind of squishy."

"Oh," the priest repeated. *"I… I assume this means that you…"*

"Yup."

Jordan looked down at the chains around his body and the flickering circle on the floor beneath his dangling feet. *"It would of course… be you. Did you… pay… for this opportunity? Did you bribe the Speakers of the Eagles to…?"*

"The Speakers? No," Anthony answered with a slight frown. "Your bosses don't even know that I'm—wait. Did you just admit that the CoAA has its own necros, too?"

"No one would believe you, even if you repeated it," the priest answered with a rasping chuckle.

Anthony snorted and spit a glob of bile out of his mouth before he tapped his eye with a metal *tink*. "Bet. Now that you know you're on cam, can you at least pretend to be polite?"

"I'm… dead? Dead, apparently? And not in Heaven." Jordan slowly retorted. *"Trying to be nice… I guess… my heart was not as pure as I thought. I… I can at least say one thing. It's important."*

"Yes?"

The priest narrowed his cloudy, tired eyes and sneered so violently that his lips briefly stretched to cover his entire face. *"You… Anthony Pierson… are an **asshole**. Go stuff yourself."*

Anthony stood still, blinked, and finally stopped a laugh with a hand over his lips. "You can't even say 'fuck you' after you're dead? That's… funny. I appreciate it, and you know what? I'll even give it to you that you have every right to say it. But we don't have time for this. Whomever has you wants you back, and I don't have the strength to fight them all damn day."

Jordan finally realized he was naked and tried to buck against the chains. When they wouldn't budge, he affixed an even angrier stare at his summoner. *"Why did you do this to me? Why am I… like this?"*

"You're in the circle because there's a whole lotta shit raining down right now, and I need answers. Why you're wrapped up in chains and look like you've been used as Satan's muffler? That's between you and your God."

"My God is your God. God is God. Universe is —"

"Careful, Jordan, careful," Anthony cautioned. "The Universe doesn't like people talking about what they've seen off-stage. My grip on you isn't perfect, and I don't want you to piss off whatever's out there."

Jordan peered at his ex-brother-in-law and focused on something that was just behind where the necromancer was standing. Or maybe just below his skin. It was a *look* Anthony had received on more than one occasion, and it never served to make him feel better. Normally, whatever the spook saw convinced them to at least play along.

Not this time.

"I see you. Who you are. You are weak. I always thought you were less of a man than my sister deserved. Still, I never knew how little there really is to you."

To his credit, Anthony took it without faltering. You didn't quite know 'emasculating' until it came from a naked, dangling, dead man. "Right. Got it. Small man. You done?"

"No. But... Kath?"

"Yep."

"Why her?"

"Hoping you'd know."

"Oh."

Anthony cleared his throat and dabbed at one of the cuts along his ribs with a wince. "The spell holding you in place gives me the power to force an answer to questions of fact. Elaborate to your heart's content. Hell, elaborate to mine." Before the priest could answer, Anthony added a warning. "Your cooperation isn't required, but it'd make things a lot easier on us both. Help me help your sister. For once, I'll even ask nicely. Please."

"I don't know if I can. I... everything is... foggy."

"I know. It won't matter. Look. I can't just plumb around in your head like this. They didn't leave enough of your brains behind for me to use your consciousness as a filter."

"I... I am unsure what that means. I... don't think I like it."

"You wouldn't. Bluntly, I'm exhausted. I *physically* don't have the strength to swallow you and rip through your subconscious, so I need you to be willing to do this the easy way. For her ass, not yours."

Jordan's spirit flickered. In the cold, clinical lights shining overhead, he looked exactly like a parody of some B-grade horror flick. *"Fine, for Katherine."*

That was enough.

"I'll take it. First: I need to know the name of the man who got you into this mess – the one who put you on the Grimshank's radar. I know they didn't squash you, but I can tell you the B&B Twins are on their way to your side of the astral."

Jordan's head silently started to jerk back and forth as he listened. "*I... there are vows. A code of...*"

"You're dead. You're released."

"*Am I? That's only for the Church and God to say.*"

Anthony stepped up right to the edge of the circle and looked into the priest's eyes. A spirit was a fascinating thing, and it was easy to get lost in just what it all meant, especially when seeing one with your own eyes. The longer he looked, the deeper he could see, beyond what Jordan's spiritual "self" had manifested. You could almost see what was beyond.

Almost.

"I don't think you're anywhere that you need to worry about keeping promises in, are you? Looks like you didn't get to the pearly gates after all, so maybe..."

"*Bastard.*"

"I know," the necromancer sighed, "I'll ask again: I need to know the name of the man who introduced you to Project Wetshell."

That earned an instant response. Jordan's spirit shook, chains and all, as fissures appeared down his head and across his shoulders. "*You arrogant – I said I can't. Look at me. Do you think I want to make this worse?*"

"No, but I can't promise it's not going to make it any better. Listen, Jordan," Anthony argued as he swung his arms out and gestured at the entire room. "You could still be feeding the masses, singing prayers, whatever. Instead, you're stuck in a drawer and trapped in a circle. Doesn't sound like you've made the best choices as of late."

"*I didn't do this!*"

"Yeah, but someone did, and they didn't like you. Someone decided to end your life and do it in a way that sent a message. Who or what, I'm not yet sure." Anthony paused, giving his words a chance to sink in. "I got to listen to you die. I've been shot at by the people who had you killed. Everyone who's come close to this seems to have either eaten a bullet or is being fitted for a box. Kath is next if you don't talk, and I'm not willing to see that happen. *So fucking talk.*"

Fresh fissures ripped through Jordan's ghost, with a ferocity that nearly bisected him at his sternum. Just as quickly as they ripped him open, his ghostly 'skin' reconstituted. "*All I can say is that the College of Eagles decid-*"

"Yeah yeah, your bosses up in NNI decided whatever you heard was worth dealing with the Grims. I know. I think I know what. What I don't know is who. So tell me," Anthony demanded.

"I CAN'T. The vows of confession –"

"I told you, you're dead. Nobody cares. Whatever did this to you *will* do it to someone else. You know it, I know it. Are you that much of a prick to hold back now, looking like you've just been run over by a tank? C'mon man," Anthony argued. "You're a dumbass, but not that bad. Not even on your worst day. Believe it or not, I don't actually enjoy seeing you like this."

Jordan flexed against the chains and kicked futilely at the ones around his feet. *"This… isn't you?"*

"You being here? Yes. The state you're in currently? No," Anthony answered. "I don't know what you did, but you did a thing to someone that's really right well pissed off at you, and for once, it's not me. Listen – I know you're confused. But if you don't answer *now,* I'm going to have to –"

"I am not confused!" Jordan yelled. Just like Blackburn, his voice seemed to migrate, sounding with a haunting dissonance just behind the necromancer's ear. *"I died. Then steel. Then pain. Pain and steel in a place where I shouldn't be!"*

The necromancer blinked – slowly – and worked his way through it as a horrible… very, very horrible… idea crawled into his head. "Nobody dies and goes to a junkyard. That's not how it works. Jordan… I… oh, shit."

"Can't you talk without swearing?"

Anthony focused on the chains across the ghost's body, and spared a very quick glance back at his corpse on the other side of the room. There wasn't a lot to tie it together, but there was enough. There also wasn't a lot more effort he could give to hold the spirit in the circle. "Are you going to answer the question or are you trying to run out the clock?"

The priest flexed against the chains that held him, shooting Anthony a withering glare. *"You know what? I can see you. I can really see you now. I knew you were an ass, but I can see* into *you now. You're… broken. I… I pity you."* As he spoke, his form darkened, like light was bending around him to try to get away.

It was little more than spectral, emotional bullshit. Those who ended up dead in bad situations had a tendency to let their trauma take control, which made them grow blind to the fact they could still find a way to be useful. Jordan qualified. There just wasn't enough time to be nice about it.

"For fuck's sake," Anthony finally snapped. "Three days ago, you were an irritating, self-righteous prick. Now that you're dead, you'd rather spend your time being a jerk than help me save your sister's ass? Fine. I'm done. Don't say I didn't warn you."

"Warn me? WARN ME?! I'm DEAD. What more do you think –"

If the necromancer cared about Jordan's latest line of nonsense, he didn't show it. He ran his good hand up and down his ribs and wiped his fingertips in a sharp downward-pointing triangle across his naked chest. Blood swelled up from the wounds and followed his fingers as he traced it out in one single fluid motion.

"For what it's worth, I'm going to try to make this right," Anthony said as he drew his hand away. A trickle of blood followed, one that flowed freely through the air in defiance of gravity and physics alike. "Sorry about this."

"You have never been sorry for a single thing in your miserable –"

"Oh that's not true. The thing is, when this shit is over, I gotta tell Kath you're okay. Since you're not okay, I gotta fix it. After the divorce, I promised I'd never lie to her again. Honestly, I have a lot of fun not lying to her. Being honest to your ex is downright delightful," he replied as he traced his fingertips through the wounds on his chest.

Jordan rolled his eyes and they briefly disappeared into his face when he did. *"If you'd lied to her less she would still..."*

"Oh, save it. Anyway. I *can* tell her you're okay because you're *not* in Hell. Someone's *bound* your ass," he exclaimed as he flicked his hand at the ghost, and the trail of blood followed along like a wet dart. "But first! Someone came to you with a confession, and it got you killed. What's their name?"

The blood spattered across Jordan's ghost and splashed across his forehead and down into his eyes. He wailed. It was agonized, mournful, and violent.

But, so was the spell. Compulsion without consent wasn't a kindness, and it was one of the least favorite parts of Anthony's job. The command was little more than an outright assault on the priest's autonomy, but that was intelligence work for you.

Sometimes, you asked.

Sometimes, you didn't.

Jordan went slack as the tendril of blood seeped across his face, into his eyes, and into his ears. Anthony watched as the small stream turned into razor-thin strands that started to root through the ghost's head without hesitation or care. Within seconds, a very poor 'map' of his brain was on full display, one powered purely by nth and the necromancer's own blood.

A few short seconds later, Jordan began to speak.

***

"Alara?"

"Yeah?"

"You seeing that?"

"The van's bouncing like its shocks have gone bad?"

Matty smirked. "Gone *great*, you mean."

She didn't dignify the joke with a response. Alara made a show of pulling her G-Locke from under her jacket, passing her thumb over the bio-metric safety. "Looks like it's a parking violation."

"Nah boss, more like a safety one. I mean, if it starts going off like that on the Free-W, it could wreck. Easily."

"Easily," Alara echoed. "Cits could get hurt."

"And we can't let it stay on the street, can we? I mean…"

"No, it could hurt someone bouncing like that."

"Really could. Driver'd lose control."

"I think that means we have an unsafe vehicle."

"I think that means you're right. We can detain it until a tow gets here."

"Nah, we wouldn't do that. Middle of day. They're not doing anything wrong. We're public servants, right? We help people?"

Matt nodded and drew his own gun with a chipper little smile. "Sure are. I ever tell you that my uncle runs a garage?"

"Nope, never did."

"Aff-O-Engies. Up near Cleveland."

"People still live near Cleveland? Willingly?"

"Parole. You stay where you gotta stay. Tax evasion, but hey, I learned some shit from him. I bet I could help them out. Give a quick look. Figure out what's making it bounce."

Alara slowly opened her door and pressed a button on her dash to start recording from all four sides with full audio. "Well, sounds like we need to go protect and serve, doesn't it?"

"Absolutely, boss."

***

The wispy form of a balding, middle-aged man with a bad comb-over took center stage in the short bit of space between the necromancer and his trapped spirit. He was an African-American with a hint of hyper-pigmentation on his left cheek, and other than that, there wasn't much about him that really stood out. One of his eyes had been replaced with an obvious cybernetic instead of a sleeker, more concealed model, but that seemed to be the norm lately in the city. If you worked in tech, it was a miracle if your entire upper skull didn't wind up crammed full of bio-cyber and decorated to match.

It wasn't like Anthony didn't have some of the same hardware in his own head – hardware that was very busy focusing, refocusing, and tracking; and that was just his eye. He had some non-over-the-counter tech he'd earned from the DoD buried behind his ocular, and all of it was happily working away.

Working on giving him a headache, but working.

Most importantly, it was recording.

"Omari… Omari Miller."

The vision flickered as the answers Anthony sought began to appear on the specter's skin. *Mechanical Engineering. Federal Safety Administration.* Others, such as Sojourn, BlackWash, and HawkCrest, were soon to follow, appearing across his forehead like brands. *HC* was worth a raised eyebrow, because they were a hefty mover-and-shaker in the Defense world; for that matter, he had some of their work embedded in his brain.

Minds worked like indexes. You had only to pull out an image, and you could watch where the connections formed. It wasn't everything Anthony needed to know about the guy, but what Jordan didn't know, there was a simple solution to find.

Or at least, a simple Fixxer-Upper.

The same numeric code he'd seen in Carlos's head and in Clare's interrogation a few hours earlier had appeared on his shoulder, too. Twice was a fluke, but three times promised to be neither coincidence nor charm. The question was why.

Jordan was in no hurry to answer. The blood seeping out of Anthony's side throbbed every few seconds and some of it simply burned away as it wound through the priest's ghost. If he sucked up much more out of Anthony's ribs, a transfusion would be needed. With that in mind, the necromancer's next question felt like an even bigger gamble.

"Why would some neckless nerd come to you in the first place? What was he doing that had him so badly upset?"

A wide-open question like that gave Jordan more room to wiggle than Anthony desired, but any geek could get involved in something shady. It was 2057, for fuck's sake. If you were working with tech and your dealings weren't sketchy, you were just good at hiding it.

Even those could hurt if you put them in the wrong spot.

The vision faded and Jordan's soul completely reconstituted in the circle. Tendrils of blood still floated around in his head, but now that the dam had been broken, the spirit hung limply in the ritualistic markings. "*I don't know the tech. He was involved in... biological/nth integration. Engineering.*"

"That's about a third of the city and half of Sil-Valley out west. Who'd he work for?"

"*I... he didn't say where he worked. But there were clues. I saw a keycard once. 'SJE' on it. A few sessions later... I told him I had invested in a few companies. He... he went pale when I said Sojourn Enterprises.*"

Anthony sat up a little straighter. "Clever boy, didn't think you would've had it in you. So, an engineer in bio-nth tech. Why was that a problem?"

"*The volunteers. They were... they were getting volunteers. Except they... he found out they weren't.*"

"Kidnapping victims?"

"*Or deceived. Does it matter?*"

Anthony pursed his lips. "No. This Omari guy was working on 'upgrading' people and found out they weren't exactly willing participants?"

"*Summarized. Yes. He was told they were paid donors.*"

"Donors? Donors of what?"

"*Parts. He... never said which ones.*"

A bit of bile welled up in the back of Anthony's throat. "Okay. So Omari was playing with body parts and found out they weren't ethically sourced. Human, I presume?"

Jordan flickered in and out of sight. "*No.*"

The necromancer intentionally made his face and tone go blank. This part had to be non-ambiguous for the recording. Alara had already opened the door for the line of questions, and E-Ve had cast it in stark relief, but this was courtroom-level evidence Anthony could not afford to screw up.

That, much as he hated it, meant he needed to sound like an idiot.

"Animals? You got yourself killed over animal abuse?"

"Don't play a fool. He came to me upset about Daems."

"Okay. Daem body parts. Still bad, but not bad enough to get killed over. What's so special about that? What parts?"

The priest hung his head and looked down at his naked, blistered toes. *"He said he was involved in the transport side. It wasn't parts. It was... full. Full bodies."*

Anthony swallowed and took a breath. Knowing where this was going and hearing it straight from the tap were two different things and making Jordan fess up wasn't half as fun as he'd hoped it would be. "Fresh bodies?"

"Very."

The necromancer posed his next question carefully. "You understand, you're confirming that this Omari guy is trafficking *Daem-Sapiens* — the *offspring of humans mating with demons* — to perform biological experimentation on. Plus, he's been doing it in the city that is run *by the Daemoness* that is believed to be the closest thing to their biological great-grandmother? Is that accurate?"

A pile of folders appeared for a moment beside Jordan's face. They were marked 'SE' and 'Project Wetshell.' *"It's why I went to the Pope. Not the police. The LSPD can't be trusted with the corps."*

"Please, the cops can't be trusted with jaywalking," Anthony muttered. "That name — Project Wetshell. Was that what he called it?"

"Yes." The ghost closed his sad eyes and tried again to push on his chains. Each move he made was noticeably weaker than the last. The chains, however, only seemed to grow in size and strength each time he pushed against them.

"Jordan... you knew about this for a while, right?"

"Yes. I learned gradually over a period of months."

Anthony let out a slow whistle. "Just to reiterate: how did you get this information? A confessional?"

The priest's ghost wavered, but he didn't fight that one. *"Yes. Several."*

"But you didn't get dead until you talked to your bosses. Your bosses' bosses, at that."

Jordan cringed. *"Correct."*

"They're the ones who told you to avoid speaking to anyone with a badge. They sent you to the Grimshanks. Why?"

"Anthony..."

"Why, Jordan? It's important."

Finally, he relented. *"Because of potential backlash if the scandal became public. They felt that discussing it with local... influencers... would end aspects of the problem efficiently enough. They would handle the rest in-house."*

Anthony's eyes narrowed as every ugly thought and clue he'd gathered started to connect. "Tell me about the CoAA's Daem resettlement program. Who runs it?"

"The Gulf Diocese."

"That's a matter of public record. But the CoAA doesn't always like to say who is the actual overseer of one program or another. Who is? Was it you?"

Jordan's soul shuddered violently as fresh cracks opened along his sternum and down his limbs. Despite sealing up a second later, the process looked absolutely agonizing. *"I didn't... know. Some did... get help. It... I didn't know, Anthony. I swear. I swear to you, I didn't know."*

"What didn't you know?" the necromancer pressed as he leaned in. "Who ran it? Was it you?"

"The Sine."

He mentally flagged the last few seconds on the video. That kind of testimony was next-to-guaranteed that the Church was going to be served with a warrant, and he didn't want to chance that it might get overlooked when the cops eventually saw it. For that matter, he wanted to watch their eyes... and see how it would play out on the news. "And, what's wrong with the program? What did you learn that got you killed?"

"I didn't know it was... related. Our resettlement efforts were disappointing. I thought it was because of... Daems being Daems. Then, I learned otherwise."

"Daems being Daems, huh? That's a lot of racism. And Kath says *I'm* bad. Good job on that."

"I'm not perfect! I follow God in a world where demons and their kin walk free," Jordan snarled. *"All this time hating the Church, and now I give you a gift with their name on it."*

Anthony would've happily punched him for that, if he could've. "You haven't given me a gift, you idiot. When I turn this shit in – and it's not a matter of if, but when – you'll have made me the poster child for this fuckup. Everybody remembers the whistle-blower; the press, the victims, and, oh yeah, the fucksticks that had the whistle blown on them. The only reason I'm not angrier at you than I am right now is because your decision to hold this information already got you stomped into a pancake, and I can't do much worse than that."

Jordan's body melted, not unlike the way a stick of butter would in the sun. He sagged, distended, and reformed; the chains maintained their hold, no matter what he did. He wasn't trying to get away, he was just struggling – literally *and* figuratively. *"I didn't know."*

"Let the record show – remnant-subject Fisher, Jordan is showing signs of emotional trauma." Anthony stretched and stood up to move closer to the dead man. "I know you didn't. Jordan, I can't fix this on my own. You can. You can help me make this right. Please, what did you learn that cost you your life?"

The priest's body melted again and reformed as a giant Bible that opened up to show some kind of weird logbook. *"The Sine-Pastor had full access to the resettlement program's details,"* his haunting voice began, *"including blood work and other testing done on the candidates. I found hard-copies of these same lists with names crossed off."*

"What was so important about those names?"

"They matched with names chosen to go to a secondary program. People would show up at a waystation, and be offered contracts. Then they'd vanish."

Anthony cupped his chin in his hand as some of the names were highlighted and then simply vanished from the pages. The phantom book faded away, and Jordan's naked body returned to form. "Is all of this second-hand information or...?"

The priest shook his head sadly as he explained, *"I didn't believe it until I volunteered to work at the hub. The... the Fontaine Center."*

"Fontaine Center? I don't know it."

"You... wouldn't. It's a mixed... mixed use. Sanctuary, lodging, pantry, shuttle hub. A waystation for Church workers and special deliveries."

The necromancer paused for a moment and made a notation in the back of his head on that. "Shuttle? What type?"

A logo appeared out of thin air and spun slowly between them. It had a rail line between the words 'South' and 'Shore,' the former of which was textured with a beach and the latter, a small ocean wave, while the rail part was embossed by the letters 'B&L.' Anthony vaguely recognized it as some local rail line.

"Bus. Truck. Auto-hauler goes... monorail station. Hon... Honest ABE. I saw them sort out people and... and that's when it clicked and I knew. I couldn't do anything to stop it. I couldn't. I tried to ask one of them... a woman. She looked like she had final say on the corp side."

"Got a name for either her or the corp, by any freaking chance?"

"*Adams. Miss Andrea Adams,*" the remorseful spirit replied. "*I don't know who she or her goons worked with.*"

As he spoke, a handful of fresh images flitted in and out of the air around them. A few security goons in gray jumpsuits; a woman in a white pant-suit with blonde hair. Her face was partially covered by a mask that fit down over her eyes. Anthony focused on a badge on one of the sec-officers arms and forced it to dominate the scene.

"Well that's a name that keeps coming up in all the wrong ways. You were visited by Blackwash Security," the necromancer clarified. "I'd bet an Ultra-Monster that the bitch with them is Sojourn, given how close they seem to be."

"*Then, if Miller was right... and I watched them go.*"

"Probably, I hate to admit. But after that, you went up north, I take it? New Northern Italy?"

"*And they already knew. Knew some of it. The confessional information... it was the icing on the cake.*"

"So this Omari guy shows up and admits to being in some shady shit. You figured out it's with Sojourn, and then you traced his supply chain back to El-Rhodes," Anthony mused – more for the sake of the recording than anything else. "You see your bosses, they send you back here to play 'pass the potato,' and not long after, you get flattened. That about sum it up?"

The ghost gave a tired look over at his old body beside Anthony and allowed his shoulders to sag. "*Yes.*"

None of it was enough to go straight to court as it was; but that was more than enough to open an investigation... or twenty, at this rate. It was a solid given that the Church wouldn't be eager to provide assistance eagerly – if they were hell-bent on covering their tracks, and it seemed that they were – then anything they offered would be under the table *if* the cops were lucky. For a moment, he could almost understand why they'd want to go to the Grims to make a deal to have them handle it.

But, as it stood, there needed to be more. As pissed off as the AGU was, any attempt to deliver this to the cops – Alara included – would run a very real risk of getting shot in the face before he had a chance to explain anything. That meant his next stop was going to have to be the local Hoover Central field office.

And they *hated* incomplete stories.

"Four questions. Do you have any idea why El-Rhodes is doing this? Blackmail? Greed? Power?" He made a point to leave off 'racism.'

A jury would check that box all on their own.

"No. I don't. I genuinely thought we were doing good. I genuinely believed we were getting people on the right path. Out of Florida. Away from the Breakdown and the gangs."

'The Breakdown.' A quaint name for the largest semi-natural event that had hit the planet since Pompeii. A disaster borne of hubris, nth, and nukes, it was the reason why Florida was... Florida... and a large part of why Los San was so big. Anyone who could get out of the Flo-Penni did. The ones that couldn't?

El-Rhode's service wasn't the first, or the last, relocation program aimed at the area. Wasn't the first or last to be tainted with corp or gang shit, either. "Are you aware of any connection to *any* of the regional gangs? Gardeners? Sub-Soua Carties? Grimshanks? Other?"

Jordan's eyes flickered around the room as the ghost began to sweat. Except it wasn't sweat – for obvious reasons. It looked more like... oil. It sparked whenever it hit the summoning circle on the floor, none of which should have happened.

Undeterred, the priest went on. *"No. Omari said nothing about gangs. I suspected, but... I also breathed. It's Los San. It wasn't until the College sent me to speak to the ones they called 'The Twins' that I even..."*

"Yeah, Clare's an absolute delight," Anthony replied with a grunt and a curl of his lip. "The evidence you said you collected. Please, for the love of everything you've ever held dear, tell me you saved it."

Jordan's ghost shook again and he violently rejected the idea. *"N... no. None. Nothing. They... they made it clear. If I kept anything then... Anthony? Is that why they went after Katherine? Do they think she knows something?"*

"You called her when they showed up," the necromancer pointed out. "Don't you remember?"

"Remember what?"

Anthony's eyes went wide – just a little. But just enough. "Oh. Oh, shit. You don't..." he began before he took a deep breath and focused on the energy at his command. Coils of nth rolled along the faint streams of his blood and the cuts in his ribs billowed briefly. When he could think past the pain, he looked the dead man in his eyes. "I'm sorry to do this. I mean that."

"Mean... what? Anthony... I...?"

"Jordan Fisher," the necromancer began slowly as he dropped both of his hands to his sides and clenched his fists. Sometimes this type of revelation didn't go well. At this rate, he was counting on it. "Jordan – how did you die? Who killed you?"

The dumbest, slack-jawed look you could possibly imagine dawned on the priest's face. It lasted long enough for Anthony to save a picture for posterity. Then the ghost *twitched.*

A roiling wave of toxic nth billowed out from the summoning circle. Uncontrolled – no, *unfamiliar*, magic attempted to burst through Anthony's spellwork like an arrow. The spike made the necromancer gag; not from the recoil effect of the blast, but for how the blast *felt* across his aura.

While he tried to re-secure the circle, Jordan's eyes went wide as his jaw dropped below his collarbone in a grotesque display. Streamers of Anthony's blood began to roil under his phantom head as an oily black glow erupted along the lengths of the chains. Jordan started to scream.

Screaming didn't quite cut it. It was a wet sound, a shrill, wet, piercing noise that didn't sound human. It was matched with a hydraulic groan and a constant thrumming that Anthony recognized from the message Kath had played.

His skull imploded. Slowly, forcefully. Phantom bones and skin split. Oily black hands manifested on the sides of his temples. It squeezed as he screamed. The rest of his body began to follow suit; his arms were crushed, and his throat was violently pulped until it was little more than the width of a candy bar.

Anthony raised his arms to shield his eyes. It didn't stop the sounds, but at least it spared him the visuals. When the racket stopped, Jordan was gone.

An unpleasantly familiar form took his place.

Jordan's voice echoed from all around the room. "*He didn't give a name.*"

"He doesn't have to," the necromancer grunted. The prick was just under six feet tall, and had a suit on that probably cost more than Anthony's annual retirement package. He had on a stupid-looking top hat with leather trim and sunglasses that dangled on the end of his nose to match. "Harold Vincetti. I know him as Slash."

"*You've met?*"

"Yeah."

"*Did you kill him?*" Jordan's voice was twinged with an odd hopeful tilt. It wasn't at all like him, though the necromancer really couldn't blame him for it.

"No," Anthony replied slowly, "but I am starting to regret that decision. This is the guy that killed you? I need to hear you say it for it to count."

There was a very long pause from the spirit as Harold's form started to dissipate. "*No. He's... he's the one that asked the questions.*"

Something about the way he said it... "Jordan, who killed you?"

The body faded. In the fog, something grew out of Slash's brief form. It was huge; easily eight or nine feet tall. It was a pile of walking cybernetics and armor plates, but right smack in the middle of it was a human, or something that had been one, once. A grotesquely modified face peered through the fog with dead eyes that locked onto Anthony without flinching.

"*I had to give them everything I had. Do you understand? I had to.*"

"Good. God. What... what the *fuck*... is that?

The figure reached out through the fog, and suddenly Jordan's head manifested in the middle of its iron grip. Jordan looked up at Anthony and shuddered. "*I... I think....*"

"What? What do you *think*, Jordan?"

A heavy **whumph** resonated through the Reclamation Center's sound-proof walls and knocked a few loose items off a nearby shelf. The necromancer's blood went cold as he shoved his hand into his pocket for his phone. A second crash was joined by a scream of surprise from somewhere near the front desk.

"*I think it's coming to show you.*"

***

Screaming. Shouting. Cursing.

A few errant prayers for help.

The gunfight had started before they approached the van. Matty had stopped halfway across the street and clutched his head; he then said a few words that Alara simply couldn't make out before he collapsed to his knees in pain. A second later, and *she* felt the same wave that had taken him out; someone or *something* had spiked a wave of psychic nth into the ether without care for whoever might be effected by it.

She wasn't half as in-tune as he was, and the power-pulse was enough to make her feel like someone had scraped the inside of her skull with steel wool. Before she could even begin to recover from that, two jackasses with semi-autos and green football jackets spilled out the back of the van. It was borderline luck alone that she had time to bring her gun up before they started to fire.

The first one went down cleanly with a bullet just below his eye. The second one opened up with a spray 'n' pray burst that she barely avoided and a pedestrian behind her didn't. The civie screamed abruptly and hit the ground like a sack of potatoes while Alara brought her gun to bear on their second assailant.

Before she could return fire, she felt *it*.

Another surge of nth rolled out of the van like a shockwave. Whatever was in the van decided it liked the automatic-wielding gangster as much as she did, and killed him before she could. The vehicle's side panel blew out and the van practically bounced as some *thing* dropped more firepower than she'd ever seen in her life through the bottom of it.

An invisible wave of nth physically knocked her partner out of his kneel and bounced his head off the bumper of some Nu-Engie Wayster parked on the street. The impact knocked his ass out cold, but she could feel his aura enough to know it hadn't outright killed him. The same couldn't be said of the ganger-with-a-gun; the van's side panel had embedded itself, edge first, just below his ribs and halfway through his torso.

Her eyes flashed brilliant blue as she reached out with an unspoken spell and grabbed Matty with all the magical strength she could muster. Telekinesis wasn't exactly a science, and fell more in the frame of 'will an object to be moved from point A to point B,' than it was anything else. Effectively, what amounted to be invisible hands grabbed him by his torso and pulled him across the street and behind cover.

There wasn't time to do anything else.

As a fireball rolled out from under the van, the *thing* stepped out of the wreckage. Alara got one good look at it, and that was more than she wanted. It wasn't human. It wasn't Daem. It wasn't a gene-mutie. Whatever the hell it was?

Cyborgs. Androids. It was 2057; they weren't exactly *new*.

That *thing* wasn't any of the above, and it sure as *fuck* wasn't alive. Except it *was*, and she could tell it *was* very much alive by the vibrating undercurrent of rotten nth it put off in its ambient aura. It ignored the burning van, the dead gangers, and, more importantly, it ignored her.

It ignored everything – and went straight to the morgue.

A few more gunshots rang out as she checked over Matty. He wasn't dead and his aura was muted, but it wasn't fading. He was going to have a hell of a headache in the morning, but he'd be okay. A cursory pat down her stomach and upper thighs verified *she'd* be okay, too, at least for the moment. When Alara peered out from behind cover, she saw an asshole in a suit put a second trio of bullets into the ganger she'd shot dead.

The thug's head popped open with sparks and a tiny burst of flame with each bullet. His murderer's coat smoldered as he dusted himself off and slotted his pistol back in his holster. For a second, she thought about trying to engage.

Instead, he ignored her and walked back to the van. He reached inside, and a moment later, he was joined by a blonde-haired woman in a singed white pants-suit. She had some kind of gas or cyber-aug facial covering that kept Alara from seeing any other facial features – with the exception of her eyes. Her blazing yellow eyes radiated nth.

A type of nth that Alara didn't recognize.

A type of nth that washed over the street like a wave before both dead gangers stood up and lunged towards the downed officers. As they staggered forward, both the asshole in the suit and the mage in white took off on a fast jog in the other direction. As they ran, the mechanoid sent a fresh burst of plasma into the front of the morgue and opened a hole where the doors had been.

The assault didn't leave her with time to do anything but react to the newly arisen ghasts. But if anyone thought that a couple of errant zombies would be enough to slow her down, they were dead wrong. When her G-Locke didn't work on the ghasts, a pair of charged bolts of nth that removed what was left of their heads from their shoulders did. There wasn't enough of them left behind to interrogate later.

She'd beat herself up for it when she had time. Right now, she didn't. A fresh blast rolled out from the Recyc Center, and the detective was quick to run to it, but not until she stopped and broke into Anthony's car.

He'd complain later, if he could.

But he'd appreciate her doing it.

***

"Anthony, run."

"Run where, exactly?" demanded Anthony, frantically shoving a table against the cooler's only exit. "I can feel it. That's where you've been. You didn't cross over; you were collected."

"Eaten," Jordan whispered. *"I remember when it crushed my head, and then I felt nothing but cold. Cold and metal and rot. Then I saw them. Wires. Cables. Dipping in and around. Through my skin, through my... It's Hell, Anthony. I'm in Hell."*

Anthony cursed as he kicked the desk into place and pulled out his phone. "That's believable. Alright. You do nothing. You can't. So just shut the fuck up."

Jordan made one last attempt to free himself from the chains and circle that bound him. *"You don't want to suffer like I have, Anthony. Put the phone down and just GO."*

"Can't do that."

"And what exactly do you intend to do?"

"The only thing I can," Anthony replied as he reached up and pressed a hidden spot just behind his ear on the left side. "Oh, he's gonna be so pissed at me…"

Jordan stopped struggling, fixing on him with a bewildered stare. *"He… who? Who could possibly be worth…?"*

"God, if really you buy into that shit" Anthony quipped as he desperately ran his fingers through his shirt.

"God has never answered a phone call in history."

"Yeah, well if not God, I'm calling someone with His ego. Fuck, where is… there. That'll do," he rambled as he noticed a one-way window that bounced his reflection back at him. He needed to be able to have his face on the recording just in case his face didn't make it through the next few minutes intact.

"You aren't making any sense. You need to run!"

He did. He knew he did, but if he didn't make it through whatever was about to happen, he wasn't going to let anyone else make it through unscathed either. A little light behind his ear flashed twice, and he started to speak.

"My name is Anthony Pierson. LI-NEC USTS-392. It is… fuck. It's 5-28-57. LWT A-1-6-6-9 is my legal and binding testament," Anthony recited before adding, "last or other. Testament contains Last Words Testimony with Abberdine, Clare; Reyes, Carlos; Fisher, Jordan. Aud-Vid-Mem notations from Pierson, Anthony. Testament is sealed for transmission. Testament is being sent to an outside third party due to hostile conditions, and should be considered to include Last Words Testimony from Pierson, Anthony, if it comes to it."

"RUN, dammit! I can't be there for Kath when you fuck up this time!"

"Oh, so you *can* curse. Cool," the necro growled as he turned away from the mirror and *connected* with the devices buried in his head. It took a moment to remind his brain what steps to take and in what order to get the overriding command system to work. It was as user-friendly as a cold fusion reactor, but when it did work, it was the greatest thing since holo-porn.

"Anthony, you are about to die! Run!"

Anthony punched in a number on his phone and dove behind a gurney as the racket outside grew louder and more desperate by the second. As he flipped it over and crouched behind it, the number rang away like mad. "The shoulder mod's connected to the/modem. The modem's connected to the/WiFi. Now hear the words I say…"

As the curse left his lips, the phone beeped and an unmistakable voice popped up on the other end. "You-you-you are aware that a bo-bo-bomb just went off right out-out-outside your location –"

"No shit," Anthony hissed. "Dropping a file to my phone, Fixx. Grab it and go."

"Gra-gra-grab what, Mr. Pierson? I'm no-no-not in the business of accepting –"

He picked up the phone and ran the front of it in an arc around the room. "Accept the damn download, Fixx. This isn't a joke."

The screen flashed a few times before a hint of raw concern came across the line. "Dead man and a dead man's soul? All in one room? Bom-bom-bombs and police-in-distress codes going off – Mr. Pierson, you've been a bus-bus-busy boy, haven't you?"

Anthony was going to reply with something witty.

It would've floored Fixxer and left him wanting more. Instead, Doc Gainsig's head burst through the door and slammed against the cabinet doors with a wet *thunk* and a clatter of shattered cybertech. The rest of his body followed a heartbeat later.

What followed his corpse was one of the worst things Anthony had ever seen. It crumbled the doorframe as it lumbered through: it was a mismatched patchwork of metal and exposed, naked skin. And in the few places where it didn't have that, it had some kind of plexiglass shell covering otherwise exposed organs submerged in a pus-colored soup of lubricants, nutrients, and God only knew what else.

A muted, "What th-th-the fuck is that?" came out of his phone before the screen went black, and the rest of the monstrosity came into view. It was effectively just a human torso with the head still attached and part of a flesh-and-blood arm bolted to a metal shoulder. The limb was wrapped in more cybernetics than Anthony had seen in his entire life. None of them seemed to *match*. The other arm was just a long, smooth barrel.

A gun, obviously.

Whatever the fuck it fired, he didn't want to find out.

It did have a jacket, a detached part of his mind noted. More of a trench-coat with the sleeves ripped out, but at least it wasn't completely naked. It wasn't much to go on, but if you threw a hat on the motherfucker it might make it through a dark street for a minute or two.

What flesh Anthony could see was mottled and gray. Its mouth hung open, slack on one side, while a mechanical piston struggled to force it closed. It was a mockery of everything and anything human, and at the same time, he *knew* some sick bastard had done this *deliberately* to make it *look* human enough to let people be comfortable around it.

They'd failed, and they'd relished in their failure.

This thing was *dead*. Anthony could smell it. Literally and metaphorically. It was a Tech-U-Up Shop wrapped in a corpse. All the hopes he'd had that he'd gotten things wrong went out the window as Gainsig's head rolled to a complete stop. Fuck the Army, fuck the Feds, fuck the NPC and the shitty mutant sand fleas that lived with them, this was the single worst thing the necromancer had seen in his life, and it wasn't even fucking close.

It was taller than a human, wider than a human, and angrier than a human. It swept the room with a cold gaze from both of its eyes — one that shone a nearly blindingly bright blue and the other that shone sickly green — and stopped with a mechanical jerk when it caught sight of Jordan's struggling ghost. It made it two steps through the room when a *third* eye implanted in a plate of metal and wires that covered the left side of its head saw the necromancer as he failed to hide behind his cover.

It lifted its right arm — the weapon attached at the elbow — and started to level it right at Anthony's face. There was barely any time to react. He shot his own hand out and willed a stream of concentrated, decay-laced nth out of his palm with what little strength he had left.

The toxic spray of magic worked like an acidic fog. Magic scoured some of the acrylic shell around its center torso and melted away the plastic in a rush of vile steam that made the necromancer gag even as he channeled it across the room. The mech tried to wave away the cloud and stepped to the side to avoid as much of it as it could, but wherever the spray touched, faux skin and metal parts began to smoke.

Aside from that?

It froze. For a few seconds. Which was something.

Green ooze flooded out from fresh holes in its chest. The mech stopped trying to track his opponent while lights around its ocular ports flashed on and off. While it tried to comprehend what had just happened,

Anthony flung flickers of less-obvious nth out to get a feel for what was inside the beast as he scrambled to find better cover.

What clawed back at him were souls – a whole hive of them. All were in pain, wracked in confusion, and hanging on by faint shreds. All of them were trapped within the shell of the putrid, loathsome wretched just feet away from where Anthony stood.

The creature dropped its head back down and fixed its remaining eyes on Anthony's face. The lights in them shifted from blue and green to a single, angry, orange. His spells had left gashes that had melted away putrid skin, but the carbon plates beneath were left unscathed.

Apparently, it had armor.

Of *course* it had armor.

Anthony didn't have time to think much else. Steel feet slammed against the tile floor as the creature launched itself across the room. Its three-clawed hand caught the necromancer by his face, and slammed the back of his skull into one of the cabinet doors without mercy or effort.

It didn't kill him, but it left him dangling a foot off the ground. Anthony's metal hand did jack and shit in equal parts to push back against the beast. A loud hydraulic hiss split the air as a strange Gregorian-style chant began to roll from the cyborg's mouth.

As the droning noise grew louder with each heartbeat, tattooed runes etched across its forehead and chest ignited with a fierce red glow. On the other side of the exam room, matching runes on the chains along Jordan's soul began to do the same – and they were joined by the scars on the priest's corpse as they lit up in tandem.

The claws tightened, and Anthony could feel scorching heat that emanated from them as if they were trying to brand him. Worse than his flesh, Anthony could feel the monster burning straight into his soul. His soul was more than a bit battered, but dammit, it was his, and he damn well intended to keep it that way.

As it squeezed, Anthony managed to get his good hand on the bastard's chest. Green slime and a foamy concoction of something vile coated his fingers, but another pulse of nth shot through the muck and into its chest like a depth charge. It stunned the beast, if only for a second. He had no idea what he was going to do next, but he didn't have to decide.

Lieutenant Dimir chose for him.

Fresh gunfire erupted into the room just as LSPD-issued armor-piercing rounds slammed into the mech's back. It wobbled and it squeezed Anthony's head even harder. The pressure was enough to make him feel his bones beginning to bend – and those were not bones that were supposed to *bend*.

Blearily, teetering on the edge of consciousness, Anthony saw Alara fling something through the air at his head. The cyborg had to have seen it too; it just didn't care.

It should've.

"BLACKBURN!"

Anthony's shotgun stopped cold in mid-air, spun, and jammed itself underneath the bio-mech's dripping front teeth. *"Well, howdy,"* Marshal said cheerily before an enormous, deafening blast erupted out of the business-end of the boom-stick.

It worked.

Teeth, flesh, metal, and bone blew away in all directions. The cyborg dropped Anthony without a second thought and took a few stumbling steps backward. Alara changed out magazines in her pistol and resumed firing into anything that even remotely looked like a squishy part as the necromancer scrambled to get out of the way.

The Marshall, bless his long-dead heart, eagerly took on the role of distraction. A second shell to the head rocked the walking corpse backward but didn't bring it down. A third went right to its chest, scattering plastic and even more chunks of foul, decaying tissue.

Anything else would have dropped. Literally anything else, but not that bastard. Alara had her hand on Anthony's shoulder in a death grip before he could push her away. "We gotta go! We gotta go now!"

It wasn't a bad idea, just not the right one. He had five seconds to decide which move to make. Right or wrong. Just five. The necromancer watched in horror as the bio-mech took a swing at Blackburn and made the spirit dis-corporate for a little more than a heartbeat.

It was Jordan who made the choice for him, even though the churcher didn't know it. Each time the mech took a swing, the chains binding his spirit blossomed to life. Each time they did, Jordan screamed. Each time he screamed, Anthony felt the souls trapped inside the monstrosity scream, too. When Jordan screamed for God to help, Anthony's ego decided to answer in Heaven's stead...

...and with a whole lot of Hell behind him.

The mech brought its gun-arm up and unleashed a blast of red-hot plasma that roasted the air where Blackburn had been floating and absolutely obliterated one of the cabinet walls in a thundering mix of smoke and molten debris. The blast sent a shock wave through the room that knocked Alara down and made Doc Gainsig's corpse bounce across the floor…

…and it also blew open nearly a dozen different coolers.

Coolers with bodies inside them.

Bodies that bounced on their trays. Trays that slid out of their storage slots. Broken men and women who had long since moved on to whatever life lay beyond this one. Bodies that were exactly what Anthony needed, even as the sprinklers kicked on and soaked the room with foul-smelling fire-suppressing foam like a bubble-rave in a slaughterhouse.

Blackburn took another hit, even as the necromancer barked out orders to Alara. There was no time for discussion, and even though she thought he was utterly insane, she followed along. Her eyes took on a brilliant blue flare as she reached out for three different things all at once:

The pathologist's head.

The pathologist's corpse.

And the bag holding what was left of Jordan's face.

As they violently tumbled across the room, Blackburn emptied another slug into the biomech's gut. The shot tore free chunks of wires and yellow bone free and brought the creature down to one knee. However, that didn't stop it from thrusting its clawed hand through the mist and spinning it like a three-pronged blender blade in the middle of the Marshall's spectral stomach.

Blackburn screamed in pain as the runes on the claw flared a bright orange while the metal spun inside him like a lawnmower blade. Whatever magic the mech was using erupted in an electrical flash that blew the ghost apart in a foggy mess. Had it launched that attack a minute earlier, it would've spelled doom for everyone else.

But it was a minute late.

Anthony punched a hole in Gainsig's chest with his left arm as he continued to bark instructions at the Aby-squad cop. She grabbed the doc's bloodied head and charged across the room with it tucked under her arm like a pro Pyro-Bowl player. Her target?

Jordan's cabinet.

Anthony's? Gainsig's heart.

The necromancer ripped his bloody fist free as the cyborg turned around and focused on him again. An arc of fresh nth followed and flowed around Anthony's arm, but not into his body. He didn't need to absorb it, only channel it. He needed to push it away and then yank on it as hard as he could.

This time, every corpse in the room responded.

Bodies bounced out of their trays. Cabinet doors shuddered. Corpses that had been rudely spilled out of coolers floated up off the floor. The monster reacted, too, and doubled forward as the force of Anthony's call worked on flesh and stolen souls alike.

Streamers of black, yellow, and white light radiated away from the bodies like clouds of steam. Jordan's spirit flickered while the circle around him began to spark on the floor. The self-inflicted cuts on his side opened wider, but not a single drop of blood spilled out. Essences and auras rushed from every corner of the room and slipped under his flesh.

Just like at the Down, it was death. It was energy. It was his.

It was his and ripe for the calling.

Jordan thrashed a bit as his body tried to roll off its shelf, but Alara had other plans. She caught his corpse and forcibly shoved it back onto the tray. A heartbeat later, it was shoved back into its cabinet by her own nth-charged will. She slammed the door shut and pushed the doc's head up against a biometric scanner in one fluid motion.

A touch of her magic made his eyes pop wide open.

A lot of Anthony's magic made the bodies in the coolers launch themselves in a macabre storm of cold skin, broken bones, and atrophied limbs. Anthony tapped almost every last bit of juice in his chest and turned the scattered bodies into a whirlwind of flesh and bone shards that clawed away at the mech's skin. Impact after impact ripped away pieces of rot, strands of wire, and bits of plastic.

The flesh storm was a useful distraction.

The real show was waiting in a little plastic bag.

Anthony forced himself upright and extended his fist down at the goo-filled bag. Chunks of the ex-churcher ripped out of the package like they were being pulled toward a magnet, but there was only one thing in the entire mess that he needed.

Probing tendrils of invisible nth worked through the material plane and sought out their prize. Every part of the corpse was dead and mastery over the dead meant mastery over the individual parts. Even the broken ones. Even the ones that he'd wanted to break himself. Organ death. Cell death.

Death was death. The bigger the bits, the more energy they had.

But death was still just death.

With a final flex of his fingertips, Jordan's jawbone ripped free of the bag and planted itself in his palm. Nth, itself, didn't seem to care about trivial human concepts like 'good' or 'evil.' There weren't a lot of signs that the universe as a whole cared, either. But, there were entities in the vast void beyond the mortal world that seemed to like things done In A Certain Way.

It was known that various *things* had inherent 'charges' to them. Actions had consequences. Not all of those consequences manifested in person. A dead holy man? If he was true to the words he professed? For some reason, that gained attention.

That attention came from Things that didn't like to share. They — whatever They were — didn't like it when Their toys were accosted. They were also, sometimes, willing to help right a wrong… if you asked nicely enough.

There was a reason why both the Catholics and the Church of Angelic America kept the bones of their Saints stashed away under lock and key. Playing a game of 'damned or divine' was a different type of metaphysical mumbo-jumbo than what Anthony liked to play with or even try to wrap his head around.

The DoD steadfastly did not give a shit. Dead was dead. Deal with it.

Anthony dealt.

As power raced along Jordan's jaw, he aimed the dripping piece of gore-streaked bone at the utter abomination. A push of nth down his hand caused skin, gum, and an errant filling to fall away, leaving just the jawbone itself in his hand. It wasn't until he spoke that the golem froze — and Alara damn near shit herself at the fierceness behind his words.

"**ENOUGH OF THIS SHIT.**" The jawbone took on a brilliant white shine as the words left his mouth. "**I AM A NECROMANCER…**"

The animated corpse took a single staggering step forward. Sparks erupted out of its bullet-mangled hip. A gray chunk of intestine slipped out of the broken plastic along its lower abdominal cavity. A deep gurgling noise rumbled out of the shredded mess it had left for a throat.

Blackburn had done a hell of a lot of damage, and the whirlwind of bones had scoured almost every piece of flesh off its body. Alara recognized a simple fact then and there: it had more than enough ability to rip an entire precinct worth of cops to shreds or wipe out an entire gang if it wanted. It was built to be a weapon, and if it faced down anything or anyone short of a tank, it'd win.

The plasma-rifle it had would've given a tank a bad day, too.

Anthony wasn't either of those things.

"**SO YOU BELONG TO ME,**" he shouted as heavy streamers of white fog whipped from the bone in his hand and lashed at the runes etched into the abomination's metal plates.

Alara didn't wait for further instructions. Her fist slammed into a big red button on the side of Jordan's cabinet. The doc's head had been enough to release the biometrics and prep the chamber to go into processing mode. When it kicked on, two things happened at once: the plasma furnace obliterated Jordan's corpse....

...and his spirit caught fire.

The jawbone ignited, too. That particular blaze was short-lived, and it faded nearly instantly. The bone was left in pristine condition as soon as the flames vanished, even as raw, visible nth lashed out from it like an organic ball of napalm.

Jordan's spirit screamed. There wasn't any way around that. He screamed, he suffered, and he burned. It was hard to say what he actually felt, but there was a transference of sensation from physical mediums to spiritual ones in certain situations. This one was textbook.

There'd be time to apologize later.

If they lived through it.

As Jordan burned, the bio-mech lumbered toward Anthony. Sickening green fluids poured out of every hole and joint it had. A half-skull made of titanium and steel shuddered with every step it took. Its eyes glistened and flashed with a rainbow of lights and activity. It stretched out its arm and leveled its plasma cannon at the necromancer's head...

...and froze.

What connection it had with Jordan's essence detonated. Feedback from the pain in the priest's soul rushed through the mech and immolated whatever controls, batteries, and tech it had buried inside its heart. The runes and spells that littered every other inch of its shell caught fire.

It froze in mid-motion as thick black smoke started to pour off its exoskeleton. Its head continued to jerk back and forth. Fingers twitched and trembled. Larger gouts of gore pulsed out of its ruined chest.

Anthony ducked under its cannon and very calmly flipped the jawbone upside down – and drove it right through the chunks of acrylic over where he assumed a heart would be. The bone slid down with supernatural force and penetrated the golem with ease.

Just like he'd done with Carlos and Clare, he wrapped his will around the first vestige of death he could get his essence to latch onto. Without a single word, he pulled. He pulled at it with every ounce of might he had left.

Every burning soul it had inside its shell followed.

There was no way Anthony could absorb them, not even at his best. As they rushed into his essence, he pushed them right back out. A torrent of necrotic energy coursed through his veins as he aimed what felt like a runaway train back at its station and let loose.

Raw, poisoned, incredibly *toxic* nth ripped into the bio-mech and ravaged it. Every last piece of organic material melted into a dripping slush. Every piece of plastic coating its organs withered and turned into hard chunks of slag. Insulated wires burned away like hayseeds introduced to a match.

The same souls that had given it power to even exist stripped it bare from the outside in and back again before dissipating from this plane of reality into the next. The only biological remnant left intact was the jawbone-turned-locus-turned-maybe-holy-relic. It quit glowing, though, and Anthony took that as a sign that the Things That Had Taken Interest were simply no longer interested.

That was fine.

It was all fine.

The mech wasn't. A reactor of some kind emitted an angry blue light buried behind the mech's heart as brand-new blue flames started to roll out of every open hole it had. As it collapsed, a keening high-pitched whine joined the fun as fresh gouts of black smoke followed.

It took Anthony five seconds to realize the light was one-hundred percent anthenium radiation, a leftover charge from the souls it had stored inside. Two more to realize it was being powered *directly* by a full-blown crydasta, and that meant that they were all about to be blown to the moon and back. As far as he was concerned, there wasn't a damn thing he could do about it other than kiss his own ass goodbye.

But anthenium was just nth in solid form.

Alara wasn't called one of the LSPD's strongest mages for nothing. She balled her hands up as the crydasta ruptured, and the flames both started and stopped in an explosive rush almost the magnitude of an old-school nuke. A single, basketball-sized fireball raged in the center of where the mech's chest had been as she forced the energy into a stabilized sphere.

A concussive wall of heated air ripped across the room and sent Anthony flying, although the detective forced the energy to expend itself right where it was and kept the bulk of the blast from going any further. The effort was exhausting, and the effects from it effectively vaporized most of the mech where it stood.

It was bad.

She kept it from being so much worse.

Once the flames consumed themselves, the resulting slag flowed into a small crater left behind as she dropped to her knees. When she could finally stand up again, Alara staggered over and took Anthony's cheeks into her hands.

Her blue eyes did their best to bore holes into his. She gasped for air as she tried to speak to him with an exhausted, "Fucking hell, Anth. I've never… fuck. I've heard of combat necros but that… you never said… you just said you were INT-OPS!"

"I was," he croaked through parched lips. "And I was stupid."

"What do…?"

He let his head roll back and quietly 'thunk' against a steel door. "I lost friends. Any fucker can shoot. Anyone. But me? Had all this power. Used it to root around in heads. Knew it could do things. When I had to use it, I didn't know how. So, I lost. Lost friends. Lost my arm. Lost my wife. Same thing. Didn't know how to deal. So, I didn't; I lost."

"That's not…"

"All the power Death has, I could touch," he rambled as blood suddenly *poured* out of the cuts on his ribs. The world started to spin and his breathing started to slow down. Alara saw the nth around him grow calm and still before she realized what had happened, and there was absolutely dick she could do about it. "Had power. Didn't use it. Happened once. Nearly killed me."

Her hands frantically dug through her pockets as she scrambled to find her phone. "Dammit Anthony, don't you fucking dare! I fucking mean it, you sack of shit; I will find someone to raise you from the dead and make you scrub the sewer; I swear to shit…"

He managed a weak smile before the room went black. "Now I've got power. Made my ass *learn* to use it when I have to. Ain't losing again. Not… not now."

Unfortunately, his heart disagreed.

7. A CRIMINAL INFORMANT
Tuesday, May 29th, 8:09 AM

There were certain sounds in the world you knew when you heard them. It was just a matter of life, of living. The engine roar of a 2001 Che-Bolt, the soft gurgle of a coffee pot, the way that rain dripped down from an overflowing gutter.

The steady beep of a heart monitor.

That last one was something of a buzzkill, especially when it was the first thing you heard when you woke up. The next noise Anthony recognized was the sound of a plas-cuff rattling, fastened securely to his arm. A familiar buzz emanated from the access node in his shoulder that basically said, 'Hey, homie. Yo shit ain't plugged in.' Hopefully it was just a SysOver-Ride plug. Standard issue for most LEOs, and an absolute bitch to unhook if you didn't have access to the datapad it was synced to.

It was intentionally a bitch.

The other, probably most important revelation: he wasn't dead.

From the dull, persistent pain in his chest, Anthony knew he should be grateful for that. A feeling that was amplified when he cracked his swollen eyes and realized where he was. There were pale pink walls with white trim along the top, and that was a dead giveaway. It was supposed to be daisies, but Kath had always said they looked like little white and yellow buttholes.

She wasn't wrong. Which meant he was in one and only one place:

University of Anthenium Medicine. ICU Recovery.

First time for a visit, but she'd talked about it enough to know.

Nor did the bad news stop there. "Ah, you're awake. Hey, so, we haven't met. I'm Matty."

Anthony forced his eyes open a little wider and took stock of his guest, and immediately wished he'd kept them closed. Had they met? Not officially, and with reason. "Oh shit. Well, at least you're not AGU."

He was, in a way, worse. AGU would shoot you. This asshole? This asshole would make your brain wish he had, if he wanted to. Matty cracked out a giggle, but didn't make it all the way through the laugh before he touched the bandages around his head with a wince. "They're kinda busy right now. Because of you, mostly. Thing is though, Cap'n Yers wants to use you as an actual punching bag, so if he gets his way, you two are gonna have time to hang out soon. Some of us are even taking bets."

"Well, that's… wonderful. How lucky can I get?"

"Not very. Even before this," Matty said as he waved his hand around the room, "you weren't runnin' higher than 5:1 on the office pool."

There was so much truth to that statement it wasn't worth being offended. "Alara? She okay?"

"Honestly, yes, and from what she said, you're each other's reason to still be breathing. She got discharged an hour ago, but she commandeered a room down the hall for a nap. Bitched until I agreed to come in and play guard. She got pretty banged up, all told. Then again, *you're* the one that had a heart attack."

Anthony carefully lifted his good hand and ran it down his chest and groaned out loud. Silver-Honey Binder Pads. Nub-Elec monitor probes. What felt suspiciously like Oni-tak stitches along his sides. Get 'em wrapped around and sewn into you once, and you'd remember how it felt the rest of your life. It was like being stuck in a damn zipper. "I did?" It also implied that someone wanted him to have a longer one. "I don't suppose they said how bad it was…?"

"Bad enough. Choice was either bring you here, or just leave you at the Rec center and let nature do its thing. Guess there was an argument about which would save the most time," Matty replied glibly. "I don't know if you care, but *I've* got a splitting headache. They've got me jacked on stims; couldn't sleep if I wanted to. Concussion, shitty one."

Anthony believed him. Cared? Debatable. "Oh. Cool."

Neither one spoke for several minutes. Talking was exhausting. Breathing was exhausting. Everything was exhausting. Matty was exhausting. From what Anthony knew of the cop, he was tiring on a *good* day. Today – whatever day today was – was already shaping up to not be one of those.

Still, it could be worse.

Finally, Matty the Hat decided to interrupt the beeping little monitors on every side of Anthony's head again. "Dude, you fucked up. You soooo fucked up. I can't even guess about how bad you've fucked up – because you've so badly fucked up, *I'd* get fired if I fucked up half of the way like you fucked up – but, Alara made me promise to tell you something in case you woke up before she got back. An' since you're lying there as exciting and fun as a bag of rocks in the border wasties, I may as well."

"Being fair about it, I just got the shit kicked out of me by some kind of cyborg that shouldn't exist so yeah, 'bag of rocks' is high on my list of life goals."

"Well, the good news is, you won't have to say much. But first," he began as he picked up a bottle of generic caffi off the floor and passed it over, "I'm going to give you a drink because I'm a nice guy, then I'm gonna have to go. But, then Alara is gonna come in, and she's gonna have a question."

"Am I going to like it?"

Down the hall, an incessant, shrill alarm split the air. A series of shouts from assorted doctors and nurses and a robotic overhead chimed in for an 'AdvanceTeam Cart.' It was just a friendly reminder that someone else was having a worse day than he was.

Undaunted, Matty carried on.

"You'll have a choice. It's entirely up to you. Which, I mean, that's scary, ain't it? We all just go about doing what we are supposed to do, or live with the choices we've already made. Our choices next to never become choices about what we can do next. It's scary as shit, if you ask me."

The necromancer blinked slowly as he wrapped his drug-addled mind around that. "You... think having choices is scary?"

"Absolutely! I mean, it's the nu-American Dream, ain't it? Have a place? Have a goal, a job, a task? A thing you're supposed to do? Know exactly where, what, when how every day? Every minute planned out? Not having that is crazy as hell."

Anthony shook his head. Or at least, he tried to. The movement sent a jolt of nausea through his gut and a matching ache across his shoulders. "I mean if you call free will hell, then sure. Speaking of – am I there? In Hell, I mean, to clarify. The question keeps popping up."

"No, no, you're not... yet."

"Yet?"

The cop raised two fingers. Surprisingly, not his middle ones. "This choice has two results. If you say no, you'll be arrested. I will take you downtown in a tank, and you'll never see sunlight again. You'll be safe and secure, and never have a worry again. We'll take the best care of you."

If that was the 'no,' then the 'yes' had to suck.

"And... if I say yes?"

"You will get to leave. Nobody will be happy about it, and you'll probably get shot before tomorrow morning," Matty replied earnestly. "But, you'll have protection. Given the bounty on your head it might not help. Some of my fellow officers are toeing the line of bankruptcy, so they may just cash in on it themselves. Still, protection offered via suicide by cop is better, sometimes, than the alternative. I'm thinkin' there's a lot of *alternatives* waiting to make your acquaintance after everything comes to light. You could make worse choices."

"And, you're of the opinion that I need protection, even if it's a bullet."

"Even if, yea. Alara is under the opinion that you're going to say yes, so I took the liberty of ordering some spare ceri-max to be sent to my room. Just my luck, I forgot about it after I got discharged, in case you happen to know anyone that'd want to put it on before they walk out the doors."

"That sounds like a yes."

He shrugged and stretched with a wince of his own. "The choice is really up to you. I don't even know which one I'd pick. On one hand, you might've started World War Four to hear the talkin' heads ramble about it. On the other, well, you've kinda started World War Four and some other people seem to be all overjoyed about it. And I... I dunno, dude. I dunno."

The casual suggestion that the 'world war' line wasn't a joke gave Anthony enough reason to try to sit up, which tripped an alarm from one of the machines behind his head. A particularly rude beep blasted through the room followed by an overly-pleasant woman's voice instructing him to stay right where he was: someone would be in for him shortly. Matty watched it all with a bemused smirk.

"C'mon man. I shot up a Reproc shop, not..."

"You don't... well, I mean, I guess you wouldn't."

"I wouldn't *what*?"

"Maybe I should just turn on the IMD for you," Matt replied as he stood up and waved his hand at a monitor in the corner. "Oh, and hey, if you say 'yes,' shoot a text to your handyman. Dude is fuckin' *pissed* about... a plumbing job?"

"Yeah, he gets like that. Thanks."

"Oh no bro, that thanks ain't big enough. I'm gonna be a really nice guy and call Yers next."

Anthony's blood went cold, and the monitor made an unfriendly 'blat' in response. "Why...? That doesn't seem that nice."

Matty smirked and pressed two fingers to his forehead before he drew an imaginary line between them. "Ab/*Psy*," he replied as a soft buzz tickled the back of the necromancer's good eye. "I'm gonna tell him your *intent* was to avoid hurting his boys, but you couldn't surrender due to extenuating legal circumstances. Actually, I'm about to be your new best friend."

"I... I like new friends."

"Ab/*Psy*," Matty repeated with a chuckle. "Don't have to try to lie when you're around me, won't do any good. Naw man. I had a good look-see. I know more shit than what hit the cloud, and I'm gonna couch it a bit."

"Why...?"

The detective shrugged his shoulders. "Because I'm not dead, and you made an effort to flatten the thing that tried to kill me. This ain't a perfect damn world, and I appreciate people trying to make it better – even if they *should've* gone to the cops first."

"Oh," Anthony whispered. "After shooting the second guy I figured that I might have to cover my ass some and..."

"And I get it, I get it man," Matty interrupted. "Besides. Necros. Psychers. We do the same shit. Only difference is, mine's with the living."

That was so damn **wrong** Anthony couldn't even formulate a retort. Matty was out of the room before he could make one, so he settled down to focus on the news – and today's broadcast du-jour was one of the national networks. Not really surprising; *Certified All-National News* was the de-facto winner of the last round of rating wars.

You couldn't walk into a doc's office, mechanic's shop, or a florist without seeing their tagline splattered across every monitor in the building. *Certified News*! *Certified Fresh*! *Certified National*! Certified bullshit half the time, but at least it was appropriately labeled.

It wasn't a good sign to see his face plastered right above it. While he quietly grumbled about the ugly as hell photo they'd used for his face, the news played out in a slow, steady chyron across the bottom of the display. No, not one.

Two. Two chyrons. Which made it worse.

So much worse.

The first clue about how bad of a mess he was in came from the date: nearly a full eighteen hours after the throw-down in the morgue. In the news business, that was practically a year. The second clue – third, if you counted the worst photo of his face ever taken – emblazoned in the top right-hand corner were the words *P. S.: The Last Words Doctrine* displayed beside a pair of talking heads in the center of the screen.

It was never a good sign when the national news covered the legal aspects of your job. Less so when the subtext below read *Leaked postmortem testimony from Pastor Jordan L. Fisher – Accusations from beyond the grave, or a shared delusion from anthenium-poisoned brains?* That was a newer argument against magic in general mixed from the competing fringes of both the Church and the national atheist movement that went by the name 'The Natural Scientific Institute.'

Between the two, they found common cause in condemning anything that couldn't be powered with a nuke, a buck, or a CPU. They were at the forefront of 'necromancy is bad' legislation, and were just an utterly miserable pile of people to get in bed with. Thankfully, the movement struggled to find acceptance, even though they could always find a cam and a microphone.

Most likely, that line of crap would be replaced in a week's time by some other insulting byline. Anthony cast a swiping motion with his fingers towards the screen. The chyron remained, but the heads changed to a static image of police and media stationed outside the Cathedral of Eagles on the Church's own private island outside city limits. It was a mega-church through and through, complete with a photo-op-enabled soup kitchen and shelter that just somehow always had exactly room to sit *one* extra person whenever the Sine-Pastor deigned to leave his gold-plated throne to come and visit.

As if on cue, an image of the Sine-Pastor's head replaced Anthony's. *"According to sources in both LSPD and the FBI, Sine-Pastor Charlie El-Rhodes is being sought for questioning in regard to allegations of illegal body-harvesting operations,"* read the closed-captioning. *"When reached for comment, neither the Church of Angelic America nor any regional LEO would verify these rumors. Nevertheless, the accusation comes following the jaw-dropping –"*

Before it could finish, the IMD was shut off by a nurse with a chip on her shoulder the size of a Ground-to-Air Anti-Material launcher. The conversation was short, to the point, and contained no less than three utterances of the words 'foolishness,' 'near-death,' and 'n-tox.' The latter wasn't surprising, though he took a little offense to the former.

She absolutely did not care.

The verdict was pretty straight-forward and utterly miserable. It was just a simple takotsubo cardiomyopathy with nth-vibrational dueling arrhythmia, or in other words, "You had two different heart rhythms for too long," and, "You showed signs of excessive nth-manipulation abuse." Which itself was another way to say, *'using nth has a physical cost, you moron,'* though she was nice enough not to say it. By their powers combined, his heart stopped.

Eventually, she finished informing him that he had a new, temporary PLA-based cardio-rythmic stimulator that would dissolve into his bloodstream by next month – a joy of the newer models of plant-based bio-med stuff. Assuming he lived that long. She also made it a point to remind him that if he'd popped his heart anywhere *other* than within a fifteen-minute call range of an Ambu-Drone Lift, he'd be plant *food* instead of being kept alive with plant *fiber*.

She also had words for the non-standard heart assistance he had stuck in his chest. She asked what it was. He declined to reply. She asked again, and he declined a second time. "I can't tell you, you shouldn't ask, and if you keep asking, I have to tell somebody you're asking. Neither you nor they will like that."

The Wicked Witch of the Gulf quit asking.

It was for the best, really.

A few minutes later the nurse disappeared back into the bowels of the hospital proper, only to be replaced not by Matty's 'woman with questions', but rather a legally-mandated social worker. She'd "come to see how a decorated combat vet" was doing after "suffering a series of traumatic experiences." She expressed extra concern about the "signs of self-harm and mutilation" on his chest, arm, and thigh.

He didn't tell her what those decorations were.

It wasn't worth the time to explain it.

She meant well enough. She would've been nicer still, were it not for the thin, flashy string of cybernetics leading from her ear to her jaw, which only served to remind Anthony of what had put him in the hospital to begin with. She bore that perfect mixture of chipper and helpful that burrowed directly beneath Anthony's skin in under a minute, flat.

Nor did it help that ten seconds after she picked up his file and timidly asked if it was true that he had been part of the Fall of New Babil that she set down her pile of flyers and dug a special one out of the middle of the stack. It was emblazoned with the American flag and a giant stamp from the Army's PR core. "We know that veterans returning from the conflict with the New Persian Caliphate occasionally have concerns about interacting with certain segments of modern American society. Please, be sure to take this, and don't hesitate to call my office at any time if you have worries."

Anthony took one look at it and rolled his eyes. It was a magazine-sized feel-good-and-fuck-your-feelings piece of public relations bullshit titled, *Daem-Sapiens: They're Just Your Neighbors.* You couldn't tell a line cook at the bar that you've served these days without getting a network code to go visit that bloody site.

The sad thing was that half the service was in need of the reminder.

The rest of them were generally just grateful for the free toilet paper. It was yet another case of 'good ideas gone stupid' straight from the Department of Veteran Affairs' 'Social Re-Acclimation Service.' which was known better as the 'Oops, We Accidentally Trained Up Some Racist Murderers And We Feel Really Bad About it So Please Forget How We Conditioned You' Corps.

The rest of the conversation was short, easy, condescending, and finished when she put her hand on his chest. "No matter what you're going through, know you can always return to U-Anth-Med. We have a commitment to anyone, and everyone, and to who they are inside." She left after she slid one of her cards into his hand and made him promise that if he ever felt unsafe about life after his service, to just let her know.

It wasn't worth the effort to remind her that he was currently on the freaking newsnets *because* he was unsafe. He doubted it'd make a difference to the psych-drone-ette and her rehearsed script even if he did. That lack of safety continued almost as soon as she left.

Anthony didn't get time to flip the news back on before one of the parties to the news came in and flipped him off. It was an impressive display from Alara, all things considered – a slightly bloody bandage on her head, a shirt that looked like she slept in it, and a skirt that looked like it came straight off a *Leather-R-Us-4-U* mannequin. All of that coupled with one middle finger on display loud and proud and a datapad in the other hand.

A datapad that arced through the air with *spectacular* aim before it hit him right over the bandage on his heart. "Two choices. I put a bullet in your head right now and piss off a couple of surgeons and a cardiologist or you sign on as a UCI."

UCI. A magic word to end all magic words. It had more power than a memory-wipe or an errant fireball. Sure, a little self-manifested pyrokinetics could always get you out of a heap of trouble in the immediate, but you still had to deal with a Fire Marshall afterwards. A UCI?

A UCI saved you from a host of sins.

If you were willing to let the cops call you an undercover criminal informant. There were reasons to be concerned about every word in that designation. Plus, you usually had to agree to it *before* you violated the law, a point that Anthony felt unpleasantly required to point out. "I don't think Yers is going to believe I was a UCI..."

"He doesn't have a choice. You do."

That was almost reassuring.

Almost. "How serious is the threat about the bullet?"

Alara sighed once, and then very casually drew a G-Locke out of practically thin air. She had it pointed dead center at his face before he could figure out where she'd hidden the holster. "Anthony Pierson, you were witnessed to be the source of a MAE in the Handed Down on May 28th, an incident that left nine officers injured. Under the provisions of the COUNTER-S.P.E.L.L. Act, you are to be execu-"

Anthony threw up his hand and waved her down before she could finish the statement, "I asked how serious, you don't have to point that at me."

"Legally, yes I fucking do," she shot back. "*Legally*, I was within rights to tell the EMTs not to revive you at the morgue. Do you understand how much shit you're in?"

"Enough that I don't think you want, '*Officer involved shooting at U-Anth-Med murders hero necromancer,*' to play on CANN."

"And take away time from how bad the AGU is getting its ass ripped for conducting a raid on faulty evidence? There's a special that's gonna air at six tonight. I have absolutely no doubt that public relations would *love* to spin it away onto you somehow, and you know they will if I give them the chance."

He cringed a little and glanced at the datapad. It had the usual wording on it that basically said he was aware of a situation, he contacted the police, and was authorized to engage in activity to resolve a situation. The extent of those activities would have to be signed off on by a supervisory officer.

Notably, the one with a gun to his face. "So help me God if you make me pull this trigger, I will find someone to bind your soul to a turbine in the sludge pit at Wastewater Treatment North. Skip the sewer; I'll send you straight into the forbidden smoothie machine."

"Peeps are that pissed, huh? I feel like I stepped in the shit."

"*In* the shit?" Alara scoffed. "Anthony, let's be realistic here. You had a tailor fit you for a shit-suit. You wear shit-brown loafers. You had a shit-sandwich for breakfast. You're going to have a shit-steak for dinner. You aren't *in* the shit, you idiot, you *are* the shit. Everything in your life right now is shit-scented, shit-flavored, shit-colored, shit-squish-to-the-touch. If I were you, I'd never so much as fart again."

"That was cute. Practice it much?"

"Every minute of the last twelve hours. Sign the damn form."

He very slowly lifted it up. "It's signed. I didn't do it."

She looked down at the datapad and shrugged after a moment. Her pistol floated out of her hands and slid back into its holster behind her back of it's own accord as she picked it up and re-read it. "Oh, right, forgot I already had that done."

Anthony looked up into her eyes and made a quiet note about how bloodshot they were, along with sunken bruises she'd gone to some care to cover up. "Gotta admit, little surprised about the life vest here. After I saw the news, I figured I'd have to at least suck on Federal cock."

"The Feds have decided that they don't want to touch this with a ten-foot-long cattle-prod, officially."

"Unofficially?"

"Unofficially, someone just field-tested a new weapons platform in a mortuary and DA Autoscis seemed to be really pissed off about a call concerning you she got from a... what was his name?" she asked before she pulled Anthony's med-monitor over. "Colonel Lyonis? Guess he was –"

The necromancer blinked once and immediately sat up in bed. Before Alara could offer even a hint of protest, he snapped the screen back around and started to pour over the details. "Fuuuuck. The Lion called? I take it back. Shoot me."

"No."

"Yes."

"I said no. Who is this Lyonis guy? He apparently gave the ER crew a hard time, too. Demanded your med records, among other things."

Anthony ran a hand through his hair and swore under his breath in a language the detective didn't recognize. "Because that's his job. Army paid for tech and he's required to check on me when it phones home. His name is pronounced Li-on-dis, yes, he's a Colonel, no, I won't say what branch, and... shit. Those numbers are off. Bad off. Shit."

"Off?"

"Yeah. Seven kilowa... shit. Should be closer to ten." He paused a sec and blinked. "Or I got hit a lot harder than... shit. Did I *die* die or was it just an on-off blip?"

"Te…" Alara started before her eyes grew even wider. "My car runs off of *seven*, you ass. What in the *fuck* do you need a ten-kW battery in your chest for?"

Anthony shook his head as quickly as the pain in the back of his head would allow. "Let me be very clear that those are your words, and not mine. For the record, I didn't say it. You said it. Not me. All I said is that it's a thing. You can ask, I can't tell. Okay?"

"No. No, nothing about this is *okay*. You went off like a warlock from a third-century fantasy story back in the rec-center, you've got tech I've never *heard of* before stuffed beside your heart, and you've got enough metal in you that I'm pretty sure you give magnets an erection," Alara ranted. "We used to be friends! Why didn't you tell me? Does Kath know how deep this stuff goes?"

"Because we *used* to be friends, and no. She doesn't need to know. Neither do you," he argued. "You walk into the Army, they give you a job, you take it. Sometimes it has perks. Sometimes the perks are metal bits. You got a freaking injection *port* in your throat because of the juice the state provided."

Alara's hand flew to the side of her neck almost instantly. "It's different and you know it."

"Meth-a-magic versus real shit, except my real shit got me blown up. It's a bit of my past I was happy to be done with, and yet here I am again, a man recently blown up a second time. Can we skip over the chunks of tech in my body? You're not the one playing with them."

Alara choked back a scream, but pushed the display back anyway. "Fine. It's fine, you arrogant… But don't you think we're done. I'm gonna tell Kath and… God. Fuck. By the way, not that you *asked*, I'm going to be just fine, thank you."

"Is that a good thing or bad?" the necromancer quipped. When thunderclouds practically rolled from Alara's eyes, Anthony raised his hands up defensively. "Kidding. I'm kidding. And… thank you… for saving my life."

"Yeah, well. You're welcome. If you hadn't dropped that thing…"

"If I hadn't, you would've," he countered with a little shrug. "You're the best at what you do. Maybe one of the best in the city."

"See, I'd *like* to think that, but I just watched you throw nth-bombs around like you're a walking anthenium reactor, so we're even. Pay me back by telling me, honestly, just *what the fuck* is up with you?"

"Which way?"

Alara crossed her arms and leaned against the doorframe. "You killed your marriage in a bottle of whiskey and buried it in a dozen different whores' beds. You skipped the Army's 'Civ-Sec-Work-Release Program,' which would've given you a flat mid-five-fig sal. Instead, you went with the post-serv disability option, and you've been working for everyone from the Grims to every third-rate corpse-consortium and funeral home along the Gulf just to buy groceries after the court spread your asshole open for alimony."

"In my defense, I only worked for them –"

"It doesn't matter how many times, it matters that you *did.*"

"Can't a guy just go through some shit?"

Alara pointed her finger right at his face. "Macho bullshit, more like. How about all the tech?"

Anthony bristled a little. "What about it?"

"I saw it."

"How much of it?"

"All the parts I can see with my eyes, you ass," she argued as she waved her hand and the med-monitor swung back over. "What the hell am I going to do with you? Or am I supposed to do *about* you?"

Anthony raised his eyebrows hopefully. "Bump the SysOverride off?"

Her glare could've done it on its own, but she flicked her fingers, and the magnetic bolt fastened to his left arm clattered to the floor a few seconds later. "Surprised you're not bitching about the cortidox."

"Corti...?" he exclaimed as he traced his IV line from his arm to a port on the wall behind his head. "The hell? Why am I on nth-surpressants?"

"After the way you fucked with Yers and the mess in the morgue? Are you really going to ask me that question?"

"Yes, but no, but c'mon. Really?"

"You didn't notice? Usually that shit makes my head buzz like a beehive."

Anthony grimaced and rubbed the back of his skull. "I figured it was a concussion."

"No, that's me," she countered. "Aura-burn, too, for good measure. Got to eat some iodine pills too, so we can add shitting my brains out for the fun of it."

"Joy. Me too, I assume?"

"Couldn't," Alara lamented, "you're too toxic."

"You know, I'm staring to take those remarks perso-"

"You're *too toxic,*" Alara stressed as she interrupted him. "So, fun fact, when an asshole like you doesn't have anyone in the system as an emergency contact or MPOA, guess who gets to know about your chart when it's potentially important to a police investigation?"

The color started to drain out of Anthony's face. "Am I the target of a police investigation?"

"No."

"That's a relief."

Alara very casually bolted the ICU door shut and leaned over the end of his bed. "You are the Goddamned investigation."

"That isn't," he lamented quietly. There was a short pause between the two. "So, you're okay?"

The detective stood back up and flexed her fingers a little. "Yeah, yeah. Don't worry about adding me to the list of Anthony Pierson's wayward souls. Blackburn is fine-ish. He's dormant, but I had his anchor checked. He'll recover."

It wasn't much in the way of good news but it was a damn sight better than the rest of what she'd said so far. "Well, that's wonderful."

That didn't mean he was off the hook. "Where's Clare?"

The lie rolled off his lips with practiced ease. "Undecided."

"Undecided? You know where she is, right?"

He wavered for a few seconds before he finally committed to an answer. "Yes, but in the interests of not implicating you, I haven't decided how best to answer that question without one or both of us going to jail, UCI status be damned."

Alara pursed her lips and worked through that argument for a minute. "Good answer. As for your third…"

"My third? What third? Carlos?"

"Carlos…? Oh, the gangbanger? No," she said as she reached into her purse and pulled out a small velvet sack. As soon as she dangled it in the air, he could feel a little tendril of *nth* probe out from it; nothing overly powerful, more like just a faint hint of electricity that wanted to find a ground.

The sight of it made his stomach drop for no reason he could easily articulate. "Alara… what's that…"

"A jawbone."

"Whose…?"

She glanced up into his eyes for a second before she tossed it onto his lap right beside the datapad. "Who do you think?"

He didn't even bother to open it. A casual "Oh," slipped out of his mouth a few seconds later, and he added a perfunctory, "fuck," for good measure.

Alara leveled her finger at his face. "Don't. You. Dare. Tell. Katherine."

For a change, the threat wasn't needed. "What the hell am I gonna do with *this*? There's absolutely no way I'm going to leave him bound and…"

"I don't know, Anthony. Maybe start a collection? *'The good, the bad, the ugly of Los San.'* I bet you could get someone to make shirts."

He carefully picked the bag up and felt the bone through the velvet. It felt like it was mostly intact, although he didn't feel any teeth. He also didn't feel any obvious consciousness attached to it, but that didn't lessen the likelihood that Jordan's ghost wouldn't eventually return to it if he didn't deal with it sooner than later. "No offense, but I don't think knockoff shirts on a street stall are going to solve my current problem."

"Napalm isn't going to solve your problem," Alara countered as she pulled up a chair and slumped into it. "And for good measure, presumably, you just got a witness killed."

"A what? That monster wasn't –"

"Not the mech," she interrupted. "*That's* another story. I mean Omari Miller. We fucked up, and yes, I mean *we* fucked up."

There wasn't a cop on the planet that liked to admit they'd made a mistake, and she wasn't an exception. Anthony sat up fully in bed and glanced back at the datapad with a frown. "How fucked?"

Alara casually tapped at the side of her head and a few moments later a familiar ding went off in his hardware, followed by a display that popped up in his peripheral vision. It took him less than five seconds to mutter his first 'oh, dammit,' and barely twenty before he dropped his head back on his pillow as a mix of schematics, A/V files, and serial numbers ran through his brain. "Who in the hell bugs a morgue?"

"Someone who wanted to listen in on a necromancer," she pointed out, as unhelpful as she was. "TEC noted it as an EOTB SeesAll. They got it in one of the bodies somehow."

"I'm not sure this counts as a *we* fucked up. *We* would have had to scrub the building top to bottom before we'd even realize we needed to look for that. You know how *good* those things are? INSCOM has a… I mean, allegedly has a contract with them."

"Oh, I know. EOTB has a contract with Internal Affairs these days, too. I know how much they charge the department, at least. But either way…"

Anthony rubbed his eyes and tried not to think how bad this was going to cost them in the long term. "Either way, anything, and everything I said got picked up on a hot mic. Presumably a hot mic held by the assholes that marched a fucking tank up my ass."

"That's my assumption. Don't beat yourself up over it."

"I'm not."

"Liar."

"I'm not," he stressed. "Omari aside, I'm beating myself up over getting involved in this mess to begin with."

Alara had to gingerly nod her head in agreement. "Speaking of, you willing to bet on if that guy is dead or if he just wants to be?"

"No, I'm not," Anthony grunted, "though I'm willing to bet we'll never find his body. So, with that hope gone, please at least tell me you have some kind of fucking idea what the hell that mechanoid was? Is? Whatever?"

"No, but TEC has a boner. That walking corpse thing just solved an entire division's collective ED. I'll send you everything they find, but you didn't leave a lot of bits behind."

"Total destruction is the best kind. It's not helpful but..."

"*TEC* has a boner," she repeated. "Ab/Psy? Cult? Go ahead, ask me how happy *my* people are. I'll give you a hint; the phrase 'burn the witch' has been uttered more than once. I overheard someone from QRD say that the Inquisition may have been right all along."

The remarks weren't the most surprising thing he'd heard so far, and he tried to take it in stride as much as he could. "Well, that thing reeked. I can't say I'm —"

She shook her head and cut him off. "You don't understand. TEC is tracking the physical parts and they've got leads. *My* techs? They *can't* identify the spellwork. What you... we... left behind of it? We can't identify the signature. I'm not entirely sure whatever put that bitch together shares even a distant relation to homo-sapiens."

Anthony went cold. Magic was magic, sure, but magic had *rules*. One of those rules was that magic had signatures, or fingerprints, or traces of the caster. Whatever you called it, you may not always be able to directly identify the *who* worked a spell, but you could identify the *what* worked a spell.

And LSPD's Ab/Psy had access to one of the largest catalogs of *whats* in the known world. "There's a very short list of things you wouldn't be able to identify. I do mean very."

"Yeah, well, if you happen to have access to that particular list, please do feel free to share with the rest of the class. The official report from my office is that the evidence was too degraded to make sense of and that additional samples are needed. Without another dip in the well, we're forced to assume whatever made that thing get up and walk was non-human, non-native."

"Define non-native."

"Too abnormal to exist on this planar shelf without Intervention."

"Divine? Please say divine."

Alara smirked. It wasn't a happy smirk. "What do you think? That I'm here to make your life easier?"

"I'm stuck in a hospital bed with surgi-baffle wrapped around my ribs. Please say yes. Please, please be here to make my life easier."

"No. But I do have warrants that might make you smile a little. And more of them keep trickling in every hour, almost on the hour," she replied with a happy little chirp to her voice.

She was scary when she was excited. Always had been, and probably always would be. "My name on any of them?"

"One."

Anthony cast a wary glance in her direction as he struggled to get the damned hospital sheets untangled from his legs. "Top part or bottom?"

"Top. With the words 'authorized to interrogate' next to it."

"At least it isn't the bottom. Speaking of, I assume there's a bottom?"

Alara casually tapped the side of her head again and a new line of text started to roll across his vision. "Andrea Adams. Here's a stack; take a look."

As it downloaded, he forced his way out of the bed and stumbled toward a half-hidden restroom. Warrants, reports, and subscreens full of mini-datadumps popped up one after another in a cascade of legal bullshit and a host of bad days for everyone mentioned. The list was extensive, and it covered most of the topics Jordan had brought to light.

Sojourn had multiple 'person of interest' notes stapled to it, and there was a filed notice of 'intent to investigate' the Fontaine Center – as soon as they could find it. There were two warrants that had been red-lined for expediency; one for the probably late Omari Miller, and the other for a subject identified only as the Gulf Operations Officer for Blackwash Security, Inc.

That was a big red flag. *He* knew who Blackwash's Gulf Ops Officer was, and *they* knew who the sec-chief was, but he *didn't* have a warrant listed for him by name. There was a story to explain that, he was sure, but the rest of the list took temporary precedence. He was barely halfway through it before he flushed the toilet and called out to her. "And people wonder why Last Words is so damn important."

"Because the process saves us money on jury fees?"

Anthony didn't bother to hide his laugh. "The other reason."

"That too," she agreed. "Alright, Mr. 'I worked for INSCOM, so my brain is huge,' what's missing from those warrants?"

He stumbled back into his room with a notable limp. "Well, the only reference I see here for the CoAA is whatever the Fontaine Center is. I presume they exist, but the DA's office is currently trying to negotiate a handover without relying on jackbooted thugs and a SWAT team?"

"We're working on getting that information from South Shore Boarding and Line, since Jordan suggested they operate it, but they're claiming that the contract is covered under the legal shield of 'Church Business,' which is bullshit.'

"The Church, who presumably, is pissed off and has no desire to help a police investigation until they get all of their ducks in a row."

"More or less," Alara started. "Ever since your phantom presser hit the cloud –"

"Really? *Phantom* presser?"

The offended look on his face made a little smile curl up across her lips as she continued. "*Ever* since, El-Rhodes has gone into hiding. The College of Eagles is very, very upset, and they're publicly accusing you of being the direct descendant of Beelzebub while saying that you're also just a conman pulling a publicity stunt."

"Their ability to speak out of both sides of their face never ceases to amaze me. What's the not-public response?"

Her smile shifted to an outright smirk. "Fire up the wood chipper because they intend to prune some branches of the Tree of Life."

"Oof."

"Big oof," the cop agreed. "They're very well aware of how bad they're implicated in this mess, and they want to make the problem go away."

Anthony lightly punched at a drawer on the wall, and was rewarded when it slid open to reveal some of his clothes. "Currently, I presume, they're fitting the Sine for a big sign that says, 'I'm the problem.' That about right?"

She shrugged. "Wouldn't know. They're doing something on the internal side, and I've been informed I can't touch them. Turns out that nobody believes you stumbled onto which Recyc Center Jordan was being stored in by accident."

He glanced up from his jeans. "Do you blame them?"

"No, but the fine on my next paycheck will. My ass in the hot-seat aside, what else is missing in that pile o' paperwork, oh wiseman you?"

He scanned through it a second time while he struggled to get his pants back on. "Andrea Adams. I've got a name, something that pretends to be a description, and that's it."

"Because that's it," Alara replied. "She's a ghost."

Anthony raised an eyebrow. "I mean you're Ab/Psy. Ghostbu-"

"You know the 80's were nearly a century ago, right? You made me watch too much of that shit in college, so don't even *think* I'm gonna let you finish that. Wrong kind of ghost, anyway."

"The last movie was in 2040 and they run reruns of the kid's show on Toon-O-Vid at two in the morning on Saturdays," he spat back. "Besides, you can take it from me that there's never a right kind. How does Ab/Psy define the *wrong* kind, exactly?"

"You have a sad, sad life – and as for wrong kind, it's more Corp-Audit than Ab/Psy," Alara warned. "Apparently, she doesn't exist outside of paperwork. Her name is in the city-corp regi; she's got a SSN and assorted other crap. Beyond that, nothing."

A series of stitches down his good arm made it harder than he wanted to admit to put on his shirt. Not that the med-techs had bothered to leave much of his shirt behind, but a torn up button-down was better than nothing. "That's not… good. You'd have to fake a lot of dirt to make a mountain big enough to enter the registry."

Alara wasn't even phased from the show he was putting on. Nor was she out of bad news to give. "More than that. She *owns* Sojourn."

In the grand scheme of things, that should've been impossible. It wasn't, because nothing was really impossible in this nightmare of a city, but it should've been. Creating a corp was easy; you could do it in under five minutes if the *LLC-Claim-A-Company*! adverts across half of downtown were right. *Owning* a corp was harder. You had to pay taxes, you had to have licensing, and most importantly, you had to register with the Corp-Regi Office.

They took everything down to the blood type of your Board.

And they were known to keep samples of it, too.

If you faked a registration? That was a crime with a capital 'C,' and they'd make sure to kick you in the C-you-next-Tuesday if you screwed around with them. The city – hell, the Feds, too – liked it when an entrepreneur found a way to make money, and they liked it more when they got their cut of your profits.

A cut they'd get one way or another. "But you don't have a photo."

"No photo, no biometrics, and a forwarding address that sends her mail somewhere in the Bronx. She's not real; an absolute corpi-ghost,"

Alara confirmed. "If this was a case of tax fraud, she'd be in trouble, but to have a ghost pop up in the middle of a mess this big?"

"Why do I get the feeling someone over in Corp-Audit is rolling up their sleeves and finding some brass knuckles?"

"I don't know, but I heard there's a bunch of very angry accountants laying siege to SJE's corporate offices right now. Ever seen a spreadsheet fired from a catapult?"

"You know, I can't take them seriously when you put it like that," Anthony mused after a moment. "All I can think of is just a gaggle of nerds using a calculator as a battering ram to get through the front door."

Alara snorted and twirled her fingers in the air. In response, the media panel kicked back on and the screen jumped around until a feed showing *'Live Coverage of a LSPD Raid'* popped up on screen right next to a declining stock chart. "I might've bought some of their stock on a short-sell order last night."

"Really? How'd you do?" he asked as he started to button up the ruins of his top.

"Gonna afford a vacation in New Miami next year if it keeps going down."

"And if you can find a ghost that doesn't exist," he pointed out.

She let out a sigh of agreement. "Yeah. A ghost that, until you turned your ex-brother-in-law into a blood-puppet, was just a name on a paper trail of weird tech purchases."

Anthony watched the feed as angry cops in silver-and-gold riot armor pushed back reporters and irrationally angry random citizens alike. Sojourn didn't have much of a front office, apparently, though the raid had managed to block off a fairly decent chunk of thoroughfare. "Any of those purchases link back to that tank?"

"What do you think?"

"I think I'm neck deep in a shitstorm."

"Cute that you think it only goes to your neck. Every single person involved in this mess has broken every EBR law we have on the books to the extent that I think we're going to need to write new books *just* to cover them."

He hesitated for a few seconds while that comment sunk in. "Damn. Fine. So, *legally*, where does this leave me on your side of this problem?"

Alara smirked in that vaguely adorable way she had. "Cute-er that you think you have more than one side. What's the other?"

"You first."

The smirk trembled and it made the dimple in her cheek vanish. "Fine. *Legally*, you are a private citizen who was forced to defend yourself from a home invasion. In the process, as a licensed necromancer, you were made aware of a potential MAE. Per established federal guidelines, you acted on that information and served as an undercover informant prior to a gang bust. The alert to apprehend you was an attempt to bring you in from the cold and to the safety of police HQ if you weren't able to do so on your own."

Anthony pursed his lips and flagged some of the paperwork in the side of his vision with an audio copy of her statement. "And I'm in the clear with that?"

"No, but you won't be charged," she answered, "conditionally."

There was always a catch. Always. "What's the condition?"

A catch she wasn't thrilled with, apparently, from the sudden catch in her voice. "Per both the DA's office and Captain Garcia, you are to make yourself available for any further encounters with those damn mechs. You broke it, you bought it. All of 'em."

"Garcia… Elija Garcia? Heads up MWAT?"

"Uh-huh," Alara replied. "Magical Weapons and Tactics."

He slunk back down onto the bed and grimaced. "Oh I don't like that condition."

"You'd like forty-five to life less," the detective countered. "First thing you get to do after you're discharged is to send him a report of everything you pulled out of that bastard. And he means everything. If you think Yers is a jerk…"

"Garcia isn't a jerk," Anthony interrupted. "He's just outstandingly good at his job and doesn't want to get killed doing it. I respect that, I honestly do. I am assuming that means you intend to put me in a weapons locker somewhere until it's time to take another one down."

The answer must've surprised her, and she tilted her head slightly as she reconsidered him for the umpteenth time. "Safehouse. State-mandated."

"No dice."

And that answer surprised her even more. "Seriously?"

"Seriously. A safehouse and a few antitank rounds aren't going to solve my problems."

"I hope by 'problems' you're including whatever you did with your wife."

He grimaced again. "Ex. And yes. And more."

"Listen, dumbass. If you thought I was leaving her out of the deal –"

Anthony cleared his throat and flipped off the monitor as GCN showed a particularly unflattering profile of his face. "You'd think these assholes would do better than the photo on my ident card. Also, I think you haven't checked the underside of the cloud lately. A safehouse *won't* solve my problems."

"I did. There's three squaddies downstairs, and two of them have anti-material tube-rifles in their trunk."

"Oh." He let the remark linger in the air before he glanced through the data-dump again. "I take it this means that the Plaza has decided to start rolling heavy?"

Alara grunted in raw annoyance. "That mech blew up a morgue and there's an unknown quantity of them left on the street. The fuck you think?"

"That I should probably be more appreciative," Anthony admitted.

"Good think."

Neither of them said anything for nearly a minute as he sat still and took stock of any residual wounds, aches, and general pains. When nothing new cropped up, he finally addressed the elephant in the room. "Look. I'll help with the investigation. I won't say I'll be *glad* to pick a fight with those abominations again, but shit with them is so fucking *wrong* that I can't ignore them in good conscience."

"Whatever 'but' you're thinking about adding, reconsider."

"*But*," he said as he ignored her entirely, "someone wants me dead. Someone wants a lot of people I care about dead."

Alara leaned forward and grabbed his good hand in both of hers. Her fingers were warm and there was a very brief electrical chill that sparked between them. It had absolutely nothing to do with feelings; more of a mutual aura check between them. "Which is why we have this magical operation called 'witness protection.' I think you forgot that part."

"Federal witsec has a 65% survival rate in the last ten years and I happen to like my face enough to not want to go through plastic surgery to replace it."

The charge faded slightly, but her grip didn't. "Fine. What's your other option?"

He took a deep breath and went for the hard sell. "Spot me the safehouse, but cut me loose. In exchange, I'll give you Kath and Callie and I'll get on the hunt for Adams. A ghost is a ghost, and last I checked, that makes her my bitch."

The charge, the grip, and the reassuring smile on her face all stopped. "Callie? Who's Callie? I want Clare."

"Oh, right, you haven't met," he mumbled. "Okay, so, you won't like her, but I got her pulled into this mess. I gotta see her through it."

She blinked. Slowly. "Got her pulled... Anthony... wait a tick. You've got TWO women stored away? For the love of the Gods do not tell me you have stuffed your ex-wife and... the way you said her name. You stuck Kath and your fucking *girlfriend* in the same dank hole somewhere?"

The comment slipped out before he could stop it. "Experience."

Her face went completely, utterly, blank. "What?"

"Girlfriend... experience," he mumbled under his breath. "But I like her, okay? She's... she's nice."

The blank stare was preferable to the look of utter disgust and rage that boiled up her neck and flared in her eyes – literally. "What do you... oh my *God* you disgusting little prick."

"It's not little. Chart says so."

Alara snapped her fingers in front of his face and a violent blue spark jumped from them as she did. "Chart says it wasn't augmented and I can fucking change that. So instead of doing the *smart* thing and going into *hiding* where people *can't* shoot at you, you want free reign of the city? *Why*?"

"Name me a bigger MAE than something walking around with a corpse as an engine and an armor-piercing plasma cannon strapped to its arm. I am required *by law* to deal with anything that's against –"

"Yeah yeah, uncontrolled magic and unlicensed abnormalities," she said as she cut him off. "You're an absolute fucking idiot, you know that right?"

All he could do was shrug. "I have my moments. Look, you can wait for the Church to send a mountain of paperwork your way and maybe put El-Rhodes in your lap if you want, but I can guarantee you he'll have suffered a stroke that'll have turned his brain into pudding and his soul will have been 'Summoned by the Holy Ghost' and be unrecoverable," he argued. "Or, and hear me out here, let me go do what I do and maybe we get an exit plan here that we can both live with."

He was right and it pissed her off. Both the fact that he was right and the fact that it should've been a mild shock to note that the Sine-Pastor wasn't already in the bed beside him. "You're aware that you actually have to *be living* to live with it."

"You're aware that if Kath goes into witsec you never get to see her again."

She lowered her hand and softened her glare. "That's low. That's low even for you."

"Did it work?"

Alara crossed her arms and leaned back in the chair. "Yes. Dammit. Call for a nurse. Time to get your ass out of here. We gotta talk about what the hell that thing is – and the two assholes that tried to feed me to some ghasts after it got loose."

***

University of Anth-Med
Medicine isn't Magic.
But Science can Make You Believe
***

Getting out of the hospital – even AMA – almost took more power and authority than Alara had. Security tried to stop them at least four different times (one for each and then once more when the rent-a-cops realized they were traveling in a group) and Anthony's doctor refused to let him get near the elevator until after he'd delivered a lecture on 'Things Not to Do.' The spiel covered everything from energy drinks to sex, and briefly brushed over the concept of not even thinking about using spellwork again anytime this month.

The lecture, of course, was forgotten almost immediately.

Alara was surprised it took that long.

The actual walk out, itself, took nearly thirty minutes. Anth-Med wasn't just *big*, it was almost a city in and of itself. A city within a city, and unlike Los San proper, a city that was significantly more diverse than the general white-and-tan that made up the bulk of the population. More than a third of the staff came from the Indo-Paci Alliance area, and another quarter of the University students themselves represented a wide host of African nations as well.

Bluntly, if you wanted to learn how to use Anthenium in medicine, you came here, no matter where you were from. It made for great choices for lunch, if nothing else. Corporate America had realized it too, and you couldn't take more than ten steps down the indoor promenade without having your eyeballs assaulted with ads for everything from *Like 'Em Long Ramen*, an anthropomorphic grill in the shape of a buxom blonde that promoted *Shrimp 'n' Barbie*, or the eternally offensive *F*in' Fried Chicken T*ts*.

The last one was a three-time winner for Longhorn Brother's 'Honest Advertising' award that never ceased to annoy the Parents Against

Marketing groups. While the ads were funny, every single one had a tagline that made Anthony's skin crawl:

Brought to you by a proud harvest from Eden Farms.

Heart and Spade might control damn near everything there was to own in Los San, but Eden still controlled everything you put in your mouth. Maybe one day that would change. Today wasn't it.

Tomorrow wasn't looking great either.

Detective Haythes joined them on their way out of the main hospital, although nobody in the trio said anything as they continued to worm their way through the campus. Long banners stretched across dorm walls and medical clinics on either side of the lengthy outdoor walkway. They advertised everything from *Tech-Connect* uplink implants to the newest *Marie Curie Lab-At-Home* fashion line.

There was an obligatory '*Master Chief Orion*' ad that briefly jogged his memory. *At the very least, that dude is one serious fuckin' narcissist...* "You know, Kath said something about Jordan doing work with Honest ABE through the Church. Part of the resettlement program. Maybe you can get info from them...? I doubt their shareholders would be stoked to find out they were being used for... whatever all *this* is. Hell, might even end this annoying advert campaign."

"What, you miss the tits-and-asses ads from Magi-Caffi?" Alara remarked as Matty suddenly had a pensive look fall across his face.

"It's the Diet Drink to Die For! Also, tits. So, yes."

"You really are a horrible human."

"I'm quite good at being human. I'm just a horrible person."

"Only you would make the difference."

The psych detective coughed once to interrupt their bickering and held out his phone. A cover for the most recent issue of '*Corporate Methods Monthly*' was stretched across it. "Their shareholders might not be as pissed as you think. Maybe pissed that they're getting noticed."

"How pissed?" and "Why?" came out of Anthony and Alara's mouths at the same time.

"Because Sojourn is their prime shareholder. Guess who contracts their security?"

"Oh, fuck," both his partner and the necromancer replied at once, though one of them – and he wasn't sure which – added an unnecessary 'you' to the end of it. "Wouldn't be hard to stick a few people on a train and say, 'we're sending you to your new home,' when the Church was interested in sending them to glory, instead," Anthony added. "Glory dispensed by the biomed company using them for research."

Alara pulled her own phone out and started to type commands into it as fast as she could. "Less '*Honest*' and more '*Bullet Express*,' if you're right," she said. "If you're right..."

"I really don't like being right all the time, you know that, don't you?"

Matty slipped his phone back into his slacks and shook his head. "No lyin' to friends, Pierson. You're happy as can be to be right all the time and I can smell it from a mile away."

"Don't sniff me. It's gross," Anthony retorted. "Aura or otherwise."

He was also right.

They stood still as a crowd of coeds wandered past them, and the silence didn't break until Alara spoke up again. "Alright asshole, what's going on in that head of yours?"

"That I need to sleep. Maybe eat something. Did they bother to feed me the last twenty-odd hours?"

"You were unconscious."

"We both know that doesn't matter."

"Do ever you think about anything but your stomach?"

"My dick, if that counts."

"It doesn't," Alara snapped back before her voice softened a little. "But food and some downtime would be good for all of us. I can't do shit until the warrants get greenlit, and you can't do anything until I clear you."

Matty stretched as they worked their way through the busy, breakfast-focused crowd. "Yeah he's gonna do things. I can hear it ticking under his breath."

Anthony gave the psychic a dirty little look and avoided the bait, if only barely. "I'm going to check on people that are pissed off. Happy?"

"No, but you promise you're not going to do anything else?"

"Not if I don't have to."

She held her tongue for a few seconds before she finally uttered a simple, tired, "Good."

It was Matty that spoke up next. "He's lying."

"I know," his partner replied.

Not that the necromancer even bothered to hide it. "Yeah. I am."

Matty stops in his tracks and looks back and forth between them. "Did you two date or something? Because, honestly, the vibe between you..."

"He stole my girlfriend."

"No, I stole your crush. Besides, she's not gay. Little bi, maybe, but."

Alara snorted and looked up at the open sky above. "Only because you beat me to the chance."

"You've had years."

"Gee, Anthony, it's almost like after she dumped your ass she's got commitment issues. Can't imagine why she's not on the open market."

"Oh, so you aren't who 'Special Red' is for?"

"Huh?"

"Merry Christmas," he replied with a small smirk. Before she could ask anything else, he popped a US-subsphere out of his coat and flicked it over to her. "I cloned Katherine's phone. I don't know how much more you can get off of it than what we scored in the morgue. Check out 'special red.' Thank me later."

Alara pinched the little ball between her fingers and held it up to see it better in the sunlight. "Huh. Normally I'd be pissed but… good job."

Her partner followed up with a happy little smile. "Why, Mr. Pierson. I take it that means you're going to fully cooperate with the LSPD's investigation?"

"It means he already copied it," Alara interjected.

Matty's smile cracked. "That too."

"Whatever other disparaging remarks you two would like to make about my character aside," Anthony replied as he pushed his way through a trio of labcoat-clad sorority sisters, "there's one big name that's missing on your pile of warrants. Harold Vincetti."

Alara flinched and from the way she tensed up, she'd apparently both had been waiting for the question and she'd hoped she could have avoided it. "Not missing; in-progress as we get more evidence. Right now we have him as a POI with Jordan's death and —"

"Jordan's testimony is enough to arrest him," the necromancer said as he cut her off. "What's the other reason?"

"Dude's corp, but you knew that," Matty answered. "The problem is *which* corp. The only thing thicker than the subdermals he's supposedly got is the wall of lawyers ready to claim 'within legal contractual limits.' I'm not saying he's untouchable but…"

"…but security corps like Blackwash only stay in business if they have an army of lawyers scrubbing down their guns. Got it," Anthony grunted in annoyance. "Except I know this guy isn't just corp-sec, he's also —"

"A Canadian citizen and a wetworker from Oregon, we know that too," the psych went on to say. "The DA had a dick-wavin' contest with H-Central about him. The Feds promised to let us know what they know."

"That and the other problem," Alara chimed in.

"What's the other problem?"

"It isn't Blackwash paying his legal bills."

Anthony paused and blinked in confusion. "It isn't? Then who is?"

The two detectives exchanged askance looks. "As best as we can tell, and as much as the Anti-Gang Unit can verify –"

"AGU?" he interrupted. "Why... no. Don't tell me."

Matty bit the bullet and confirmed the necromancer's thought. "The legal-eagles over at Edwards, Alfonz, and Mustang are under personal retainer for Susan Sands. If there was any doubt about his connection to the Gardeners..."

"...then that doubt just got buried under a mountain of legal briefs, got it," Anthony grunted. "Wait, the ads that they run. Cybernetic and anth-augments, right? Their legal specialty?"

Alara nodded. "You called it. From what we can find on public record, Vincetti has more tech than some armies buried under his skin," she added. "We can't touch him. Couple that with the mechs, and it all really, really pisses me off."

Anthony heard the shift in her voice and even Matty had to grimace. "Why?"

"Because before that biomech *thing* went after you, a pair of Gardener shitbags tried to shoot the two of us up," Matty interjected before his boss could. "Then it blew the shit out of its delivery van."

"I got the greenjackets," Alara added. "After I put their asses to sleep, the mech stormed out – and Vincetti ran off, along with someone else – a bitch in white."

The necromancer stopped walking and glanced back and forth between them. "I'm guessing he's not dead and you're not happy about it."

Alara grumbled and let her shoulders sag a little. "Didn't get the chance. The woman with him? She's bad, Anthony. I got the vibe that she's some kind of necromancer, but somehow worse. Worse than you by a mile."

He pursed his lips as he processed *that* idea and tried not to take excessive offense to it. "Thinking she's the source of these machines?"

"Maybe? They're nothing we recognize and she's nothing I could recognize so..."

"No chance you got a description...?"

"Wore a mask," she admitted, "and Matty was unconscious, so no read. Yellow eyes, and had a power pulse when she pulled the ghasts up. Not on par with the one you used back there but it was sickening. I felt like I wanted to vomit just being near it."

"Not a lot that can do that. Usually it's just –"

"Yeah, yeah, I know how nth exposure works," Alara interrupted. "Lab couldn't get much residual off of the bodies; guess I didn't let them wander long enough. All I can tell you is that she was wearing a HawkCrest AirModule 3. Only reason I can tell you that is because TEC ID'd it on cams."

"Hawk… isn't that on some of the papers you sent me?"

Matty nodded. "Yeappers. They are the second-largest shareholder in Sojourn Enterprises. Primary? Andrea Adams, the SJE CEO. But guess who's on HC's public disclosure statements as their Zonal Director for the South American Gulf? Give you a hint; her name is all A's."

Anthony took a second to whistle under his breath. "You know, there's keeping shit in the family and then there's outright incest. And you still can't get the DA to find a judge that can cut a warrant on Vincetti *why*…?"

"Blackwash donated the corp-max to the Mayor's election campaign," Alara replied disgustedly. "It's in progress, but when it goes through…"

Anthony grunted and then had a sudden thought that hit that was just as much good as it was bad. "So, this bag of dicks has been hired or tasked with getting everyone even tangentially involved in this dead, apparently. He *can't* be so stupid as to not realize his time is about up. From what I've heard about him, he's something of a completionist on his contracts."

"Which means we'll have more bodies soon, but he's a known merc," Matty replied. "Maybe you can pay him enough to hop off into the sunset for you."

Anthony pulled up his phone and tapped a few commands into it. A moment later, he glanced at the cop with a raised eyebrow. "Blackwash is estimated to pay their top execs around $335k a year. I can't even fathom how much his lawyers cost. How much do you think they're paying the guy pulling the trigger on their cleanup?"

"Can always play MegaBucks and hope for the best," the detective happily quipped.

"The lotto isn't going to help anyone do anything," Alara said as a set of double-wide doors opened open to clear their way to the outer promenade. "I get where you're going with this. I just can't do anything about it."

The necromancer grit his jaw so hard he felt a molar try to crack. "Fine. But you need to tell Autoscis that this isn't the time for the gears of justice to grind slowly. The second that this Mr. Slash is fair game for you to pick up I've got a feeling we're going to see fireworks go off."

"If half of what you've said, suggested, recorded, and hinted at is accurate, the Cloud's gonna be so lit you'd think it's Moscow circa 2027 again," Alara shot back, "nukes and all."

"Remember when the best thing that came from Russia was vodka and dumb games about falling blocks? Not the wandering, irradiated bodies of random dead Bolsheviks?" Anthony complained. "Because I miss those days."

"You weren't born in those days."

"Doesn't mean I can't miss them. You miss it when synth-leather was actually fashionable, and you still wear it all the time."

Matty choked on his tongue while Alara drew herself up to her full diminutive – yet oddly terrifying – height. "Say that again and see if I miss you with a 9mm –"

"*Enough*, you two," her partner interrupted as the trio pushed their way through the University Hospital's main entrance. While the crowd had died down a little, there were a handful of orderlies at the exit with Hovi-Med-Chairs and overly pleasant smiles on their faces for this time of day. "Ya'll aware that I can feel the sparks rubbin' off in the air around your auras and I *don't* mean the fun kind. I'm gonna go get a CometBall and a side of Lizie-Sticks. Get over your shit by the time I'm back, okay?"

As he stomped off and braved the crowd a second time, Alara and Anthony made their way through the final set of glass doors. A giant archway sign loomed overhead with an aggrandizing tagline: *The Heart and Spade Foundation. Proud Sponsor of Bio-Medical Advancements Worldwide*, just in case you forgot who paid for what around here, they were happy to remind you.

Once they were finally out of the hospital, the unhappy pair stood in silence until the necromancer gave up. "Look, we cool?"

Alara looked up at the sun and cut loose a sigh that belied the size of her frame. "No. Yes."

"Which?"

"Both," she replied after a few long heartbeats. "I'm pissed."

"At me or...?"

"*Because of*," Alara replied almost instantly, "though damned if I can blame you for much of it. You're a hammer, Anthony. A convoluted, alcoholic, fucked-up hammer. Every problem looks like a nail to you. Or maybe a grave. Maybe you're a shovel, not a hammer. I don't know, but the real problem is that we don't live in a world of nails and graves. We live in a city of glass walls and people get cut when you chuck them through the panes."

To his credit, Anthony took the blast of vitriol in stride and he didn't even crack a frown. "We really do live in a world of graves, but I get the point... and you're right. That's your thing, too. Always being right, always having an answer." he admitted in one brief glimpse of self-reflection. "But are we cool?"

She kept her eyes locked on the sunrise and tried as hard as she could to ignore the din of the city on all sides. "I'm keeping you out of jail. Does that answer your question?"

"Mostly. Christmas cards this year?"

"Don't press your luck," Alara finally replied with a tired chortle.

Her response drew the first real smile he'd had in days. "Good. Because I think this whole damn mess is out of our pay-grade, and there's something going on about it I don't like."

"Other than all of it?"

"Other than all of it," he agreed. They stopped beside an empty valet booth that lorded over the hospital's entrance drive like it was the judgmental seat of God Himself. "You've got advanced weapons tech... advanced *illegal* weapons tech. You use it to stomp a priest flat, then blow up a morgue. *Why*?"

Alara blinked as she looked out at a veritable sea of auto-cabbies that shined under the Texas sun. "Showing off, I guess."

"When was the last time you heard of a criminal showing off?"

"The 2056 Congressional Elect-"

"Okay, *valid*," he agreed curtly, "but *in general*. This isn't just some prick that robbed a post office. How many corps are in the crosshairs on this because of a fucking *priest* getting stomped with a mech that could go toe-to-toe with an APC?"

He had a point and he could see how much she hated it the longer the realization dawned in her faintly-shimmering eyes. Even without actively being amped up, the residual signs of anth-use were present all the time. The sun brought it out more often than not. Some peopled liked it.

All she did was reach into her jacket and pull out a pair of shades. "Hadn't looked at it like that before," the detective admitted finally. "There's blunders, and then there's blunders."

"And then there's billion-dollar blunders. How much research went into that thing? How hard is the Church tied into it, and the Daem community? This isn't some gangland spat or even a pair of Weap-Tech companies going to war in Afghanistan and LSPD has already tanked a few million dollars worth of company stock on their *first* raid and you aren't done. This is an open, flagrant violation of international law in the middle of the one fucking city that has *just enough* of the right people to investigate it without sending out for help. Someone *wanted* this much attention."

"People that want this kind of attention don't care about who gets hurt, either."

"Obviously," Anthony agreed as a limo pulled up behind him and stopped just a few feet away from where he was standing. "Damn, I thought you got me an auto-cab, not a –"

"I did," she interrupted as the doors opened...

...and a trio of very big men in very dark suits with very big guns stepped out. Her hand didn't even have a chance to glow before the first beefcake put a hefty semi-automatic pistol to the back of Anthony's head. The other two pointed two top-of-the-line SMGs at her face. "Not. A. Word," the pistol-wielding gunman ordered. "Car. Now."

Anthony, for once in his life, shut up and did as he was told.

The guy with the gun didn't leave him with any other choice.

People screamed – briefly. The screams were quieted almost instantly as the limo doors slammed shut, and the gunmen vanished without a single shot fired.

Alara, on the other hand, had other ideas – ideas that were short-circuited by a sudden stab of pain in her right arm. The world started to spin immediately, and she fell back into a Hovi-Chair that she hadn't realized was behind her. A hand clamped itself around her mouth as she started to scream, and a very calm voice spoke just loud enough for her to hear. "I'm sorry Detective, but you're frightening some of the clients."

She tried to speak up around the hand, but couldn't get a word past it. Her assailant turned her chair around and she saw Matty slumped back in a matching one a few yards away where he was being tended to by U-Anth staff. Alara tried to kick, but her legs had gone to sleep, and dark clouds had built up around her vision.

An Anth-Med doctor strolled up out of the edge of her sight and squatted down in front of her chair. "Good morning, Miss Dimir," he began, "you're confused about what's going on, and I understand, but you need to calm down."

"I'm not confused about sh..."

"Mr. Pierson was discharged twenty minutes ago," the doc firmly – and loudly – replied. His voice was enough to placate the handful of people that had witnessed the kidnapping, and every last one of them scampered off to pretend they knew nothing about anything.

Alara felt a haze of some kind of psychedelic fog drift down over her shoulders. "But the gun… suit… men…"

"I'm afraid that due to an unexpected side effect of the traum-meds you were prescribed combined with a malfunction of your anth-port, you're feeling a little chron-lapsed."

His mouth said one thing. The playing-card-shaped tattoo on the side of his neck said another. "You're one of…"

He touched the black spade on his skin with his fingertips as the world around her head went dark. "Please understand – the Heart and Spade Foundation is a very large donor to the university."

***

***The Meta-Planar Assessment Bureau
A & Nth: The True Ascension of Humanity is Waiting in Your Genes.
Visit us at our offices in Spade Down today!
***

The floor of a taxicab had a worse taste than the floor of this particular limo, but even this one left a decidedly tangy feeling on his tongue that he didn't like. A familiar – but unhappy – voice chimed in from overhead as he spat a mouthful of carpet fuzz out. Red carpet fuzz, of course.

"Usually, I'm the one tied up on the floor like that," Emiline sighed, "Or I used to be. You know, I almost miss them."

Anthony glanced up at her and wiggled himself around until his back pressed against the rear seat. It wasn't perfect, but it'd do. "Almost?"

"Okay, fine. I don't. But there were perks."

"I will pay you if you promise not to tell me what those were."

"You're broke," she deftly shot back, "and not in a position to offer anything. We, on the other hand, are, though… well, I'm still under some obligations."

She was also dressed, for a change, and unsurprisingly looked good even in a suit. A full suit, too; nice clean and corporate-crisp-proper, down to a tie and a conservatively braided ponytail. When she shifted slightly and crossed her legs, he caught a faint hint of either a red blouse or bra – and knowing her it could be either – and the glimpse was intentional. "Do those obligations include untying me?"

"Eventually," Emiline replied sardonically, "but not until you're a good boy and earn it."

"You know that's not half as sexy as you think it is."

"The right mood hasn't been established," she admitted as she pulled a small-caliber pistol out of her jacket and pointed it at his face. "Better?"

"No, but I appreciate the effort," he answered after a very short moment to consider if she planned to use it or not. "Clare?"

Emiline nodded once. "Clare. Where?"

"Safe."

"From who?"

Anthony carefully rolled the answer back and forth on his tongue before he decided to go with the honest one. "Nobody you'd be happy about. I take it you want her back?"

"Uh-huh."

"Do I get to live after I turn her over?"

"Live? Yes. Be happy about it? Not entirely decided yet; I'm not going to lie. Not to you, anyway."

He finally managed to wiggle into an upright sitting position as the limo hit a pothole the size of a dragon's skull. "Yes, I have her," he admitted. "No, I do not want to keep her. Yes, you can have her back. Yes, you were on the call list to –"

Em leaned forward and pressed the barrel of the slender ceramic pistol right to his head. "No lies. That's the rule."

"– contact once I figured out what to do with her," he finished.

"That's not much better but it's appreciated," she finally answered as she flipped the safety on and slid back into her seat. "Presumably you were going to shop around, see who you could bribe to get out of the mess you're in?"

"Well with both of them gone it seemed to make the most sense at the time, but honestly if you haven't noticed I've been a little busy."

"I did. I heard. I saw some of what you put out to the news," she agreed. "We almost had an entirely different conversation. I had to speak highly of you to certain parties to keep this chat tame."

"I don't think I want to know."

Her eyes flashed and she gave him one of the least reassuring smiles he'd ever seen. "*Very* highly, Anthony. I'm going to cut this quick because you're about to be busier than you want to be. We get Clare; you get Susan Sands. You also get to live because you got me out of the Down before everything went to Hell, and you're not hanging upside down over a smelter because of how much I *appreciate* that."

Anthony let out a not-so-subtle sigh of relief that was replaced by a feeling of sudden, intense confusion. "Why do I care about Susan Sands of all people? I mean yeah she's connected to the Gardeners, but I –"

Emiline stretched her little leg and nudged the center of his chest with the toes of her appropriately corp-classy burgundy boot. "How much work have you done for us?"

"As little as possible, honestly."

"True, I suppose. But. Do you know the difference between a 'need' and a 'want,' as the world uses it?" The question was apparently rhetorical, as she continued on without waiting for him to reply. "If you fill someone's 'want,' you scratch the surface. You entertain them, sure, you give them a reason to keep going as they seek to fulfill their needs. But, once you fulfill a need, you've proven yourself as more than just a source of serotonin and smiles, Anthony; you secure yourself in their life as a source for their continued existence in their life as they know it, or ironically, want it."

"I think I see where this is headed. Fine. Why do I *need* Susan Sands?"

Her smile took on a slightly kinder sheen as streetlights made her lipstick glisten in the dark limo. "Do you really think the Gardeners would make a play for the throne without her authority? Or her involvement?"

Coming from anyone else, that might've been idle conjecture. Coming from her? It felt like more of a statement of fact. "She's not the ultimate shot-caller though. That's the Organicist."

"He likes to keep his US involvements to Florida. Everything else is her providence," she replied with a little smirk. "Assume that in the here and now, not only is she calling the shots – she's loading the guns."

That, love it or hate it, was a lot of information to digest and implied a lot of things about life in the Gulf in general that he didn't like. Still, it was worth making a note of before he asked a pointed question that had to have an answer. "Is this a suggestion to solve one of your problems or mine?"

"Why can't it be both?"

"Because you're scary when you smile like that."

"Am I?" she asked as she touched the edge of her mouth and wiped her finger across her lips. "I don't have to be."

There was a lot to unpack in that line, and he decided to... not. "I'll give you Clare, but I need her for a bit first. Even if you give me Sands trussed up on a chrome platter, it doesn't do shit for the hit on my head. Until I'm in the clear, nobody's in the clear."

"Again, your honesty is appreciated, and I actually do respect the situation you're in. I don't want to see you come to harm, but I have interests to protect of my own, and I am very sad to say that you *aren't* one of them, Mr. Pierson."

"I'm one of them to the extent that I had her in my head and already put some of her soul online," he countered.

"Oh, I know. I assume you've already made appropriate backups of assorted tidbits that information to ensure you don't get stabbed by a random knife at some point," the Grimshank's presumptive new boss shot back. "Or did I overestimate you?"

Anthony bit the end of his tongue to stop his first thought, and eventually replied with a simple, "A bit of column A, a bit of row B."

"Oh look at you, excelling in sarcasm," Emiline mused before any hint of happiness on her face vanished. "Give me Clare and we'll put Sands in a hole so deep even *you* won't be able to dig her out. Instant trade."

"Instant as in, 'I have her hanging in a closet by her toes,' or, 'I have her *jol* on a sub-sphere in my bra,' instant? Because those are two different things."

"The latter, but you can presume there's an added offer of help using the shovel."

"To dig the hole?"

"Or to hit her in the face until she falls into it. Whichever works."

Her candidness was appreciated, if not chilling. "You didn't answer my question. You're telling me why *you* want Sands dead, but you're not telling me why *I* need her out of play."

"Who do you think has authorized the hit on you? The second one? The first attempt was purely accidental; collateral damage more than anything else."

Anthony looked deep into her eyes and studied her face for several long seconds. "Susan Sands doesn't know I exist."

"She does and you'd be happier if she didn't. You're costing her money, time, and people. All of which are why I'm happy to have you as my friend."

"We're friends?"

"Of course. Friendship is always better than the alternative," Emiline warned. "I also... respect you. A lesser man wouldn't have gotten involved in this mess to the extent you have. Then again, a lesser man wouldn't have earned that arm the way you did – wouldn't you say?"

The necromancer grabbed his steel shoulder out of instinct as his blood went cold. "I served. That's all."

"There's serving and then there's sacrifice," Em pointed out.

"I served," he repeated.

"So says the official story," she replied with a glint to her eye and a tone in her voice that made him want to run away. Run away, and never

ever look back. "I want to work with you in the future. You have to have a future in order for that to happen. Right now, your odds of a future without accepting help are… forgive me, but they're grim."

Every word out of her mouth was loaded with more meaning than a copy of the Webbie World Word Tool and most of them implied she knew a shit-ton more about his life than she should've. And a shit-ton more than he wanted her to. "What makes you say that?"

"Aside from the obvious?"

"You don't deal in the obvious."

Emiline laughed a little and leaned back in her seat. "Some of the things I know about your situation are things I can't speak of. What I'll say is that there are people who are in positions of power who have known about this problem long before you did. They can't touch it because it is a family matter of sorts between two very different parties – and I can't explain more than that. What I can say is that you know more about magic than I ever would pretend to. To wit, I assume you know how some bonds are worth the blood they're written in."

For someone that didn't want to say much, that said a lot.

It didn't say *enough,* but it said a *lot*.

"Fine. Next question: how the living *fuck* does getting rid of Susan Sands solve my problem with the Gardeners?"

She ran her hands down the length of her shirt and upper thighs with a slow and happy sigh. "It won't. It'll improve your standing with Heart and Spade. In fact, I am willing to bet that by the time that all of this is over, HaS will make sure that any *concerns* you have will be resolved as long as *our* concerns are resolved. Not just Clare, of course. But the other, larger issues."

"Considering the size of those issues, that's a big bet," Anthony replied. "You do know that right now my blood, sweat, and tears are pledged to the cops so I don't end up buried under a prison somewhere, right?"

"We don't want your blood."

"Well, that's –"

"Just your soul."

"That's not."

Emiline smiled and carefully reached over to put her hand on his thigh. "I'm kidding, of course."

"No, you're not."

"No, I'm not," she agreed. "I said I respected you. Unfortunately, I have a boss. My boss doesn't know enough about you to put that same measure of faith in your success. My advice? Prove your doubters wrong."

Anthony thought about pulling her hand away, but it just felt so *warm* and *nice.* More of her synth-bio implants at work, probably. Hopefully. "I didn't think the HaS got involved in family matters."

"Apparently," she replied thoughtfully, "it depends on the family."

"I also didn't think that they'd tell the Grims to contract out to a third party to eliminate some spokeswoman. I'm not an idiot, Em; you wouldn't be here if you hadn't been promoted to fixer status."

"You say that like I haven't been playing secretary for years," she countered as she wrapped her knuckles on the glass dividing wall between the front of the car and their cabin. "You do have another problem: time. In the interest of seeing this resolved with some measure of expediency, make a note: Mexico – outer Ocosingo, August 17th, 2055. January 9th, Port Putnam, Florida, 2056. I know you don't fly the clouds, but you have friends that do. Ask them to take a look, and you'll see things that make sense."

"I'm not going to like any of those, am I?"

"No," she replied. "But, I do have a name for your monster. This 'Project Wetshell,' as my dearly departed Maitre and Maitresse had named it? I would put your search bar towards a '*centurio inanis*,' if I were you."

"Centurio... inanis? That's a mouthful," he remarked after a second.

Emiline shrugged in disinterest. "Latin, I am told. A 'Void Centurion,' which sounds about as pleasant as a metal allergy in a cage."

"I think I like it less in English," Anthony replied after a few more moments. "There's some really ugly implications that suggest where these things are from."

"Accurate ones?"

He pursed his lips and had an unbidden memory of how badly the mech reeked. "I'd wish 'no' but I doubt it. Damn." After he replied, he pulled up the names and locations in the back of his head and fired them off to Fixxer. The limo's door opened, and a neon-yellow autho-cabbie greeted him just beyond. "You know Em, I was already having a bad day..."

"I know," she said with a slow smile. "Could always ask for a kiss to make it better."

He thought about it. And he wouldn't deny that he did. When Emiline's car pulled off, he slumped back against his ride and wondered if he'd regret missing the chance before the week was over.

He did.
It didn't even take the week.

8. CORPSE CAPITALISM
Tuesday, May 29th, 10:17 AM

In a sane world, getting behind the wheel of an auto-taxi and overriding the *auto* part of it wouldn't be a great idea. Fortunately, this was Los San, and sane was a matter of principle and the size of your bank account. Not that Anthony had much by way of either, aside from the escrow he'd confiscated from the Grimshanks. While Alara hadn't left him with much more than the bloody clothes on his back, Matty's 'forgotten' cerimax, and his shotgun — wrapped carefully up in his duster, as not to worry anyone that might see it — he didn't have much else to work with. According to one of the emails vying for his immediate attention, the rest of his stuff they'd recovered from the morgue had been sent on to his new, albeit temporary, apartment.

After all, he wasn't the subject of a criminal investigation. He was a subject, who was a criminal, contracted to do an investigation. Semantics: they make the world go 'round.

With the rest of his joy and life was a carefully wrapped, well-hidden shotgun, tied up with a nth-dampening Surgi-Baffle cable. (*Surgi-Baffle: For when you don't want your magic to vibrate to the nth degree!*) The very first thing he did was to pull the cord off and do the metaphysical equivalent of checking for a pulse. It was there, thank the Gods of your own personal choosing, but Alara hadn't been lying about how badly Marshal was wounded.

He'd be fine. It'd just take a while.

A while that Anthony both had and didn't have. As soon as Em had let him go, he'd popped open a network port on his arm and connected straight to the NeuroCloud to see what awaited him in the dark of this bleak little night. The email explosion he'd gotten in ICU had been bad enough, but the moment people realized he was finally awake…

It's not that he was trying to be doom and gloomy about it, but every third HeyU! in his inbox was bright orange and glowing with 'Open me first' and 'Sender knows when you see this' notifications. Two of them caught his eye more than the others. He hoped the first one was good news. It wasn't, but it could've been worse.

Anthony:

Check in on your girls; the yippy one is irritable.

And – thank you. I do not believe that all in the Church wish my people dead, but to have their hatred exposed so brightly is a terrible boon for the cause of my community. But be careful; no good deed goes unpunished.

I have asked the Others of the source of nth-disturbances. They say you are at the eye of the storm. They say that the result is man-made; the tools were not. This is beyond what humans call normal. The cause itself may be beyond what my people call tolerable.

- E

A thanks and a watch your ass from E was always nice, but less pleasant was the matching email waiting for him from Fixxer, which offered one solid piece of advice that could not be easily ignored. Advice that not only was he not going to ignore, it was advice he decided to act on.

Before the car could veer off into the westbound lane, Anthony had an override pulled up and a few fresh directions plugged in. A quick note to Alara went out next so she knew he was still breathing, although he left out where he planned to go next. She'd be pissed, but she'd have to live with it.

A:

Send a warn-warn-warning before sending my bots to kill-vids, than-than-thank you. Te-te-tend to your Gardener pro-pro-problem first – then we need to talk.

- Fixx

***

!!BIO-BAGEL!!
America's #1 Fast-Break Bagel Breakfast!

***

You couldn't take a break in the city without having an advertisement flashing in your face. Everywhere you went, you got an ad – and the only people that knew where you were better than you yourself did were the regional marketing agencies. Step out of your house, and face-track software would sell your activate location to every interactive billboard on your route.

The Walk/Inn the auto-cabbie had pulled up a block away from was absolutely no different. No sooner than he put his foot on the sidewalk than several displays changed from holistic health services to pharmaceutical-grade painkillers, caffi-cans, and some AI band with a 'new' synthwave album. The ads kept playing even as a few drone-heads near-aimlessly ambled into through the tiny, cramped corners of the bodega that served as its front office with the necromancer.

Food in front, beds above, and by-the-minute showers in the basement. College kids and Docs-Without-Offices adored the franchise. So did Callie, for similar reasons.

The holographic ad that served as the Inn's door switched to something about *America's Next Top Skyline Model* as Anthony approached and 'encouraged' him to walk straight down an aisle that was more Valley of Plenty of Ass than groceries. Any other day, he'd have found it amusing. Today was less so, and his irritated growl caught the attention of the clerk behind the desk.

The sod behind the acrylic-shielded counter didn't look much better. He was just some bored-looking twenty-something in a red tie and blue button-down. The clerk looked up, glanced at Anthony's burnt and bloodied shirt, looked at the circles under his eyes, and shrugged before he turned his attention back to the pad embedded on the counter.

"Sooo... Dah!, $3.99. Happy-Menths, $4.50 pack. Showers are $25 for twenty min; rooms are $100 for an hour, $250 for three."

The necromancer started to say something important that died on the tip of his tongue. Instead, he sagged his own shoulders a little. "Diet on the Sooo, and do you have anything related to a muffin back there?"

He answered without even looking up. "Sug-free Ras-Berry Fresh Poppers. Under-tongues, not chomps."

"You know, I miss the days when we'd actually get to chew our food," Anthony muttered under his breath.

"Still can. New wrappers. Flip 'em inside out and munch away."

Anthony looked up at the wall of snacks – nothing but bagged chips, dried-out fruit and vegetable 'supplemental substrates,' and a dusty shelf full of under-tongue body-fuels. The idea of actually eating the packaging sent a chill through him that made his monitor give a single agitated beep as the cashier went back to work.

As soon as Anthony paid for dinner with a swipe from the back of his robotic hand, the clerk returned to his pad without a second thought, then he paused, looked up, and pointed to a kiosk by the door. "Hey, there's a HealthMed kiosk there. Looks like you've gone through the shit. Gives diagnostics; $35 a symptom, $50 a script. Takes insurance. Healthy Hands network."

"Yeah, about that. What's your name?"

The clerk hesitated before he slowly pointed at a little rectangular button on his lapel. "Roger. Pronounced Rah-g-rrr."

"Fine. Roger Pronounced Rah-g-rrr, listen man. I'm gonna need to speak to your manager."

The clerk rolled his eyes and lowered his head to try to hide behind his ratty blonde bangs. "Corporate office: 361-883-"

Anthony put his right hand up on the plexi-shield, just below the silver plastic grate they were speaking through. A flash of pale yellow welled up along the scars in his chest, and a matching indent on his palm radiated a similar shade. "Your other manager."

Roger's eyes went wide and he took a single step back as he reached under the counter. "Hey. I'm just here sellin' rooms and booze man, I ain't –"

"Don't," the necromancer uttered quietly.

"Like I said, corporate office is 361-"

Anthony's left hand shot under the plastic and caught the clerk by his dangling tie. A quick tug and pull, and he slammed Roger's face down against the countertop, "Hit that alarm, and the message your people get is from a corpse; we clear?"

Roger struggled, though only for a second. "We… we clear. No alarm."

"Good man. Listen, you just want to get through your day, I want to get through my night. Roll up your sleeve. Left one."

He loosened his metal grip on Roger's tie as he uttered the instruction, and the clerk made a show of keeping both of his hands above his waist as he rolled up his sleeve. There was a tattoo of a corn stalk poking out of a skull above his elbow, under his arm and near his shoulder. "How'd you know?"

"You're working the desk at a Walk/Inn; why the hell did you think I wouldn't?" the necromancer demanded.

Anthony slowly and deliberately reached into his pants pocket and pulled out a data chat he'd imprinted on the way over. "I've got a gift for your upper management. Clare Abberdine, the Wannabe-Francias Bitch herself. You know her?"

"Yeah. I know she's dead. Why?"

"Yeah, she's dead," the necromancer agreed with a disgusted scoff before he added, "and your people should know by now that where I'm concerned, that kinda thing doesn't fucking matter. Make sure your cams are on because I'm only saying this once."

Roger reached over his head and made a show of pointing a small little pen-sized recorder at Anthony's face. "It's live-streamed. They already know you're here, and it'll take 'em less than five to get here and kill you, you know that, right?"

"I know that'd be a really dumb idea," Anthony retorted as he looked up at the mini-cam. "Hey, assholes. If I die, my ex dies, my current dies, or anyone I know and/or love gets so much as a stubbed toe? You lose your chance on a datadump the likes of which you've never dreamed of. *And,* for good fucking measure, everything she ever knew about you little shits goes right to LSPD and Hoover Cent both. I can fucking promise you she knew more about your org than any of you thought she did," he called out before he turned his gaze back to the hapless clerk. "As for you?"

"Chief, I ain't got nothin' to do with shit and –"

"You do now. Tell your crew it's time to cut their losses. Or better, straighten their Slashes."

"What the hell is that supposed to mean?"

"Harold Vincetti," Anthony challenged. "So help me God, before this week is out he's gonna be public enemy #1 if I have any say in it and trust me kid, I do. If your people burn him and put his ass out in the cold, I'll make sure that Clare's soul becomes the biggest harvest they can possibly imagine. A trade for a trade – the cops or a grave get his head, your bosses get Clare's soul."

Roger with a purring 'r' blinked slowly and made sure both of his hands were safely on the counter before he replied. "I've heard that name. I ain't heard yours, and I don't want to. The cam picked up everything."

"I suppose you're gonna try to find some way to slow me down before your greenbacked assjacks get here?"

"No chance, hombre, none. I know that name, and now I officially do not give a fuck about anything but closing down early tonight. We cool?"

"Cool, then we're cool," Anthony answered before he ran his hand over the glass barrier and focused on his palm. Cracks appeared as the plas-glas began to melt under his palm. When he was done, a dripping message was left behind. "Top one is my direct line. Your boss can reach me there. Bottom one? Last four of an account number. Your boss will know what it is. I'm not putting up the whole thing because you seem like a nice guy and they'll gut you sideways if you know all of it."

"I am a nice guy," the clerk huffed as he picked up his phone and snapped a picture of the dissolving plastic. Anthony smiled for the camera and pointed at both lines as Roger took the picture. "You don't know what she does to *nice guys,* though, do you?"

"I have an idea or two," Anthony admitted as he tapped his fingertip on the counter. Another yellow flare radiated out from under his skin as he dissolved another address into the plastic sheathing. "Dimir. She's local PD. Call her after you call them, or don't, I don't care. She might help you out for being a *nice guy.*"

"Man, I was gonna catch the Pyro-Bowl match tonight. Orion 'imself is supposed to be on the –"

"Dude, I could give less of a shit about a guy who runs trains for a living. Depending on how the rest of your night goes, you may end up being tied to the first tracks outta town. We both know you don't really have a choice to pass this on, right?" Anthony pointed skyward to the cameras tracking his every movement in stony, mechanical silence.

Roger rolled his sleeve down and took a picture of Alara's contact info before he pocketed his phone. "I don't get paid enough for this, ya know? How about you get the hell outta my store?"

Anthony stopped, looked up at the mirror, and then reached for his wallet and tossed the poor sod an extra fiver. On his way out, he grabbed a bagel off a display and wandered back to the autocab with a happy little, "Thank you!" and a wave.

***

Happy-Menth!
Another Healthy Stimu-Smokable Food Alternative from
Your Friends at Eden Farms.
Remember: Who's Tending Your Garden?
***

The drive through the city was as peaceful as it could be, however little that honestly was. The autocab helped; the throbbing pain in Anthony's chest did not. It only took half an hour to cut through uptown, but those few minutes of relative peace made all the difference in the damn world.

'Peace' didn't mean a nap. Or a rest. Or anything other than the sound of heavy traffic blaring around his head in every direction, no matter how soundproof the cabin was supposed to be. He'd taken the time to turn off the cab's popup media panel when it started blaring another ad for the esteemed otherworldly 'benefactors' of the city – *The Heart and Spade Foundation: Our Love Comes from the Bottom Up*. Even so, it did nothing to cut down on the deluge of holograms and flat-casts dotting the highway in a constant stream.

At least the ad revenue kept the potholes fixed.

What it meant was that he had a chance to breathe. A chance to think. A chance to finally ignore every voice screaming in his head and to give a middle finger to the voices outside of it. It also gave him a few minutes to hammer the side of his head against the window. There were too many headaches in his life with distinct names, and they all wanted a piece of his peace.

So, he pulled them all up, one by one, in his internal HUD.

Sojourn Enterprises. A bio-*mech* firm that, as Clare had deftly pointed out, specialized in advanced sub-dermal and mixed-organic 'pep' enhancements. On the surface, they didn't look like much; perky tits and tight asses dominated their corporate info-sheet. However, if you dug deeper, some of their performance stats showed numbers more in line with sub-cu body armor and bone-deep hazmat protections.

They weren't cheap, either. One full skin-job would set you back close to a quarter mil, and if you were looking for bone replacement therapy or external form-jacks, you were *starting* in the range of a year's rent in a midtown apartment. That cost targeted a very specific market—the byline on their 'tissue investment' page made it clear who the company was selling to.

'*Ask about corp-wide rates! Protect your bottom line with sapien-organic defensive systems today!*'

Except... that was just their public face. Alara had Corp-Regi send over a full breakdown package, complete with a tidbit regarding ownership – HawkCrest, as Matty had confirmed earlier. Anthony knew that name for the same reason everyone else did... and then some.

Even if it hadn't been plastered all over Omari's face from Jordan's testimony, he'd have known it by logo, name, and mailing address. HawkCrest wasn't just a major player in the DoD's 'full-scale, full-service, full-return' post-deployment programs; they were considered one of the top destinations for anything that involved physical rehab and biologic redevelopment. Their headquarters even had an aviary in their lobby for added style points.

They had contracts with multiple national governments valued on the low end of a couple billion, and that ignored their state-funded agreements for public insurance and recovery. That made two links of a chain. As for the third, you didn't make billions by outsourcing one of your most important internal necessities.

Needs like mil-grade sec.

Needs like street-level logistic defense.

Needs that a sec-firm like Blackwash could solve.

Needs that had gotten incredibly *sloppy* without *any* viable reason. All of it boiled down to four chains connected to an anchor named Harold 'My AKA Is A Verb!' Vincetti. That anchor was right in the middle of a seabed of mechanical parts and festering corpses that made up whatever the so-called Project Wetshell was.

Somehow, those chains hung off of America's Bullet Express.

There were some otherwise pertinent questions he hadn't brought up with Alara that had been nagging at him since he had learned who the players were. Necro-anth research was illegal as cooking *azul* in your bedroom, and a hell of a lot more expensive. Whomever was funding it didn't *care*, and that was a ticket to an entirely different carnival ride of nightmares.

And then there were the questions of, 'Why Daems?' and, 'Why in the US?' and 'How long has this been going on?' that needed to be answered. Em's comments sure as sunshine made it sound like it'd been going on for a while, and he was sure he wouldn't like those answers when they'd eventually come up. There was one more problematic issue:

Why was the cover-up so freaking *bad*?

That question deserved an immediate answer, but it wouldn't be delivered anytime soon. While he pondered it, the peace and quiet of the info-dive came to an end when the cab pulled up to a Pop-Up! Tower Complex. The name was the only cheerful thing about it; this week, it'd be apartments. Next week, half of those apartments would be rented out to office drones doing data-entry-by-night jobs. A month later, there would be a club on the top floor and a laundromat on the bottom. The locals would complain about gentrification. The developer would complain that nobody wanted to sign a long-term lease.

Then, PUT Corporate would find another chunk of mildew-filled real estate, flatten it, and put another condo there. The cycle would repeat itself ad nauseam, and God help you if you suggested the words 'rent control' within earshot of the development board. Even so, Pop-Up! was known for its solid security and ample lighting, making it the go-to locale for LSPD and the private sector alike. If nothing else, the extra lighting kept most of the street-level trash from hanging around too much.

The lobby of the PUT had exactly two people in it: one was the full-mask desk drone that had half of its attention buried somewhere in the NeuroCloud, and the other was some tranced-out chick with neuva-dreads down one side of her head and a pink side-ponytail on the other.

She was too blasted on azul to remember her own name, let alone his face. The drone took one glance at his ident card and buzzed him through to the elevator. Neither of them gave notice nor care to the obvious shotgun-sized package under his metal arm, and the only other biometric device in the lobby was an intercom system he had to give his name. Whatever security the hotel offered was likely built around the idea of 'nobody knows so nobody cares,' which wasn't as reassuring as he figured it was supposed to be.

Apparently satisfied he was who he said he was, the building security system kicked him off on the fourth floor. A few minutes later, and he was face-first on a bed with every intention to sleep the next eighteen hours away. If intention ruled the world, it would have been a much better place.

And, if some motherfucker would shut the fuck up and let him sleep…

Anthony picked up his buzzing phone an hour later, looked at the masked number, and unleashed a plethora of profanities into it the moment his thumb brushed 'accept.' The caller took every ounce of it, then in a flat monotone voice, asked simply:

"*Ar-ar-are you done ye-ye-yet?*"

"Do I need to repeat it?" he grumbled as he pushed himself up and into a sitting position.

"*Ye-ye-yes, but not to me-me-me!*" Fixxer's violently cheerful voice retorted. "*How's the heart? Broken? Battered? Bruised?*"

"Yes, yes, and yes. It hurts like hell, Fixx."

The phone's speaker made a distinctly comical sound straight out of a 1990s sitcom, complete with a 'waa waa' noise and a canned laugh track.

"Well then! Let's patch that hole and play a ga-ga-game! Do you want the go-go-good news or the bad?"

Anthony groaned and dropped the phone on his bed. With a gesture from his cyber arm, he flicked the video screen display over to the wide-panel TV at the end of his bed and watched as Fixxer's face-of-the-moment jumped into full view. "Does any of it mean I get to sleep before dawn?"

"Sleep is for the dead," the digital avatar exclaimed joyfully, *"w*hen *people like yo-yo-you let them rest."*

"Since when did you get to be so Goddamn judgmental?"

"Since you started prep-prep-preparing to be an executioner," the digital face mocked as a black hood popped over his head. *"Which you are la-la-late on."*

The necromancer's noncommittal grunt carried all the weight he deigned to give and was greeted just as warmly. "Finding people takes intel, Fixx, *actionable* intel. Something I've been light on."

"Not that li-li-light. You've been waging war on yo-yo-your own. You missed getting our master of ver-ver-verbage when you were playing pa-pa-paw a corpse at the morgue. Bad news first: you are a wa-wa-wanted man by anyone who avoids a badge. Slash has been turning over ev-ev-every rock in the city looking for you."

"He hasn't found me, so he can't be that good at it."

"Oh no! He found you! He kn-kn-knew which hospital you were in. Thank LSPD for ha-ha-having the wherewithal to lock their ICU down. He knows you're go-go-gone, too; he just hasn't quite cracked where to yet!"

Anthony cut loose with another slew of profanity before he caught himself uttering more blasphemies than he figured he had earned good-boy credit to use. "Do I have you to thank for that?"

A little laugh bounced out of the speakers as a handful of mirthful emojis bounced across the screen. *"There may be si-si-sightings of you from South San to the Port of Anthi. Just may-may-maybe. Make no mis-mis-mistake, he wants you go-go-gone. Breaking his toy at the Reproc did not put him in a good mood."*

Another string of curses filled the room, followed by an outright self-loathing crimination. "Well, that's too fucking bad. That toy deserved to be broken."

"More than you kn-kn-know," Fixxer agreed.

As tired as he was, Anthony almost let that slide.

Almost.

"But you know…"

"*So does the blonde Grim-shell, it so seems,*" the digital voice answered with an unpleasant flux behind the words. "*Those dates she told you? She couldn't have pa-pa-paved the yellow brick road with more gold if she'd tri-tri-tried.*"

"Oh shit. What'd you fi—"

Fixxer was only happy to interrupt him. "*That tiny blonde bimb-bimb-bimbette called it a Centurio Inanis, yes? I-I-I call it a walking ni-ni-nightmare. I think you'll agree.*"

The words died in his mouth as the flatscreen display opened three new windows on its own — and each one displayed a different way to embrace the Geneva Suggestions. Two of them were titled with the regions Emiline had named, and the third had a geo-tag that set it somewhere near the city-state of Port-au-Prince. The trio played out roughly the same way; each looked like they were recorded on early 2000's grainy-cam, or at least, someone's third-world-hacked-together ocular feed. The one in what used to be known as Haiti had more of an urban combat feel, though that wasn't horribly out of place.

All three videos had a different version of the bio-mech that had trashed the morgue, too. In the oldest one from Mexico, the mech was more meat than metal; long metal stilts had been grafted into and through its legs, though the torso seemed relatively untouched except for the head. A year later, in Florida, a different mech had been rigged with a multitude of oxygen tanks and heavy metal plates that made the corpse look like a submersible trashcan more than it did a weapon.

But in Port-au-Prince, three months ago? It had more tech wrapped around it than the one in the recyc center. There was a lot to unpack; a mix of realizations that the one in the morgue hadn't been some kind of one-off prototype, the fact that there actually were more than one of these, and the fact that Fixxer had been able to find out about them relatively quickly.

The latter was worse than anything else.

Because if Fixx could find these videos in a manner of hours...

...then there was no doubt that a lot of other people knew about them, too. Knew and hadn't done anything about it. Knew, and hadn't made it public. That tracked with what Em had said, but there was a difference between 'hearing' and 'realizing.'

You could hide a lot under the Cloud. But even if you hid it, the Feds knew it. They may not know *who* or *why,* but they knew *it,* whatever *it* was. There were just enough big and bad implications to these videos existing on the cloud that if what the mechs were *doing* in the feed wasn't enough to make him throw up, the suggestions about who might know about them absolutely were.

And to reiterate, they hadn't done anything about it.

Or if they had, they'd been quieted.

Somehow, that didn't make him feel any better at all.

"Please," Anthony began as he watched as a woman's head was slowly ripped off of her neck, "tell me that these were hard to find."

"You know I'd alwa-alwa-nev-never lie to you, Mr. Pierson! Once you told me where to look..."

"Okay. Well," he replied slowly as he sank into the mattress, "that's a lot worse than expected. Are the full broadcasts as bad as these snippets?"

The screen focused on the video from the Penni, where two black men with heavy machine guns poured lead into the mech facing them down. Bullets ripped necrotic flesh off the mechanoid's frame, and the injuries didn't seemingly do anything to slow it down. Anthony turned his head away when the mech wrapped its hand around the face of the closest gunman and started to squeeze.

"Yes."

The word was punctuated with a distorted scream and a wet crunch. "Anything *useful* from them, or are they just snuff videos?"

All three screens spun out at once with a global map and a half-dozen different overlays that popped up over and around them. Every window Fixxer pulled up had some measure of pertinent data on it; locations to the nearest known Sojourn or Blackwash office, names of the predominant gangs or other underworld figures, and in the case of the video from Mexico, a couple of identities to go with the bodies. The latter wasn't as helpful as it sounded, though Anthony made a point to catalog the names for Alara later.

"No."

Anthony leaned back and braced himself up by his elbows. Emiline wouldn't have dropped these bombs without a reason, and making him take a forced view of a bloodbath probably wasn't it. "Alright. That just means that there's something in them we aren't seeing. Set it aside for right now."

The screen seemingly *bent* inside itself as a disgusting tunnel of eyes opened up and swallowed the three main windows and all of their children in a cosmic-horror inspired *gulp*. As the necromancer gagged, Fixxer cut loose with a few choice words of his own. *"I see everything, Mis-Mis-Mister Pierson. You know that."*

He took a long breath and touched the exposed bandage on his chest. "What I know is that those don't look like prototypes to me. Judging by the way they were being used, they also look like the Sub-Soua Carties are running them."

"Weeds in the Garden," the shapeless avatar answered. *"Banned from doing business in the USA, but their fert-fert-fertilizer-prone brethren are underfoot too much as of la-la-late."*

"Not wrong. Both want to exert more influence in Los San than what they've got, but c'mon, the cartels have more brains than to use this kinda tech on this side of the border. South Am? Sure. Hell, pick half the countries on the other side of the planet, and you could get away with it. We both know there's worse shit than this brewing in the Indo-Pak-Paci sphere, so why the fuck *here*?"

The screen flashed a picture of the modern-day globe, complete with country flags and marks pointing out levels of infrastructure available. *"You can get Daems any-any-anywhere. The chems for anth-biologics? Go where the man-man-manufacturing is. There are seventeen chem plants in the i-i-immediate Gulf area that cover the types of polymers needed for —"*

Anthony glowered at the screen as countries ticked off the map one by one until only the US, the South-Indi Republic, and the Tech-Monarchy of Madagascar were left on the screen. "Fine, but why *use* it here and not just Fed-BOX the stock to a lab of your choosing run by friendly slave labor that will keep their mouths shut? I mean, honestly. It's like they've got their own private highwa…"

As the thought slowed to a crawl, he leaned forward and tapped his fingers on a marker for Port Putnam, Florida. It was on the outer edges of the Flo-Penni 'Anth-logic Quarantine Zone,' or as politely known, the edge of the Breakdown. The inhabitants had a different name for it: Hell's 4th Circle.

They weren't that wrong.

"You have the face of a man having a revelation," Fixxer intoned as Anthony studied the screen and quietly pulled up a couple of different maps in his HUD.

"Bring up the rail lines and their owners that go through… Perry, Houston, and… there… Nuva-Mex City."

Fixxer did just that, and a small handful of different names popped up. One of them was all too familiar. *"In Mex, it's Soci-Gov owned and —"*

"— and all the hippie-commie stuff is corp PR bullshit," the necromancer interrupted. "Who pays for them?"

There was a very short pause before the digital avatar came up with the expected answer: an immediately recognizable logo. "I... I don't like where this is going."

"South Shore Boarding and Line. Third time they've come up, which means it sure as fuck ain't coincidence. And wouldn't you know it — they've got the lines that go from Nor-Flori to Oregon, right?"

"Ye-ye-yes and no. With their main transfer hub in Tucson that converts to their sis-sis-sister corp, West-State IronRoad," Fixxer confirmed.

Anthony cut loose with a burst of profanity that made the digital presence put an anime sailor on the screen, complete with a blush that went from head to toe. "Fuck me. I get it."

"I'll say that you're not my ty-ty-type, but I..."

"Shut up. Listen. It's a mobile lab. That's why it's being centered out of here. SSBL has lines that funnel this project to every city with a vested interest in this shit. They get their bodies out of Florida and have them unloaded, sorted, tested, whatever they're doing, and then processed *here*. The ones that don't pass their checks get moved on to wherever the Church is putting on their public face, and the ones that *do* get approved for further processing end up getting bundled with their biomed supplies. It's easier and safer than sticking them on a plane and less likely to get pulled over on the freeway."

"Or reported by a nosy nei-nei-neighbor," Fixxer added. *"Assuming from there, then, they get to go on a choo-choo tri-tri-trip to parts unknown."*

"Parts known, I guess. I mean, look at that video from Ocosingo. According to the map, that's pretty fucking close to the Atlantic, and that means global shipping for any interested buyers."

"Well, then, you'll lo-lo-love this," Fixxer crowed. The screen returned to all black, replaced moments later with a rainbow-tinted holding pattern before he finally spoke up. *"I ca-ca-can't find an O-O-Omari Miller that's ever worked for Sojourn, Crest, or their im-im-immediate tech-or-bio subsidiaries. He cou-cou-could be through an outside agency or a firm with investments, but not anyone that wou-wou-would have access to internal pro-pro-project specs."*

That wasn't just a headache. It was a *headache*.

"Hold up. You're telling me that Jordan got killed over a guy who doesn't exist? I'm not questioning your work, Fixx, but —"

Fixxer flashed a series of gold question marks across the screen and played the theme from an old question-and-answer broadcast show. *"I wor-wor-worked hard on those internal da-da-databases,"* he whined. *"I am not as per-per-perfect as you are, but he doe-do-does not exist in their public connected ser-ser-servers."*

Before Anthony could comment, a steady stream of names began to cascade down the side of the display. Specifically, *one* name — Omari Miller — and a running total on top that finally ended at seventy-eight thousand records in the US alone. A few seconds later, the list of Omaris in the south crested around ten… which changed a heartbeat later to ten *thousand*.

"Okay, I get it. There's a lot of him. Fine. You can't find him; I ain't mad. Odds are good whoever contracted Slash has already fed this idiot to a wood-chipper anyway."

"Odds are," Fixxer agreed. *"But… I do have some go-go-good news. The nu-nu-numbers you've been seeing in the mem-taps? I fo-fo-found them."*

"Alright, spill. I'm beyond curious. I assumed it was gibberish."

"An-An-Anthony!" Fixxer exclaimed. *"I'm sho-sho-shocked! You don't usually miss a clue."*

"It's been a week."

A double-stack train appeared on the screen before the avatar answered. *"SBAL is the company ID for a double-decker mag-lev cargo hauler owned and op-op-operated by, you guessed it! — SSBL! And! For bo-bo-bonus points, it's marketed under ABE Re-Re-Relocation Services. 131718 is the car ident-ident-identifier."*

Anthony's jaw dropped a second time. "No way. You didn't —"

"I-I-I believe this is called corroborating evidence. It's a sha-sha-shame I'm not allowed to go into court."

"Yeah, your circuits would catch fire and everyone's phones would start speaking Yiddish the moment they tried swearing you in on a Bible to tell the whole truth and nothing but. Backward Yiddish, at that," the necromancer pointed out. "That said, I could kiss you…"

"I-I-I would much prefer if you di-di-didn't," the avatar replied, as a happy laughing emoji bounced across the screen. *"Your ans-ans-answers are in the numbers, and the numbers are on the rails!"*

The number flashed on the screen again, and then changed to footage of a newscast with a bored-looking local reporter (not one of the national talking heads) standing beside one of the new monorail stations that had cropped up downtown over the last five years. It was part of a new 'national transit' investment from the suits out in DC. Advertisements promoting the damn things were everywhere. *Single Rail. Single People. One Nation on the Line.*

"…and with the backing of Honest ABE, the South Shore Boarding and Line rail specialists are happy to announce the new Double Stack Nth-Trans will be able to haul twice as many traditional mono- or dual-rail service lines. Using their new Nth-Lift Engines, South Shore expects to revolutionize the logistics industry by…"

Fixxer muted the blonde before she could ramble on any further, though the real focus was the ad stamped across the leading car's faceplate. *'Ride into the Future with Master Chief Orion. Ride with Honest ABE.'*

Anthony stared at the advert and felt the muscles in his shoulders start to cramp, "I swear to God I need a flowchart for this."

"I ca-ca-can provide one!"

"Don't… just. Don't. Corporate links aside, I still don't get it."

"It seems fairly straightforward."

"No, it doesn't," he argued. "This isn't a case of some kind of runaway Frankenstein. This isn't a lab experiment gone wrong. This was targeted overkill, twice, with a treaty-breaking corporate no-no machine. I mean, half of the EBR laws are enforced by the UN, useless as they generally are, but still enforced by them. You don't break those and then go mosey off to Europe for a vacation without having every alphabet agency on the planet put a tank-sized hole in the back of your neck."

A slew of '?' marks rolled across the screen before his semi-partner finally answered. *"What if it's a case of a runaway middle finger?"*

"What do you mean?"

The corporate HaS playing-card-and-spade logo popped up in the background. *"The Spades knows about these. Angry about it too, if they choose to be this obvious in how they fe-fe-feed you."*

"And?"

"Whoever is funding this program just showed those corporate hed-hed-hedonists that they can put it in their backyard any time they want."

That was an unpleasant point to make, but it had all the signs of being the right one… or at least part of it. "Huh. 'We have nukes, and we're not afraid to use them,' type of threat?"

A quiet video started to play of archaic nuclear tests from way back when. *"A tale as old as the split atom,"* the avatar intoned.

"Even if that was the case, they surely wouldn't have used them against the Church – not for something this high profile. Stomp a corp agent or something, sure. Something Jordan isn't. I mean, not unless you *want* an all-out war. Gotta think there's better ways to start one than this."

"But you al-al-already believe the Sine ordered the hit."

"El-Rhodes passed what he knew about Jordan on to Slash or Adams or someone. I don't doubt that. I doubt that he knew they'd use… whatever that mech was. No. There's something else here. Something I'm not seeing."

*"In that case, we work another ass-ass-**ass**pect of this problem,"* the Avatar intoned with just the right level of inflection to be offensive. *"We make a point to just hack the Slash."*

That was another accurate, albeit repetitive, point: "Gotta find that blade to dull it."

"Then do your job," his handler answered succinctly. *"I hi-hi-hired you to get rid of him. Instead, you've opened a can of cor-cor-corporate worms – complete with gangland offers for hits on your side and theirs. Not my fa-fa-fault you don't like that they're living ones and not gu-gu-gummies."*

The necromancer rubbed his steel hand across his lips, desperate for the sensation of something solid. Fixxer was absolutely, one-hundred percent *right*, and it didn't help. *At all.* "Yeah, well, now that you mention it, as much as I am not a fan of premeditated murder, Em's promise of a world without Susan Sands in it would be a better one for everybody with a heartbeat."

"If you're going to find my opposition, then yo-yo-you just need to figure out why the Spa-Spa-Spades want you to hunt a ghost."

"No, I need to figure out why both the cops *and* the corps want me to hunt a ghost," he countered. "One is bad enough. Two is problematic."

"Not the kind of menage-a-trois you'd like to be in."

"No. Fixx, I hate to say this, but getting rid of Slash isn't going to solve much. If he's running security for this bullshit, his boss is the problem."

Fixxer's avatar flicked a few times in between bursts of static. *"A you problem. Not a me problem."*

"That depends on how you look at it. The deeper this goes, the worse it gets."

"That's cor-cor-corporate life."

"That's *attention*. If LSPD doesn't resolve it, Hoover Central will. You're involved."

"Because of you."

"You said Slash is your direct competition, and you put a name to his face for me," Anthony countered. "If he's doing work you're wrapped up in on the side, then the Feds will start digging around in his deals and –"

The screen shifted to static again. *"Sav-sav-save it. I dislike it when you have a poi-poi-point. You hunt Slash. I'll look for Ad-Ad-Adams."*

"Both mean Sojourn," Anthony answered with a mild groan. "On the other hand, he may be less of a headache for you soon. Once the DA's office can get through a mountain of red tape, they're going to unleash the hounds on him."

"What are they wai-wai-waiting for? An engraved inv-inv-invitation?"

"A check to clear, I think. I also put out a feeler to the Gardeners for a trade; if Slash becomes persona non grata at their doing, I've got a lead on some non-*this* stuff enough to negotiate a treaty. It's whoever gets to him first that's gonna be the question."

Fixxer's smiley-faced avatar reappeared on the screen with a cartoonish frown and a wagging yellow finger. *"Or if so-so-someone gets to you. It's a race to see who ends up staked out in the desert!"*

"Speaking of being tied up and put on display, Callie said she had encounters with the suits at Sojourn before. Maybe she knows something we can use to get through this."

"You just want an ex-ex-excuse to check on your ex-ceptional —"

"Ugh, don't even say it. Let me make a call."

"You do-do-do that, but hu-hu-hurry."

"You're not one to be impatient. What's wrong?"

"Aside from being worried about your con-con-continued health? Am I not allowed to just be a fri-fri-friend?"

Anthony sat up and gave the screen a very blank stare. "No."

A giant bandage flashed across the flat-panel. *"You wo-wo-wound me, good sir!"* Fixx complained.

The screen went blank immediately after.

***

Phone calls at eleven in the evening generally went one of two ways: 'Are you free to fuck' or 'Help me, I'm fucked.' Either way, the woman on the other end of the line responded succinctly upon answering. "Do you have any idea what time it is? Get fucked."

"If I thought I could, I would."

"Oh my God! Are you okay?" The question came out loudly, with a lot less indifference than Callie had planned for whenever she heard from him next. She'd even rehearsed it quietly in the bathroom, not that she'd ever admit it.

"It's been a long couple of days," Anthony admitted after a painfully long, drawn-out pause. "Are you two alright?"

"We're… living," Callie answered as Katherine slowly opened her eyes and lifted her head off her pillow. "We haven't killed each other yet, so there's that."

"Please don't," Anthony feebly pleaded. "That would kind of undermine everything I'm working towards, and… yeah."

Katherine scooted across the bed, leaning in even as Callie tried pushing her back. "Is that Anthony?" she whispered.

Callie waved her off with a dirty look and a sneer. "He's mine, go away."

"What was that?"

"Uh, nothing. Okay, so we're all alive. What's going on?"

"Listen, I'm trying to dig us out of this shit, and it keeps getting worse. You two are safe but not in the clear," Anthony replied. "The guys that tried to kill Kath still have a contract."

Callie cursed under her breath and felt her shoulders sag. "Dammit. How about me?"

"Me, you, her," he replied in resignation. "Half the Daems in Texas. The chucklefucks who tried are pissed they didn't succeed, and they're trying to earn back their reps."

"Oh good, because if there's one thing that murderous sociopaths need, it's a strong rep," she growled under her breath.

Katherine chimed up with a very quiet, "Actually…"

Before Callie could utter something in response, Anthony cut her off. "Was that Kath? Good. I need to talk to her, too. But, first, I need something from you."

It took every ounce of strength she had not to *gush* in response and to remember that, yes, she actually was pissed as hell at him. "Yes, I mean, why in the world would I –"

"You've done work for Sojourn Enterprises, right? Didn't you say that?"

And that wasn't the question she'd been expecting. It wasn't even in the same zip-code. "Uh, yeah? A lot of us do."

"Why?"

"Why?" she asked as she blinked. "I dunno. Hard dicks? Usually the reason."

"No, I mean, why are their corporate bosses dropping titties on their crew? Don't they have wives, girlfriends, whatever? You don't see a lot of corp-sponsored fuck-'n-sucks for the middle-management types unless they're overseas or platformed off-shore."

She perked up almost immediately, "Oh, that's easy. A lot of them are travelers. Their people work all over the states. Load us up on a train, and away we'd go."

There was a long pause from him as he brought up Fixxer's map in his head. "Really. Any idea why?"

"Not really. I know that they've got a campus by the Westlake Mono-Hub. Wouldn't know it to see it; don't think I've ever seen a sign on it, just a dorm."

"A dorm by a mono-hub?"

"Dorm, hotel, whatever," she remarked. "They used to hire on for cross-country trips. Hop on here, get fucked all the way to the west coast, suck dick on the way back. Kinda fun. We should – I mean, you should try it sometime. Or not. I don't care."

Katherine rolled her eyes. "Used to?"

Callie caught herself and thought about it for a second. "Used to. Last time they threw something that way was, eh, six… eight months ago? Probably just got a diff agency."

"Different agency… yeah," Anthony repeated slowly. "Got an address?"

She did, and a few seconds later, she had it sent in a message from her phone. "So why do you care about a bunch of suits gettin' laid?"

"They're trying to kill us."

"They are?"

"Well, not *them* specifically, but yeah," he replied. "Thanks, Callie. That helps way more than you realize."

The escort shrugged. "Yeah, yeah. When the fuck are we getting out of here? I'm kinda not into the whole kidnapping kink. You get me?"

"You'd like the 'fucked in a morgue' kink even less," Katherine retorted icily.

"That's not true."

"Of course it isn't," Anthony's ex replied with a disgusted sigh. "Gimmie the damn phone."

Before either party could argue, the older woman had shoved her pillow into Callie's face and knocked her onto her ass on the floor. Katherine tore into him as Callie's protests raged in the background. "I swear to every God in the Alternates that if you don't get me out of this apartment, I'm going to kill both of you, and then myself. I'm *done*, Anthony. Get me the *hell* out of here."

"I'm working on it," Anthony whined. "Listen, it's not just me. I'm sending someone for you in the morning. Be gentle with her. She's pretty banged up."

"Oh. Oh, I see," she snarled. "You're sending me another 'banged up' woman. What, you have time to go get some new skank while –"

"G'damn, Kath. It's *Alara*. I made arrangements to get you two into pro-custody."

Katherine's protests and indignation died on her lips. "A... Alara? She's helping you?"

"Yeah, like I keep saying, I'm *trying*," he retorted. "Honestly, I'm doing my fucking best over here. Not like this is a vacation. I've been shot at, blown up, hunted by the cops, worked for the cops... I had to talk to your brother; I had a heart attack..."

"You had a heart attack?!"

Callie jumped to her feet and went straight for the phone. "He had a *what*? Anthony, are you okay?!"

His ex shoved her away and clutched the phone to her cheek. "And what do you mean you talked to my brother? He's... oh. Oh no. Tell me you didn't. Tell me you *fucking* didn't!"

Callie watched the blood drain from the slightly-older woman's face and took a step back on her own. "Didn't you say that your brother is... oh. And he's... *ohhhh*."

"Well, you don't like it when I lie to you, so take your pick," Anthony retorted. "Wasn't what I wanted to do either."

"But you did it."

"Yeap."

"He's gotta fucking hate you."

His reply came after a few seconds, and he sounded so utterly exhausted she almost felt a twinge of pity. "He's hated me since we first met. Look, I didn't really have a choice. He was in a bad spot, and things didn't go as planned."

"Are you implying there was a plan?"

"I decline to say if it was a good one," Anthony muttered, "but honestly, it was for the best. You don't want to know what they did to him."

"The actual absolute Hell I don't. He's my brother. I deserve –"

"He's your brother, is why I'm *not* gonna tell you *shit*," the necromancer retorted. "His soul is safe right now. I'm going to help him move on soon."

Tears started to form up in the corner of Katherine's eyes as her voice fell flat. "Safe place *now*? Help him move on *soon*? Why. The fuck. Is he even. *Earthbound*?"

He heard her tone shift. Not only did he hear it, he knew exactly the kind of look she had on her face. For the safety of everyone involved (up to and including Callie), he decided to pick his words *carefully*, just this once. "They killed him, then abducted him. I helped extradite him from his… detention," he mostly-honestly replied. "Unfortunately, now he's bound. The better and worse news is that he's bound to me. Getting him unbound is high on my list of interests."

"How high? I swear, Anthony, you better fu–" Before she could finish the threat, her phone buzzed, and a copy of his hospital stay flashed on the screen. The curse died in her throat as she scrolled through the breakdown and slowly hunched over the phone. "What is…"

A matching copy of it flashed on Anthony's side, along with a little smiley-face from Fixxer that included a note that read, "*You three aren't fu-fu-fun to listen in on.*"

If Kath registered the comment, she didn't note it, even as the color left her face. "Oh. Good. God."

"Learn any new self-admin treatments for n-tox? I'm feeling kinda sore."

"You… you're going into protective too. *Right*?"

"Kinda."

"You're going into protective custody too, *right*?" she repeated.

Different tone. Different look. It even set the escort back on her heels. "When people are done shooting at us, yes," he finally agreed.

It was the best Katherine was going to get, and she knew it. Finally, after she finished reading through the notes, she caved. "Is Jordan okay, at least? Mentally?"

Anthony's lip quivered a little. "Kath… let me just…"

"Is he better with you than where he was?"

"Better with me. I swear."

Her shoulders tensed up, and her eyes widened a hair. Callie didn't see it, but her ex recognized the fury almost instantly. "Dammit. Are you going to be able to help him?"

"I promise I'm doing everything I can. When I can. That's just going to have to wait a while."

Her eyes sank a little. "I hate that I get it, but you're telling me everything *later*," she conceded, "and you're still a fucking idiot. So, when are we getting out of here?"

"Tomorrow is the plan. Just hang tight, okay?"

"Right." She looked over at the escort as Callie continued to hover just a few feet away. "You wanna talk to your girlfriend *experience* again or…?"

It was a tough call, but… "Please?"

When she took the phone, there was a mumbled mutual 'Hey,' and then nothing but awkward silence until Katherine finally rolled her eyes and slid off the bed for the bathroom. "Oh, just tell him you miss him and get it over with."

"I…"

"Yeah, same," the necromancer replied. "You two getting along okay?"

Callie glanced over her shoulder as Katherine scratched her panty-clad ass on the way into the lavatory. "If I had to pick between living with her and raising the dead for the Army, I'd have bought a shovel, too."

On the other end of the line, Anthony couldn't help but cringe. "That good, huh?"

"She's scared, Anthony. I'm scared. I'm scared I'm gonna end up having to leave town, she's scared she's gonna end up having to bury you… for some reason." Callie's voice was so soft, Anthony had to strain just to hear it. "Can't say I'm thrilled with the idea of being shot, myself. You, I'm not so sure about but…"

"No… no, I'm not either," he answered with a tired yawn. "Listen. I'm about to do something to get them off of our backs and put this all behind us. It's not going to be easy, but… just trust me. I got you into this, I'll get you out of it."

"*You* didn't get me into shit," Callie countered, "but *you* lied to me about what you did for a living. Security consultant, wasn't it?"

"What did you say your name was? *Sunny Jubilee?*"

"I gave you my real name after our third date, *Silver Hand*. When were you going to tell me you preyed on dead people?"

"We both work with stiffs," he countered. "Mine are just a bit… colder than yours."

Callie pinned the phone to her shoulder and crossed her arms. "And they probably stay stiffer much longer than some of the ones I'm used to."

Anthony heard Katherine's laugh echo over the line as he tried to formulate something even remotely witty in response. When all efforts failed, he broke down. "I'm sorry," he said simply.

It must've taken her aback for a moment, because when she finally spoke up again, her voice seemed to waver. "Yeah, yeah. You just… keep that arm of yours in good condition, alright, *Silver*? You fucking owe me one."

"I… I owe you several."

"Damn right you do," she agreed, "so don't die."

"No promises, but I'll try."

The phone beeped once in her hand as he disconnected the call. Callie let it fall to the carpet as Katherine worked on a fresh bottle of wine in the bathroom doorway. "You lying bitch."

Callie looked up at her and blinked. "What?"

"You. You two. You knew."

"Knew *what*?"

"That he loves you," Katherine challenged. "I could hear it in his voice. For fuck's sake, girl. We've been here for how many days and you can't even be honest about that?"

The escort rolled her eyes and waved the older woman off. "He loves getting his —"

"I was married to the man," the nurse interrupted. "I know what he sounds like when he's hoping you're not as angry as he thinks you are. He's in love with you. Kinda disgusted by it, but whatever. You're both… adults," she grumbled before she gave Callie another one of her patented *looks.* "Even if barely."

The younger woman huffed and gave the phone a little nudge with her big toe. "Yeah, well, wouldn't be the first client that got a crush. Not like it matters."

Katherine wandered over and sat down with the bottle in her hands. "Doesn't it?"

"The hell does that mean?"

"You love him, too."

Callie froze like a deer in the headlights. Her eyes went wide and her lips parted as words — any words — tried to form on the tip of her tongue. "Love… him? Lo… *him*? Give me a damn break. He's a fun ride. He's also a fucking psycho that plays with dead people, but hey. He was fun. *Was*."

The nurse took a swig from the bottle and crossed her legs on the bed. "You so sure?"

"*Positive*," the escort snapped.

Katherine pointed a single finger accusingly at the phone. "Then why'd you spend the last five minutes holding onto that chunk of plastic like you'd never hear his voice again?"

The escort stopped herself from picking it up and just sorta sat there in a half-hovering position. "I… why… wait. Why do you care? You sound jealous."

"Ex. Wife," Katherine clarified. "I'm allowed."

"Oh? Is that 'Ex. Wife.' or is it… 'Eh, I'm his *ex… wife*,' sister? Because we both know there's a *difference*."

It was Katherine's turn to freeze and she pressed the bottle to her lower lip as she mulled over her own response. "Oh, fuck you."

"Fuck you too."

Katherine took a swig from the bottle as they sat in prolonged, awkward silence. Finally, she let the bottle rest between her legs and let loose with a depressed, frustrated sigh. "I... I hope he's not about to do something stupid. Again."

Callie nodded her head and reached for the bottle. "We know he is. Gimmie that."

***

Anthony wasn't off the phone more than two minutes before Fixxer's voice popped out of the flatscreen's speaker. *"Th-th-that went well! I'll get eyes and cams on that hub, and –"*

"Did you have to listen in?"

"Of cor-cor-course! I wouldn't be helping if I didn't know everything that was going on, and I've known too lit-lit-little as of la-la-late for my own personal sen-sen-sensibilities," the avatar answered as a weird, almost cruel modulation warped his voice on the last word. *"Spea-spea-speaking of, what's in the bag?"*

The necromancer glanced over his shoulder and realized he'd left the reliquary bag lying out on his pillows. Except he would've sworn on a stack of Bibles that he *hadn't*, and he *didn't* like the implication that the bag had moved on its own. "Jordan's safe place."

"Sleeping with your brother-in-law? How positively bi-cur..."

"Oh, for the love of God no."

Fixer cut loose with a mocking chortle. *"But you know what you do have?"*

"What?"

"An address," Fixxer pointed out. *"Use what your girl gave you and get me into their har-har-hard systems. Once I'm there, I'll get you an-an-anything you want."*

That was the type of offer that was a great idea and a horrible one all in one shot. "Fine. Get me an idea what kind of sec is on that campus, maybe some floor plans, and I'll start looking at ways in for both of us. Then, hopefully, you can find enough to shut this shit down."

The screen flashed on and Fixxer's polygonal, pixelated face positively shivered. *"Thre-thre-threaten me with a good time. I'll send a wo-wo-*

worm to your headset for upload. AND! Because I am ben-ben-benveloent… let me hel-hel-help you out a little. Free."

Free and Fixxer weren't two concepts that meshed. Ever. Before the exhausted mage could even ask, the screen changed to a pair of very buxom, leather-clad, toy-equipped women.

"Why do they look like Callie and…?"

As the older of the pair grabbed the other by her neck and pushed her to her knees, Fixxer laughed through the speakers. "*Just helping you fe-fe-feel at home!*" The speaker dinged quietly as he disconnected the call. The only remaining sounds in the apartment came from the half-fake moans of the porno.

Anthony watched for a long minute before he sighed and unzipped his pants. "The shit I put up with, I swear…"

9. FIRE FIGHT-ER
Wednesday, May 30th, 5:37 AM

No matter what the old movies or ritzy e-books said, intelligence work was rarely sexy. Sure, you might – *might* – get lucky enough that the drop-dead blonde hitting you up in a hotel bar worked for the Ru-Chi Block and was about to pull you into a secret black-ops spy adventure, but chances were, she was just trying to put a skimmer in your back pocket to tap your credit. The former would ruin your career, but the latter would wreck your bank account.

Priorities mattered.

Either way, the kind of intel that Anthony worked rarely had hot blondes or bars – Emiline excluded. If he wasn't trying to pop some grouchy stiff out of his grave or trying to use a wheelbarrow to drag a body across a battlefield for a pop-'n-talk, there was paperwork.

Reports. Video feeds. Corporate registries.

The latter wasn't as big of an issue where he'd been stationed to deal with the NPC, but you could replace 'corporate registries' with 'neighborhood warlord lists,' and it amounted to the same thing. People that wanted your money while they influenced the region. People that'd be happy to kill to do either.

And all of it meant that he had a quiet day in his room unbothered by absolutely everybody. For the first time since Kath had shown up at his door, he could relax. Even if the financial reports were so dry they made his eyes bleed, not being at risk of imminent death had a lot to be said for it.

And that held true for the rest of the day and most of the night.

Until Alara started to (figuratively) blow up his headware.

Since she had the gall to do it just after 4:30 in the morning, he had a feeling it was less of the 'wanna fuck' and more the 'we're fucked,' type of call. She'd never offered the former, and the latter was perfectly in line with how the month had gone to this point. When the detective said to turn on the news, he did.

For once, the news was actually pretty good.

For him, anyway.

Sine-Pastor Charlie El-Rhodes, on the other hand? Not so much.

As Anthony had assumed would happen sooner rather than later, the Pastor had been put out to pasture. From the initial coverage, the cause of death was 'under investigation.' Before he could even send a 'holy shit' in text, Alara sent over a prelim scene note that undercut the lies LSPD's PR department had fed the news.

.50 cal, incendiary. One in the gut, one in the heart, and one in the head. Order uncertain; overkill was accomplished on round number two. The bullets had gone into him from right beside a bullet-proof window, which proved the old adage that your defenses were only as good as the efforts you were inclined to take when putting them in.

Remember – you had to reinforce the walls, not just the glass.

The rounds were, Alara noted, presumed to be dep-anth. It was one of a few solid ways to ensure that doing anything magical to the corpse would take a shitload of time and a migraine's worth of effort to do successfully. Depleted-anth rounds were commonly found in sidearms Army-wide and anyone on any kind of para-military force worth their salt kept them on hand to deal with other-than-natural concerns.

The whole thing was sad. Very very sad.

He cheered into his follow-up head-text and was about to go to bed when she had him turn on *another* news network. The screen at the end of his bed flicked from Gulf Coast News to Certified All-National. Lo-and-behold, they had a certified asshole on their front story, too.

"And in related news, a spokeswoman for a joint task force between the LSPD Ab/Psy Division and the FBI's Enhanced Threat Unit has released a statement involving this man, Harold Vincetti, a fifty-three year old male with dual-citizenship between Oregon and Canada, who is wanted in connection with multiple murders and two, yes two, magical anomalous events that have struck the city in recent days. Regular viewers may recall that Mr. Vincetti had been named in the investigation into the death of local hero, Jordan Fisher and –"

Before the brunette-haired drone could even finish, Anthony had his phone in hand and Alara on the other end of a call. "Did you burn him first, or did someone else?"

"Autoscis received a hand-delivered message this morning that Vincetti had been removed from his duties at Blackwash, and as an added bonus, the lawyers from Eden Farms that were interfacing with our office have informed us that they are no longer interested in covering his case."

She couldn't see the smirk on his face, and he probably should've been grateful for it. "So, the Gardeners are tired of losing their farm help and have decided to cut him loose."

"Someone has decided to make a point in separating the wheat from the chaff," Alara confirmed, "with a frigging plasma-torch. This wasn't pure luck. You do it?"

"Let me re-read the UCI contract, and I'll get back with you."

A few seconds of silence gave way to a slow, "Anthony…"

"Do you want me to lie to you or not?" he asked as he swung his legs off the edge of the bed. "Be honest."

"I want to give you good news without you turning it into a whole damn drama production," she countered, "if that isn't too much to ask. Swear I'm gonna change your name to 'Broadway' in my contacts."

"What is it now?"

"Asshole."

Anthony pursed his lips and shrugged after a trio of short seconds. "Fair. So, what's the move?"

A familiar buzz went off behind his left eye, and his HUD was filled with a fresh warrant and a handful of technical notes. "MWAT is prepping to hit the Fontaine Center now. I have an appointment with some desk-plant from the FRA at 7 to move on that front."

The acronym went completely over his head. His nearly-ruined white shirt followed suit. "FRA?"

"Federal Railroad Agency," she clarified. "I did read what you sent me. You think this shit is on the rails, then we gotta get the rails involved."

"I think this shit went off the rails if you can excuse the anachronistic slang," Anthony muttered back. "This week has almost made me miss the efficiency of picking up a gun and shooting in whatever direction a Master Sergeant ordered."

The remark earned him his first real laugh from Alara's lips he'd heard in months. "Yeah, well, I have some news on that, too. I got a rude little email this morning with a Tec-Trak ID on it for a snythi-limb; a Geldar 35a. Comes complete with an internal sword sheath and semi-biologi flesh."

He stopped fighting his shirt and tilted his head for a moment. "Any idea who the tracker belongs to?"

"Sure do. Why do you think I went to the trouble of waking you up?"

"Where is he?"

It wasn't so much a question as it was a demand and the way his voice went flat put a cold chill down her spine that she'd never, ever admit. "Last pinged at a movie triplex at Devon and Radley. Near exit… 37 on the Skyline."

He had to admit that a trip on the Skyline at this time of day would be a brief bit of urban beauty, but that sounded… uncomfortable, and he couldn't put a finger on why. "What's the name of it?"

A map and a secondary overlap popped up in his ocular that noted the area — and known less-than-legal affiliations assorted property holders had. It took a few seconds to populate, and Alara was happy to add live text as it loaded. "The triplex? Checking," she replied. A few seconds later and she answered, "Oh, he's at the StarDome. Glad to know he's able to take in a movie after a hard day's work murdering witnesses."

Anthony was off the bed before she finished talking. "Fuck, fuck, *fuck*," he thundered.

"What's your problem? Not a fan of Hollywood?"

"He's not done, Alara. Get a tac team and send them to 1996 Devon. Get MWAT there too, and right fucking now."

She didn't reply right away. When she did, it was as much of a threat as it was a confirmation. "You better have a damn good reason for that," the detective replied, "we already have a Warrant Team dispatched for Vincetti, but that's three blocks away."

"It's Kath. That's where I have her. He's going for the girls."

He had his gear together and was out the door before she sent her reply. "There's a squad car waiting. And if you see Vincetti —"

Anthony killed the call before she could finish, and answered to the silence and the silence alone. "If I see him, I'm shooting him."

***

StarDome Theaters
See the Stars — Under the Stars!

***

The Tabletop Stay on Dudley.

285

The first of a long-running chain of town hostels that had popped up in the late 2030s. They promised a respite of the insanity of city life, and a place for ruralites to enjoy the favorite things the city had to offer – all for the same price no matter the block they were on, with an open-to-all greenscape-style roof complex at every location.

It was wonderful if you were into inner-city-being-cozy shit.

It was also on fire.

The notice had come in while Anthony was still six minutes out. His driver – some street-level traffic cop with a mid-cali short-rifle holstered next to the passenger seat that was big enough to make Blackburn jealous – had responded with all the eager gusto of someone who normally spent their days pushing digital files back and forth. When the fire alarm went off, he punched the lights and slammed the generator straight into overdrive.

By the time they arrived, the city's Volunteer Hi-Burn Team had arrived staged with some of the newest and shiniest of fire-fighting equipment known to man. The truth was there were two things the city did well: the first was to make sure that fires didn't spread. Period.

The second was blatant displays of discrimination and racism.

For once, they found a way to make it 'reasonable,' – because if you were human, you didn't make it onto the team. There was a stark contrast between the VHBT and the MWAT teams just for that reason. VHBT didn't take anyone but Daems and MWAT didn't take anyone who wasn't pure-blood human.

Only one of them came under fire for it.

The other was celebrated because they were practically immune.

Anthony was out of the car with his shotty out at a dead sprint as soon as it slowed down. He got the immediate attention of a couple of different cops who tried their best to intervene, but he had his hand on the VHBT chief before they could stop him. He was a big guy – even for a Daem – but he was smart enough to pay attention when someone offered help and flashed a shotgun at the same time.

"I'm a freelancer. On contract with LSPD," he blurted out before the firefighter could say anything. "There are two witnesses being housed in there. Important ones. I need to know if they're alive, right now."

"Sorry, *hermano*, nobody's still upright according to bio-therms," the Daem grunted. Anthony had to take a sec and admire him. Most of his kind tried to cover up their genetic aberrations. This guy? He wore his horns with pride, and he hadn't done anything about the dragon-like scales around his eyes. "Fire's been raging like a bitch. Something wiped the fire-sup systems. We could barely get the power to the block shut off through the network."

The words hardly escaped the chief's mouth before a second-story window blistered out and shattered. Molten chunks of plastic rained down on the street while a mix of yellow-and-orange-clad first responders fired a mix of shoulder-mounted fire suppression devices into the upper windows. Clouds of smoke and foam answered their barrage as a ceiling shattered inside the hostel.

"Chief, it's worse. There's already people dead in there," Anthony replied as the chief turned his head back to the blaze. "I can smell them."

The Daem's eyes narrowed as he watched a rush of flame belch out from a third-story building. "Mage?"

"Close enough."

"How many?"

The necromancer took a deep breath and closed his eyes to focus. A few seconds later, he answered with a tired, pained, and worried, "Too many. Five, minimum. Ground floor for most. One... second floor. Nobody third."

"Fuck," the bigger man replied immediately. "Tell me anything else?"

"I can get you more info on what's inside if you don't complain about me doing shady shit. And if you do complain, I'm gonna do it anyway, but I'll probably have to punch someone, and I don't wanna do the fucking paperwork."

Sometimes, a reputation has its perks. The firefighter looked down at Anthony and pointed to a spot a couple of yards away behind some of the assembled emergency vehicles. "Wait... I know you."

"No?"

"Yeah. I do. The news. And E."

Anthony rolled back on his heels a little. "She's been keeping people I care about safe in there. Let me help. Please."

The bulky alt-human gave it more thought than Anthony probably deserved and relented after he looked back at the car the necromancer had shown up in. "Said you're contracting?"

"Yeap."

"Get my men hurt, and I'll drag you into that hell-pit myself."

Sometimes, those perks came with threats.

Either way, it helped. "Let me make a big noise, and I can put a spirit out and –"

"Mage support is six away. Get your spook here before they get theirs, and I don't care," the gruff, rough, and professionally pissed-off Daem replied before he stormed off to bark orders at his men. "LISTEN UP YOU SCALED FUCKS – MAGE SUPPORT IS ON-SITE. WATCH YOUR HEADS AND GET THAT SHIT PUT OUT."

The ease and speed that the conversation went left the necromancer in shock – for all of five seconds. His cop escort was by his side before he made it to the safe spot, and the poor bastard made the mistake of asking what he could do to help. Anthony's answer made his jaw drop even as the former serviceman pulled out a special little toy to use.

Anthony's insistence made him patch into the on-scene command chat and issue a warning to ignore a single imminent gunshot. Even if the cop hadn't done it, the shot would've been fired anyway. As it was, the necromancer had his shotty placed against his shoulder and aimed at the far corner of the structure's rooftop where nobody else was standing.

Normally, Blackburn didn't need to be fired to manifest.

Given how bad of a state he'd been in the last time he'd been able to pop out and say 'Hi,' Anthony assumed he'd need a little boost. Plus – there was something extra mixed in the slug that he needed. It was something of an, 'in case of emergency, break glass,' type of moment. Except it wasn't glass.

The slug slammed into the rooftop corner with an appropriate crack. Brickwork shattered as the silver-coated round split open and decorated the edge of the hostel with a mix of powdered anth and Anthony's own blood. A single shard of bone buried inside disintegrated on impact as well.

As Anthony's familiar manifested, the necromancer dropped the gun back to the mag-holster on his hip and went right to work doing the type of stuff that his heart wouldn't like, and honestly, he didn't care. He hadn't lied to the fireman; there were at least five dead in there. There was also something else hidden in the churning mess of ether that he couldn't quite identify – but it was calling for him.

Which couldn't, in any possible way, be a good sign.

The heat from the fire washed over his skin as he shoved his coat off and rolled his sleeves up as far as they could go. The ground was soaked with scummy filth and debris, so a focus-circle was out of the question, and his chest was too bloody to play pick-a-spot with his knife. It ruled out dragging a soul out of the blaze to him so that only left one other option.

Blackburn didn't manifest all the way. The fight in the morgue had done more than enough damage to leave him a malformed, flickering, barely functional shadow of himself. The crystallized nth and the chunk of an 'in case of emergency' reliquary he fired with gave Anthony enough 'oomph' to not just give him the strength to take form…

…but the strength to see what his familiar saw.

The effect was a step below astral projection, but as a quick-scout method, there were worse options to use. Anthony reached up and grabbed his escort's arm and in a short, flat, no-nonsense order, instructed him to relay whatever he said to the fire crew. The cop didn't bother to argue.

It probably had something to do with the way that Anthony's eyes had taken on a yellow glow. Or the way that the scars up and down his chest had a matching glimmer. Or the blood seeping out from under his bandages.

Whatever the reason, the officer listened.

While he listened, Anthony *watched*.

The view from inside Blackburn's head was distorted at best, and the fire didn't help. The High-Burn Team had managed to knock it back a good bit, though he didn't think there was going to be any way to stop the blaze from taking out the third floor. As the spirit twisted through a hallway near the building's core, a wave of flames rushed over and through him that would've incinerated anyone still living with ease.

Anthony let loose an involuntary scream as the blaze rushed over his familiar's shoulders. It was reflex, nothing more, nothing less, but even Blackburn recoiled as a wall of heavy smoke swallowed them whole. When the ghost pushed beyond it and through a smoldering wall, they found the first body – and it told them almost everything they needed to know.

Even with the corpse on fire, there was no mistaking who he worked for. Green jacket, Hispanic descent, teen, maybe early twenties. Erica didn't employ or offer a haven to anyone that kept their gang affiliations.

Blackburn turned away from the body as quickly as he could.

There were some things you didn't just need to see.

Nor had Anthony been wrong about the rest of the dead. Blackburn dipped into an elevator and sunk down to the ground floor without much urging. Death left more than a small ripple in the currents of the ether around the world and tracking it didn't take much effort.

Blackburn lingered over the first two bodies in the building's lobby for longer than either of them wanted. The fire had mostly been knocked out of the front of the building, and a second crew was busy trying to break through the back. The two corpses had been tied to barstools and it was hard to tell which had done more damage: the bastards that had murdered them, the fire, or the impact of hundreds of gallons of high-pressure water.

The spirit reached down and touched each one in turn. He gave them a little tug and came back with enough of their essences in his hands that Anthony was able to rule out either woman as his – and he hated the fact that it mattered. But it did. They weren't his, and that was three of five corpses accounted for.

Before Blackburn could do anything else with them, Anthony saw a canister careen into the lobby from an exterior wall. His familiar had just enough time to escape the room before a violent shockwave of air and suppressant flattened the room and coated the ceiling in a mix of hardening foam and flame-nullifying gel. The impact made the whole hostel shake, but it did its job in a hurry.

It nearly destroyed the bodies, but that was what DNA was for.

The kitchen offered the last two corpses up, though the smoke was so thick and the flames had been so thorough that it was hard to tell where skin ended and fixtures began. If Anthony had to take a guess, this was where the fire had started. One of the bodies was a complete stranger; thank your pick of Gods. Their soul was still attached enough to their corpse that he could see its silvery form through the smoke as clear a cloud in the sky.

The other one?

If he had to guess, he'd have assumed the fire started on the stove. With her. With her face pressed against a burner. With her hands tied to the oven door. With her body burnt and mutilated beyond hope of a proper funeral.

Anthony let go of Blackburn and shunted as much of his strength as he could possibly manage into the woman's body. She was too far away to just pluck her soul; he'd have to take other measures.

And he hated himself for it.

When he could open his eyes again, his original escort was long gone – and Alara wasn't in the least bit happy to see him. She was a hell of a lot less happy when he collapsed with both hands on the ground and tears in his eyes. She had her hands on his arms to pull him out of the muddy puddle before he could do more than unleash a few heartfelt sobs of grief. "Don't tell me, please don't tell me..."

"It's not them," he croaked out. "It's not."

Relief cascaded down her face as tears rolled down his. For a few scant seconds, she finally got to see *him*, the real *him,* as emergency lights illuminated his face, reflected off his metal arm, and shone off of the fake bio-fluid that made his ocular look like a real eye. He was just a tired, beaten-down asshole.

He'd never really claimed to be anything else.

She just hadn't realized he'd been telling the truth all this time. A singular flash of nth in his God-given eye broke her from her brief reverie as he stumbled to his feet. "If it's not them, then who? Anthony, talk to me."

He didn't. There wasn't time, and he had less than little interest to discuss it. The crew beat him to it regardless with shouts of, "We've got a survivor!" and, "CIVIE COMING!"

One of those statements was right.

Anthony did his best to shout them down – no, it wasn't a survivor, and don't get close. They didn't listen, and in hindsight, he couldn't blame them. The ghast made a beeline right for the necromancer and ignored everyone who tried to stop her; their hands couldn't hold onto her burnt flesh, and the firefighters quit trying when one of them accidentally pulled a chunk of her charbroiled shoulder off.

A sudden hush fell across the scene as the fire crackled behind them. She was everything a firefighter hated, all in one. A reminder that they couldn't save them all, and a reminder that dying in a fire was the last thing any of them wanted to face.

Someone threw a fire blanket over her shoulders.

It fell off when Anthony wrapped his arms around her. "Fuck me, Erica, I am so, so sorry."

Her corpse made a single, pained 'mew' sound.

"ANTHONY – WHAT THE HELL ARE YOU DOING?" Alara demanded as she stood behind him. The smell coming off Erica's corpse was more than enough to make her gag, and she couldn't wrap her brain around what she was seeing.

When he stepped back, he was covered in soot, ash, and char. "Erica, I am so, so sorry. Erica I... fuck...you can't talk," he said as he realized just *how* bad of a shape she was in. "*Fuck.*"

"Erica... is that... is that *Erica Veight*?!" the detective finally realized; a little slow on the uptick, but she got there eventually.

"What, you thought it was the Pope?" Anthony snapped back as he cupped Erica's sagging head in his hands. "God I need... I need to know what happened to them. Erica, can you hear me? Can you tell me what happened?"

Maybe her soul could. Maybe it couldn't.

But all her lifeless *corpse* could do was let her head droop to one side as a chunk of her hair and scalp fell off her head. When it came down to it, Daems were fire *resistant* but far from fire *immune*. Flesh or scales, it didn't matter; torch a body long enough, and it stopped working like nature intended.

The detective watched how Anthony did his best to ease the ghast down to the ground and onto her back. Even in the middle of all the chaos, he was nothing short of immaculately respectful to her as he laid her down in the middle of the debris-strewn street. When he was done, her eyeless face gazed up into the pre-dawn sky directly above.

"What can I do to help?" Alara finally managed to blurt out.

"Shoot anybody that stops me," he answered as he placed his hand on her face and closed his eyes, "and shoot me when this is all done." The corpse made a gargled, 'Nnnnnn...' noise that ceased a heartbeat later. Nth flashed in the palm of his hand, and he quit responding to Alara's questions.

***

The All- Volunteer High-Burn Team
Fighting Fire – With Hell-Born Firepower
***

Erica resisted.

For all the years of their friendship, she hated him for what he could do – for what he did do. He knew it, and she knew it. He wasn't overly fond of her methods and even less fond of some of her religious beliefs, but at the end of the day, they respected each other. She'd never come over for a beer, and he'd never go over for a harvest grill, but they were still friends.

If there was any other way...

But there wasn't. And she resisted. And he hated himself.

The inside of E-Ve's head was a scrambled mess. Instead of a hallway of memories, there were flickering vine-like tubes that encompassed every inch and every direction inside of her subconsciousness. Some of them had thorns, and it only took one brush against them to learn that they meant absolutely *do not touch*. With the warning in mind, he manifested a machete and went to work to try to clear a path.

Every swing made the vines convulse. Every cut made a pained noise echo through the translucent, opalescent green stems. Every push through felt like torture – though who it hurt worse was a matter of debate.

He didn't have to cut his way through for long. Once the vines gave way to burnt tendrils and ember-covered brush, he knew he was close enough to start reaching into them. A singular lily hung limply off a cluster of burnt leaves, and the second he reached for it, he could see what she'd seen.

Or at least some of it.

Her memories were as scrambled as her mind. A series of rough images played through his head; someone knocked on the door to her midtown penthouse. When she answered, there was a gun. Just a gun, a comically giant gun aimed at her face.

Other semi-static scenes rolled over him like a movie being played out in a waterfall. He saw faceless foot soldiers in green jackets that ripped through her apartment. He saw a distorted white suit with green eyes and a black void where her skin should've been that ordered them around.

He saw a tophat hovering on the edges of her peripheral vision.

Then he saw the creature in white step forward with some kind of tool. An angle grinder, maybe; possibly a drill. Anthony clamped his eyes shut but couldn't do anything for his ears as he pushed through the scene.

He saw Katherine and Callie, clear as clear could be, thrown into the back of a van while Erica watched. They were bruised, beaten, but alive – or had been when she'd seen them last. She watched them get loaded up through glass panes of a hotel lobby.

She watched the person in white order more of her green-jacketed thugs around. There'd been gunfire; sporadic, brief. One of them died. The memory showed the gangbanger simply breaking apart in a haze of green glass.

Another scene popped up – an older memory – a much, much older memory. It was the first time they'd met – he'd been in a back alley, and in her mind, there was black oil pouring off of him as he'd retched into a dumpster. Fragmented as it was, it hadn't been far from reality.

She'd reached out to him.

The memory shifted again to the white suit and the shapeless figure in it. The suit grabbed her outstretched hand and put a torch in it. Then, her face had been slammed onto a stove. He heard a hellaciously loud *hiss* erupt. Gas, maybe. Erica had always had a thing for classically-cooked meals.

He didn't need to know the rest.

He felt it. Felt the heat start under his jaw. Felt the flames start to roast the inside of his mouth. Felt her horror, heard her screams, felt her struggle. Watched as her eyes were lost in blistering ash.

He fell out of her head and onto his ass with a terrified cry of his own. His skin burned, and he felt the water under him sizzle as he landed. Hurt the soul, hurt the body; it was a risk you took when you dived into someone's mind unprotected. Her last scream rang out in his ears, and it followed him back into the real world.

Alara's voice cut through the fog as reality… settled… back around him. "The hell do you mean you can't find him? Trak said he was –" A blast of a fire siren cut her off before she could continue. "I'm looking at it right now; he left the Dome over half an hour ago. You should be right on him."

Anthony screamed as Erica screamed. A single word and a life-ending amount of pain on it. A word that, truthfully, the detective had never heard him say. "*MOTHER! MOTHER!*"

The detective cut her conversation on the phone short as he came to. "Oh shit. I gotta go. Go find the motherfucker. He's not a Goddamned sewer turtle and he doesn't have wings, so he's *got* to be on the ground or in a building. I don't know, just put a bullet in him." As she knelt she added a curt, "I don't care if it's on the warrant or not, *slag him.*"

Erica's scream buffeted his consciousness while the pavement dug at the back of his skull. He grabbed at his ears as 'Mother!' repeated over and over again in the back of his mind. "Fuck make it stop. I can't, I can't…"

"I'm here, I'm here," she replied as she grabbed his shoulders and felt a mini-seizure rip through him. Bloody and frothy specs of saliva had started to foam up at the edge of his mouth. "Kath… is she okay?"

He shook his head, and she hoped he meant 'yes.' She was wrong. "N… no. Slash has them. Or… fuck. Bitch in white does. Car… cargo van. Black."

She didn't reply directly but tapped a spot behind her ear. "All units – issuing an APB. Black cargo van, last seen in the vicinity of StarDome Entertainment. Kidnapping; Fisher, Katherine. Attach to active warrants for Vincetti, Harold." When she finished, she placed her index finger on Anthony's forehead. "Time for you to check out."

"Please. Knock me… no. No, don't," he mumbled as he tried to push it away. "Can't, gotta –"

"Oh yes, I'm gonna," Alara interrupted. "You gotta downpulse, Anth. You're about to vibe off the damn planet. Five minutes for a shunt. That, or you get to enjoy a heart attack. Again," she lectured.

It was a quick, simple spell. It'd disrupt his aura long enough for his natural nth-patterns to stabilize. He'd be out cold for half an hour, but it'd save him from a week-long migraine; first-aid 101 for nth-abusers. It just took someone who knew what they were doing.

She knew, and he knew she knew. He relented.

And then the shot rang out.

***

Veight Community Services
Building Organic Communities from the Bottom Up
***

Blackburn felt it before he saw it.

There wasn't any way to miss it, not after the first time. The fact that it had survived the firestorm was a testament to its durability, or at least, a testament to the chems pumped into what was left of its decaying flesh. This one was more machine than dead man, but that didn't stop it from walking.

As soon as it saw Anthony's familiar, it reacted. A burst of nth went off from it like a concussion wave and almost completely dispersed the long-dead lawman on the spot. The rush of magic didn't do any damage to the building.

The blast of plasma did.

***

The Tec-Trak Modifi Tracker
Your Enhancements Shouldn't Walk Away on Their Own.
But They Might Have Help — And Now You Can Find Them.
***

The bullet hit Anthony dead center in his left shoulder.

The ensuing storm of shrapnel hit Alara across her right cheek. Blood burst out of her mouth, along with pieces of skin and a chunk or two of a tooth. The shock knocked her back on her side and flat on her back.

It saved her life, too.

The VHBT's pump truck was designed to resist temperatures of over two thousand degrees. Weaponized plasma charges were rated at nearly twice that. When their truck exploded, it sent a mix of supercharged water and chem suppressants flying along with chunks of steel and molten aluminum. The impact outright killed two of the firefighting Daems, and knocked almost everyone else on their ass.

Whatever the blast didn't kill, the monster that emerged from the smoldering hostel was only happy to finish off. Another sizzling discharge of plasma obliterated a squad car. A few seconds later, and a firefighter that didn't move fast enough was summarily picked up by his horns before the mechanical monster shoved its orange-hot cannon into his throat.

The beast pressed until half of the Daem's neck melted away.

Anthony didn't fare much better than the other wounded. The bullet punched through the steel and chrome that made up his bad arm and cored it almost effortlessly. The impact alone left him dismembered; when the bullet exited, it effectively ripped the faux bone interface that made up his shoulder blade out with it.

Blood flowed from the wound as freely as the electrical sparks and silvery bio-hydraulics that followed. The shock from exiting E-Ve's head had been enough to nearly knock him out. The shock and interface-feedback from losing his arm?

There wasn't any real way to stay conscious through that.

The last thing he heard was the sharp crack of a second sniper round, followed by a meaty thump that turned Erica's head into a blood, bone, and asphalt mist. By the time Alara could recover enough to make a scream of her own, he was out cold. Her howls of pain lasted until a jackbooted Blackwash goon kicked her in the face hard enough to shatter her jaw.

10. LITTLE BATTERY-POWERED ARMY MEN
Wednesday, May 30th, 9:09 AM

A light came on somewhere in the back of his head.

Scratch that. The light came on in the front of his head, just behind his eye. It came with a steady glimmer of life that jogged the rest of his unconsciousness back from the darkness – and into a whole lot of pain.

All manner of unpleasant sensations came back slowly, but they ramped up exponentially the longer the light behind his eye blinked in an increasingly furious tempo. When he could finally part his eyelids to see, there wasn't much; just a frosted-over plex-shield with a limited view of the outside world.

Pain was an understatement. After the initial shock wore off, Anthony felt like he'd been hit by a truck. There was an obscene amount of bio-feedback pouring out of the stump of his left shoulder, and when he tried to take a deep breath, his ribs suggested that he shouldn't try to do that ever again. There was also the feeling that he was cold.

Cold was another understatement. He was borderline hypothermic, and that errant thought convinced him to glance up. The words, '*Emerg-In-CY #3211*' had been stamped into the metal just above the plex covering, which was everything he needed to know.

The Army used this same brand to move injured troops.

INSCOM used them to move uncooperative assets.

Presumably, someone had decided that Anthony would be less than cooperative after shooting him. They were right, but there were reasons why Intel liked to use these for prisoner transport. Those reasons usually involved things like 'forced sedation' and 'if a wound is frozen, it isn't bleeding.'

Throw in a couple of restraints, and you didn't have to worry about someone making a break for the outside world until you were good and ready for them to enter a dark cell buried a mile under some General's shitter. Except, at the moment, he was just cold and not entirely frozen through and through. He was also bleeding if the trickling feeling from the right side of his temple was anything to go by.

All of which suggested he was either intentionally trapped in a stasis-pod turned coffin, or the outside world had other things in mind that didn't require sedation. He didn't intend to wait and find out, but before he could do much more than get a feel for how much nth he had left in his system, his headware decided to send him a message again. This time, literally.

A wall of text began to fill up the HUD in his cybernetic eye. Most of it was just shattered pixels and chunks of regurgitated ASC-3/Mo-Python server garbage, likely just corrupted data from system shock – literally – incurred when his arm had been blown off. Just thinking about the shot sent a spike of pain through the receptors in his shoulder.

Anthony was halfway through trying to remember how to send a debug command when some of the broken text put itself together in less-broken words that had some very bad connotations. Words like, 'Gun,' and 'GPS_undefined_error.' Eventually, the words turned into sentences.

'DefGrid Box. Keypass 9187.'

And then another – a little less cryptic but a bit more succinct.

'Leave. Or. Dead.'

The line flickered in his headset for a few seconds before it vanished into the digital ether that had spawned it. As soon as the words were gone, the In-CY pod's latch popped open with a rush of warm air, and he promptly spilled out of it onto his face. The ground was less accommodating to his injuries than the pod had been, and after a moment, he came to the worse realization that the ground wasn't the ground.

The ground was a floor. A metal-plated floor with a slight vibration to it. A metal-plated floor in a dim metal-composite storage room that was just about the right size for a train car. A cargo car, if he had to guess, and he didn't have to take many guesses on who owned it.

Every realization took him another moment as he pushed himself up onto his knees. The pod's sedatives had enough grip on him that he wasn't entirely sure of his footing, and whoever had stuffed him into it hadn't gone to any effort for wound care or even basic first aid. It was pretty obvious that they hadn't intended for him to wake up until they were good and ready. It was just as obvious that they had, unfortunately, taken anything useful out of his pockets.

A problem that was resolved when he stumbled to his feet and found the lockbox his mysterious benefactor had marked in his headware. A few mumbled curses and a couple of key presses later, as he slumped his ruined shoulder up against the side of the gunmetal-colored crate, the box spat out a shelf with a gun and a box.

The box felt more important than the gun.

He popped the lock on the old wooden case with his thumb and snagged his obsidian knife free of the protective felt padding it was buried in. Everything else in the box had been broken, used, or outright missing, but the knife alone was enough to do some serious damage if used in all the right ways.

The same couldn't be said for the gun. It wasn't his, and he didn't know where it came from. There wasn't anything too special about it other than the fact that it was *there* and someone had left it for him, so he did the rational thing and picked the snub-nosed semi-auto up.

As he did, he heard a rifle's deafening report cracked through the cabin with arguably more thunder than the bullet that preceded it. The bullet barely missed Anthony's skull, and it sent a chunk of shrapnel and debris up from one of the myriad crates toward the rear of the car. He didn't have time to aim, only to figure out a general direction. He only bothered to put one round downrange in someone's general vicinity. Compared to the rifle that had nearly turned his ribcage inside out, the little pistol had a decidedly flaccid 'pop' instead of a thundering report.

It did the job. He saw two figures scramble for cover as he tried to do the same. Unfortunately, there wasn't much of any. The cabin had boxes stacked across both sidewalls, with several more pods to his right and nylon-strapped crates on his left. It wasn't designed to be a fortress by any stretch, and it felt more like a cattle chute than a battlefield.

It was pretty obvious which side of the slaughterhouse he was on.

A second round absolutely shredded a heavy-duty plastic box less than three inches away from Anthony's face and sent enough hard debris into the air that he couldn't see what he was doing. As the crack of the shot died down, Slash's unpleasant voice rang out as clear as a bell. "Back in the pod, Mr. Pierson. Either under your own power or with a bullet in your heart; I don't actually care."

"I'd believe that if you opened up with 'halt,' or, 'stop right there,'" Anthony countered. "Not sure I believe it now."

"Heart it is," Slash shouted before he depressed the trigger on his rifle again.

The bullet obliterated the crate the necromancer had been leaning against just a few heartbeats prior. Anthony ducked and sent a trio of bullets out to pepper the other end of the car. The rounds forced Slash to duck back into a doorway and made the Blackwash trooper duck for cover. He glanced down at the pistol and swore silently; the shitty little thing couldn't have more than three bullets left in the mag at most.

"Maybe we could, I dunno, *talk* about this?" Anthony shouted. "Little tired of you trying to –"

Two distinct shots burst through the train this time. Neither came close enough to Anthony's body to inflict any real damage, and he could tell that the hitter was just trying to keep him pinned down. It wasn't as reassuring as it should've been. "You killed my men, destroyed a Centurio, and because of you, our stock price has been in free-fall. Why should I not want you dead?"

"Literally just self-defense!" Anthony countered.

"Wouldn't have been if you'd just handed over the girl!"

For one brief second, the necromancer thought about conceding the point. A brief, fleeting second. One that was interrupted by the black-clad tacti-cool Blackwash thug that had finally found the balls to make a move down the cabin.

He had two seconds to make a choice and three seconds to carry it out. Anthony leaned out from cover and tucked his elbow into his stomach as tightly as he could. Anyone could make a shot with one hand, but not everyone could make a shot with one hand while moving between cover with their other arm lying in a ditch somewhere.

Even fewer could if they'd spent the last few years relying on their tech to make the shot for them. His stance was shit and he'd get his ass chewed out if anyone from boot would've seen him do it, but he did it. The Blackwash thug took two rounds to the chest fair, flat and square.

It helped when he was the only thing in Anthony's line of sight that he could've possibly hit. The sec shithead hit the ground with a mighty thud and a cry of pain, although there was absolutely no chance that the bullets could've done more than slam into a quarter-inch of cerimax plate. The fucker was bruised but not dead.

"You know, I'm not stupid," Anthony called out. "Try harder."

"I know, but I'm willing to make sacrifices for bait."

He had three seconds to comprehend the meaning behind the word 'bait' before a door at the rear of the car opened and Hell strode through it. It was another Centurio – but thinner, fleshier, and more agile than the two Anthony had run into before. You would've been forgiven for mistaking it for some tech'd-up chromehead wandering the subway at two in the morning if you didn't know better.

Anthony knew better.

The last bullet he had just pissed the mech off.

The shot didn't do more than lacerate a piece of dead skin across the Centurio's forehead as it ricocheted away into oblivion. Undaunted, the mech reached down, picked up Anthony with one hand, and launched him over the fallen Blackwash guard right to Slash's feet. He purposefully landed on his blown-out shoulder, and as bad as it hurt, it kept him from breaking the other one from the force of his landing.

The impact was, however, more than enough to rattle his already concussion-staggered brain, and it didn't do any favors for the rest of him. As the Centurio advanced on him from the rear of the car, the corporate hitter at the heart of all of his recent headaches planted his feet on the other side of Anthony's head and leveled the barrel of his rifle at the back of the necromancer's skull. "I respect that you convinced the Gardeners to cut me loose. Honestly, I had planned to retire soon as it was. You expedited that, but I have a reputation to uphold."

Anthony managed to cough up a wad of blood and a pain-filled groan as part of his answer. He tried to push himself up to his knees, but neither gravity nor his aching bones were willing to comply. "No chance we can talk it out?"

The hitter had an answer to the question. It didn't even involve a bullet. Whatever it was, he didn't get time to say it. Anthony's right hand shot out from under his chest and grabbed the assassin just above his left ankle. Before Slash could pull away, the gunman began to scream.

Necromancy was death magic, but death was just entropy given an endpoint. And entropy could be sped up if you knew how. The right intent, the right vibrations, and nth could manifest as a fluid, or as a flame.

Or as acid.

A harsh, wet sizzle accompanied Slash's scream of pain. The shock was so severe that he dropped his gun before he could pull the trigger, and the magical attack was so vile that he fell over a second later. The assassin collapsed and fell backward into the hall connector that separated the cargo car with the next one.

The bottom part of his shin and left foot stayed where they were.

When the Centurio picked Anthony up by the back of his shirt collar, the necromancer twisted around, and a stream of acidic nth rolled off his hand and all over the mech. Toxic magic coursed across the monster's gray flesh and exposed metal-alloy coated wires. Within seconds, a cloud of corrosive spellwork had enveloped the Centurio's head and completely obscured its face.

Even as its face dissolved under the assault, it didn't let go.

It did, however, use its other hand to punch Anthony square in the chest. Wrapped in solid steel plates that fit its decaying hand like a glove, the blow crushed the necromancer's ribs and cracked the hardest part of the bones covering his heart with ease. Almost instantly, his heart simply stopped from the shock.

His body went limp, and the spray of nth from his hand ceased immediately. The blow did enough damage that the heart attack he'd had earlier in the week decided to come back for round two. He didn't even have time to *think* of a response before his lights went out and his brain checked in for a nice quiet vacation in oblivion.

The Centurio's face fell off as it dropped its prey. While the necromancer landed on the train's floor with a hard thud, skin and assorted biomechanics sloughed off of the mech with wet splats that revealed a half-metal skull and two bony nodules on both sides of its head; remnants of its prior life as a Daem. Arcs of nth danced across now-exposed wires between them like little lightning bolts, though if it hurt, the mech seemed to be completely oblivious to it.

Slash continued to howl in pain from the cabin door as he clutched the stump of his leg, and the Blackwash guard made matching, muffled noises through his gas mask a few feet away. The necromancer was the only person not to make a sound, except for a strange, high-toned keening noise that came from his chest. The Centurio looked down to admire its handiwork as Anthony died.

Except he didn't.

The Army made sure of it.

Tucked under a sheath of now-broken bones, a small little box with a small little light woke up. The light shifted from green to black, and as Alara had breathlessly complained a few days prior, an even smaller cylindrical tube tucked away in the small box — complete with a literal red flag emblazoned on it — did exactly what it was supposed to do.

In the event of a minor heart attack, the box would've tapped into its internal battery and induced a quick discharge to keep its host alive — just like a pacemaker. But a myriad of sensors nestled here and there in

Anthony's body were already pissed, and enough warnings had gone off on a technical level to trigger a more... robust... response. One last fail-safe tripped when an EKG stored in the box went flat across the board with no rhythm left to indicate a natural return.

Six seconds.

That's all it took. Two for his heart to stop. Two more for the sensors to send out an SOS to the CPU nestled right beside his ventricle. And two for the system to activate.

A valve that was supposed to be held open by the flow of blood through a small artery closed. When it didn't open again, an electrical circuit completed. A charge raced from a tiny battery through an even smaller conductor, and it hit a piece of explosive material no wider than the size of the head of a pin that had been wrapped around a piece of crystal. The charge detonated with a pop so small you couldn't hear it without a stethoscope.

As a whole, the Army loved that dead men could tell tales.

The brass preferred that they waited to die on friendly territory.

The sliver of anthenium the charge had been delicately attached to, however, went off like a firecracker. Raw, manufactured magical energy coursed through Anthony's body like he'd stuck his fingers into an electrical socket. The charge didn't just jumpstart his heart; it activated a slew of bio-mechanical functions embedded around it and even triggered a few in the back of Anthony's head. Just in case there was *critical* damage, assorted biomechanics went to work to ensure that his heart actually beat – beating on its own was optional, as far as the docs were concerned. It just had to beat so the user could live.

Dead men could tell tales. But living ones could do it in complete sentences. If the dead man was lucky, he wouldn't stay dead. If he was really lucky, maybe he could get a heart replacement later. If.

If was a matter of time. Time, this time, was a matter of seconds. Ten.

Ten seconds of being dead. Ten seconds that the next world had to gnaw at periphery of his soul. Ten seconds that he wasn't supposed to remember. Ten seconds he barely did, but he remembered enough.

Anthony's eyes flew open and yellow light poured out of them as reactor-grade anth pumped through his system unchecked. His heart roared back to life against its own will, and the sudden rush of both blood and adrenaline that shot straight into his brainbox pulled him out of the Void's less-than-comforting embrace and back into the waking world.

The Centurio watched with glassy, dead eyes and a singular blinking occular that tracked his every violent, spasmodic movement. Without a word, it bent down and picked the necromancer up by his shirt collar and allowed him to dangle in the air. A moment later, and it decided a second punch was enough.

Anthony couldn't do anything about the flesh-and-metal fist that pulled back to deliver a blow that was aimed right at his face, but he could do something about the way it looked at him. In his heightened state, he could see the raw sparks of anth that danced from one horn-stub to the other, and that was a weakness he could exploit. Before the punch could land, the necromancer grabbed hold of the closest stub and directed more power than was humanly safe down his arm and into its head.

Out of his own reserves, there wasn't a chance in Hell he'd be able to do it; the monstrosity had been built well enough to mitigate most magic, as he'd seen so far. The battery in his chest, however? The question was, 'You and what army?'

The answer was 'Uncle Sam's.'

Anthony's blast turned what little bit of brain the Centurio had into a pudding cup and nearly incinerated every last inch of made-to-order tech that had been buried under a shell of poly-alloy steel and good old-fashioned bone. The monster froze solid as jets of flames erupted out of every orifice on its face for several long moments before it went completely slack. A few seconds later, the necromancer was free – on the floor and bleeding, but free.

His prey wasn't.

A visible tendril of nth had wrapped itself around the Centurio's head and through the air to Anthony's hand. The phantom rope spiraled through the monster's eyes and mouth and down into the belly of the beast, where it found a burning, unstable, and fully-charged power-cell of sorts. A power-cell made out of a single angry soul with a destroyed brain and its essence bound to a block of anthenium, much like the one in the necromancer's chest.

Without any control, the Centurio was a walking bomb. With control, it was going to be a *problem*. Slash recognized it; he recognized it too late, but he recognized it.

Anthony rolled out of the immediate line of fire as he forced the mech to take heavy-footed, lumbering steps toward the hitter. There wasn't much in it he could control, and there weren't any obvious weapon systems built onto it. Then again, the entire concept of a giant armored biomech was that it *was* all the weapon you needed, especially if you couldn't stop it.

Slash tried. Repeatedly. Maybe it was the agony from having his foot burned off. Maybe it was simple shock. Or maybe it was outright terror. Whatever the reason, his rifle barked until it couldn't bark anymore.

Chunks of flesh, bits of steel, and ample slivers of debris blew off the Centurio. The bullets managed to drop the monster down to one knee, but it didn't knock it out. That was fine. Anthony didn't need the mech to take Slash out.

He just needed the power it had.

When it dropped down, the necromancer shoved his hand into the mech's mid-back and pulsed enough nth through his veins that it melted flesh and steel both. Angry glowing sparks and crackling electrical discharges ravaged his palm and blistered his skin, but it opened a clear path into the Centurio's reactor. Anthony gritted his teeth through the pain and locked his fingers down on the anthenium core's housing with all his might.

The better he could make contact, the more power he could draw.

The more power he could draw, the heavier the spell he could use.

If a mage was powerful enough to bind a familiar, they could summon their anchor. The further away the familiar's anchor, the harder it was to summon; the walls of space and time didn't like to bend. But there was a trick to it, and it wasn't a trick very widely known: you didn't summon the anchor.

Anthony's scream cracked midway through, and he collapsed as he finished it. Cracks appeared in his vision, and a sharp ringing noise erupted in his ears. Blood trickled down his nose as he felt a heavy *crackle* pop out of the Centurio's chest and into his arm. A stab of violent, uncontrolled *power* flowed through his arm and stopped just at his shoulder...

...where a phantom's hand grabbed him and held him still.

In Los Santuario, the law was what you made of it.

And a ghostly lawman was only happy to see it through.

Blackburn manifested in full as the Centurio's reactor spilled into Anthony's aura. The ghost absorbed the brunt of the sudden shock and channeled it through his spectral form. As the biomech fell flat on its face, the last thing Slash saw with his living eyes was the antique that appeared in the air behind it.

The shotgun fired. Once.

As Slash's corpse slumped to the floor, Blackburn flipped the weapon over and extended it to his friend. It took a few moments, but Anthony was eventually able to pull himself up enough to sit up against a crate. All the ghost had to do was take one look at him before he sunk to the ground beside the necromancer in a show of quiet support.

Almost a minute later, Anthony coughed up a wad of something slick and pestilent onto the floor. "You didn't bring a cig with you, did you?"

"*I ah, no. Think there's a pack of 'em in my coffin though.*"

"Got room for me in there?"

"*Maybe if you lose another arm,*" Blackburn replied. "*Boy, you look like shit.*"

"Better than I feel," he half-croaked out as he looked down at his hand and admired the burns all over it. It had already started to blister, and the parts that weren't blistering had started to crack open. "Bring any iodine instead?"

His familiar looked him over and saw through Anthony's wounds a bit deeper than the necromancer could himself (and more than he would've wanted to). "*Bullets, but not enough, I am afraid. Do I… uh… need to save one for you or… you just gonna let nature take it's course?*"

Anthony kicked the Centurio's boot and grunted. "Not a God-damned natural thing about this mess. Not that it matters. We're dead as soon as someone checks the cameras."

"*Well then m'boy, why don't we try to find a way around that? Just because my bones are already in the ground doesn't mean yours should be in a hurry to get there.*"

"As if. Kath'll have mine ground to dust and used for mortar to pay off back alimony."

The Marshal tilted his head to the side and inadvertently exposed the gash in his neck for the world to see through. It wasn't a pleasant sight no matter how many times Anthony had seen it, and he gagged accordingly. "*Speaking of which, I swear I —*"

"Two down," Anthony interrupted as he waved toward the back of the car. "Saw her while I was dodging bullets. Callie is next to her. Alive, I think."

"*Alive,*" his familiar confirmed after he glanced down the hauler's hallway. "*Hurtin', but alive.*"

"Well, that's two of us."

"*Three,*" Blackburn corrected. "*The ah, man in black right there? Still has a pulse. Tryin' hard to pretend he doesn't, but he does.*"

Anthony slowly turned his head to look at the Blackwash corp-head. "Oh. Yeah. Hey, you. Asshole. Give it up. The ghost says you ain't dead, and I can't make your ass twerk yet, so quit trying to fake it."

Wisely, the corporate shithead lifted both of his hands in the air before he rolled over and adjusted himself so he was on his knees. "Listen, hombre, I was just following –"

Blackburn racked a shell in his namesake shotty and leveled the weapon at the guard's head. *Son, has that line ever done anything for the sake of anyone that's ever found themselves on the happy end of a weapon in the history of ever?*"

"He's got a point," the necromancer added as he squinted and tried to read the Blackwash goon's name-tag. "Alright. Bob. Listen."

"Uh, my name is –"

"Bob," Anthony interrupted. "Your name is Bob because I don't give a fuck what your mom called you. So, Bob, you're gonna take off that mask so I can see who the fuck you are, then you're gonna answer one helluva important question for me. You got that, Bob?"

"I... I got it," Bob the Guard answered with just a little hesitation. "If it... if it makes things any better, Mr. Vincetti is the only one with cam access. He oversaw all the transports and –"

Anthony and his familiar exchanged brief glances. "That's helpful."

"Only iffin' Bobby is tellin' the truth," Blackburn countered. *"Bobby, you tellin' the truth?"* the ghost asked just before he warped across the cabin and pressed the muzzle of his shotty up against the guard's head.

Wisely, Bob nodded along in agreement, and then he carefully pulled his helmet away. He wasn't anything to write home about, though he had that grizzled handsomeness you might find on a home direct-sales network. "Listen man, it wasn't personal and –"

"Bob?"

"Yeah?"

"Drugs. Where are they?"

Bob blinked. Blackburn blinked too, though it didn't have quite the same effect. "Drugs?"

"Drugs."

"I uh... we don't... we aren't..."

Anthony waved his hand dismissively. "Yeah, yeah. You're genocidal maniacs, not dealers. Fine. I don't care. You fuckwits have been running a biomed lab on the rail lines for God only knows how long so I am presuming someone on this fucking train has some azul. Or crack. Or oxi-ram. If it ends in -cet or -ine I'll pop it right now. So. Where are the fucking drugs?"

Bob swallowed and slowly lowered his hands. One went to his pocket, and despite Blackburn's insistent nudges, he pulled out a thin vial with a swivel top. "Subdermie aspirin?"

There was a long, drawn-out pause between them before the necromancer finally extended his hand to take it from the guard. "You're a shit person, Bob. Do better."

When Bob handed it over, Anthony's hand didn't cooperate. The shot fell to the floor as his fingers hung loosely in the air. The necromancer said something short and to the point before he gave up and let his arm drop down to his side. "Shit."

"*Ah, Anthony, I don't think —*"

"Yeah, I know."

"*But, Anthony —*"

"I said *I know*," he growled from under his breath as he took stock of the spreading blisters and blackening skin up and down his fingers. "Alright, Bob, here's the deal. I don't have a lot of time to dick around, and I need a hand and I want some answers. Or… fuck. Two. Maybe three. I hurt too damn bad to count," Anthony ranted as his voice trembled with pained cracks every few muttered words. "The question is: do you help me now and get to have dinner tonight, or do I shoot you and dump your corpse off of the train?"

Bob chose wisely.

The next few minutes were a mess — literally and figuratively alike. By the time the three of them were all done, the cabin floor was absolutely slick with blood and a few stray pieces of *parts* that didn't need discussed. The fun didn't really start until after Bob hauled Slash's corpse over to the necromancer for a little bit of a Q&A session.

Anthony couldn't do much with his hand other than lay it limply over Slash's bloody face. It took damn near the last of his reserves to tap into the hitter's brain, and the limited connection the hardwired sociopath had between body and not-so-dearly-departed soul proved difficult to get a grip on. Throughout the entire experience, the necromancer didn't move an inch — but his aura did.

With every inch he took from Slash's mind, the spread of decay and anth-radiation poisoning took another inch out of his own body. Vincetti fought every step of the way, but that was okay. Every step was something new that the corpse gave up, and every ounce of information only served to piss Anthony off even more.

By the time it was over, his arm was all but dead from the elbow down.

But by the time it was over, Anthony knew everything.

Starting with who the hell Andrea Adams was.

"Bob."

The guard hadn't made a sound for the last ten minutes. He was content to stay that way, too, but Blackburn nudged the back of his head until he responded. "Ah, yeah?"

With a hateful gaze that accompanied the jaundiced yellow discoloration in his right eye, the necromancer made sure to get every word out crisp and clear. "You are going to put a tourniquet on my arm, and then you're going to find me a knife."

Once again, Bob complied.

Bob wasn't as dumb as Bob looked.

"Anthony, you're gonna need to have more than some rent-a-cop with a nail file doing work on you. You… you do know that, right?" Blackburn quietly pointed out.

"Yeah, well, if you've got a medic stashed in those slugs…"

"Not in the gun, but there's one in the chamber."

It took his partner a second to realize what he meant, and Anthony did his best to shut the idea down as quickly as possible. Unfortunately, he spent the next minute with violent wretches and bloody vomit that stained the side wall. There wasn't anything anyone could do about it; at best, Blackburn managed to brace his partner with the stock of his shotgun to keep him from going face-first into the floor. *"Boy, you –"*

"It's n-tox, BB," Anthony managed to croak out between dry heaves. "That battery only goes so far."

"And does some rank-and-vile bullshit to your body, too."

"Rank-and-vile bullshit is better than being a corpse."

"Which you're about to be," the specter pointed out.

"But not yet."

"Semantics, Anthony. Those are what we used to call 'inconvenient details,' you know."

The necromancer sagged to the floor and took a ragged breath, "Lecturing me isn't going to help. So, whenever whoever is running this shit show realizes I'm not dead…"

Blackburn gave him a pensive stare that spoke volumes. *"So given that you aren't interested in having the common sense to die quietly per their request, I suppose that this problem is going to have to be managed by the three of us."*

"Three? It's just –"

"Three, Anthony," the ghost repeated. *"Boy, you need help. More help than I can give. You have to know that."*

"I do but –"

His familiar reached down and put his hand on Anthony's ruined arm. *"Then for once in your life, accept that there are some people in this world that might be willin' to risk themselves for you, instead of just you riskin' yourself for them."*

The Blackwash asshole stopped digging in his pockets and vehemently shook his head. "Now listen you two; I'll do a few things but if you think I'm some kind of –"

"Oh, shuttup Bob," the Marshal retorted as he swung his weapon through the air...

...and drove the stock right into the control panel on Katherine's In-CY pod. When that didn't work, the ghost did the next best thing and shot the controls point blank. Her door opened as fresh emergency lights and a very displeased gender-neutral voice started to make a series of announcements/lectures/warnings/and other to anyone that would listen.

She didn't even ask if he was okay.

All she asked was a simple, "What the fuck did you do now?"

***

Katherine's help was invaluable.

Katherine's help slowed down about the same time the knives came out. Everyone in the cab learned a few things about both themselves and general anatomy by the time that the necromancer was done with his work. Kath even learned a new level of respect for the batshit insane nightmare he'd lived through during his service...

...because nobody sane would've had the ideas he did.

They also learned that Slash had a reason for his nickname, and it was a good one. It also made Anthony pretty freaking grateful they'd never engaged in hand-to-hand combat, because he'd have lost. Cleanly. With perfect cuts.

When it was all said and done, the cargo compartment hadn't necessarily changed for the better, but it had changed. Barely visible cords of nth hung limply in the air between Anthony's chest and the bodies of both Slash and the Centurio. With the guard's help, Slash's head had a new home, and so did his phone.

His beeping, swearing, phone.

His beeping, swearing, phone with an open line to two different people who were equally pissed off, but for different reasons. Anthony hadn't bothered to explain himself; he'd just made a conference call and said, "Track me, sorry, bye." It didn't make much sense to drag it out any further than that.

They'd live with the curt ending. Hopefully.

Blackburn also looked a little pleased with himself, "*Think she'll forgive you*?"

"Nope."

"*Want her to*?"

Anthony wrinkled his nose as his two temporary minions did all the heavy lifting and most of the hard work. Sadly, Bob had lost the ability to form coherent thoughts after everything he'd seen the necromancer do, and he was only happy to oblige the instruction to open the car's cargo door. "Yeah. I do."

An immense roar ripped through the cabin as Bob keyed in a safety override that allowed the side doors to pop open. The second that they did, an explosion of air blew through the car and nearly sucked the guard out. The only reason the corpses didn't move was because Anthony simply wouldn't *let* them, and the only thing that stopped *him* and Kath from flying out into the great Texas waste beyond was a pair of crates he'd wedged himself in between.

The train didn't approve, either.

Warning klaxons fired off at a decibel suited to terrorize an entire city block while the whole car – and from the reverberations, the next two or three in line – shook so hard it nearly jumped the tracks. It *did* noticeably slow down, and it was a given that the handful of security Slash had stationed on the train was about to burst down the doors in the next few minutes at best. But for once, a few minutes was all he needed.

"Bob, do you know that the assholes you work for have been systematically murdering innocent people?"

The Blackwash guard looked up at him and winced. "I just collect the check, hombre. The corp provides security for –"

"Bob. Genocide, Bob. Textbook definition."

The goon looked at Anthony – or what was left of him – then glanced at Blackburn. The Marshal wasn't half as bemused as his partner, and the phantom's gun hadn't wavered very far from Bob's head. "Out the door?"

"Out the door. The train slowed down and –"

"No, Anthony," Katherine interrupted. "I don't care. No."

"He's got armor."

"Not enough," his familiar added, *"much as I hate to agree with your ex-missus and all. I'm sure you both understand."*

The necromancer gritted his teeth and glared down at the professional asshole at his feet. "Fine. But we can't leave him conscious."

Before Bob could attempt to negotiate a different idea, Blackburn spun his anchor through the air and connected the stock of the shotgun right against the side of his temple. The swing would've been a solid home-run back in the 90's; as it was, it knocked the guard out cold. From the bloody drool that trickled out of the corner of his mouth, Anthony had to assume it knocked him into a date with a dental surgeon, too.

Nobody said anything immediately after Bob drifted off to a concussion-induced dreamscape. Neither of them had much of a chance. The sirens cut out suddenly, only to be replaced by a single high-pitched tone from speakers hidden overhead. The tone was followed by an announcement from a less-than-amused woman...

...and to make it worse, they knew exactly who it was.

"Mister Pierson. If you're done trying to derail my train, I'd like to see you in the front of the cab to discuss our arrangement. Security has been ordered to stand down. Do be quick, darlin'; we're going places, and you might not like those places if we can't work out the details."

Anthony looked around for a button to hit. Any button, anywhere. He finally found a comms device on Bob's body that he was able to fumble on with nearly-dead fingers. "This... this Andrea Adams, I guess?" His voice lingered for a moment before he dropped a small bomb of his own. "Or Susan Sands?"

A long silence greeted the pair before her voice crackled back through the intercom. *"I don't have a clue what you mean."*

"Sure you do," Anthony replied slowly. "Vincetti had a lot to say about you, starting with the fact that you know how to do some basic illusions— change form, change faces. The Wholesome Farmhand of the Sunday-morning news circuit is doing double duty as the ghost CEO of Sojourn Enterprises."

More silence hung in the air before Susan answered him with a bit less cheer in her voice. *"You've been finding out things you shouldn't know."*

"You sent your boy to kill a necromancer. What'd you think would happen if he didn't do his job?"

"Now that's a valid point, but do understand that my invitation isn't to be ignored."

"Can't ignore it. I pulled... pulled a profile on your ass before... before I knew who you were. Cocky. Arrogant. Sadistic. Powerful; fucking powerful. You've got nth talent I don't think anyone human has. You'd have to to write the spells in the Centurios like that."

"If all this is flattery…"

"No, this is me saying that I'm not doing shit for you until I get some answers. This is also me saying that I know I have something you want: Clare."

"You're a wounded man on a train full of security who would be happy to chuck you off the rails, darlin', so I'd reconsider what kind of leverage you think you have. Only thing you've done now is to ensure that everyone in that car goes the kind dead you don't get up and walk away from. I don't need –"

Blackburn smirked and watched Anthony work. Susan's voice went from bemused to irritated faster than usual, which was a good sign, kinda. "I'm still alive, so, yes, the fuck you do," the necromancer shot back.

Silence reigned again before she finally answered his taunt. *"As I said, I am willin' to discuss our arrangement; but I want you to understand that if you make things difficult for me you can be sure I'll find ways to make what's left of your life difficult on you."*

The line went dead when she finished. Anthony glanced at his familiar, who looked nervous – even for a ghost. "Oh, we're fucked."

*"Dunno what could've made you think that. The voice of Susan Sands herself on the overhead? Or the fact that this train is radiatin' **death like** a rave in a graveyard?"*

"It is, isn't it?" Anthony replied with a slow blink of surprise. "I hadn't noticed it. Well, it gives me an idea."

"You didn't go and notice it probably because you're bleedin' all over the place," Blackburn said, with an unnecessary finger point to boot.

"If I'm not living through this, neither is anyone else. Trust me, please. I've got an idea."

"Good one or bad one?"

"Both." Before his familiar could comment on the vagueness of *that* particular statement, Anthony pointed his chin at Slash. "Now gimmie some help. Like I said; I need a hand."

Blackburn looked down at Slash's mutilated, headless corpse. *"You've already popped him up. What more do you want?"*

Anthony shrugged his one working shoulder and gave his curled, blackened fingers a wistful look. "How many times do I have to say it? I need a *hand*. Maybe two."

11. NECROMANCER'S BULLET
Wednesday, May 30th, 9:31 AM

As she'd promised, Susan Sands was waiting at the front of the train in all of her, *'Look at me! I'm a personification of a marketing manual for the Southern US!'* attire, down to the hair bun and button-up plaid-print faux-cotton shirt. The only thing she was missing was a stalk of hay sticking between her teeth and maybe an Ameri-Buddy beer in her hand.

Not that she would; the latter was sold by a subsidiary of Heart and Spade. Lust *loved* freedom because it meant you could act on your desire. Still, he was almost surprised she didn't have a cup of coffee to complete the look.

"Ah, there ya are, darlin', thought you might've gotten lost. Oh, and I see you brought a guest. Would this be the vaunted Marshal Marshall Blackburn?" she asked as he stepped into the train's cab. "I see you managed to – how should I say it? Re-arm yourself?"

She was right; he had.

The joke was so tasteless that the necromancer emptied a shell right into her face to get her to shut up. Susan's head whipped back at, more or less, the speed of sound as a single G-Locke 9 bullet punched a hole square in the middle of her forehead. The only noise she made in reply was a satisfying thud when her body hit the train wall and slumped down into a bloody puddle.

Wasn't easy, but at that range, you couldn't miss.

As far as the ghost that lingered in the corner? It wasn't Blackburn. For that matter, it was barely half-formed. Still, it was outright amazing what you could find lingering around on a train full of dead bodies stuffed in freezer units. It was, however, angry. Silent and angry.

Angry enough that Anthony felt stretched thin keeping control.

As far as the train itself went?

Of all the things that Slash had offered up, security codes to get through the freight liner were almost on the top of the list. SSBL had designed the train so that its anthenium-fueled engine could offer additional wind displacement to lower the problems with air resistance and drag; he didn't want to try to figure out how and didn't bother to ask. The net result was that instead of just being *long*, the train was *tall*, with eight of the front-end cars being double-deckers.

From the front, it looked more like a shark fin than anything else.

Four of the cars were labs.

None of them had the same material Anthony had seen in Carlos's head from what felt like a lifetime ago, but they were biological experimentation chambers. Three of them were meant for 'resource preparation,' by the signs and the freezers. One of them was meant for disposal.

If he'd had either the time or the strength left, he'd have made a point to ensure the storage units were full of Sojourn assholes. Fortunately (or unfortunately, depending on how you looked at it), the Sojourners, Blackwash security, random hookers, and whomever else didn't leave their spacious berths unless they had to. Most of the 'had to' included several different labs, assorted storage compartments, and the main engine bay directly under the main cab, along with the 'special' storage right behind it.

South Shore's special anth-reactor gave off all kinds of bad vibes throughout the entire electrical system from the mag-levs on the underside of each car down to the freaking flickering lights. The train reeked of death on a level that couldn't really be put into words. Whatever the reason, the end result was that both the necromancer and his minion felt like they were walking through some kind of nth-inductive charging station.

The only person that had given them any problems was a lone custodial worker who, apparently, had seen it all, said most of it, and didn't give a flying fuck about either of them. On any other day, it would've been amusing. As it was, she provided an unwelcome delay although Anthony was distinctly certain he overheard Blackburn ask for her number after they'd locked her in a spare cabin.

Why, he just didn't even want to guess.

As Susan slumped over lifeless, the necromancer took the time to note that her blood wasn't *red*, but that was a problem for future Anthony. *Current* Anthony was a bit more preoccupied with the mangled pile of wires, flesh, and LEDs that had been looped around and through a central figure strapped into the conductor's chair in the middle of the cabin. On the surface, it looked almost like another Centurio, though a closer inspection made it clear that he'd been bolted directly to the chair and had no chance of getting out of it.

They'd given the poor bastard some kind of nightmarish throne to match the full-face helmet-turned-crown that it wore. The bio-hacked corpse sat in the middle of the train's control deck. The consoles spanned a hundred and eighty degrees around the cab, with a web of wires and pipes that ran from station to station and directly to ports built into the engineer's chest and under his crown.

Three giant screens hung from the ceiling over each section. One showed irrelevant tech data about the train, and another depicted regional rail routes. That one was lit up with dozens of warnings and orders to cease operation that had come straight from the feds via the Railway Administration.

It was far from the most important thing in the world to worry about, so Anthony didn't. It was nice to know that Alara cared enough to put out a stop transit order, but he wasn't willing to bet if it was to try to save him or shoot him. Probably the latter.

The one closest to his head had everything he needed to know, and most of that came from bits and pieces that Slash had eventually offered in the dank pit of bullshit that had been his mind. "Was that... necessary?"

"No, but it made me feel better," Anthony replied as Susan's wet and raspy voice complained from behind the chair. "Didn't think it'd kill you. And if it had, well, I could've lived with that."

"I would've done the same. I assume you did your homework?" she croaked as her jaw shifted back into place and her teeth regrew.

"Honestly, no. Vincetti did. Ab/Psy and Cult figured out they were looking for something that wasn't supposed to be in town; I just don't think either of them expected to have to look so high up on the corporate food chain. I mean, inhuman magic is one thing, but..."

"Inhuman?" she scoffed. "I'm what humans wish they could be."

"Don't give yourself that much credit," Anthony grunted. "I want to be surprised, but I don't have it in me."

"Not even a little bit curious?" Susan challenged. Her fake southern drawl made the menacing suggestion sound a lot more chipper than it should, but the end result was just a brand-new way to make Anthony's skin crawl.

The necromancer sized her up slowly and silently as she stood up and crossed her arms. The green blood smeared all over her shirt and jeans faded into nothing as the fabric seemingly drank it all up to the last drop. "A lot of curious. I don't think it matters, but I'm a lot of curious."

"I think all of that is gonna depend on how you've decided to view our agreement. Remember what you offered Roger?"

"Clare for Vincetti."

She smiled and allowed her eyes to flicker to Anthony's arms. "Seems you have him; more of him than I expected, actually."

More than he'd expected, truth be told.

Anthony lifted his hands and stared at them. It wasn't the kind of trick you got to train for; just the kind of trick that you figured out if you had to. Half of Vincetti's lower right arm had melded with Anthony's anth-irridiated stump stump while his other arm had been tightly impaled into the ruins of his cybernetic shoulder. Every time he moved it, it made a noise like a lemon stuck in a juicer.

Nth held everything together but did absolutely nothing to dull the pain. In what was assuredly a bad sign, his ruined limbs felt like they were okay; both wounds had stopped throbbing three cars back. "So, that was your game, huh? Pop my pod; let him know I was loose. Two men enter; one man leaves?"

"You gave me the idea," the brunette bitch pointed out. "I burn him, I get you. He kills you, I still get you. Either way, it resolves a loose end."

"Except for Clare."

Her hairline rolled as her skin shifted from her nose to somewhere behind her back in a singular wave. "No, you get to tell me either way. Where is she?"

If she was trying to intimidate him, it was working. Anthony backed away from the Centurio-engineer and put his – well, Vincetti's – hands on the control consoles. "It just... it just hit me. I'm alive because I fucked up, aren't I?"

"Yes," Susan admitted. "I want Clare. You have her. You shouldn't have gotten her, but I want her. If the cops had... honestly? Honestly, darlin', I mean no disrespect but I personally couldn't care less about you aside from the fact that you have her."

Anthony took a deep breath and locked eyes with his familiar for a few seconds before he sagged down and tapped a couple of commands on the console beside him. Two of the three vid-screens popped up with two packets of information – one for Susan Sands and the other for Andrea Adams. The living RP specialist-turned-nightmare blinked in brief surprise, but didn't do anything else.

"I have to admit how impressed I am. I've known some brilliant people. No matter how good they were, they couldn't have pulled this off. You're PR for Eden Farms. Direct control over the Gardeners and their distribution network, for all intents and purposes. Then, in your spare time, you're the on-paper CEO of a biotech firm, and you funneled — slowly, I'm sure — all kinds of magical hacks and manuals over to Sojourn and HawkCrest R&D to make your little freakshow real. I honestly don't know how you managed to do it."

Susan preened a little bit and basked in the flattery. "Ghostwriters, AI assistance, spoof emails. Honestly, you'd be surprised how many people will believe you aren't you when you don't have a face," she replied as she covered her lower mouth with her hand in an intimation of a mask. "Masks and muzzles work just as well in Corporate America as they do damn near anywhere else."

A little light went off in the back of his head — figuratively, this time, instead of literally. "For both of our sakes, remember you said that later. Thing is, I want to live through this. Let's make a deal?"

"We *had* a deal," she countered forcefully, "and sunshine? I hate to be the one to say this an' all, but what you want and what you're gonna get are two different things. Your heart is a cow's spit away from being part of a worm's well-balanced breakfast. The question is more one of, 'Do I get to die with all my teeth in my head, or die after the pretty girl in the tight jeans pulls them out with her fingers?' wouldn't you agree?"

"Oh come on," he grunted as he tapped the keys again and Andrea Adam's biography and data-log became the center focus of all three screens at once. There was a *lot* to it, and frankly, it was intimidating. "Ain't gonna matter. Hell gets to pull them out or you do."

Susan's face shifted again. This time it didn't just roll; her face *shimmered* and her pale Caucasian skin started to crack as faint scales pushed up against the fake flesh that she wore as a cover. The scales were quickly joined by a pair of horns that unsheathed themselves from the edges of her forehead before they curled around to point to the back. "You know *nothing* of Hell," she promised as her southern accent melted into a deep, twisted groan with an undercurrent of a reptilian hiss. "I do."

"I'd say he does, too," Anthony replied as he pointed at the Centurio while he tried to keep his composure.

The demoness smiled and it made her face move in a way that wouldn't have quite been possible for a human. Or at least he thought it was a smile. Maybe it was. Hopefully, it was. "He earned his throne."

"Why do I fucking doubt it?"

Susan slid her hand around the back of the engineer's helmet and fondled it carefully, "For the same reason I doubt you're taking me seriously. I want Clare. I want her now."

"I don't want to die."

"Too bad. You're human."

"And you're not," Anthony countered. "You've got a fuckton of med supplies on this train and you can't tell me –"

Susan lunged from behind Orion's chair and wrapped a single hand around the necromancer's throat in a single, supple move. He couldn't react in time to stop her, and Anthony's quiet 'guest' in the corner didn't try to intervene. "Screaming or in your sleep; I don't care. I want that fucking wannabe French bitch in my hands. Where is she?"

Her fingers sent lightning bolts of pain racing through his skin and across every bone left in his body. It didn't just *hurt*, it felt like she disrupted every ounce of nth he had left, even if it wasn't much. "Here, I have her *here*," he wheezed and spat, with the last word punctuated with a little bit of bloody froth. "Not for… not for long."

Susan's eyes turned a sickly, jaundiced yellow as she pressed her face so close to his they could kiss. "What do you mean?"

"I mean, when I die, she goes away. You don't find her. She falls off this train and you spend the next fucking year digging her out of the desert. I don't think you have that kinda ti-"

"You are a fucking LYING sack of SHIT!" Susan roared. "Do you think this is some kind of GAME? I WANT HER!"

"AND I DON'T WANT TO GO TO HELL!" he screamed back. "You wanna know where she *was*? Have a fucking look!" Anthony opened his mouth and twisted his head to the side. His tongue pointed out the obvious: a hole where a molar should've been.

Realization dawned across the demoness' face and disgust followed it immediately after. "You. Little. Worm."

"You could've had her any time you wanted if you hadn't popped me outta that pod," he spat. "Jaw-pockets. With the right dentist, you can store a lot of things in your mouth. Now, keep me out of Hell and you get your soul."

It worked – in a way. Susan let go of his chest, and her features slowly slid back to those that were a rough approximation of a human. "That is what you really want, isn't it, darlin'? You want to avoid the other side more than you care about your women."

Anthony sagged down onto the console and tried to catch his breath. His heart was racing so hard he could hear it in his ears, and at the same time, every harried beat was joined by a stabbing jolt through his chest. "Mostly," he croaked. "Maybe. Maybe I just think you're gonna be too busy running from everyone you've pissed off to go back and collect them."

"Or maybe I'll make an example. All the Master Chief did was go to a priest and try to clear his soul. Imagine what I'll do to the woman that went to the cops. Or better, imagine what I'll do to make you suffer. You'll be much better off playing nice, darlin'. I mean it."

That wasn't just some casual threat. The necromancer's breath stuck in his throat as he realized who sat in the chair beside him. "Omari Miller. He's…"

"Was. Perks of keeping him under a hood."

"Fuck."

Susan focused her eyes on Anthony's chest and licked her lips slowly, "You could say that. So. You don't want to go to Hell. You think I can be your savior."

"I think I'm fucked no matter what."

"Darlin', you are absolutely positively bonified *boned*," she promised. "So, if you think I'm going to save you… let me show you from *what*."

Anthony screamed once and sharply as she wrapped her hand around his face. Nth unlike anything he'd ever felt before washed over him and pulsed into his mouth and eyes. The sludge-like etheric substance permeated his consciousness, and he saw… it. Hell.

And Her.

First Susan… and then he saw *Her*.

***

The worst of the worst of the memhalls he'd been in hadn't prepared him for this one. He wasn't sure if it was *his* or *Susan*'s, but it wasn't *pleasant*. The train went away the second she pushed her way into his head and the hallway that manifested was as cold and dead as moon rocks – with just as much color to go with them.

Only the rocks weren't rocks.

Most of them were bones.

Bones, mixed with mortar, shoved in with chunks of misshapen bricks. If you'd ever seen the London Catacombs, you had an idea of what it was like. At first, it wasn't impressive. It wasn't until he realized that some of the heads still had faces that his stomach dropped.

Faces he knew. Men he'd served with. Men he'd seen die. Men he'd ripped the souls out of their still-warm corpses to get them back to base. Men that he'd shepherd from the sandy shit-pits in the middle of NPC territory to back stateside. A few he'd said goodbye to at their funerals.

And then there were the ones he'd personally shoved into the next world, usually face first, with lead, dep-anth, or whatever was handy. Maybe they deserved it, maybe they didn't. Uncle Sam thought they did.

In the heat of the moment, it was what it was.

In here, their fingers reached for him. Their mouths worked as a foggy glass plug at the end of the hallway moved... melted... broke. The cracks in the glass bled as they spread. Every piece of the plug that shattered felt like a knife in the top of his head. Every chunk of the foggy mess that broke was echoed with the unmistakable feeling of a ball-bat across the back of his skull.

He started to scream; from pain, mostly, though fright wasn't far behind. The second that he made a sound, a withered hand with bones that had worn through the skin punched through the barrier of the hall and wrapped itself around his entire upper torso. Rigid knots of bone dug into his ribs while talon-like nails dug into his back and spine.

The hand *pulled* him through the remnants of the glass wall of his future-to-be and dropped him at Susan's feet. Contrary to popular belief, they weren't cloven. In fact, they barely could be classified as 'feet.'

Slash had shown him Susan's plans, and had given him a chance to peer behind the curtain at what she *might* be. The demoness was only happy to show him exactly what she was. She reveled in it. She delighted in it. She started to laugh as he began to convulse under her palm and that laugh dominated everything he could hear.

She was more than *old*.

He'd profiled Andrea Adams as a cocky, overconfident, semi-psychotic, and sadistic corporate shithead. You couldn't turn on GCN without forming an opinion of Susan Sands either, and for one brief pained heartbeat, he kicked himself for not seeing it earlier. He was right about all of it, except for the 'semi' part.

She wasn't psychotic.

She simply wasn't human. Human concepts didn't apply to her. Behind her, the realm that unfolded – literally before his eyes – was a place that defied the meaning of the word *time*. A sea of shifting mountains and clouds full of souls that snapped from one location to another like screaming, floating bubbles.

Time didn't exist here. There wasn't a point in trying to measure between experiences because the experiences never stopped. They repeated, returned, and changed. Everything was different, and everything was new all at the same time, and every last heartbeat of it was *agony*.

Beyond her? Beyond the horizon offered of her scales, claws, fangs, and worse? Below her status as an evolutionary link between humanity and the detached and diffuse planes that hung on the other side? Below the sadism and boredom; below the emotions that might be distant cousins to feelings like loathing and hate?

A glimpse, nothing more, just a glimpse of the afterlife.

It made the taste he'd toyed with a few minutes before feel like a joke.

Then he saw Her. A single striking form of beauty. A mountain in Her own right; one that was the size of a dime one moment and the size of Mount Rushmore the next. She was humanoid but not human. Demonic, but at the same time, nothing so trivial. Her face was as gray as a 1950's sitcom starlet; Her features just as comely and inviting.

She locked Her eyes on him and shook Her head 'no.'

Supple fingers emerged from the roiling carnage-red clouds of writhing souls and ever so intently, *flicked* in the air. A rush of force buffeted his face and stripped the skin from his body. He felt his eyes melt and his bones dissolve. He heard a whispered cry of pain try to pipe out of his throat.

Then it all stopped, and his ashes vaporized in the maelstrom.

***

Anthony could still hear his own scream in the engine cab when he regained consciousness. When Susan let go, it took his brain a long minute to process that he was in the train cab. It took another one for his brain to process that train cabs were still real. It took less than that for him to find the strength to look up at her and croak out an accusation.

"You're an Elder Daem... you're... just a crackbreed."

It only took a quarter second for her to kick him so hard in his stomach that he threw up all over the floor. When the vomiting stopped, she sneered down at him. "I think the phrase you're looking for is *pure-blood*."

Anthony looked up at her from the floor. "I think... I think the phrase I'm looking for is... is you are purely *fucked*," he groaned. Drool and fear dripped off his face and onto the floor as his heart continued to throb off-tempo. The jumpstart wasn't supposed to do more than wake his ass up and get him moving. It wasn't supposed to get him in a fight with one of the Pentaship's fucking earth-bound first-born.

"I'm fucked? *I'm* fucked? Says the man who can't even stand up. Fine. You know what waits for you, and you know you're about to be Hell's little bitch in just a few minutes unless you quit this bullshit and tell me where she is."

"I will, I promise, I will," he croaked as he finally found the strength to pull himself up off of the ground. Slash's left arm was utterly useless in the process, and it hung loosely off of his shoulder with a hint of barely visible nth to keep it attached. "Just… why… your own kind? Humans, I'd get; animals, whatever, but yo…"

The back of her hand rocked his face hard enough to bruise his cheek and eye both. "My *kind*? You fucking think that I am one of *those*?"

"Elder… Daem," he croaked from a few inches above Orion's lap. "It's in the name."

"Because *humans* have this pathetic mandate to *name things*," Susan raged. "*Pathetic* little Adam and Eve hangers-on. And just like them – *just like them*! – my Mother turned Her back on Her truest of the true! Oh no, a new little creature to play with. Look at what happens when you put a rutting whore and some fucking brainless cock in a room together. They make half-breed *bullshit* that isn't worth stepping on… Her *children*. She has the fucking gall."

The vitriol behind her voice was enough to take his breath away… if he could get one. "Wait… wait. Please. You're mad… all this. Picking and choosing them. Slaughtering them. Turning them into weapons. Parading them under Helesiki's ass. All of this… because you're mad at your fucking *mom*?"

The Daem sank her fingers into the hair on the back of his head and wrenched him upright to stare into his eyes. The yellow was still there, but it literally burned at the edges of her face. "Oh you can't just kill them. Sure, you can get some people willing to do it. I tried. No. No, you have to give a *purpose* for it. You have to have a *reason* because that's all your kind demands, purpose and *fucking* reason. So, I gave them one. 'Home the lost, heal the sick, feed the poor.' Humans like that kind of message. And in the process, I made every single one of the pillars of your so-called society rot."

Anthony stared at her as his mouth dropped.

He just stared.

"Billions of dollars spent and now on fire. Countless lives destroyed. Murder. Torture. Geno-*fucking*-cide. Your big… big plan was just to… let two or three of those things fucking… wander… through the city. All of this for that? That… minuscule little… in the history of the city, this is barely an inconvenience for everyone except for the guy that has to wash out the body bags. You thought that you'd get your revenge… by stomping out Jordan *Goddamn* Fisher? THAT was how you thought you'd get…?"

A sneer ripped across her face even as her scales pushed back to the surface, "No. No. I was going to unleash these on the *world*. They were going to bring down Spade Tower by force and the whole world would know what could be done with just the right mix of tech and the wrong mix of blood."

"Oh, so… generic terrorism?"

"*Knowledge,*" she countered. "The tower falls and five minutes later every fucking warlord on the planet would want one. The pathetic half-breed Daems would be seen for what they are – tools to be used for the glory of all Hell, not just Mother's narcissism. They'd be exterminated by the fearful and harvested by the powerful. It was going to be *beautiful.*"

Anthony started to sag in her grip. "Then you throw it away for *Jordan*? You're calling your mother a narcisi-bitch, and you waste this plan on *JORDAN*?"

"That was one of you fucking humans. All. Vincetti's. Fault. When I'm done with you –"

"I watched you do it. I saw you. The order."

It was the first thing he'd said that made her pause. "Excuse me?"

Anthony swallowed hard as her fingers drew blood on his scalp. "Bitch, I was in his head. I fucking watched you do it."

"Darlin'. What in the name of your worthless God…?"

"Vid-call," he clarified slowly. "You did it in your Andrea Adams skin-suit. I *watched*. You assholes have fucked up my headset but I can try and get you a –"

She placed her thumb up right below his good eye and pushed. He screamed as her nails dug into the skin just below his eyelid. "Your kind. Your people? Ya always think that you can get away with lyin' to anyone, but then you forget who introduced the concept of falsehoods and… and…"

His laugh started low in his chest as tears flowed down his cheeks. "And you can tell when… when we are. I know." The Elder Daem froze as she poured her focus into his head. It felt like a thousand bees rolling around his brain all at once as her expression cratered.

"Go on," he croaked. "And what?"

The realization hit like punch to the face. "You aren't…"

"Not a single… single word," he replied with a giddy chuckle.

Susan dropped him back to the chair and blinked slowly as her eyes shifted colors from yellow to a more human brown. Her body began to change shape, too. "I… I didn't. I…"

When she finished shifting, 'Susan Sands' was gone, and 'Andrea Adams' had taken her place, but it didn't matter. None of it mattered now. She just didn't realize it.

"You know, the way… the way you lost your shit over it? Vinci figured he'd have to kill you, too. 'Cept he didn't know about the whole Susan thing. Just thought Adams was some psychopathic CEO. Not like there aren't a dozen of them in town," he added as he spit some blood out of his mouth. "Wanted to clean us up first. Just to… just to cover his own loose ends."

"His loose ends? *His*?" she repeated back. The air around her started to take on a nearly visible nth-charge as a literal inhuman rage roiled off her skin. "Explain! Now!"

"What's to explain?" he croaked between laughs. "You spent years bouncing between Adams and Sands to play both sides against the middle. You didn't stop once to think that someone would do the same to you."

"What —"

"You got played. You both did. Twice."

Susan/Andrea had her hand pulled back to strike him when she froze almost completely solid and looked into his bloodshot, swollen eyes like she'd lost her keys in his head. "Twice? Oh, do you think you're somehow as smart as I am? Is that what you're playing at? Win me over by showing how innovative the human mind is?"

There was some baggage to unpack there. He just didn't have time to do it. "If only. So, um. Have you ever heard of Frank's Hardware?"

"Don't waste my —"

"You know, Frank of Frank's Hardware?"

Susan looked at him like he'd lost his mind. "You're… serious? No, I haven't heard of 'Frank's Hardware.' You're dying and you're asking for a recommendation on *screwdrivers*?"

"No. No. Just… just wondering if you knew him. Because I think… I think he knows you," Anthony replied as he straightened up against the cab's wall. The scars on his chest erupted with busy little yellow lights that were streaked with red and putrid, rot-green as he focused the last bit of his strength through them. "Can I be honest with you?"

"Please, humor me."

He pointed up over her shoulder at a small plastic dome with a blinking red light in the corner of the cab. Almost immediately, all three display panels flickered to bright life. The center panel flipped to a security feed of the train. The other two flipped to duplicate feeds....

One that was being carried by Gulf Coast News...

...and the other by Certified All-National.

The color drained from Susan's face in-person and on the monitors both as Anthony laughed. "Bitch, I'm dyin'... but you're live."

***

Frank's Hardware

Having a bad day? You just need a Quicker Fixxer-Upper.

***

For once in his life, Anthony had left simple instructions. "Move two cars back, you'll find a terminal... wall-mount. Call C-Phone-Search, say *'Frank's Hardware,'* then say, *'All the fixin's.'* Once you do, follow the instructions you get," he had said as he had forced his hand into the Centurio's stomach. "Without argument."

Katherine protested.

She did that a lot, but it didn't do any good.

"Blackburn is going with you. So is this hunk of shit. Anything that tries to hurt her, shoot them," the necromancer said as he turned to address his familiar and the barest hint of a consciousness he'd let the centurio have.

His ex pocketed the bloody phone as her hands shook, but she still made the effort to reach over and touch his face after. "I don't want to leave you, Anth..."

"Bull and shit," he grunted as he flopped onto his ass and admired his work. "You want to live through this? Go and get it done."

"What happens after I call this magical hardware store? Last time, they sent a car. What should I expect this time, a verti?"

"I have no idea," he admitted. "Frank wants in their system, kinda think he's going to have some fun with it. Just... wait for my call. I need... I need their attention focused on me."

"You can barely fucking walk, you idiot," she seethed. "You're stretched between… fuck, I can't even *tell* everything you're doing. You're branched out like a bloody spider web. You *might* make it to a med-station *if* you pull back from the spellwork but…"

"But none of us are getting off this train if I don't," he countered. "So you let me do what… what I need to do, and we'll call it even. Okay?"

It wasn't okay. It wasn't even remotely okay. "What makes you think you can distract anyone? Let alone tell us when —"

Blackburn put a ghostly hand on her shoulder and she flinched away from the oddly cold touch that lingered behind. "*I would trust that the boy has a way of getting' a message across, especially if he's sending me with you. Which itself is a request I don't take kindly.*"

"Three's a crowd," the necromancer retorted as he stood up on wobbly legs. "Come on. That bitch isn't going to wait."

"What are we supposed to do until she gets her hands on you?"

"I don't know; play dead," he grunted. "Anything, just… do it."

Fifteen minutes later, Katherine did it. She dialed the number.

Then she listened for instructions. She carried them out.

And then she backed away in horror as a digital face appeared on the flatpanel and started to *laugh* at her. When it stopped, the screen went dead and every light in their car went off. Every light except for two blinking red dots on two different black oval domes on different sides of the cab.

When nothing else happened, Katherine caught her breath and looked at the ghostly figure that idly floated just a few feet away. "The only person allowed to kill that sonofabitch is me. You got that?"

Blackburn nodded and glanced at the monitor as it came back to life. There was a simple message on it, and he did as instructed — by both of them. He vanished and his gun blipped out of existence a moment later.

No sooner than he was gone than a very pronounced pair of *ca-chinks* echoed through the cargo room, and she felt the train immediately slow down. Emergency lights flickered on below the grated floor as sudden deceleration nearly dropped her to her knees. A voice toned overhead that calmly announced that an unscheduled decoupling had occurred, and that emergency services would be enroute as able.

It wasn't half as reassuring as it should've been.

It was less than that when she glanced up at the scrolling text across the screen and felt her own stomach drop. She looked up at one of the cams, and very slowly waved her hand at it. "Uh, hi?"

Susan's scream could be heard through the entire train. It was nothing more than raw, inhuman, rage. Anthony weakly lifted his chin and gave her a single little smirk. "Kill me if you want, but what you need to do is run."

Blinded by rage, she tried.

The ghostly figure in the corner manifested in full and blocked her path. She froze for a few scant seconds as Vincetti's ghost *pushed* her back with a violent pulse of pure nth that buffeted her shifting flesh. It did little good, and she charged again.

This time Vincetti didn't just push, he *pulled*.

Spectral dead simply couldn't move things around very well... unless the item was their anchor. In the grand scheme of things, very little anchored a ghost like their own dismembered corpse. It was a lesson in magic that Susan should've learned by this point of her otherwise remarkable existence. The longer of Slash's arms detached from Anthony's shoulder and shot through the cab like a bullet.

A fleshy bullet that disgorged one of the long blades he was known for from the top of its forearm. The Elder Daem couldn't dodge it in time, and the carbon-fiber blade punched right through her chest and out the back of her spine. The impact forcibly nailed her to the back of Orion's chair and lobotomized the tortured engineer in one go.

It didn't do much to slow her down. She was a pure-blood demon; low on the totem pole, for all intents and purposes, but a pure-blood demon all the same. You couldn't kill one just by stabbing them through their heart. They were generally a lot more resilient than that; and she was no exception to the rule.

The Daem ripped the necrotic arm out of her chest and sunk her fingers into Slash's etheric skull. Spirits couldn't touch much, but a nth-based entity could touch a spirit. She sunk her fingernails into his essence and *ripped* him in half with barely a thought. An agonized, human wail erupted as his ghost broke apart and vanished into the air like phantom silk until nothing but a faint echo remained.

It couldn't have happened to a nicer asshole.

Just as quickly, a nicer asshole made a point to make sure it didn't.

She managed to get her hand on Anthony's chest before a solid chunk of steel and wood spun into the air and delivered a perfect uppercut to the point of her chin. The impact hit with enough force to nearly knock her off her feet, but not quite. Susan screamed in a language Anthony didn't know and wasn't in a hurry to learn.

She shut up when the barrel lodged itself between her front teeth.

Anthony gave the command and Blackburn pulled the trigger.

You couldn't just shoot a demon and expect it to die nobody could. Not a pure-blood. Not an *elder* anything. Low-grade monsters? Sure. Daems in general? They were human enough, if not thick-skinned. But an actual honest-to-God demon?

Nope.

Even to wound one, you had to have special rounds; something coated in depleted anthenium, or maybe silver. Pure lead didn't work on anything except for stubborn ghosts that refused to move on. Just on the chance that he might've been a little worse than the average undead bear, Anthony had seasoned a few of the shells with a little special fun before they'd even gotten onto the train.

Shards of plastic, burning gunpowder, a little bit of near-molten brass and two teeth slammed into the roof of her mouth and pulverized the demon equivalent of a brain into pudding at sonic speeds. Blood, bone, and pulp burst out of the top of her head in a spray of gore that got caught and streamed on live air for the whole damn nation to see.

Two teeth from a holy man.

Two teeth from a *murdered* holy man. Two teeth from a murdered holy man that found themselves inside the skull of the hellion that was responsible for his death, torture, and non-consensual resurrection as a battery pack. Two teeth that had more than enough nth of their own to do some damage if used properly.

Putting them inside a demon's face counted for 'used properly.'

Blood and gore were followed by a jet of burning hot nth that erupted out of the back of her skull, her blown-out eyes, ears, and nose. Blue and green flames carried an inhuman screech that nearly blew out Anthony's eardrums by the time it finished. When the sound stopped, Susan's head was nothing more than a puddle of lifeless gunk.

The rest of her body nearly melted to the floor. It largely lost cohesion, and quickly devolved into a steaming pile of worm-like tubes and limp bones with the consistency of overcooked spaghetti. Blackburn stepped back from his handwork with an utterly horrified look on his own face.

"What in the actual fu-"

"Well… shit," Anthony mused as a chunk of her skull fell from the ceiling and hit the floor with a wet plop. "If I thought that was all it was gonna take…"

Blackburn looked down the barrel of his gun and made a quiet gagging sound. *"Boy I have been dead for a very very long time and I haven't ever seen anything like that before. Be quite happy with you ifin' I never do again, especially not with my own stick, you understand?"*

"Take it up with your next owner," the necromancer replied with a wet cough. "Though you may wanna consider… jumping on the next, um… train, I guess… to the next… yeah. I really should've thought of it sooner, fuck."

"You didn't know what she was, and to be fair, you're a few heartbeats left. What can I do to help?"

"I'd ask for a guided tour of Hell, but…"

"She already gave you a glimpse, huh? Heard they can do that."

"Go bind yourself to a church when I'm gone."

"That bad, huh?"

Anthony looked up at him with a single, bleary, bloodshot eye. His cybernetic eye had gone limp and simply pointed down to the ground. "Thanks Black. For everything. Dunno how to say it… but, love ya man. You've… fuck. You've been there. Repeatedly. Thank… thank you."

"Aw now don't be like that. You don't do well with sayin' that shit and I, sure as the fact that my body is cold as dust, I don't like listening to it. We can get you back to the pod and…"

"C'mon BB," the necromancer croaked. "I know when shit's dying, not just dead. We're in last… last fucking words territory here. Too much… n-tox. They'll have to bury… bury me in a fucking Superfund site."

Blackburn knelt and put his hand on the center of the runes on Anthony's chest, *"Yea boy, but you keep the dead up and movin'. That special jumper switch in your ribs is doin' the same thing, ain't it?"*

"Yeah, but I have to be alive to do it. Can't… you know… juice runs out, lights go off. Nobody's home to… to reset the breaker."

"So you need some power."

"Black…"

"Now, now, hear me out and stay with me boy. I ain't done with you yet. You're on a train powered by anthenium, literally a battery, the type of battery in your chest."

Anthony looked down at the ghost's hand and felt the edge of an idea start. A terrible idea, but an idea. "It's not that… well. It is. But it isn't. I'd need a medium. A filter. Biological."

"You got one right there," Blackburn replied as he pointed down at what was left of Adam's body.

"I've got one right… what?" he asked before his familiar's meaning dawned on him. "No. Oh. Absolutely no."

"Your pick," the lawman replied. *"Go through her or… well. Bonfire, I guess. With you the guest of honor."*

Anthony looks back and forth between the corpse and the ghost for a long minute he didn't really have to spare. Finally, he started to crawl across the floor with a grunt and a wheeze. "You know what. I take it back. I hate you."

"I know, I know. Hate you too."

***

Hours later…

A blast of hot, stale air washed over Callie's face and jogged her awake. Her eyes didn't quite focus at first, and it wasn't helped by the brilliant flashlight in her face. The Texas breeze stole the chill from her skin almost instantly, but it didn't do a damn thing for the rest of her.

A stabbing headache was the third thing to reach her consciousness, followed by the sharp pain of an obviously broken rib and the unpleasant sensation of at least one IV in her shoulder. As miserable as all of that felt, it was a soothing voice and a pair of soft hands that coaxed her to focus on the angel in front of her. Or… no. Not an angel.

A cop.

A cop in tac gear.

A cop in tac gear with a disarming smile and a voice that cut through the fog of her borderline delirium. "Hey. Hey, can you hear me?"

"Yea… yeah, yeah I can… who…?"

"You're safe," he started. His voice coated her ears like a soft glove. "Just relax, I'm using some nth to help you through this. Do you consent?"

"Use… use whatever you want," Callie purred… or at least, tried to. Her voice was raspy and rough, and the purr sounded like she had a bad case of strep.

He chuckled as he took her by both of her shoulders and helped her sit up in the pod. "I'm Detective Haythes. Do you know where you are? What's the last thing you remember?"

Callie tried to get her eyes to focus on… anything. The sky was as wide open and clear as she'd ever seen it in her life, down to the actual stars above. She could see a small small handful of vehicles parked around an empty wasteland; mostly off-road types and at least one EMS low-lev. "I… I was…"

"Take your time," he replied. Every time he spoke, pale pink ripples escaped his lips.

"So pretty," she mumbled as an EMT took hold of her and started to check her over. The IV popped out of her arm and the brief stab of pain helped her clear her thoughts a little. "In a hotel… Katherine. Then someone came and… oh fuck, oh *fuck*," she exclaimed before Matty reached over and took hold of her chin with practiced ease.

"You're safe. You're okay," he repeated. "Katherine is safe, too."

The grip he had was enough to turn her into a defrosted puddle all by itself, but she somehow she managed to keep her focus. "Ev… Erica? Erica. They had her."

"She… I'm sorry, she didn't make it," Matty answered, "but do you know what happened after?"

"I… pod? They stuffed me in a pod and…"

"They did. Do you know what happened after?"

Callie shook her head slowly. "N… no? Where am I?"

The detective rolled back on his heels a little. "Nowhere, if I'm being honest. Someone chucked you off a train dead smack in the middle of the T-Waste. You're a good hundred miles from civilization."

"I'm… what? Off a train? How did you find me?"

"Your pod has a tracker. Someone called it in."

She swallowed slowly and watched the world come into focus. Waste was right; the only things that even looked *remotely* like civilization was a series of mammoth pillars and the monorail line they supported. "Who? Anthony? Tell me it was Anthony. Tell me Anthony is *okay*."

"He's… alive," Matty answered more or less honestly. "But he left a message. We needed to know if it meant anything specific. Because… well, Anthony is Anthony."

Callie laughed. It hurt a lot to laugh. "Yeah, he is. What message?"

Matty nodded at the faceless, mask-wearing EMT beside him and the med-officer lifted the door to the pod back up. The message was short, sweet, and etched into the inside of the plas-glass. She read it. Twice.

"What the…? 'Sorry for the head?' What in…?"

"That's what we were hoping you could tell us. Do you remember anything that he might've said or done? Did he give you anything?"

She shook her head and struggled to scoot in her seat. In the process, she felt something roll across her foot. "I haven't seen him in… wait, what's that…?" As she did, Matty bent forward and shined his flashlight into the pod and below her thighs.

Harold Vincetti's dead eyes flashed back.

Callie's scream echoed for miles in every direction.

12. REBOOT
Tuesday, June 5th, 2057

Hell wasn't as hot as he'd expected. It actually felt almost climate-controlled. It was also quieter. Anthony had imagined there would be screaming. For that matter, he expected to *be* screaming. He hurt, but not bad enough to scream.

To curse under his breath, yes.

To scream, no.

An IV pump went off somewhere behind his head. A heart monitor beeped twice. Someone was talking in a nearby... hallway? Room? A reassuring voice in his head told him it didn't matter. It wasn't like Hell would worry about his health.

No, he'd seen enough of that to...

Anthony blanked. He knew he'd seen it. Susan had shown it to him. But the memory was outright gone. Not hazy, not foggy, just gone. There was a hole where he knew it was supposed to be. It felt like a neurological 404: File Not Found.

Whatever sign that was, he was pretty damn sure it wasn't good.

He didn't get time to think on it, either. No sooner than the idea went through one side of his brain and out the other, a sorta-familiar voice chimed in inside his head, prefaced with a digital 'ding' that he knew well.

Far, far too well.

New user access detected. Initializing software.

If you had tech, you knew that voice. It was just inhuman enough to ensure you knew it was AI without menacing you to the point that you'd want to run away if you heard it when you woke up in a strange hospital. When you expected it, you welcomed it. When you didn't...

"Initializing...?"

Bi-neural handshake commencing. Hardware interface activating.

The sting hit before he could brace for it. A single jolt of lightning spiked in his eye and a matching lancet stabbed through his skull. A few seconds later, another pain pulsed through his left shoulder and into his ribs. When it finished, the 'soothing' focus-tested computerized voice chimed in again. This time it was accompanied by a HUD screen that appeared over his vision for good measure.

Initialization complete. User registration completed.

User: A. Pierson. UBCI-O45-98776-13. Thank you for your purchase of Tru-Cam Ocular model 19-7-IW-E.

User: A. Pierson. UBCI-LA58-98776-15. Thank you for your purchase of GripMaster Enhanced Arm Replacement.

User: A. Pierson. UBCI-UT20-98776-17. Thank you for your purchase of HeartDef Dermal Plating & Subdermal Resuscitation Systems.

Please press or say 'yes' to continue.

"Good God. What the fuck is... how..."

Please thought-press or say 'yes' to continue.

The words scrolled across his field of vision as the room flickered between monochrome, color, and something that might've been UV light as his new ocular tried to make sense of the world around him. As the text finished, a giant red holographic 'yes' button appeared right in front of his face.

"What... those are... that's... that's expens..."

Please press or say 'yes' to continue.

Press or say 'no' to recycle the initialization process.

"God, fuck. Yes. What the hell..."

The HUD cycled on and off and for a heartbeat, his vision went completely black. When it came back on, the room was back to normal — live and in perfect color. A quick query into his headspace came back with a single flashing notice that felt a little too uncomfortable to give him any peace.

Communication Services Disabled.

Please see System Security Director for access.

The words left a lump in Anthony's throat and dried out his mouth all in one go. It may have been his head, but it was someone else's game, apparently. The who was answered a few short heartbeats later when the text faded and a symbol appeared in the corner of his vision.

A black rectangle, shaped like a playing card.

A white spade with a black heart in the center of it.

The Heart and Spade Foundation.

A med-assist notice went off behind his head to alert the room of a sudden spike in patient blood-pressure as he pushed himself up from the bed and swung his legs around. Another beeping notice went off as a handful of wires fell off his chest to reveal another bit of concern: a whole lot of fake flesh and a decided lack of the DoD's handiwork.

There wasn't much to it that he could see, though there was a significant swath of surgi-flesh that stretched from one nipple to the other. The fake skin and scarring from the DoD's emergency system had been removed and replaced, and a cursory touch suggested that someone had covered his heart with some flex-steel for protection. They hadn't just repaired him; they'd gone full-bore bod-mod.

If they planned to bill him for it, hopefully they'd already taken out a kidney. Those still had use, he'd heard, because if not... well. The 'if not' meant there'd be a cost he didn't want to pay.

Which meant that's what someone had in mind for him.

Nobody came in to check on him, and nobody stopped him from leaving the recovery suite. In all his life, he'd never stepped foot in a building this clean. There wasn't a speck of dust anywhere; not a single smudge on the onyx-glass walls that made up the sides of the hallway or a black streak on the cold porcelain floor.

Monitors adorned every other door down the ward, and for as occupied as the screens made them seem to be, they were silent. So silent that every grippy-sock step he took echoed down the hallway. When no clear-cut path presented itself, he went for the closest waiting area and... waited.

***

Los San stretched out in front of him like an eager lover.

Spade Down had a view unlike any other. Apparently, the med-wing was situated somewhere around the 60th or 70th floor, with an enclosed glass promenade that circled the entire level where you could walk out on in spots if you wanted. For that matter, there was ample seating and workspaces to toil away at along the edges – just in case the office drones were allowed to have a view, he supposed.

Indoors was just fine. There were a pair of RealLeather™ couches that offered visitors a look out the window and over the city skyline. Dusky sunlight made the Gulf shine like nothing else, even as the city cast a shadow across the turbulent waters. A perk of being up so high, he supposed; Spade Down was smack in the middle of the city, but the spires that gave it life did their best to overlook just about everything else that Texas had to offer.

But the city?

The gorgeous nightmare of a city?

Every twinkling light was a dream. Every window was a chance to see someone's hope. Every street corner, a choice; every alleyway, a promise. Every person, a threat; every shadow, a guarantee of darker times ahead. Every screaming LED billboard... well, those were there to remind you of what you were:

The customer? The product? The medium for both?

Or the victim for all the above?

After an hour waiting, he had an answer to which of those he was.

"The press; they never pronounce it right," a familiar voice called out from the hall behind him. Her heels had made all the noise necessary, and he was too tired to bother to look away from the ships in the bay to see if he was right about who it was. Those footsteps and that gait... he'd only met one person that could make her *heels* swish in tune with her hips.

"Your name?"

"My name," she agreed. "They always think it's *Line-ah*."

"It's pronounced *lean,* I assume?"

"Lean-*ah*," the woman corrected warmly. "Do not forget the -*ah*. Not here, not up here."

"But downstairs?"

"We all have our hobbies."

"Your off-hour hobbies included playing secretary for the twins?" he asked with half a grunt to go with it. "Starting to think everyone's got a side-gig these days."

Emiline... no, Emilin-*ah*... stopped next to him and smiled. She wore a latex suit with a matching corset and boots that nearly reached her knees. It was the kind of outfit that suggested she was dressed for either sex, murder, or to sign a corporate contract worth a few mil. "Was there not a President who once said, 'It's the economy, stupid?' Because... well."

"Don't know why I didn't realize it. Everyone knows that the Grimshanks don't spit on the sidewalk without permission from Lina Lohas; their HaS-corp liaison. I'm an idiot for not realizing..."

"Liason and VP of Corporate Security, you mean. The truth is? Secrets hidden in plain sight are the best secrets," she interrupted. "But certain things are a secret. I suspected you knew after you absorbed Clare. Are you telling me that you did not?"

"I knew not to fucking ask," Anthony countered. "Some blood-money bank accounts, sure. Who they were in bed with? Didn't need the visual. Or want to sign my own death warrant."

"Once again, I underestimated your interest in survival."

He took a deep breath and focused his eyes on some yacht off in the distance. With the new headware, he realized he could zoom in and pick off the name emblazoned across its hull without any effort at all. "I get the feeling that your people have decided to invest heavily in that."

"We are people of our word," Em replied evenly. "We promised that if you resolved the Sands situation, we'd take care of you. We just didn't expect you to resolve the Sands situation in a way that would've made the McHelmsley family jealous over missing the Pay-Per-Stream rights."

He flexed his new arm and watched his fingers curl up under the lounge's soft lights. "I take it you approve."

"Of a public execution? No, actually, I don't," she lightly chastised. "Of the public humiliation? Some days, there can be room for business and pleasure in the same breath. You will be pleased to know that Eden Farms is now effectively out of business in our great city and their stock price has plummeted to a depth rarely seen by any except for deep-ocean harvesters."

Anthony choked at the casual way she dropped the statement. "Uh. Because of me? And you think I'm happy about that? No... no I'm not."

"Oh?"

"In my experience, broke billionaires make for bad days, especially if you're the one that broke them. I don't..." Anthony began before his voice trailed off. "Em, after the last fucking week, I'm not up for any more bad days."

"Amusing that you think it's only been a week."

His eyes widened as he tried to do another call into his headset, only to be denied again. "Em..."

"Don't panic," she said as she put a comforting hand on his lower back, "it's only the 5th. We wanted to be sure that the surgeries had time to heal. And to ensure that the ground game was prepared for you."

"Ground... game?"

Finally, she turned her head to look up at him. His disheveled, bruised, and drained reflection bounced back from the crystal-clean glasses she wore. "Monsieur Pierson, in short, you are the victim of your own success.

You have two options and that itself is an illusion, because you won't pick one of the two."

"What's the one you think I won't?"

"I don't think that you'll take your shiny new hand and break that window," she replied as she pointed off to the Gulf, "and I don't think you'll jump off of the balcony immediately after. I think if you did, you'd wonder very hard about why you can't remember what Mademoiselle Sands showed you of the world that is behind this one on your way down, and that will terrify you more than the fall. I think you'd regret it immensely, but more importantly, I don't think you're a coward."

He took a slow deep breath through half-clenched teeth. "Okay. So what's the other option? Work for you?"

Emiline's laugh was short and sharp. Somehow, it was also insulting. "For me? Ah, no. You do have numerous new toys and existing skills that may be useful in the future should opportunity present itself, but if you fear that I am next to send you down to human resources, no. I promise."

"Then what?"

"You live your life, that's all."

"That's a load of bullshit. It's not that simple."

"I said you *live*, Monsieur. I said nothing about it being *simple*. You live. You leave here once our physicians are through with you; you surrender to the police and allow them to ask of you their questions. You will sign their witness agreement; you will be offered lodging – of the non-concrete and steel bar kind – and you will accept. You will take their stipend, follow their instructions and go to court to testify against whom you are told to testify against. For the media, you will state the basics and offer no comment on anything you may have seen that may be too… fantastical… for the average person to need to be burdened with."

Anthony listened to her spiel and felt his stomach fall somewhere below his knees. "You so sure that I won't jump?"

"I am certain that the wheels of justice will be encouraged to move quickly," she replied firmly, in a no-bullshit tone he'd never heard her use. "Over which period you will learn to use your new equipment, and as your ex-wife happened to demand, that you, how was it, 'Fucking rest and don't let him cast a single Goddamned spell,' I think."

"For how long?" followed a moment later by, "Is she okay?"

"Yes, to the latter. Mademoiselle Fisher is alive, and well, and as you likely assume, safe and employed with us. As far as tapping into nth? Her belief is that you should never, I think, and our doctors concur that you are on a magical hiatus for a few weeks at worst."

That… that could've been worse. "Callie?"

The hand on his back flinched while her smile remained the same. "Ah, yes, her. You have interesting taste in women, Monsieur. I… I cannot profess a fondness for her… let's say just simply, *for her* that yes, she is safe; she is infuriated, but she is safe. Mostly, she is concerned over your health, a personality feature which may be the only admirable one she possesses."

"Oof. What'd she do to piss you off?"

Emiline took a moment to give him a pensive look. "It is a matter of both my personal and professional policy to not engage in the private life of a client or a contractor," she started, "unless specifically asked. I would not be opposed to offering an opinion. *If* asked."

On a better day, that would've been a fun conversation to have. "But she's safe? Both of them are?"

"Yes, both of them are, and both of them have been kept in the loop regarding your care. Your familiar is safe as well; but we would like to have a discussion with you about him and how exactly he kept you alive on the train, please."

"Uh, he didn't…"

She slowly shook her head 'no' and glanced down at the floor. "Monsieur, do you remember what happened… all of it?"

Anthony tapped the side of his head. "After I repainted the cab? No. Not… a lot. Feelings, mostly. Some haze."

"Not surprised. From what we can tell you used both your familiar and Susan's corpse as a medium to… interface… with the train's electrical system. Ingenious, but with… complications for all parties involved. But your familiar, again, is safe."

Anthony put his hand on his chest and quietly squeezed the faux flesh that covered his heart. "Does that explain the fuzziness? I can't really get a feel for the nth in here."

"It is one of many reasons, I think. For obvious reasons, we weren't able to allow your companions access to this floor. I'm sure you understand. I will ensure that you are able to place calls to both of your women once you retire back to your room to rest for the remainder of the night. As far as the Marshal, he will be returned to you upon your discharge."

"Okay, a ghost running rampant in ICU is bad news for the rest of the people here, I get it. But Kath? Callie? What reasons?"

"I said they were obvious," Em retorted, "but I can forgive you for not seeing them given the situation. Now, having said all of that, you are not in a position to do more than provide cogs for the gears of justice at a Congressional hearing at this moment. Once you endure your punishment for the handful of good deeds you've done…"

Anthony cleared his throat and rolled his shoulders back. "I was waiting for this part. It's not going to be an 'or else,' I know. You're going to give me an offer that I can refuse, but I won't want to."

"No, no, Monsieur. I respect you. In a week, you did what we could not do without unnecessarily unpleasant complications for months. There will be parties who will be unhappy with our involvement to the limit we've expressed it and less happy with what we do after, yet they would have been irredeemably infuriated had we acted direct or alone," Emiline countered deftly. "I will not denigrate who you are by framing your future in such a way."

"That's a reli-"

"I am giving you an order," she interrupted, "and you will follow it to the best of your ability."

"That's not."

"Too bad," Em stressed. "Monsieur, you will do your civic duty and then you will enter yourself on the Corporate Registry. Records and Financing on the 23rd floor will handle that for a fee to be assessed later once you sign a document we prepared during your recovery. You have had a file opened with Spade-Sec service as a contractor agency for our affiliates and you will be given a choice of office locations in the downtown area."

Anthony backed away and brushed her hand off his back. "Hang on a minute. You just said I wasn't going to work for you."

"And you aren't," she replied. "You will never receive a stub from Heart and Spade Foundation, Incorporated. My name will never be on an invoice. You will ensure that you are available for the needs of our partner-and-child divisions when at all possible, and it will be very possible. In exchange, you will have enough clients – either us or ones we recommend to you – to be comfortable. For a time."

The necromancer stared at her with a face full of frustration and a gut full of dread. "Look, no. The corp life isn't for me. Absolutely fucking not. I'm fine drawing a pension. I'm fine fucking off in the alleys. I don't want… *this*," he said as he swept his arms out. "I don't mean to be ungrateful for the fix, but I'm nobody's fucking wage slave."

Emiline stepped back up to him and took the end of his chin in her fingers. She was short but powerful, and the single move shut him down on the spot. "Nobody. Is. Making. You. One. What we are doing is recovering an investment, and no, *you* do not have a choice."

"The Hell I don't," he argued. "I'm not some –"

"Anthony. If you decline to comply, then when you step out of this building, you will find out how very small you are compared to how very large that city is for someone who has angered the people you have angered. I do not mean this in a manner of corporate speak or business deals. There are powers out there beyond street gangs and boardrooms that, as I speak, are *livid* and worse yet, *embarrassed,* so they seek someone to vent their stress on. With us, you are not that person. Without?"

"Without? What, someone else is going to shoot at me?"

"If you choose to decline our involvement in your life, I will go and open that window for you myself to spare you the unpleasantness that will define your life for however long you're cursed to keep it."

The way she said it? The stone-cold, absolutely all-encompassing way she said it? "You're serious."

"I ask that you use the security code on the door there," she replied as she nodded her head towards an opening to the balcony, "5-6-1-3-5. If we've made the wrong choice, at least allow us to only waste the money on the modifications and not the glass."

He thought about arguing.

He also knew she was right.

A new voice interrupted their conversation, and it spoke with such weight that it took Anthony's breath away – figuratively and literally. A pressure wave of nth, unlike anything he'd ever felt before, accompanied each word like it was magic itself that spoke. "Mister Pierson? If you're wondering if you should accept the offer? You should. I would, were I you."

The voice's owner was arguably the most beautiful woman he'd ever seen in his life. She had hair the color of the sun and eyes that matched. Her body was the kind you either gave up carbs and lived in the gym to get, or the type you dropped the GDP of a small country on a surgical suite to procure. Either way, she had it.

She smiled and flashed a mouth full of *perfect* as he tried to pull his eyes away from hers even though they seemingly *demanded* he lose himself in them. She wore a tight-fitting black dress that left absolutely nothing to the imagination, and that couldn't have been unintentional. Callie would've been jealous. Katherine would've been annoyed.

The necromancer knew exactly who she was the moment she came into view. She flexed the corner of her mouth a little as he stared at her in a mixture of awe, fear, and minor disbelief. When she smirked, her reflection bounced off the black mirror hall panels.

Her real reflection was the crimson maelstrom of the realm she belonged in. The mother of all storms that ripped through the world of ruin. The storm that settled around her shoulders like a halo.

The mirrors snapped back to reality a heartbeat later, and Em bowed her head in respect. "Lady Helesiki. I didn't expect you."

"Few do," the Daemoness replied in that same melodic voice. "As I said, Mister Pierson; you should take the offer."

Anthony swallowed back on his tongue and, to his credit, refused to budge from where he stood. Though to be fair, it was a mix of completely petrifying fear and the fact that he was so emotionally exhausted that he couldn't just bring himself to give a shit. Later, yes. Now, no. "Because it's from the Pentaship?"

"Because it's from a mother," Heart and Spade's CEO replied, "no matter how many times removed. You aided my children, intentionally or not, and removed a threat to their lives from the board, for which I am grateful."

"Why... me? I saw videos. That shit... it had to take years, lots of years. You can't tell me you didn't know."

Maybe it was the tone of his voice. Maybe it was the honesty. Maybe it was just the balls it took to call one of the most powerful creatures on this side of the planar walls out. Whatever it was, Her smile cracked.

But only just a little.

"The ills of the world are... complicated," Helesiki began, "with boundaries and rules that are set in stone, the likes of which defy mortals knowing or understanding. Those of mine who suffered have gone through their trials. They are not suffering now; they are rewarded. Those that aided in their suffering? That profited from it?"

She didn't answer the rhetorical. He almost did. "It comes down to choice, doesn't it? Always does."

"It does. Any of them could have blown the whistle. Only one of them decided to, the poor man. While I give no love to the Pastor, he, too, did the right thing. So did you. My home is for those that deserve it. For the moment, you do not. But we can at least offer to pay the toll for your services."

"You know, you two pack so much stuff into your words I feel like a baggage handler at the TSA. Respectfully? Please – please know I do mean this with full respect – I don't buy it. You could've."

"Monsieur Pierson please –"

"No," Helesiki interrupted, "from where he stands, he isn't wrong. I cannot judge someone for their thoughts when they have no reason to consider them otherwise, and I don't expect him to be able understand why."

He shook his head and tried to calm the steady thump bouncing around under his ribs. "Try me. Please. You don't owe me shit; I get it, but I'm not gonna be able to sleep…"

The Daemoness bowed her head in deference. Something told him that *wasn't* a gesture she did often, if ever. "I understand. Do allow me to suggest it is a *family* matter. I will say that a direct hand, or a directed hand, would have unleashed Home in a way that would not have been kind on any of us."

"Beyond boardrooms and gangs," Emiline repeated as she slipped her hand around the necromancer's wrist.

Anthony swallowed slowly again. "Why… why are you two doing this? It'd be easier to kill me and sweep me under the rug. A lot cheaper, too. What am I missing? No games. No riddles. What the fuck am I missing?"

Helesiki and Em exchanged a short look that made both of their eyes glisten and gleam as the last vestiges of the sun dropped down below the horizon. "I have been a poor mother to my children and their children and their children for too long. It isn't… it is not in my nature," she admitted with a bit of difficulty. "So, at the very least, I can start now."

"Okay, fine, so the Daem community…"

"*All* of my children," she stressed.

Anthony's heart thumped. Twice. Out of rhythm. "Uh, excuse me?"

"Monsieur, I did mention that the method you used to stay alive was most ingenious," the VP of Heart and Spade's Corporate Sec replied with a terrifying little smile. "It took us a while to get to the train. You filtered anthenium through a pure-blood Daem. You didn't think that there wouldn't be consequences for that, did you?"

"What is it humans call my children?" the Lady asked. "Hell… mutants?"

He shook her hand off his wrist and started to pat down his chest, his back… and then his head. His eyes went wide as saucers as he felt a pair of little nodules where little nodules shouldn't have been. "Wait. The fuck. What? What in… what am I supposed to do now?"

"Live," Helesiki replied. "Which is more than others get to do."

There wasn't a good response to that.

Emiline, however, had one that sufficed. "Accept the offer," she began as she tapped the end of his nose, "and do as you're told. I even workshopped it a bit for you while you were out; how does NecroTek Security Consultations sound?"

Anthony swallowed nervously and slid his fingers around the lumps on his hairline. "Campy," he finally admitted.

"But catchy, Monsieur?"

"But catchy," he agreed as the sun set over the bay.

EPILOGUE
ONE MONTH LATER.

A screen flickered to life on the cruiser's dashboard just in time for the 9 PM news. *"At this time, neither my office nor the LSPD will have any further comment on the matter. Be assured, we will work diligently with Mother Esmeralda from the Office of Cultural Norms to ensure that the displaced families of the Daem-Sapiens are united after this incredible tragedy."*

That promise came from the mouth of Eagle Bergeron; the Sine-Pastor's replacement and superior. He'd taken over the Gulf Diocese before El-Rhodes' body even had a chance to cool off. He wasn't necessarily an unpleasant man, or even a bad one. He was just a man stuck in the hot seat.

And he had terrible people to keep him company on all sides.

The view shifted to a Congressional hearing with the headline, *A Necromancer Goes to Washington* in bold letters across the top of it. The hearings had been as contentious as they had been hyped up; you'd have been forgiven if you thought the playoffs for the Cinder Cup were being held front and center in the Capitol Building. The best part about it?

The utter look of misery plastered across Anthony's face.

The second best part of it? The way he managed to piss off every self-aggrandizing bastard there just by breathing. The man had talent. Honestly, Alara always assumed he'd missed his calling because judging by the look on the Secretary of Energy's face, he was being a great advocate for blood pressure pills.

Heartburn pills, too.

It was worth a laugh as she settled in at a parking spot and picked up her phone. *"Frank's Hardware. Ah, Detective, how can we be of assistance today?"*

Alara looked out over the Gulf and took a long, deep drag on a cigarette with a faint blue glow to the tip. "I wanna speak to your boss."

"Frank is unfortunately busy at this time and –"

"You knew who I was before you even answered the phone. I'm not in the mood; put your boss on the line."

Dead silence greeted her. Off in the distance, the sounds of the city drifted up the valley to the water towers at her back and the glowing billboards on top of them. *"De-De-Detective Dimir! It is a ple-ple-pleasure to finally talk to you!"*

"No it's not."

A little pause answered her at first before the joyfulness vanished. *"No, It's not. You aren't an established cli-cli-client with us, Detective. I am under no ob-ob-obligation to –"*

She pressed a button on her phone's screen and a little email icon spun around like it had been flushed down a drain. "I know how you work; trade for trade. There, five cops. Each one dirty as fuck and on the Gardener payroll. AGU won't let me touch them, so I can't do shit about it. Do with the list what you will."

"That… that sounds like a yo-yo-you problem more than a me gi-gi-gift," Fixxer replied. *"But interesting. Go on."*

Alara took another puff of her cig and sighed. "Before Anthony turned Sands' face into a jigsaw puzzle, she denied having her pet biomech stomp Jordan's head in."

"Yes. I-I-I saw."

"Thing is," she continued, "it occurs to me that his death being a spectacle was probably the only way to get eyes on her bullshit in a way that couldn't get ignored."

A series of ellipsis and question marks began to roll across the display. *"That does seem like a val-val-valid observation."*

"Eden's out of town now, both the Grims and the Gardeners have been decimated by Yers, the Church got caught with their pants down, and even Spade Down took a rep hit. What's the PAC ad running? 'Can you trust a corp that can't take care of their own?' You know. The PAC that *magically* appeared out of nowhere and is funded *entirely* by 'grass roots' donations?"

The question-marks turned into little smirking faces. *"Am-am-amazing how that happens."*

She gazed into the bay and watched as a few glowing embers from her cig bounced off the toe of her boot. "Slash had more in his head than Anthony knew. Can't blame him; he was busy trying not to die and all that, I guess. Slash realized *quickly* that Sands hadn't given the order to use the mech… so he took the blame for it. Came up with an excuse that kept him outta the ground. Smart play from the asshole. He just couldn't figure out who did."

Alara's phone went blank for a few seconds before Fixxer's head floated into the middle of it. *"What makes you thi-thi-think I do?"*

"Because I know who you are. I know what you do. You're the self-stylized Game Master of Los San. Frank the Fixxer. The problem solver with the hardware solution to your every need. That about right?"

"It's clo-clo-close. Do you think I-I-I did it?"

"Yeah. I do. I think you knew about the kill order and you ran the numbers. You *could've* passed word on to stop it, but you didn't. You let it play out, you just interfered so it would play out *messy*. You're the one that faked the instruction to use the Centurio to kill Jordan. You *knew* it would get attention and then you jumped at the chance to get Anthony involved. You *knew* you could control him to make sure it played out like a mess and that he'd *have* to ask you for help."

"That's a ver-ver-very interesting accusation, Detective."

She smiled down into the phone as the billboard overhead cut to silent static, "None of the power players in this town profit from this mess. None, I've checked. Who paid you, Fixxer?"

His face disappeared from her phone and a battery indicator popped up to replace it. As she watched, nearly half the charge vanished at once. A woman's voice chimed back in over the line in lieu of a reply. *"Thank you for calling Frank's Hardware, Detective Dimir. Please enjoy the rest of your night."*

The rest of her battery died as every light along the hillside followed suit. Sparks popped out of the rear port as she dropped it to the ground and stepped back with an uttered, "What the fu-" that died on her lips as she looked up… and around. Every billboard within a mile had changed screens to a single corporate logo and tagline. The cig fell out of her lips as she read the line of text and lost what was left of her bravado all at once.

***

Guth Energy Services
Power. Absolutely.
Proudly Serving Humanity as the First Chair of the Pentaship.

The Global Council of the Pentaship
You Have Friends… In Places.

***

END
Necromancer's Bullet
The First NecroTek Novel
***

Dead Men Tellin' Tales
I listen to the voices in my head.
Then I write books about 'em.
***

A note from the author!
If you've made it to the end – you're awesome! I hope you enjoyed
Anthony's first adventure and the general feel of NecroTek.

If you did, do you mind doing me a favor?
Whatever you thought of it, can you do me a solid and drop a star or five?
Sorry to ask, but authors like me need them to know what we're doing
right, wrong, and to appease the all-knowing Algorithm.

Anthony and I will see you soon… maybe even sooner than you think.

Oh – and if you enjoy swords and sorcery fantasy, and not just urban?
Welllll… keep reading into the backmatter! I have a whole slew of other
titles published for fans of grimdark swords and sorcery, gratuitous
violence, and even more magic…

OH. And if you really like what I do, feel free to follow me on social media.

You can either head to my website or my FB page for links to everything
else! Plus, you can grab my newsletter for exclusive notes, early-release
info, and so much more!

Facebook:
Joshua E. B. Smith, Author
@sagadmw

THE SAGA OF THE DEAD MEN WALKING

Year 512 of the Queen's Rule
The Snowflakes Trilogy
Book I: Snowflakes in Summer
Freshly minted by the Order of Love, a young exorcist is sent to the edge of the Kingdom of Dawnfire to deal with a 'small, simple haunting.' Between a winter that won't end, a girl that doesn't belong, and people being eaten in the woods, only one thing is for sure: he's over his head, and utterly out of luck.

Book II: Dead Men in Winter
As the search for the Coldstone continues, new allies enter the fray in the mountains around Toniki, and in the streets of the City of Mud. But new blood only means new bodies, and Makolichi seeks to provide those in excess...

Book III: Favorite Things
It's time for Usaic's Tower to ascend. Truths will be revealed, blood shall be spilled, and suffering shall become legendary. But it's not just the living who should fear the Coldstone being set loose. For though the dead will rise, the damned had best be ready for Who comes next...

Year 513 of the Queen's Rule
The Auramancer's Exorcism
Book I: Insanity's Respite
Beaten, broken, and battered, Akaran is sent to the Safest City in the Kingdom to recover from his battle against Makolichi, Daringol, Rmaci, and the rest. What he expects is peace and time to heal. What he finds instead is that insanity knows no bounds and offers no respite...

Book II: Insanity's Rapture
In life, the woman in his dreams had been a spy – a murderess, a liar, a fraud, and a thief. Sentenced to burn for her crimes, her screams have haunted his sleep since the moment she was set aflame. As both the city and Akaran's mind descend into chaos, only insanity offers rapture.

Book III: Insanity's Reckoning
The most dangerous man in the city is about to get his magic back – and

he's got a murder on his mind. As he prepares to hunt a sadistic vampire, his past is about to come back to haunt him in a way he never could have imagined.

Book IV: Insanity's Requiem
It's time for the madness to end, but the insane have no desire to find peace – and peace will only come when Basion City is turned into an open grave.

Origins of the Dead Men Walking
Year 512 of the Queen's Rule
Slag Harbor (An Interruption in the Snowflakes Trilogy)
After battling Makolichi in Gonta – and before facing him down for the final time in Toniki – Akaran decides to leave Private Galagrin behind in the City of Mud to make sure that nothing got missed in his sweep. What he finds is more than just stray shiriak; it's an answer to an unasked question...

Year 513 of the Queen's Rule
Lady Claw I: Claw Unsheathed
Who's to blame when a young girl is accused of murder? Did she do it, or did her father? And when she's cornered and the claws come out... does it matter?

Year 516 of the Queen's Rule
Fearmonger
Years after Toniki, a grizzled Akaran serves as a peacekeeper to the Queen – and nothing wants the peace to be kept.

Year 517 of the Queen's Rule
Blindsided
Stannoth and Elrok couldn't be any more different. Trained mercenaries in the Hunter's Guild, they absolutely hate each other – but they don't have a choice but to work together.